I0557837

Scorched at Stevens Street

Stevens Street Gym Book #2

Charlie Roberts

Sisters Romance

Copyright © 2022 Sisters Romance

All rights reserved

The characters and events portrayed in this book are fictitious. Any similarity to real persons, living or dead, is coincidental and not intended by the author.

No part of this book may be reproduced, or stored in a retrieval system, or transmitted in any form or by any means, electronic, mechanical, photocopying, recording, or otherwise, without express written permission of the publisher.

Chapter 1

Madeline

I click the link in the body of the email to complete the Velvet Playroom Application. The first set of questions are your basic questions, name, address, phone number, date of birth, etc. The very first question in the next section reminds me what I was filling out.

Tell us about your first sexual encounter, check all boxes that apply.

Immediately my mind went back to Scott Henderson. I was two months shy of my sixteenth birthday. Scott was a senior, had just turned eighteen. I felt so special to be dating him. He was popular and all the girls wanted to go out with him. I also knew he had a reputation of expecting sex from his girlfriends. The weekend before we had come very close. He had undone my bra and felt me up. It was the first time a guy had done that. He'd also put his hand inside my panties, also a first for me. It was exciting, and terrifying.

"Fuck are you wet!" he had said to me. I didn't know what that meant. I guess I was pretty naïve. "I want you," he had moaned in my ear as he rubbed my hand over the front of his pants, over his hard penis. "Do you want me too?" he had asked.

"Yes, I want you," I had said.

I got hold of my older sister's Cosmo magazine that next week. I read it cover to cover and was shocked by what I had read. So, when he picked me up that Friday night, telling my parents we were going to the movies and meeting a bunch of friends, I was shocked and excited when he took me back to his house. To his empty, parents-free house. They were gone for the weekend, he proudly told me. As soon as we were inside, he told me we were going to do it. Thanks to Cosmo, I now knew exactly what that meant.

He led me up to his bedroom. His kisses were like the ones the previous weekend, heavy and intense, his tongue nearly choking me. His hands were all over me. He took my top off, undid and removed my bra, and gazed at me. The smile on his face scared me, but I didn't tell him to stop.

"Your tits are fucking beautiful," he had said.

I was embarrassed and self-conscious, standing there bare-chested. Then his hands felt me up again. I now knew that what I was feeling was sexual excitement. His mouth then kissed and sucked on my nipples. He was moaning. It was embarrassing, and it seemed wrong that his mouth was on them.

He tore his shirt over his head. Now as a thirty-four-year-old woman, I had to laugh at the little boy pretending to be a man, but at the time, I was mesmerized by his body. I shyly touched his chest and my excitement rose. He grabbed my butt and pulled my pelvis up against his. I felt his erection, proud I made him excited, me Madeline Shaw, I got a guy hard. Little did I know eighteen-year-old boys got hard when the wind blew.

Then he undid my jeans and pulled them and my panties off. I was standing before him, completely naked. I was scared to death! He took his own off and he pulled me with him over just steps from the bed. I was petrified, but I didn't say stop.

He put my hand on his hard penis again and grasped his hand over mine, jacking him off. He moaned and his face showed an anguished expression. He stopped me, kissed me again, and then his hand ran slowly up my leg. My mind was focused on what he was doing, and I realized I was excited, and I wanted this. I jumped, startled, and I'm sure I let out a scream when his fingers penetrated me.

"Fucking wet and ready," he said. "Never been fucked, have you?" he taunted. I wanted to seem experienced, not like a little girl. As he backed me up, my knees hit the bed, and I was pushed rather hard on to my back. "First though," he moaned, straddling me, his penis in my face. "Lick it," he commanded.

I had read about oral sex in that magazine. It said it felt great. The article also mentioned many guys liked to receive, but not give. "I will after you do," I said.

"Oh, you are a naughty girl," he said, his voice strained.

He flipped around and leaned his head down between my legs, pulling them apart with his hands. His tongue penetrated me, and I screamed out. He leaned up, his gaze meeting mine. It felt...incredible, and scary, wrong that someone would do that, embarrassing that his head was there, but I wanted him to do more.

"Don't stop," I told him, finding courage some place that I didn't know existed.

His lips curved into that scary smile again and he went down on me and licked and sucked. Then his fingers penetrated me while he did it and I couldn't handle what I was feeling. I knew I was wriggling, trying to get away from the sensations that were overwhelming me.

He stopped and came over me again, his hard cock poking my lips. "Your turn," he said.

I grabbed hold of it and licked it like a lollypop like I had read about in the Cosmo. It was awkward and gross, and I felt like I was doing something really wrong, but I didn't stop.

After a few minutes, he grabbed my chin. "Suck it as far down your throat as you can," he ordered.

It was horrible. I gagged, and he laughed at me. But he kept pushing it into my mouth. After a short time, he pulled it away and grabbed a condom. He put it on, spit on my pussy, and settled between my legs, spreading them wide with his knees. Panic was rising. I didn't want to do this.

"I love you, baby," he said. Thinking back now, I had to laugh at that. At the time, I believed him.

He kissed me as he pushed his cock into me. It hurt. I told him to stop. "Not a chance," he said snidely. He held me tighter and pushed harder. It hurt worse. I pushed against him. He grabbed my hands and pinned them over my head. I turned my head to the side, away from his kisses that were suffocating me, and he kissed and bit my neck. Being only eighteen years old, it didn't take long for him to come, though I thought it took forever.

The relationship only lasted a few months as he went off to college in the fall.

I realize now that Scott had been the least vanilla sexual encounter I'd ever had. He had restrained me. He had issued orders to me. He had taught me what sex was about, well, the mechanics of it. My teen-self thought his moaning was embarrassing. My grown woman-self envied his unbridled expression of his pleasure. I had been more excited that night with Scott than I had been with several of the last few men I'd been with.

I pulled my mind back to the present, took a sip of the glass of wine I had gotten as soon as I had come through my front door, and got busy checking the boxes of what I was looking for.

One box mentioned the use of restraints. I had suggested tying each other up and driving each other crazy to Dave, my last boyfriend. He thought I was nuts. The thought of being restrained while a guy drove me crazy, having to take all the sexual attention he wanted to give me, turned me on. I checked that box.

Dave had also refused to spank me, something I had read about in the erotica romance novels I loved but had never experienced. I really wanted to see if it was a turn-on, if it heated you up like the books said. Another box checked.

I had even wanted him to issue me orders of what he wanted me to do to him while I kneeled before him and role-played, acting out any fantasy he dictated. He told me I was warped, that people didn't really do those kinds of kinky things. I knew he was wrong. Two more boxes checked. The heat rose up my cheeks as I read the options, clicking off box after box. I knew it wasn't the wine heating me up.

After saying goodbye to Dave, I knew I couldn't contain my curiosity any longer, nor could I face another unfulfilling sexual partner. I had surfed the internet for weeks and followed link after link to finally find a site for a club in downtown Lexington called the Velvet Playroom, which promised everyone's fantasy be fulfilled. It also promised to match up each eager participant with a partner who shared his or her interest in erotic pleasure.

I had tried the traditional sex within a relationship route all my adult life and it just didn't work. Running my own restaurant is time consuming and I know I am not always the easiest person to get along with. I know what needs to be done and I do it. In and out of the bedroom. And with the last few men I went out with, I just did not feel fulfilled in the bedroom. Perhaps this would bring me the fulfillment I yearned for. Perhaps keeping sex separate from the rest of my life, and outside of a relationship, would be the ticket.

I pulled my thoughts from my head and got back to the form.

The third section asked me what specific lifestyle I was looking for, suggesting a Dominant and Submissive relationship was where my section two checkbox selections were leaning towards, my interests landing me squarely in the Submissive realm. It gave a narrative of the lifestyle and what taking on the role of a Submissive would mean and what it would give me. I'd read a lot of erotica books that dealt with Doms and Subs, but this narrative really helped to explain the relationship and the balance of power.

I knew I wanted to give it a try. I took a deep breath, and I clicked yes. The form was submitted.

Butch

It had been a quiet shift at the firehouse, which we were due. It was midafternoon, and I was heading to the gym on Stevens Street. Its owner, my friend Andy Stevens and his new wife Kenzie, had gotten back from their honeymoon late last night. I had texted with him and saw posted pictures from their week-long honeymoon in Aruba, but I had not actually spoken to him since before their wedding, which I didn't make it to.

The department was still reeling from the five-alarm blaze that broke out in the large, abandoned warehouse that day. Two firefighters, friends of mine died there, four more were injured. The warehouse contained a squatter's city. Hundreds of homeless had set up a shanty town in that dilapidated wood structure that burned to the ground when an open flame for cooking caught the building on fire. Five of the homeless lost their lives as well.

We battled the blaze long after Andy and Kenzie had said 'I do'. I was supposed to stand up for Andy. I felt bad that I couldn't be there with him. He was a good friend, and I was thrilled he had found happiness with Kenzie. I could have made the tail-end of the reception, but I stayed at the hospital with Sophie, my friend Lucky's wife.

Lukas Lucky Dupree had been very lucky! He had been on the roof when it collapsed. He suffered a few burns, a broken back, broken arm, and broken collarbone, but he lived. That night, he had surgery and I couldn't leave Sophie alone in the surgical waiting room. The firehouse was stretched thin. Many of my fellow firefighters held vigils with the widows and their families and with the families of the other injured firefighters that night. We were truly a family. That was one of the many things I loved about my job.

I push open the door to the gym and throw a smile at Logan, Andy's number two, at the gym. Logan stands by the main counter. "Hey, what's up?" I ask.

"Nada," he says with a smile. He steps forward and we shake hands.

"Are Andy and Kenzie around?"

"Yeah," Logan says, glancing behind him into the office.

I look around Logan and see a very sun-tanned Andy sitting at his desk. He's on the phone. He smiles warmly at me and holds a finger up, silently asking me to wait a minute. Logan and I shoot-the-shit for a few minutes until Andy hangs up and comes out of the office.

"Hey, man," Andy says, coming around the counter and embracing me.

"Welcome back. I don't even have to ask you how it was. The pictures I saw looked incredible," I say.

"Yeah, it was gorgeous there. We had a great time," Andy says.

"I'm really sorry I didn't make the wedding." I had told

him in a text message, but I wanted to say it to his face.

"Not an issue. I'm glad you weren't hurt. That was a hell of a fire from the news reports I saw. What was the final death toll?" Andy asks.

"Two firefighters and five of the homeless that were living in that death-trap," I say.

Andy frowns and shakes his head. "And Lucky? How is he doing?" He had met Lucky. He had come with me to the gym a few times.

"He's got a long road ahead to recover. I'm not sure he'll ever be back at the firehouse."

"Man, that sucks," Logan says.

Just then, Kenzie descends the stairs from the apartments above the gym where they live. Kenzie is glowing. She has as dark of a suntan as Andy and she looks very happy.

She comes up to me, smiling, and gives me a tight hug. "Hi Butch, it's great to see you. I'm so glad you were not hurt in that fire. God, that was horrible."

"Hi Kenz, welcome home," I say. "I'm so sorry I missed your wedding because of it."

"No apology needed." She releases me from the embrace. Then she turns her attention to Andy. "You're sure you don't mind if I go try that yoga class out with Ashley?"

"No, babe, that's fine," Andy says. "Go, have a good time."

I'm surprised. Ashley hadn't been very nice to Kenzie. Were they now friends? I watch Ashley come down the stairs. Her blond hair, which is held high in a ponytail, bounces as she takes each stair with a little hop. I still couldn't figure her out. I'd originally thought Andy and she had something going, but Andy set me straight on that pretty quick. Same was true for Logan. I think she may be the only woman in the greater

Lexington area that Logan hasn't slept with. I never tried to go there, even though she has always flirted like crazy with me. She isn't my type.

"Hi Butch," Ashley says, coming in way too close. Her blues sparkle an invitation to me. She practically slides against my body to get by, which she doesn't need to do. She has plenty of room to maneuver around me to go behind the counter.

"Hi Ash," I greet. I step back so she'll have more space as she comes back out holding her yoga mat.

"I'm sure you can do all the poses. Just please be sure to tell the instructor you're pregnant so she can give you any modifications as needed," Andy tells Kenzie. She smiles and nods. He places a kiss on her lips. They both smile, their eyes locked onto each other's for a few seconds before Kenzie steps away and leaves with Ashley out the front door.

The smile on Andy's face is telling. My friend is ecstatic. I'm happy for him but I'm pretty sure I won't ever find that kind of contentment. I thought I had it once, but it had disappeared faster than kindling in a raging inferno. Kenzie had wanted to introduce me to one of her friends, but I honestly didn't know if I wanted to meet anyone yet.

"You here to work out?" Andy asks.

"No, not today. I just came by to see you. I was on at the firehouse the last twenty-four hours, and I need to get some shit done this afternoon. My brother's been busting my balls to get some work done for him, so I'll go take care of that first to get him off my back."

Andy and Logan laugh.

"That brother of yours is a trip," Logan says. "Man, talk about two people who are polar-opposites."

I knew Logan was referring to Cosimo's taste for the finer things in life. He had embraced the status of our upbringing and the winery business that had been in our family for generations. He was all about our Italian roots and loved to stay at the family villa in Tuscany. I preferred beer or whiskey to wine, liked to spend the money, but wasn't a slave to it like Cosimo is. And the family villa in Tuscany, well, all I ever felt there was drama and expectations. No thank you. I liked my life here, away from all of it just fine.

"His membership is still active, but I haven't seen him in here working out in months," Andy says.

It didn't surprise me. The only time Cosimo liked to sweat was in the act, preferably with his partner tied to something, but I certainly wouldn't divulge that little fact about my brother. "I'll see if I can get him here to workout with me next week sometime. I'll remind him his muscles will go to mush if he doesn't. That usually does the trick," I say with a laugh.

Madeline

I'd been rushing all morning, like usual. My food order came in short lemons. I ran to the downtown market to grab some. I hated paying retail but had no choice. I buzzed through the produce aisle and ran right into my girlfriend Kenzie at the checkout line.

"Kenz!" I squeal.

"Madeline!" she replies in kind as she engulfs me in a hug. "What are you doing here?"

I hold the bag of lemons up. "They forgot my lemons in this morning's delivery."

I hadn't seen Kenzie since her wedding. I knew she had gotten back from her honeymoon a few days earlier. We had text messaged and were trying to figure out a day to meet for coffee. I'd seen the great pictures from Aruba she had posted on her social media pages, but I wanted to hear all about her trip and her new life with her hunky husband.

Kenzie's cart is full of all sorts of healthy foods. Andy has had quite an effect on her, for the better. I consider making some smart-ass remark about it, but she beats me to it.

"Bet you never thought you'd see the day I had kale in my cart?" she asks with a laugh.

I guess I'd been staring at it. I laugh too. "But do you eat it? Or is that for Andy?"

She laughs again. "You would be very surprised by what I eat now."

That takes my mind in a direction it shouldn't have gone, that I definitely won't voice to my friend. "I'm sure I would," I say. We chat as we check out. I wait and walk out with her, helping transfer her many grocery bags into the trunk of her car while we talk. Yes, I am in a hurry, but I want to spend these few minutes with my friend. The restaurant will have to wait.

"Did anything ever happen between you and that server from the bistro when we had coffee?" Kenzie asks.

Huh? How did she know about him? I had not told her I was seeing him. "Yeah, I hired him," I say.

"That wasn't what I asked, and you know it," Kenzie says with a smile.

"Yeah, that crashed and burned quickly. The first time was good, and it went downhill from there."

"What about the relationship part?" Kenzie asks.

"What does it matter if the sex sucks?" I ask.

Kenzie laughs. "Yeah, I can definitely agree with that."

I knew her new husband did not disappoint her in that way. I was genuinely happy for her, a new husband with a four-year-old daughter, and a baby on the way, not that I wanted any of those things. I loved my life the way it was. I honestly could say I was not sure if I ever wanted to have children. How could my life of early mornings and late nights work with a kid? And I had worked so hard to make my restaurant what it was. I knew I would never give it up.

"You know, I've come to the conclusion, I am just too busy for a relationship," I say. *And too demanding*, I think, but I don't say that aloud. I can't tell Kenzie about the sex club I applied to. She'd never understand. I knew what I wanted, though, and the relationships I'd had for the last few years didn't even come close to satisfying me. "And I intimidate men. That isn't what I want, but it just happens. Guys learn I own and run a successful restaurant and they turn into, I don't know, these sexual wimps. I hate having to be the aggressor."

Kenzie laughs. "Are you sure they just weren't sexual wimps all along? I think you've just been seeing the wrong guys. Please let me introduce you to Andy's friend Butch," she begs.

I felt my mouth twist into a smirk. I didn't want to hurt her feelings, but I wasn't up for it. The club was what I knew I would try next. "Kenz, really, I'm sorry. I'm going to have to pass. I'll tell you if I change my mind. The restaurant is really keeping me busy. We got this great write up by a food critic while you were on your honeymoon and reservations are crazy! I'm booked solid! I don't have a lot of free time these days." *And I want to fill it with something different from what Kenzie would think I would.*

"But you will come work out at the gym with me, won't you? You promised. You'd be surprised how much energy you'll get out of a good workout!"

I think about it for a second. Getting some definition in my muscles wouldn't hurt my appearance either. The thought of being at the club I applied to thrilled me, but it also made me feel insecure about my body. I liked food way too much to diet and let's face it, I'd always carried a few extra pounds around. It never bothered me until now with the thought of what I may be doing.

"Sure, I'll come work out with you tomorrow after I get my food order in and straightened out after the morning delivery, about ten? Will that work for you?"

"Perfect," Kenzie says with a smile. "I'll put you in the appointment book." She giggles. "It'll be in ink, so you can't back out."

Butch

It is ten a.m., and I am just getting off work. I go to my locker to leave my work shirt. My helmet, number thirteen, sits above it. I shuck the shirt off, leaving my white t-shirt beneath. I usually preferred to work out in a tank top, but I had forgotten to pack it in my gym bag, and I'm not about to go out of my way and go home to get it, so this t-shirt will have to do. I grab my gym bag and head to the Stevens Street Gym to workout.

We'd only had one call from midnight to five, which was extremely quiet for an overnight shift. I actually got five hours of uninterrupted sleep. I felt rested and wanted to push myself with a good workout. I wasn't sure what else the day would bring. I was due back at the firehouse at ten tonight for another overnight shift.

Our shifts were still all messed up because of the fatalities and the injuries from the big fire. I was working with the captain to shake out the shifts to something more regular for the crew, but until we got it hammered out, I was flexing my schedule all over the place to cover shifts as needed. I didn't mind.

I'd been dodging calls from my brother, Cosimo, for two

days. He always wanted me to do something down at the club, a business we owned and ran together. I had tried to step away, wanting to be more of a silent, uninvolved partner, but he kept reeling me back in. I guess that was fair. I had made a commitment by going into business with him.

He just didn't understand that my mind, heart, and soul weren't in it, probably for the past year. It had been a rough year, not that he fully understood. How could I expect him too, when I had not confided in him all the feelings that had run through me the past year?

A year prior:

This was the night I made sure everything was taken care of not only at the station house but at the Velvet Playroom. All the guys wished me good luck. I doubled checked the reservations earlier today at a high-end restaurant I wanted to try. A small table with a very intimate setting. Candles and wine at the ready. I had pre-ordered what we are going to have based on her likes.

I finish my shower, trim my beard, and put on my favorite black suit, black shirt, and black tie. Catrina's favorite. I open the safe in my closet and grab the little blue box from Tiffany's. Inside the box is a Tiffany Novo three Carat Emerald-cut with Pavé Diamond Platinum Band. I take one last look in the mirror, go over what I am going to say, and then head out the door.

The car that I hired is waiting in my driveway. The driver opens the door and I slide in for the thirty-minute ride to her house. For once in my life, I am actually positive about everything. I want to spend the rest of my life with her, not only as her husband, but as her Dom. I have never had a Submissive so in-tune with me and my wants.

The car pulls up to the front of her house, and I let myself in. The front of the house seems to be dark, but I see light coming out of her bedroom. It is just like Catrina to be running late. I walk down the hall and crack the door open to surprise her. I let my eyes adjust to the light and I look over to where moaning is coming from her bed. I freeze. Catrina is hand-cuffed to the bed, naked as the day she was born. Her legs are spread wide-open, and I see a blonde head between her legs. What the fuck!

Catrina is aware of me in the room, opens her eyes, and smiles. "Hello Drago, I am running a bit behind schedule, as you can see," she purrs.

I am seeing red at this point. Just at that moment, the man turns, and surprise of all surprises, it is Michael. I haul him off the bed and nail him so hard in the nose that he falls back and hits the wall.

Catrina screams and starts crying. "What the hell, Drago?"

I look over and Michael is getting up. I look at him and hiss, "you better stay where the fuck you are if you know what's good for you!"

I give Catrina one last look of pure hatred and turn to leave her house. My heart has shattered into a million pieces. How could she do that to me, and with one of my best friends from the Velvet Playroom? She and Michael are now dead to me.

I walk back out to the car. The driver gives me a questioning look, but opens the door, and I slide back in. He then asks me where I want to go, and the only place I can think of is the Velvet Playroom to talk to my brother, Cosimo, and drink some of his bourbon. I need to get drunk out of my mind to wash away the betrayal I just witnessed.

Madeline

I shouldn't have been surprised by Kenzie's comfort in

the gym. She greets me wearing a Stevens Street Gym tank top and tight crop pants. She still isn't showing. I have to look closely to see the tiniest of baby bumps in her abdomen, which is still flatter than my normal tummy.

With no small talk, we quickly begin our workout. She shows me how to use the equipment. She adjusts the seats and weight amounts for me as we travel between pieces of equipment. She shows me how to use one, then hops on the machine next to me so we can chat while we both do our reps. Before I know it, we had used almost all the weighted machines.

"Hey, quick, look at that guy," Kenzie whispers to me as a man walks by. I turn my head to only catch a glimpse of his white t-shirted back as he disappears within the weight room at the back of the gym. "That was Butch, that guy I wanted to fix you up with."

Damn, I hadn't gotten a good look. He looks strong and solid, the little I did see of him. I didn't see his face though, not that I am interested. I kept an eye out in that direction as we finished our workout. As we step back near the counter, at that angle I catch sight of him, barely, but enough. Wow! He is hot. He is seated on one of those slightly reclining benches. He's talking and laughing with Logan. He sits reclined; I can't see his face, just a very manly, clean-shaven jawline pointed towards the ceiling. I watch as he chest-presses more weight than I could fathom, even pushing or pulling across the floor.

Logan sees me and waves. I smile and wave back. Another hottie. I almost wish I had gone after him the night of Kenzie's wedding. I bet it would have been amazing. I could have, Logan made that clear, but Kenzie had told me to stay away, warned me what kind of man he was, a player who specialized in one-night stands. What good was one incredible night of sex if you wanted more and could never have it? And I'd never want Kenzie to hear I had a one-night stand with her husband's best friend.

Kenzie looks to see who I waved at. "You didn't, did you?" she asks.

"What, just wave at two hot guys?" I say with a lusty smile.

Kenzie laughs. "No, sleep with Logan."

"I wish I had, though, girlfriend, if I was in bed with a man like him, I wouldn't be sleeping." We both giggle. "That Butch, yeah, from the little I just saw of him, he's hot."

"Are you changing your mind on that intro?" Kenzie asks with a smile.

"Maybe, I'll let you know," I say. I might as well leave my options open.

Chapter 2

Butch

I shrug on my leather pants. Thank goodness, I don't have a raging hard on, or these pants wouldn't tie shut. How in the hell did I let Cosimo talk me into this? Why did I ever agree to train a new Submissive is beyond all thought control? Usually, Cosimo takes care of that side of the business. Security of the club is my forte. It has been a long time since I have had to handle a novice Submissive.

As I walk through the club, I notice details I hadn't noticed in a long time. The main area is furnished with comfortable couches covered in velvet, soft lighting, and mirrors adorn the walls. Soft music plays throughout the room, adding to the ambience for the evening. Many walks of life are here, from the Mayor's Assistant, to one of the high-ranking police officers from the local precinct, to construction workers, and sales clerks. This room is decorated specifically to invite everyone to drop their inhibitions as they enter. Cosimo paid an interior designer a lot of money to create this effect.

The number of Submissives present is overwhelming tonight, and every Dom and Dom in training have smiles on their faces. As I make my way to the office, I pass through the private rooms of the Velvet Playroom. As it is early, most are unoccupied. However, the reservation list is full for the evening.

I open the door to Cosimo's office and drop into the soft, supple leather chair in front of his desk. "Tell me again why you feel I am the best candidate to deal with a newbie who, from all accounts, is scared shitless about this whole process?" I ask Cosimo.

Cosimo sighs, running his hand through his short black hair. "Because, my dear brother, you are the most gentle Dom in the place, and if you don't get back into the game, you will get rusty."

I run my fingers over the plaque on the desk, the Velvet Playroom, our place, this place. We're partners. I don't take orders from Cosimo, I don't have to deal with this woman if I really don't want to, but I haven't told him no and here I am dressed and ready. I gaze at Cosimo, giving him my best 'I don't give a shit' look, but he knows I will do what is necessary to keep the club going. I may have stepped away a bit in the last year, but I'm still committed to the club's success.

"Besides, just because she wants to wear a mask in the public rooms doesn't mean she's scared shitless. It just means she wants to keep her anonymity," Cosimo counters.

"Who is she?" I ask.

"She wants her identity to remain unknown to everyone, including her Dom, and that is you."

I laugh out loud. "If she's anyone famous that I'd recognize, that will blow that one."

Cosimo smiles devilishly. "Interesting choice of words, blow. How long has it been since a woman's lips were wrapped around your cock?"

I shoot to my feet. "I'm not having that conversation with you again, dear brother."

Madeline

All new Subs in training must check in at the front desk in the foyer. As I walk through the door and wait to register with about a half dozen other girls, I take in my surroundings. I am amazed at the taste in the décor. I guess I really didn't know what to expect, maybe a dungeon like atmosphere since we are beneath street level. The mirrors on the walls are of all different shapes and sizes, all adorned with gold frames. The wallpaper is a beautiful red and gold, very subtle with a touch of class. The only place to sit is on a very large, round, red velvet circle settee. A beautiful antique crystal chandelier is directly over it.

I hear the receptionist call out the name Charlotte, while staring right at me, and then I realize, that is the name I chose to be called while in the club. I walk up to the registration desk, more than a bit nervous. After signing in, I am given a full mask, which was one of my stipulations before signing the contract with the club. Anytime I am in the public areas of the club, I will wear the mask. She also hands me a keycard. It is solid red with no lettering on it. It is my key to enter the door of the club after tonight.

I am advised to follow the Dom that will come shortly for me. I wonder if he will look like the Dom's I've read about in all those erotica romance novels that I have spent a small fortune on. Not all men can be hot, but for this to do what I want it to for me, I at least have to be attracted to him. I'm glad the contract allows for the refusal of a potential Dom if compatibility does not exist. That would be my out if I am not sexually attracted to him.

Fifteen minutes pass, and most of the girls that arrived before me have been taken away by men, their potential Doms I assume, all of whom have been drop dead smoking hot. The woman running the front desk alerts me that my Dom is on his way. I am starting to lose my nerve, wondering if I have lost my mind to even consider doing this when a very large man walks into the foyer.

He stands about six-five. He has just the right amount of hair on his chest. As my eyes move further down, his abs are incredible. The washboard look was never something that turned me on until now. Holy shit, I wish I had laundry to do right now. The leather pants that he is wearing leaves nothing to a girl's imagination, and if the bulge in front where the pants tie together is any indication of how well-endowed he is, my books have let me down! Apparently, reality can be better than fiction.

As I finally look up at his face, those eyes hold mine. He has blue eyes I could drown in and stare at all day. I didn't know anyone's eyes could be so alluring, like the beautiful water in the Caribbean. I note he has long jet-black hair that is pulled back with a thin leather wrap. What looks like a two-day shadow adorns his Adonis-looking face. My Dom walks to me. He reaches out his hand and introduces himself simply as Master D. I reach out to shake his hand, and I am surprised that he flips my hand over and places a light kiss on the palm. Shivers run up my spine, and I close my eyes to regain control of myself. He chuckles to himself and then starts to speak.

Butch

My cell phone buzzes; a text from the front desk. My Sub has checked in and is awaiting my arrival. Her name is Charlotte, her chosen Sub name for the club. As I walk through the door leading to the foyer, I see her sitting on the circular sofa, fidgeting with the hem of her skirt. She looks to be a petite but curvy woman. When she looks up, I see doe eyes trapped in headlights coming from behind her mask. I could swear she is ready to bolt. If this evening ends badly, I am going to kick Cosimo's ass for having me handle her. But if I play this right, I just may have this frightened kitten purring in my arms.

I walk right to Charlotte and take her hand, turning it over and placing a light kiss on her palm. She is so nervous. Her anxiety is radiating through her entire body as she closes her eyes. I need to find something to put her at ease. I chuckle to myself and that is when she opens her eyes, and I see the most unusual dark chocolate eyes with 24 karat gold specks in them. She has very large eyes, and long dark eyelashes adorning them. She doesn't seem to be wearing any type of eye makeup, which makes me wonder if she is a natural beauty under that mask. Those types of women are so rare these days.

I immediately become the Dom by telling her to please stand up, bring her things with her and to follow me. As we walk down the inner corridor to the locker rooms, she is following me as a good Submissive should. I think to myself, *"She has done some homework. Perhaps this won't be the worst experience of my life."* We stop in front of the ladies' locker room. "Please go to locker number thirteen, place your personal belongings in the locker, and put on the outfit I have personally chosen for you to wear this evening," I advise her. Charlotte just nods her head and heads through the door of the locker room.

Madeline

As I follow him to the locker room, my eyes are glued to the large dragon tattoo that adorns his entire back. The yellow eyes have me mesmerized. When he walks, the tattoo seems to move with his muscles. As I look at his long black hair that is gathered at the nape of his neck and secured in a leather tie, it looks so soft and the natural wave in it invites me to touch it. I've always loved men with long hair that was kept neatly. And that voice, I never thought a voice like my Dom exists, at least not outside of the books that I have read. Smooth and rough all at the same time. I wanted to drop to my knees then and there, but from the research and the erotic romance novels I have read, that would have been disrespectful.

As instructed, I go into the locker room and find locker number thirteen. I pull out the outfit chosen for me by him. To my surprise, the leather mini dress looks as if it will cover most of the parts of my body that I would have chosen to keep covered for my first time here. The sleek black leather mini dress has a halter style top with a plunging front. Studded straps in the front and at the sides. It reveals a lot of skin, but nothing I would be too upset about. There are knee high leather boots with three-inch heels. The boots might be a problem, but after putting on the dress, which hugs every curve of my body, the boots go so well with the dress that I will make my best effort to not trip and fall on my first night.

I walk over to the mirror to take a look at what this outfit reveals, and I am shocked at what I see in the mirror. Although I have ample curves, the mini dress actually accentuates all of my curves and minimizes my flaws. I smile to myself, thinking that I can do this, and I am hoping to experience a lot this evening with my Dom.

Taking a deep breath, I open the door to the locker room, and he is leaning against the wall. My breathing accelerates. He is the hottest man I have ever seen. It could be the adrenaline pumping through my body, but I am beyond excited to start our session.

Butch

While I lean against the wall across from the women's locker room, my mind wonders. Why is it I cannot find a woman that meets my needs as well as satisfies them? Although I have an enormous wall around my heart, I know deep down I want a woman that can satisfy my sexual needs and love me unconditionally, if that is truly even possible. I thought it was, before Catrina swept through my life like a hurricane.

My thoughts are interrupted by the door to the locker

room opening. My new Sub-in-training walks out, and I forget to breathe. Damn, for a moment I forget I am the Dom in this situation. She is a vision in her leather mini and leather boots. I can picture her with a crop in her hand, giving me orders instead of the other way around. I let a breath out that I didn't realize I was holding. I gaze into her eyes behind that damn mask she insisted she wear in public, and her eyes have something smoldering that almost looks like lust. The way she is fidgeting shows she is nervous about what will happen tonight. Good, I don't want someone who is cocky, that I would have to punish the first night.

"We are going into the main room, and you will do whatever I instruct you to do. Is that understood?" I ask.

"Yes Sir, I understand," Charlotte answers back. That brings a smile to my face. Her voice is low and sultry. The way Sir rolls off her tongue makes me hard. I really need to control myself tonight.

As we enter the main room, I can see her eyes darting all around the room. There are Doms and Subs in various stages of training and those who are long past the training phase and come just to play in the sexual atmosphere of the club. Most of the Doms are sitting in very plush velvet chairs, while their Subs are on their knees, eyes down, palms up, waiting for instructions from their Masters.

We walk over to the chair by the large fireplace. Everyone knows the chair located there is never to be used other than by Cosimo or myself. Tonight, I am the lucky one taking a seat by the warm fire. As I sit down, I instruct Charlotte to kneel to the right of the chair and to place her palms on her thighs. I can see that she isn't comfortable in the high heel boots she is wearing. I decide to cut her some slack as she kneels.

"Stop, Charlotte, come and stand in between my legs. Place your right foot on my knee." She complies, and I start to unzip the boot. I can tell that she is relieved as the first boot comes off. "Now the other foot," I instruct. That boot is placed on the floor next to the other boot on my left. "Please continue with the instruction I gave you." Charlotte kneels down to my right and places her hands on her knees. She looks up at me, wondering what I am going to ask next. My eyes burn into hers as I reach out and touch the side of her neck. "Eyes are to remain down," I tell her in a forced, terse voice.

My Sub's heart is beating like she is running a marathon. I know I can intimidate, but for this arrangement to work, I have to get her to relax and trust me. "Charlotte, look at me," I command. As she lifts her head, those dark brown eyes seem to look into my soul. "Although this is your first night at the club, you seem to be very obedient," I say. "I would like to walk you to a room that is having a very specific scene going on tonight."

"I would be honored, Sir," Charlotte responds.

After some discussions about politics with one of the other Doms, I get up from my chair and place my hand out for her to grasp. As she places her smaller hand in mine, I notice it isn't as soft as most women's hands. However, her fingernails are well manicured and have a beautiful shade of pink on them. She bends down to grab the boots, and I instruct her to leave them.

We walk through the hallway and stop at a room that contains a small stage with approximately 30 chairs in a semi-circle in two rows. Several Doms with their Subs are already seated. I lead my Sub to the front row, center and sit down, telling her to assume the position of a Sub, which she does beautifully. I watch other Doms in the room staring at my Sub.

Charles, one of the long-standing members of the club, taps me on the shoulder and asks what the deal is with the full mask. I explain it was a stipulation of my Sub before joining the club. He smiles and makes the comment that she is definitely someone he would like to fuck. I turn back around.

However, if Charles could see my face right now, he would know that he is out of line, and for some reason I don't want anyone else touching her. Wow, where did that come from? I have just met her and have exchanged little conversation with her. I guess I really need to get laid.

Master Christopher brings his Sub-in-training onto the stage. He places her with her back against the St. Andrew's cross in the center of the room. While Master Christopher ties her hands and ankles to the cross, I watch Charlotte's reaction. I can tell her breath is erratic, and that she seems to get completely turned on with something simple as being bound to a cross. Interesting. As the scene plays out, Charlotte's breath becomes quicker, and she is starting to squirm where she sits, so beautifully I might add.

I lean down and whisper in her ear, "would you like to try that after they are done, my sweet Sub?" Charlotte's eyes become as big as saucers, and she is still breathing erratically. "Well, I am waiting for an answer."

"Yes Sir, I would enjoy that very much."

I hope that after the scene is over, she will still feel the same way. The scene takes a turn that I hope doesn't scare Charlotte. Master Christopher has just finished eating his Sub's pussy and kissing her deeply. Makes me wonder if there is more going on there than just training, but I decide to mind my business, for now.

Master Christopher then calls up another Sub in training. Her name is Carol, I believe. Master Christopher, with the permission of Carol's Dom, instructs Carol to finger fuck his sub. While Carol is following his instruction, Master Christopher gives himself a hand job. When he is ready to explode, he instructs Carol to go back to her Dom. He then finishes up and jets warm cum all over his Sub's pussy and legs. She moans with complete pleasure from the act. However, he isn't done with the scene.

I happen to look down at Charlotte, who hasn't moved an inch, and I can tell that she is very intrigued by what just happened in this scene. However, her eyes show a different reaction as something is suddenly scaring her. As I look over, I see that Master Christopher has taken a crop from the wall and has starting using it on his Sub's breasts. His Sub moans in pleasure.

I again lean down and whisper in Charlotte's ear. "Are you sure you still want to proceed, my little lamb?" Charlotte nods, and I give her a stern look.

She remembers where she is by responding, "Yes Sir."

I cannot wait for the scene to end. I have some plans for her, and I am so hard I feel like I am going to explode.

Madeline

As I sit with Master D and watch the scene play out, all the books that I have read over the last few years don't prepare me for what I am watching. I never thought that watching a girl finger fuck another girl would be such a turn on, but I feel my pussy dripping wet after the scene ends. The fact that my Dom wants to try out a similar scene with me has my heart pounding and my nipples are so hard that the leather dress I have on is begging to be released from my body.

The room clears out and I watch Master D walk to the door and lock it. My breathing has become more like panting, and I am dripping wet with anticipation. He tells me to stand up, take off my mask, but keep my eyes down. Master D walks to my left side and gently takes my left hand in his. He whispers to walk with him, and he guides me up on the stage and then turns me around in front of the St. Andrew's cross. I am told to look at him while he lifts each arm and restrains my wrists. He instructs me to move each leg until he is able to restrain those as well. I become very excited waiting for what is in store for me next.

I then watch as Master D walks right in front of me, and slowly starts to unzip the front of my barely there leather dress. I suck in my breath. This is moving too quickly for me. I didn't know things could progress this fast. But I want this. I have craved non-vanilla intimacy with a man for a long time. The last few relationships I've had have been disappointing. And the truth is I am just too busy with the restaurant to try another relationship that would probably end up disappointing me again.

"How do you feel right now, Charlotte?" Master D asks, breaking in on my thoughts.

"I am fine, Sir." I respond. From the way his eyes seem to light up and the slow smile that forms on his face, I feel as if I have pleased him.

"Charlotte," he continues, "before we begin, we need to discuss your safe word," Master D states. "There are a few rules we are going to discuss before proceeding. Your safe word will stop anything we are engaged in immediately. Please remember that if you are feeling uncomfortable, that safe word stops all play. However, if you are just feeling nervous, or need an explanation other than what I supplied you before we move forward, please ask. We are building trust between the two of us, and I never want you to feel distressed during our sessions."

I nod, and then he asks what I would like to use for my safe word. I look up and blurt out "Paris."

He nods and says, "Interesting choice for a safe word. We will definitely discuss that at a later date."

Master D runs his index finger of his right hand down my throat and stops between my breasts. His touch is feather light, but his finger has a callous on it, making me wonder what he does for a living. As his finger moves to my right breast, my breath hitches. I feel like I am going to internally combust. I have never been so turned on by a man's touch, not that I have had a lot of experience with exciting sexual encounters in the last few years. As his finger wanders over to my nipple, it almost sounded like Master D had a small hitch in his breath. I know I cannot hide my emotions on my face. What the hell is wrong with me? This isn't a relationship; he is training me for my future Dom that I want to have a long-term sexual relationship with.

As my mind wonders, I wasn't ready for what happens next. A very sharp pain assaults me, and then a very foreign tingling sensation in my pussy occurs. "Have you ever had a nipple clamp placed on those beautiful breasts of yours, Charlotte?" Master D questions.

"No Sir, never." I whisper in a very shaky voice.

"How does it make you feel?" he asks.

What can I say? It hurt like a bitch, but now I am so wet I want him to fuck me. No, I don't think that is what he wants to hear. Just as I am getting ready to respond, I feel the same beautiful pain on the other breast. Whoa, no warning or preparation for that one. Master D is so close to my body at this point, I can smell the woodsy outdoor soap he must use. If my wrists weren't restrained, I would love to run my finger down his chest all the way to his chiseled abs. But that isn't happening today.

Master D tugs on the chain that is hanging between the nipple clamps and asks again, "What is your safe word, Charlotte?"

I respond, "Paris, Sir."

"Good, shall we proceed?" he asks.

"Yes Sir, please Sir," I respond. Gee, I don't sound needy now, do I? I just want to be fucked so bad, but I know I am hoping for too much during my first session.

Master D walks behind me and starts to place a blindfold over my face. "Permission to speak, Sir?" I whisper.

"Yes, Charlotte, what is it?"

"Do you have to blindfold me? I had an awful experience once when I was blindfolded," I share.

"I need to blindfold you for the next part of the scene, in order for you to feel the complete experience of it. In order for this to work, we need to build trust. I need you to understand that I would do nothing to hurt you."

"I understand Sir," I reply. A blindfold is put over my eyes. It is a red silk scarf of some kind, which seems to cover a good portion of my face. I need to get out of my head, this isn't that asshole that hurt me when I was blindfolded. I can get over this. Breathe, breathe, breathe.

Master D drops to his knees in front of me, but with this damn blindfold on, I cannot see anything. Just as I am wondering what will happen next, I practically jump off the cross as Master D's finger slides through the folds of my lips. I hear him take in a sharp intake of breath as he slowly runs his finger up and down through my wet pussy. He then inserts his finger and I feel like I am going to orgasm right then and there. Seriously, even my vibrator doesn't make me feel this way. He slowly pumps in and out. I feel a second digit enter as well. My hips move in rhythm with the pumping of his fingers.

Before I know what is happening, he growls, "don't you dare orgasm until I grant you permission to do so."

That woke me up, but the deep need inside is too much. I scream, "Master D, Sir, I cannot hold out! this is so new to me. I need to come, please Sir."

He promptly removes his fingers and stands up.

While he unbinds my ankles, I cannot figure out what

just happened. Did I displease him? He then walks behind me, places my mask back over the blindfold. While lost in my thoughts as to what I might have done wrong, he releases my left wrist and then my right, and he scoops me up and carries me down the hall. We stop, and I hear him enter a code on the number pad, and I hear a squeak of what I can only assume is a door. My mask and blindfold are removed. Very soft, low lighting pops on. We are in a room with a very large king-size bed with a beautiful black and white satin comforter on it. Master D walks to the bed and lays me on it. The comforter is already folded back. "I am going to remove your dress, Charlotte, do you understand?"

"Yes Sir, I do." I wonder why he had to ask if I understood. Once the dress is gone, he tells me to lie down and he covers me with the comforter. He walks to the table beside the bed and brings a bottle of water with him. He sits on the edge of the bed and instructs me to drink as he lifts the water to my lips.

"We are done for the evening, Charlotte; do you have any questions regarding your training tonight?"

I have so many questions, I don't know where to start. I must begin somewhere, so here I go. "Did I do something wrong, Sir?"

I can tell he is thinking about what I just asked. "Why do you feel you did something wrong? You are a very quick learner, and I was surprised we went as far as we did this evening."

"I was wondering why you wouldn't let me finish my orgasm, Sir," I blurt out, without thinking.

He shakes his head, and I know I should have kept my mouth shut. "Charlotte, as your Dom, I decide when you climax, not you. Is that understood?"

"Yes Sir, I understand. My apologies."

"Charlotte, let me explain a bit of how this works. A Sub exists to please their Dom. It is always the Dom's choice whether their Sub orgasms and when. I know this is your first night in the club, and I will let your insubordination go this time. However, in future sessions, you will be punished. Is that understood, Charlotte?"

I nod, knowing that I really screwed this up tonight. I also question if this is for me. I am the one normally in charge. But that was one of the points of trying this to relinquish control. Despite that, I wanted to orgasm. I was so close.

"Aftercare is very important for a Dom to look after their Sub, making sure that they are coming down from subspace slowly and comfortably," he explains, breaking in on my thoughts. "Although you didn't reach that tonight, I want you to get into the routine."

We sit there. It seems like only a few minutes. However, when I look at the clock, I see an hour has passed. Master D gets off the bed and hands me a red plush robe. "Please go back to the locker room and change to go home. I will have the front desk call you an Uber."

"Thank you, Sir, I do appreciate that." I have a lot to think about before my next session.

Chapter 3

Butch

Well, this evening turned out differently from how I thought it would. After having one of the staff put Charlotte into an Uber, I go back to the offices to find Cosimo sitting at his desk with two glasses and a bottle of Kentucky Derby Woodford Reserve Bourbon. As I walk in, Cosimo points to the guest chair in front of his desk. Without saying a word, he pours us each a glass, neat, and hands me one.

"Your evening seemed to go very well tonight, Drago," Cosimo says. A smiled appears on his face, which I want to slap off. Even him calling me by my given name pisses me off. "I have never seen someone respond so quickly to a Dom that they ended up on the cross their first night here. You definitely haven't lost your touch, my brother."

I take a long swig of my bourbon, loving the feel as it travels down my throat. I run my hand through my hair, having removed the leather tie from the back. This day wasn't the worst day of my life, but it wasn't a day I was looking forward to either, until I walked into the foyer to find my new Sub sitting there. Although she wasn't tall, thin, and blond, she had curves in all the right places. Her dark hair and beautiful brown eyes, with those gold flints in them, almost had me on my knees. It really has been too long since I was with a woman.

When she removed that damn mask her overall effect was that of a goddess, one I need to have.

"How long did you watch our training session tonight, Cosimo?"

He looks at me and grins. "The whole session, Drago. I was worried about you since you haven't been in the game for a while, and that is why I insisted you get back out there. I am hoping this will fuel your desire to be with a woman after what Catrina did to you."

I groan, swallow the rest of the bourbon, which burns all the way down, and take a deep breath, exhaling hard. "Well, I hope I didn't disappoint you with my performance tonight, Cosimo," I sarcastically add.

"Drago, she is exactly what you need right now. Her responses were amazing, and I think you can teach her exactly what she needs to know to get her to where she wants to go in the lifestyle. Her file indicates she is open to almost anything her Dom will show her, but she has some hard limits you should probably review, again, before your next session. Which, by the way, is a week from today. She is only available on Monday evenings," Cosimo says, but his voice is not condescending.

I know I have been out of the game for a long time. He has every right to be concerned about me, but still, him treating me like a Dom in training pisses me off. "I was really surprised she didn't use her safe word the first time I put that nipple clamp on her," I share with Cosimo, not sure why I am. "In fact, she was so wet and ready, it took every bit of self-control, not to go down on her and enjoy that sweet pussy of hers."

"Welcome back," Cosimo says and then lifts his glass back to his lips.

Cosimo and I say our goodnights. I do a final security

sweep of the facility to confirm that all our patrons had left the premises. I stop by the room with the St. Andrew's Cross and replay the night in my thoughts. I have had no one that was so responsive their first visit.

I was so hard during that session, I really thought I was going to have to fuck Charlotte right there and then. But I know that isn't what she wanted. She wants to learn the lifestyle, and I will be the one to show her. No other Dom in the place will touch her. Again, where the fuck did that come from? I don't even know this girl, but she's already gotten under my skin. Talking about skin, that little birthmark she has right behind her left ear is very sexy. It looks like a heart, and at first, I thought it was a tattoo. However, every time I whispered in her ear, I would check the mark out and it was definitely a birth mark.

After locking up the last door, I head to my Harley-Davidson FLSRCI custom cherry red motorcycle to head home for the night. Ha, it was three a.m. Who was I kidding? It was morning, Tuesday. I decide to pull into an all-night diner to get some breakfast and the best coffee in the state of Kentucky. The waitresses all know me, and within ten minutes, I have my breakfast and black coffee placed in front of me.

I again replay the evening's events. Her eyes captivate me. Her hair smells of sandalwood and lavender and is a beautiful dark shade of brown, with natural waves. My hands were itching to run my fingers through that gorgeous head of hair. I can be patient. Next time, I promise myself.

I am going to work up a new scenario for my next session with Charlotte. I hope that when she starts to trust me, that damn mask will be removed in public areas. She is no one famous that I recognize, so I have to believe she is being overly paranoid. I want to show her off, and in the back of my mind I hear "mine."

***

My alarm goes off Wednesday morning. I have a pretty good idea of what my next few weeks will look like. We have four new firefighter trainees showing up at nine a.m. this morning for the first week of training. As one of the lieutenants of our firehouse, I need to be present for their arrival. I have a meeting with the captain at eight-thirty a.m., so I jump into the shower. I make it a quick one, grab a cup of coffee and head out the door dressed in my uniform pants and a white t-shirt.

The weather looks as if a storm is brewing, so I decide to leave the Harley home and I jump into my other ride, a 2014 BMW M4 Convertible. As it roars to life, I mentally thank my grandfather for buying it and leaving it to me when he passed away last year, along with a very large inheritance that I haven't touched. I love my life as it is. My job doesn't pay as well as the wine business, as Cosimo is always reminding me, but I get satisfaction from it that my brother doesn't understand. I would never leave the firehouse just because of some old family money in an account with my name on it.

And I was right. The drops start to fall before I even make it out of my subdivision. Rain equals an increased number of motor vehicle accidents, or MVAs in fireman speak and we respond to a lot of them as well as to fires. Most shifts we respond to more accidents than fires, not that I'm complaining. I hope the rain is done by the time I am done with work. I'd like to put the top down and scream down some of the beautiful country back roads as the sun drops below the horizon. That always relaxes me.

I make it to the firehouse in record time, giving me ample opportunity to have one more cup of coffee before the new trainees are assembled in the briefing room. The captain, two other lieutenants, and I go over a few items before we stroll into the briefing room. From what I can see of the new lot of trainees, only three are going to make the cut for this firehouse. Of the four, one seems a bit too timid, and his physical appearance is sub-par, at best. But hey, we could be pleasantly surprised, so I will try to keep an open mind.

After introducing ourselves, the captain explains the training schedule and rotation. Since I am not working with the trainees until Friday, I welcome them and then take my leave. I have paperwork that has been sitting on my desk for nearly a week that requires my attention. As I dive into the stack, the alarm goes off, an overturned box truck on the ramp exiting the interstate and I am off to another adventure. This is why the paperwork never gets done.

Thursday rolls around. It had been a quiet shift at the firehouse, which we were due. It is midafternoon, and I head to the gym on Stevens Street. I have already put in over eighty hours in the last ten-day cycle, so the captain granted my request for comp time knowing that I will begin working with the new recruits the following day, Friday. I will be on for three twelve-hour overnight shifts, all weekend, with them. I smile to myself thinking that after that, Monday night will come and that will be my next session with Charlotte.

Madeline

"Francois Blanchet is a no talent hack, a fraud, and a miserable human being!" I exclaim in response to her bringing up the Lexington Food article he was quoted in, winded from my run on the treadmill. "And he's not even French! His real first name is Frank, not Francois."

"Tell me how you really feel about him," Kenzie says with a laugh. As she is just walking on her treadmill beside mine, her voice is normal.

My eyes scan the buildings in front of me, across the street from the window of the Stevens Street Gym. I'd never noticed before, but the main offices to a winery are housed in the building at the end of the block. "I had that great write up by the food critic and then what does Frank do? He goes out of his way to deep six my restaurant."

"You did kind of fire him," Kenzie reminds me.

"No, I rejected him as a partner in my restaurant. My restaurant, not his. We were both sous chefs at La Palm when I got my inheritance and was planning to open the Toad and the Hoot Owl. He's the one who wanted to horn in on my dream and partner with me. I never even entertained the idea," I correct her.

"But you let him come work for you last year," Kenzie adds.

"As a favor for an agreed upon time of three months, part-time, while he got his permits in for his little French Bistro. He wanted to renege on the agreement, and he wanted to stay longer and got mad when I wouldn't let him stay on. That wasn't the agreement. I was happy to help him, but it became clear he was still looking to horn in on my place."

"What he said in that article was pretty bad," Kenzie admits. "You have every right to be upset."

Upset? I wasn't just upset. I was livid! "The article wasn't even about me. He made it about me when he brought up the Toad and the Hoot Owl, and he attacked me personally. I did him a favor and now he does this."

"Certainly, your patrons will not believe that your kitchen is filthy, your food source ingredients are low quality, or that you treat your employees poorly, as he alleges."

"Maybe." I appreciate how Kenzie is trying to make me think it's not as bad as it is. But the truth is, people are fickle. I had that fantastic write up by the Lexington Food Critic and my reservations exploded. I am quite sure this new article with his allegations will cool the reservations. It could even turn a few of my loyal patrons off.

"Can't you sue him for liable or slander?" Kenzie asks. "None of what he said is true."

"No, it's not. But a lot of it is subjective, opinion. I think a better defense would be to take him on with my own offensive, call him out on his motives, on the cleanliness of his own kitchen, the quality of his food, and the state of his own employee relations. He doesn't have such a good track record going."

Kenzie shrugged. "Sounds like a pissing contest."

"There is no high road to take on this one. He went out of his way to attack me and my restaurant. He's going to get it back in spades."

"Did you sleep with him?" Kenzie asks, stopping me dead in my tracks.

I turn the machine off and stare at her in disbelief. "No! Have you seen the man? He's a toad."

Kenzie laughs. "And some would call you the hoot owl."

"That is not where the name of my restaurant came from," I insist.

Kenzie laughs again. "Be careful calling him a toad. You don't want that picked up by a reporter."

"Oh, my God!" I exclaim. "You know damned well my restaurant's name came from the made-up fairy tale my grandpa used to tell me as a child."

"I'm just saying, be very careful where this guy is concerned. It sounds like he has it out for you and will take anything he can and run with it. You don't want to play into his hand."

"Thanks," I say. "You're right. I need to keep my cool where he's concerned."

I step down from the machine. I point to the bathroom and excuse myself.

Butch

Pushing through the front door into the gym, my gaze sweeps the room. Kenzie crosses over to me from the row of treadmills lined up against the front window. "Hi Kenz," I greet.

"Hi, it's nice to see you," she says, giving me a hug. "Andy wanted to talk to you, was going to call you later. He's down in the MMA area."

"Thanks. I'll go see him before my work out."

I drop my bag in one of the cubbies by the doors to the bathrooms. The doors are both closed. I have to wait to change anyway, so I cross the gym and take the stairs down to the basement area where the MMA training space is. Andy has been talking about expanding and building changing rooms. It will be nice when he does.

"Hey, bro," I call over to him. He's in the center of the fighting ring.

He hops down and with long strides, closes the distance between us. He greets me with a hand shake. "I was going to call you later."

I glance back at the ring. "What about? You're not thinking of doing that, are you?"

Andy laughs loudly. "Me? Oh, hell no! Not that I'd want to, but Kenz would kill me. Mason and Blake asked about hosting some matches down here and having a paying audience in attendance. I was wondering how do I go about requesting EMTs be on call or in attendance at the event? I haven't mentioned it to them, but Kenzie and I think it would be a good idea, if it's possible."

"I'm glad you're thinking about that and asking in advance. To have a couple of guys here, it's going to cost Mason and Blake both EMTs salaries for the duration of their being on site. We'll let them park a unit outside, just in case."

"I'll tell them."

"If they cheap out and don't go for that, make sure you let me know when this match will be, so we are staffed for any potential calls. I'll want to have it noted in our schedule at the firehouse," I say.

"You got it," Andy guarantees me.

"Oh, and did you file a special event permit request for it?"

Andy smiles wide. "Isn't that what I'm doing right now?"

"Okay, okay, I'll file it for you. Text me the dates so I will have it in writing from you."

"Will do." He points at the stairs. "You here to work out?"

"Yeah, going to hit the weights. You available to spot me?"

Andy slaps me on the back. "I thought you'd never ask."

I laugh as we both ascend the stairs.

Madeline

Kenzie is near the desk when I come out of the bathroom. Her eyes are on the white t-shirted back of a man, who I barely get a look at as he goes down the stairs at the far end of the room. "Is that the same guy you pointed out before? Who you wanted to fix me up with?"

"It sure is," Kenzie says. "He shouldn't be downstairs long. I can introduce you when they come back up."

"Oh, I wish I had the time," I say, glancing at my watch.

"I have to go so that I can get home, get a shower, and be at my restaurant by four to prep tonight's special."

"In a few months, we'll have showers and locker rooms here," Kenzie says with an excited smile. "Andy and I have been brainstorming how to improve the gym."

"That's great," I answer. "But I still really need to go. I'll meet him another time when maybe I'm not sweat soaked."

"You look great," Kenzie assures me.

The truth was, I had no intention of meeting him now. Not since my experience at the Velvet Playroom. I had given the night a lot of thought over the past two days. I know I want to give it at least the six visits I signed up for, my training sessions, like I really need six more sessions to figure out what a Sub does and doesn't do. Master D is hot, and I was so sexually excited while with him. I am completely okay with sex outside of a relationship and I think this will be easier for me with my schedule. To know that I am going to have sexual contact with that hot man every Monday, sex that is new and exciting, is exhilarating.

"Another time. I promise." I give her a quick embrace and then grab my bag from the floor near the treadmill and I rush out the side door.

Butch

Kenzie is at the main desk when Andy and I reach the first floor. "You just missed my friend, Madeline, who I wanted to introduce you to."

I smile and shake my head. "I'm sure she's great, Kenzie. And I appreciate you think she and I would hit it off, but with my schedule, a relationship isn't that easy. And if she's as busy as you say, it sounds like it would be frustrating to try to get together." Besides, if it was meant for us to meet, we would have. "If we both happen to be here or at your place at the same time, great. I'll meet her then."

"Well, she did say she'd help us move, so if you are still off and can help, maybe then," Kenzie says.

"Yes, I am still good for helping with the move. I'm not scheduled to work." I chuckle. "And I know that won't change now that I'm making the schedule. Things are crazy because we are still down a few guys at the fire house."

"How's Lucky?" Andy asked.

"Lucky," I say. "He's healing well. I talked to him last night. He is doing good, considering."

Andy taps me on the shoulder and nods to the back where the barbells and weight plates are. "I only have an hour before a client is due. Let's get to it so I can spot you."

"See you later, Kenzie," I say with a smile.

"Hey, did Andy or Logan tell you about Logan's new kickboxing class?" Kenzie calls as we step away.

Andy throws his hands in the air. "I was getting to that," he says to her. "She's like a marketing machine. Having her work here is going to be so good for business, cross selling our offerings." He chuckles.

"I'll check a class out," I call back to her.

Chapter 4

Madeline

T he week is flying by. The new dishes that I have created have been a success and patrons have requested that they be incorporated into the main menu. I will have to give that a bit more thought. I am so thankful for the rave reviews the food critic gave the restaurant. However, I find my mind wandering back to my first session with Master D. Monday cannot get her quick enough.

Just as I am getting aroused just by thinking about it, I hear a loud crash in the back of the restaurant. I race back to the kitchen to find the entire rack of lamb that was being prepared for tonight's large group that has reserved the entire restaurant, sitting on the floor. Shit! Could this night get any worse? First, I walk into a pipe that was leaking in the Ladies Room, then trying to find a plumber that would take care of an emergency repair was a bitch. Next, I find out that the truck carrying the wine for the large group that is coming in tonight had a minor accident and the wine was destroyed. Now this! I am so used to running a well-oiled machine that this has really messed with my routine.

As I watch the staff clean up the lamb mess, I rack my brain how to fix this, so I don't have to cancel their gathering at the restaurant or sub in a different meal. After all, they had requested the lamb. I open my contacts on my cell and find the number for my friend Makarios over at Agathias Restaurant. If anyone has lamb in the quantity I need for tonight, it is Makarios.

Within forty-five minutes, the lamb arrives, and my staff is hard at work getting it ready for the group that is coming in at six-thirty. Now the wine issue, they had requested a specific wine be served with the lamb tonight, a Chateau Musar Red. This will be hard to replace on such short notice and in the quantity I need. I contact my sommelier at home and ask him to do his research and come up with a wine that is comparable to Chateau Musar Red and to get a case of it to the restaurant as soon as possible.

I am so glad that I have hired competent, knowledgeable, hard-working members for my team. I know that they won't let me down. And with that thought, Dave Walsh invades my mind. He was the exception. Not competent. Not knowledgeable. Not so hard-working. And although hot, not good in bed. I guess I really got lucky that he got pissed off when I broke up with him and he quit. Saved me having to fire him.

As I am putting on the finishing touches for tonight's large group dinner, my phone dings. I have received an email from the club that upon my arrival on Monday; I am to go straight to the ladies' locker room and change into the outfit chosen by my Dom that will be in locker number thirteen. What is with the number thirteen? Even most buildings and ships don't have a thirteenth floor.

***

Monday night arrives, and I find myself walking up to locker number thirteen, telling myself to breathe. I open the locker door and find a beautiful black corset with thousands of rhinestones adorning it. Along with the corset, I find a red garter, a black thong and black fishnet stockings and three-inch red high heels. Thank goodness, I don't have to wear those damn knee-high stiletto boots. That was a challenge, to say the least. A note also indicated that after I was changed, I was to walk to the wall phone and dial 111 and Master D would come and get me for my next training session.

After slipping into the outfit left for me by my Dom, as instructed, I walk to the wall phone and dial 111. The voice on the phone is female. She tells me that Master D would be there shortly and to wait for him to knock on the locker room door so he could walk me to the main room. The anticipation is killing me. Will our encounter be as hot as the first training session last week? I really hope that I didn't disappoint him, and that I become a good Sub for my permanent Dom.

I hear a knock on the door and slowly open it. Master D is standing there, black leather pants, hugging each inch of his magnificent body. Again, he is shirtless, and all I want to do is run my hands over his chest. I notice him intently watching me, and he seems to smile at me, me of all people. My imagination is running wild, and I want to ask him if he ever modeled. I cannot figure out why GQ hasn't been knocking down his door to photograph him.

"I am ready for the evening, Master D, and I want to thank you for the amazing outfit you chose for me to wear for you this evening."

"Charlotte, you would look fabulous in a trash bag. I just wanted you to sparkle this evening. We need to discuss the scene I have planned for this evening, so you fully understand where it is going and what is expected of you."

"Yes Sir, I cannot wait to hear what you have planned for me." I put my mask on and we start down the hall to the main room.

Once in the main room, Master D sits in the same chair by the large fireplace as he did last week. "Assume the position, Charlotte."

Immediately, I drop to my knees, palms up on my thigh and my head bent.

"Beautiful Charlotte, just beautiful."

"Master D, you have a beautiful Sub, and I hear she will be looking for a permanent Dom after her training is complete."

"Master Dante, if you would like to be considered, please let the main office know of your intentions."

"I will definitely do that Master D, thank you," Master Dante answers.

"Charlotte, tonight's scene will be a bit more public, and I want to make sure you can handle that before we proceed. Are you able to handle it, Charlotte?"

"Yes, Sir, I trust you."

"We will go up on a stage, and I will place your hands in soft handcuffs, and I will hook them up above your head. Then your legs will be spread out with a spreader bar. Another Sub will come up and untie your corset and remove it for everyone to see those beautiful tits of yours. Another Sub will spread whip cream over those amazing pink nipples for me to suck off. However, you are not to orgasm until I tell you that you can. Do you understand, Charlotte?"

"Yes, Sir I fully understand." My pulse is racing just thinking about it.

Butch

"Are you ready to be out in front of everyone tonight, Charlotte? I don't want to worry about you using your safe word if you have any misgivings about the scene tonight."

"Yes, Sir, I feel I can do this. I want to please you, Sir."

"That is just the beginning of the scene. I want to taste

that sweet pussy of yours Charlotte, do you want that to happen tonight?"

I cannot believe what I am hearing. A drop-dead gorgeous man just said he wants to go down on me, Madeline Shaw. Unbelievable. I feel as if I won the lottery. Sure, he is doing his job, but damn, he is doing it to me. Hell yes, I want this to happen. I respond, "Yes, Sir." Probably with a bit more zeal than I intended, but fuck yes.

Master D chuckles and shakes his head, standing up to take my hand to lead me to the stage. My stomach now has butterflies. Isn't this what I wanted to experience? I filled out the application and laid it all out there. Get your shit together Maddie!

The room is dark, with a single spot light shining on the stage. I can see Doms and their Subs filling the room. All Subs are kneeling before their Doms. Can I do this? Once we start up the steps to the stage, there is no turning back.

"Breath Charlotte, I am here, and I won't hurt you, please trust me."

"I do, Master D. I know you won't hurt me."

"Good Girl, now please turn around." As I turn, I stumble right into his hard chest. His large, muscular arms encase me until I regain my balance. Wow, a girl could get used to that chest. He slips off my mask and slips on the blindfold.

As he turns me around, he instructs, "please put your hands out for me Charlotte. I am going to put handcuffs on them and then raise your hands and hook you to the chain above your head. With the blindfold on your experience will be more intense." My heart rate is starting to pick up as Master D leans in and whispers, "your application indicated that you were into being blindfolded, and I hope I don't disappoint you tonight, my sweet."

My breathing is getting as fast as my heart rate. Yes, the blindfold makes this more intense.

"Now, spread your legs apart and let me know if the stance is too wide, as you need to be as comfortable as possible for the next 30 minutes."

I nod my head. My nerves are starting to settle in. You want this Maddie, breathe.

"Charlotte, we will begin in a few minutes, and I want you to adjust to this new position."

"Yes, Sir."

After what feels like an eternity, I finally hear Master D request that Sub Marta come to the stage. My breath hitches. Here we go. I hope I can make it through the scene and not disappoint Master D. Sub Marta unlaces the corset, and the rush of cold air on my breasts brings my nipples to attention. I feel hands run up and down my left arm, and someone blows into my ear. I have shivers running down my spine.

This is what I wanted. I smile and then I feel the left nipple being covered with whip cream. My right arm is now being stroked, and I feel someone's warm breath in my right ear. I feel like I am going to come right now. The whipped cream is sprayed on my right nipple and then total silence.

I hear Master D explain that this is my first public scene, and that he is very proud of me taking this first step after only one session. I can hear the other Dom's commending Master D on having such a responsive Sub. After thanking them, the room is silent once again.

Suddenly, something soft brushes my right breast. I moan, and I hear Master D chuckle. He then whispers in my left ear, "are you ready Charlotte? There is no turning back."

"Yes, Sir, I am ready."

Without warning, his mouth clamps on my left nipple and he is sucking off the whipped cream. He has an amazing mouth. The things he does with his tongue are sending me into orbit. A sharp pain and then pleasure invades me after Master D nips my left nipple. "Very good, Charlotte, you are doing great."

All I can do is nod, so afraid that I might explode right there. Master D moves on to the right breast. I don't know how the experience could get any better, but shit, what he is doing feels like nothing I have experienced. Too soon, he removes his mouth from my nipple.

I hear Master D instruct Sub Kara to come to the stage. He asks her to remove my thong by cutting them off with scissors. Cold air rushes between my legs. Immediately I feel a strong finger rub my clit, and I don't know how much longer I can hold out. I haven't been given permission to release my orgasm. This is sheer torture.

A warm breath is blown on my pussy and without warning, a warm tongue plunges into me. I don't think I can hold on much longer. Master D grips the sides of my thighs and I can feel him burying his mouth into me. The stubble on his face tickles the inside of my thighs, but the need to come is overwhelming. Right as I am on the edge of losing control, his tongue is gone.

"Charlotte, I know you are ready, but I haven't given you permission to come, but you are handling this very well. The next time I go down on you, you have my permission to lose yourself, and I will be there to bring you down from the experience."

Master D runs his hands down my thighs and once again plunges his tongue into my wet pussy. Within a minute, I am screaming from the major orgasm I have just experience. He then moves back to my breasts, and I feel a smaller finger invade my channel. Another finger is added, and the rhythm makes me want to orgasm right then. Master D stops sucking on my breast and whispers if I come, he will punish me. Like what is happening right now isn't punishment? I lose track of time. It seems to go on for quite some time.

Just as I was getting used to the rhythm of a female's finger, I feel a finger try to invade my ass. At first, I wasn't sure what was happening, but then as Master D bites down on my left nipple, a small plug is placed in my ass. It burns, but after a few minutes, my body adjusts to the feeling.

Finally, the fingers leave me and are replaced with two much larger fingers, and the pace is such that I will not last very long. Thankfully, Master D commands me to come and I moan and scream as my come dribbles down my legs. I drop my head down. I'm completely spent. The spreader bar is removed from my legs. I am unhooked from above and I am immediately lifted into powerful arms. I hear the handcuffs being removed and completely fall into Master D's arms. He thanks everyone for their attendance, and I am swiftly carried away.

I feel myself being placed on a soft bed and I hear Master D asking me to open my mouth so I can drink some water. I croak out the question of how long we were up on the stage, and Master D indicates it was approximately forty-five minutes. No wonder I am so exhausted. I have experienced nothing quite like that, true euphoria.

After Master D is done administering his aftercare, I am left alone to take a shower, change, and catch the Uber that I am sure is waiting for me. On my ride home, I contemplate what happened tonight. I also think about wanting to be the best Sub to Master D. Tonight rivaled any fantasies I've ever had.

Chapter 5

Madeline

It is a Friday night, and the restaurant is rocking. Evidently, Frank's nasty commentary on my establishment hasn't turned that many people off. The bar is even packed. I check the reservations for rest the weekend. Yes! I am fully booked. Then I make the rounds, welcoming guests and engaging in brief conversations with each table.

As I finish speaking with my patrons about their meals, and start walking towards the kitchen, I see Kenzie and Andy come through the front door. I forgot I had invited Kenzie to come in tonight. I greet them with hugs and kisses and escort them to their table. We chat for a few minutes and then I excuse myself. I need to check on the kitchen staff.

Just as I reach the kitchen doors, a steel grip on my arm stops me in my tracks. I am shocked to see Dave. His facial expression is that of pure anger. He drags me to my office, slams the door, and locks it.

"What the fuck, Madeline?" he erupts. "I called the employee line and was told I no longer have a job."

I laugh and say "are you serious Dave? You quit. I told you we were through with our relationship. You're the one who quit in a very public display. What the fuck are you doing here? I thought I made myself clear. I didn't want to see you here ever again."

"You know, the only reason I quit was because you broke it off with me. I need this job, Madeline," Dave shouts, moving a bit too close for comfort.

I can smell the alcohol on his breath, and I shove him away.

"You need to rehire me, or I will file a sexual harassment suit against you," Dave threatens.

"You have got to be joking. You quit in front of witnesses, and I have their statements in your file!" I shout back.

"You bitch, you're going to regret this!"

"Get the fuck out of my restaurant and never come back!"

Dave turns and storms out of the office, slamming the door behind him.

Take a deep breath, Madeline, I tell myself. I hope that our shouting match wasn't heard by the staff. That would be awkward. I take a good five minutes to calm my breathing before I leave my office and walk over to the bar and pour myself a very large glass of one of my favorites, 19 Crimes Banished. It is a very smooth dark red wine that I keep in stock for my customers. Fuck Calgon, Master D, take me away! The encounter with Dave reminds me I am looking forward to Monday evening and my next session with him.

None of the staff or customers look my direction, so I am reasonably sure no one heard what took place in my office. I still can't believe that Dave came in and accosted me and screamed at me like he did. After I broke it off with him and he quit, I honestly didn't think I'd ever see him again.

Later, I walk over to Kenzie and Andy's table to see how they are enjoying their meal. I force a pleasant expression, but

I can tell that Kenzie sees right through it. "How was your dinner?" I ask.

"It was good, but what's wrong? And don't lie to me. I know you too well," she says.

Shit, I am not good at making things up on the fly. "Can we talk Monday when we meet for breakfast? It's a long story. And not appropriate for here and now." At least she didn't mention hearing the screaming or hearing the door slam. I am not looking forward to that conversation, as I really don't want her to know that I have failed miserably in yet another relationship.

"Of course," Kenzie says. "But call me before if you want to talk. I can see that something is really upsetting you."

"Yeah," I admit. "Thanks. I'll see you Monday morning. Looking forward to it." I shake off the anger that is still coursing through me from that fight with Dave. I have to put on my game face to get me through the rest of the evening. It is only eight p.m., and we are booked solid until ten with reservations. "Anyway, I hope you enjoyed your dinner."

"We did, thanks, Madeline," Andy says.

***

Monday morning arrives, and Kenzie is at the restaurant waiting outside at a table that sits in the sun. I greet her with a hug and a kiss. "I am so glad that we started meeting for breakfast to catch up on our week. Since you met Andy, and the restaurant has become one of the city's 'up and coming' places to dine at," I laugh at my own cliché reference to my restaurant, "we haven't been able to get together at the last minute like we used to. I really look forward to these breakfast dates because they are very relaxing for me."

"Me too. But tell me, what the hell happened Friday night that had you so upset?"

I think for a moment, and say, "I don't even know where to start, Kenz."

"From the beginning would be a great place, Maddie."

"You know I was seeing the server that I hired, Dave, remember?"

Kenzie nods her head. "And you told me you broke up."

"I did. He made a surprise visit to the restaurant on Friday night. That's why I was upset. I didn't know he was there. He must have slipped in through the back door because all my other employees would know to tell me if he came in through the front. He didn't leave on good terms."

"What happened?"

"He grabbed me and pulled me into my office, and we had a fight, as in screaming and swearing at each other. I was so pissed! He threatened to sue me for sexual harassment for firing him, but I have witnesses he quit."

"Oh no," Kenzie says. "That isn't good. You don't need any bad publicity like that after Frank Blanchet's statement regarding your relations with your employees being an issue."

"I know! And don't tell me how stupid I was to hire him and have a relationship with him. I know that. I know better than to mix business with pleasure." I rub my forehead and avert my eyes.

"I would never tell you that you're stupid," Kenzie says, laying her hand over my other hand which clutches the table. "So, why did the relationship go south?"

I stare at her, considering what to say. "At first, I really enjoyed being with him. The sex was wonderful, but a bit vanilla for me. I suggested we try a few things to spice it up. You know how I love those erotic romance novels, and some things they describe I really wanted to try." I see Kenzie roll her eyes. She has never been a fan of those books and cannot believe how I love them. "Don't give me that look, Makenzie. Dave wasn't exciting in bed, not as bad as Missionary Mike, but a close second. I just wanted him to be a bit more exciting."

"Forget the sex for a second. What about the rest of the relationship?"

"What does the rest matter? If the sex sucks and he isn't willing to spice it up, what's the point?" I could see in her eyes she wanted to comment on that, but she held back. "You obviously do not have that problem."

Kenzie blushes and laughs. "Okay, I get it."

I laugh too. "Yes, you sure do!"

We laugh for a few moments at the sexual meaning of my comment, only stowing it away when the server takes our order. Once she moves a way, I continue. "But after I told him what I wanted to try in bed, he went off on me, telling me that I was perverted, and he couldn't understand why I wanted to try those things."

"So, you broke it off, then?"

"That was the end of the relationship. I think he knew it even though I didn't officially call it quits then. Not until a few days later. There was an incident. He cornered me in my office after watching me talk with some of the regular customers, telling me I was a flirt, and that I should keep my hands to myself, and not cheapen myself by flirting with and touching the male customers."

"Wait, you're telling me he acted jealous and possessive?"

"Yes. And then I broke it off with him. I told him he was welcome to stay on as a server, but it would be strictly a work relationship after that point. I told him going forward that I would be just his boss and would not tolerate what had just happened."

"You did that immediately following the incident?"

"Yes. I would not allow him to talk to me like that. His behavior was border-line aggressive, and I would not let him go a second longer thinking we were together."

"So, when did he quit?"

"He took a week off, but the next day he was scheduled to work. He came in with a major attitude. He didn't like any of the jobs assigned to him, acted like some kind of prima donna, too good to roll silverware for the table setting presentation. And when he was asked to help set up the bar, he lost it. The funny thing is, he asked me to get bartender training, knew that was where the big tips were. Setting up the bar before the restaurant opens is part of it. Dumb shit. I was giving him the opportunity he asked for as a peace offering." I pause and shake my head, remembering how horrible that day was. "He quit on the spot. It was very public and very nasty. My other employees knew I had been seeing him, well, any who didn't knew after that. I was so mad, I was shaking."

Kenzie grips my hand. "Oh, sweetie, I'm so sorry it went down like that."

"Well, you can believe I learned my lesson about hiring a guy I'm dating. So, that is why I'm not ready to meet anyone right now. Besides, I've come to the conclusion that I suck at relationships, and I need to just focus on my restaurant."

"Good riddance to that asshole. You don't need that type of negativity in your life. If he ever comes back to the restaurant, I can have Margot pay him a visit. As you know, she can be very intimidating when she needs to be."

"I don't think that will be necessary. I believe this last discussion, if you want to call it that, did what I needed it to do." Besides, I think sicking a cop on him would just piss him off more and maybe cause him to come back at me for retribution.

"You know Maddie, what you need is a way to get rid of some of your stress on a weekly basis. A regular workout schedule would do that for you. Logan is starting a new kickboxing class I think you would love. And not only is it a great workout, hitting and kicking something really helps rid you of stress. Plus, I would love to see you more often."

"I already promised to come once a week and work out with you."

"This would be besides that. One day a week at the gym is better than nothing, but two to three days will really have you feeling amazing!"

"Seriously? You know my schedule. Where will I find the time for two or three days at the gym?"

Kenzie laughs at me. "Really? You can't find one additional hour in your week to do something that will benefit you?" She pins me with a look, calling me out.

"I'll think about it."

The server brings our breakfast orders. I devour my vegetable and cheese omelet. I check my watch. I know I should get to the restaurant. Even though it is Monday, and the restaurant is closed tonight, I have to get my food order in for the next few days and I have paperwork to do. Plus, I want to catch a nap before I get ready to go to the Velvet Playroom. My mood lifts at the thought and I'm pretty sure my pulse speeds up too. I can't help but smile.

"What?" Kenzie asks, seeing my smile.

I wish I could tell her. But she would never understand, so I lie. "I was just thinking about hitting or kicking something, envisioning it to be Dave." I giggle. "Okay, yeah, I'll check out Logan's kickboxing class. Can you text me a schedule?"

Kenzie smiles wide. "Yes, I'll do that as soon as I get back to the gym. I think you will really like it!"

"I hate to have to cut this short, but I have to get to the restaurant. Not only do I have my normal work, but it's also nearly the end of the quarter and I have to get all my financials to my accountant."

"That's what Andy was working on too when I left to come meet you," Kenzie says.

"Owning your own business is not all glamorous. A lot of it is boring paperwork," I say. I drop enough money on the table to cover my portion of the bill, tax, and a generous tip for our server. I give her a quick peck on the cheek, and I am off for another fun and stress-filled day.

Butch

I finally have a day off from the firehouse. I wish I would have been able to sleep in, but that didn't happen. Changing shifts like I have the last few weeks is hell on your body. I had worked three twenty-four-hour overnight shifts in a row. And each shift was hectic. I got very little sleep. It was a great learning opportunity for the four trainees assigned to me. They got to see multiple MVAs and even a few dumpster fires each night. Unfortunately, it looks like we have an arsonist loose in the city. There is no way that many fires occurred accidentally or randomly. Someone was setting dumpsters in my territory on fire on purpose.

I was switching back to day shift tomorrow, which would necessitate tonight's meeting with Charlotte at the club be cut short so I could get home and get a good night's sleep. I have a meeting with the captain and the fire marshal at nine a.m. tomorrow morning. And I'd yet to write up my report on the four trainees from the weekend.

My mind wanders to what I had planned for Charlotte tonight, and I can't help but become very aroused. I'd only been with her twice and damn; she's gotten to me. I had to consciously keep her out of my thoughts when I was at work all weekend. As I think about her, my hand finds its way to my cock. I only wish it was her hand gripping me.

My phone chirps a new text message. Cosimo. He wants me to call him as soon as I am awake to talk about work at the club and how early I can come in tonight. So much for the day off I have. All I had planned for today was a good workout at the gym, something I didn't get to do during the last three twenty-four-hour shifts.

I set the phone back on my nightstand and rest my head back on my pillow. My thoughts again go to Charlotte and my hand that's on my cock gets down to business. Cosimo is going to have to wait. It's been nearly a year since thoughts turned me on enough to actually want to pleasure myself. And I will not let Cosimo ruin the mood.

***

I eventually get out of bed, but I don't call Cosimo. I text him to let him know I am beat from my three long shifts. I tell him I will be in an hour earlier than usual. And that's the best I can do. I leave no room for argument or negotiation. Then I grab a protein shake and my gym bag. I mute my phone and throw it into the bag. I don't want to know if he messages me back. The place could be on fire, and I wouldn't care. Well, okay, I would. But otherwise, I don't want to hear from him.

It's a beautiful day, so I take my bike. I feel absolutely relaxed as the wind whips over me and the sun beats down on me. I go a bit out of my way to enjoy the ride and make it last longer. I go through the downtown area and see Kenzie just getting up from a table on the outside patio of a coffee bar. I pull over and cut my engine.

"Hi," I greet. "How are you doing?"

She smiles. "I'm good! How about you?"

"Couldn't be better. I worked the last three days, but I'm off till tomorrow. I was just heading to the gym." I see the dishes from two people on the table. "Is Andy here with you?" I glance towards the inside of the restaurant, looking for him.

"No, I met a girlfriend for breakfast. Madeline. You just missed her. She left a few minutes ago. I was just finishing my coffee."

"Ah, the elusive Madeline," I joke. Kenzie keeps saying she wants to introduce us. I'm sure she's great, but my sexual direction is so specific, I've found a normal relationship doesn't work for me. Not many women are open to the Dom-Sub lifestyle, and I can't imagine being in a relationship that doesn't include that aspect.

Kenzie laughs. "Not elusive. You both are just very busy people."

"Sounds like a match made in heaven or a disaster waiting to happen." I chuckle. "Are you heading back to the gym? Do you need a ride?" I offer.

"No thanks, I have my car," she says.

"Okay, I'll see you later." I smile and then restart my bike.

***

My day flies by. After a great work out at the gym, I return home just as Anna, my housekeeper, finishes cleaning. I have her in once a week if the house needs it or not, and usually it doesn't. I'm home rarely and I pick up after myself. Not only does she clean, but she also does my grocery shopping and cleans out my fridge of anything that went bad that I didn't get the chance to eat or drink, though that is not much of an issue as she has been with me for years and knows my schedule and eating habits well. The one place Anna never goes is my basement playroom, which I haven't been in, in the last year.

For a second, I allow my thoughts to drift to Charlotte, and I consider what it would be like to have her as my permanent Sub, in and out of the club. I can honestly say that I want to see if she could fit into my life outside of the club. I think I may be ready to move on. Given that I've only had two sessions with Charlotte, I am shocked that I am even thinking about this already. I tuck that thought away, for now.

When I arrive at the club, I go to see my brother. His office door is open. He motions for me to close it after I have entered. "What's up?" I ask.

"I know you have been busy at your first job, so I told Danny not to bother you with this," he begins.

Danny is our IT guy for the club. He's a contractor, supports our business and any IT issues we have. "Is it security related?" I ask.

Cosimo nods. "He has identified several attempts to breach our firewall."

"What?" I demand. "I should have been notified right away!"

"I'm notifying you now. As you've said before, your first job takes precedent, and you cannot be disturbed when you're there. Relax, the firewall stopped them. He's beefing up our firewall security and wants to talk to you about it. Make an appointment with him tomorrow sometime. He was in today, but you couldn't be bothered this morning."

I'm instantly pissed. "You didn't tell me it was this serious this morning."

Cosimo raises an eyebrow, trying to call me out for dismissing him this morning. Damn him and his games. He knows damn well had he told me it was a security issue, I would have called him and would have evaluated if I needed to come in or not. But no, he is always wanting me to come in when I don't need to. A lot can be dealt with over the phone.

"I dealt with it," he says coolly. "I approved time and the work needed for him to beef up our security, and the funds to pay for it. He was here for six hours today and will be back tomorrow. You can hook up with him then."

I nod, still seething. "I will."

Chapter 6

Madeline

J ust like the past two sessions, I arrive in an Uber, sign in, and head to locker number thirteen in the ladies' locker room. One thing I have to say is that Master D has exquisite taste in bondage clothing. Tonight's outfit consists of a red Basque set that has push up cups, black lace ruffles, g-string and red sheer lace top thigh-high stockings that attach to the garters. Again, he knows how to make my body beautiful, and I can't believe I have tried nothing like this one.

Once again, there is a note. However, I am not to call for my Dom. I am expected to walk into the main room with no escort. Can I do this? I have always had Master D as my security blanket, and now I am on my own. Coupled with the fact that the outfit tonight leaves nothing to the imagination, I am a bundle of nerves.

I don't know if I can do this. I sit in the chair by the door for what seems an eternity when someone walks in. It is another Sub, based on what she is wearing.

She introduces herself as Marta and she has come with a message from Master D that if I am not standing next to him in the main room in the next five minutes, he will drag me out of the locker room and administer my punishment in front of everyone present.

I thank her for the message and ask her to let Master D know I will be there in less than two minutes. Fuck, he means business, and this is what I signed up for, right? I walk over to the bar that is on the right side of the room. How have I never noticed there is liquid courage available? I pour myself a shot of Pinnacle Chocolate Whip Vodka and swallow it quickly. Taking a deep breath, I turn and walk to the door and open it. Walking down the hall to the main room, I keep telling myself to breathe, all will be well.

As I enter the main room, a hush comes over it. All eyes turn to me, and the only eyes I want to see are Master D's. As if reading my mind, he rises from his chair and walks over to me. Taking my hand, he places a soft kiss on the inside of my palm and leads me down the hall.

Master D steers me into a room that has been closed on my first two visits, but apparently this evening, we are going to use it for a private session as he closes the door behind him. I am thankful that if I am going to be given any type of punishment for tardiness; it is behind a closed door.

"Charlotte, you are ready for something a bit more exciting. I'm going to remove your mask and put this blindfold on." I turn around and he removes my mask and replaces it with the blindfold. Once it is on, I begin to turn, but he stops me.

"Although you look beautiful in this red Basque, I insist that it be removed."

I start to tremble as I remove the first garter, when I feel large strong hands on my waist.

"Did I instruct you to remove your outfit, Charlotte?" he asks.

"No, Sir, you did not," I respond and stop what I am doing.

"It would give me great pleasure to remove your clothing. Please allow me."

I feel his body against mine. Slowly he bends down and unclips both garters, lifts my right leg, removing my shoe and then slowly rolls the stocking down my leg. By the time he starts removing the left stocking, I am practically hyperventilating. His hands are on my legs, leaving searing marks as they travel to my ankles. His body slides against mine as he stands back up, and I feel his rock-hard chest against my back, and I hear him breathing behind me. His body is what dreams are made of.

"Charlotte, please raise your arms so I may remove the rest of your clothing."

I do as I am told and just then, I feel a chilly breeze over my nipples. What the fuck, completely nude at my third session. I am so self-conscious of my flaws; I cannot believe he is asking me to do this. I sense he has moved in front of me. It is confirmed when he runs his hands up and down my arms, sending shivers up my spine.

I hear movement, and I suspect that Master D has moved away from me. I hear what sounds like him taking a seat in the chair across from me.

"Charlotte, please turn 360 degrees for me." His voice is a quiet growl.

As I start to turn. He tells me to go slowly, and I comply. As I finish, Master D rises from the chair and walks up to me, so close I can smell the soap he used when he showered. It's amazing the heightened senses I have with my eyes blindfolded.

"You are perfect, Charlotte, beautiful. Thank you for your trust." Master D then pushes me forward until I hit something that feels like a table.

"Charlotte, I am going to turn you around and lie you down. Please relax."

I comply and he lifts me up like I weigh nothing and softly lays me down on the table. Shit, the table is cold, and I start to shiver. Suddenly, something very soft and warm is placed over my body.

"How does that feel?" Master D asks.

"Wonderful, thank you Sir."

"I have a quick matter to attend to, Charlotte. Please relax and I will be back shortly."

"Yes Sir, thank you." I hear the door open, then close. I wonder if he has really left the room. Or is this a test to see if I will remain in this position with the blindfold on while he's gone? And I can't imagine what matter he'd have to attend.

Butch

As I contemplate Charlotte coming into the main room in the killer red Basque that I picked out for her, I wonder what it would be like to have her as a full-time Sub. All of a sudden, the room becomes silent and still. I look up and see Charlotte standing there. She is a vision, and I can see the lust in the Dom's eyes that are present. Fuck that. I stand up and walk to Charlotte, taking her hand and placing a soft kiss on her palm. I don't dare say anything at this point, as I am losing my shit here.

As I escort Charlotte into a private room, I am not sure whether I should continue with this session that I have planned. The room itself is softly lit with a table in the center and a chair to the left of the table. After I sit in the chair, I instruct her to turn around for me so I can fully inspect my Sub. The perfection is undeniable. I have never wanted a woman more than I want her right now. Why did she come into my life now, when I am still trying to get my shit together? I want nothing more than to fuck her until she screams my name. My inner dragon is rearing its ugly head. I gasp at the sight of perfection. I can tell that Charlotte is a bit nervous, which is understandable as we are only at session three, but I am pushing her to do something normally covered around session five.

After I lay her on the table, which I know is cold, I cover her with a heated blanket to keep her warm. I excuse myself to figure out why these feelings are hitting me so hard. Unable to figure it out on my own, I walk to Cosimo's office to get some guidance from him.

When I walk in, Cosimo is standing at the monitor that is displaying the scene in the room where I left Charlotte. He turns and hands me a large glass of our favorite libation. He looks me in the eye and begins. "Drago, what are your intentions with this Sub? I have been keeping tabs on your sessions, and although she is excelling, I cannot believe that she is ready for the scene that will be played out in that room tonight."

All I want to do is defend my actions, but he is right. I am pushing Charlotte, and I really don't know if she is ready for this or not. "Look Cosimo, she is so responsive, and I can tell that she is ready for this next step. My cock is definitely telling me we are both ready for this. She understands the relationship between us, Dom and Sub. She will be okay," I defend myself.

"Suit yourself, brother. But I am warning you, don't complain to me when this Dom-Sub relationship spirals out of control."

I finish my drink and slam the door behind me as I leave. I have a very willing and responsive Sub waiting for me and the things I want to do to her cannot be contained any longer. Why did I think I would get anything close to guidance or support from him?

Madeline

After what seems like a lifetime, I hear the door open. The warm blanket has become cool, but I am very comfortable despite the hardness of the table. The blanket is suddenly removed, and a pillow is placed under my head.

"Are you ready for your next training session, Charlotte?" Master D asks.

"Yes Sir, I am ready to learn how to make you proud of me as a Sub," I answer.

I hear Master D walk over and start opening what sounds like drawers. Small clanking sounds on the small cabinet that I saw when walking into the room make me wonder what is in those drawers.

Master D walks back to the table and his first touch to my breast practically makes me catapult off the table.

"Relax, Charlotte, I need you to turn over, and I will help you, so you don't fall off the table. I am going to be placing the nipple clamps on first. You have already experienced these, so take a deep breath for me please," he instructs.

As I take my first deep breath, the first clamp is put on. Yup, still fucking hurts. As I take my second deep breath, the second clamp goes on and I hear Master D walk away again. When he returns, I feel his finger run up and down into my folds and he circles around my clit. Heaven for sure. The nipple clamps aren't hurting anymore, in fact, they are aiding in my oncoming orgasm. As Master D pushes a finger into my hot, wet core, I lose control.

Master D whispers in my ear, "Let go, Charlotte, come for me, my sweet."

I comply and scream so loud I scare myself.

Master D chuckles and tells me what a good Sub I am.

"Charlotte, I am moving on with this session. What is your safe word?"

"Paris, Sir," I answer.

"Good girl. Now spread your legs for me so I can get a view of that beautiful pussy of yours that is so wet."

I feel Master D blow a hot breath across my pussy, and it is a decadent feeling. I remember what he did with his tongue during the last session, and I have to say, it was very enjoyable. He once again enters one finger into my wet core, and I start to move to his rhythm. A second finger is added and as he hits that sweet spot, I am going to explode.

As I start panting, he removes his fingers, and the loss is felt immediately. I am lifted from the table, flipped over, and placed on my stomach. The nipple clamps push against my breasts, but erotically, not in a painful way.

"Charlotte, please get on your hands and knees for me."

I comply and wonder what is going to happen now. Soon enough, I find out. Master D grabs my hips and pulls me closer to the edge of the table. I hear Master D step away, but he seems to return fairly quickly. Without warning, I feel a sharp slap on my left butt cheek. Master D then rubs small circles around the area he hit. Although it hurt immediately following the slap, it is now warm and sending tingling sensations to my core. Before I can register what is going on, another slap to the left butt cheek is followed by a rubbing sensation.

"Charlotte, do you need to use your safe word?" Master D inquires.

"No Sir, I was just a bit taken by surprise."

Two more slaps to each butt cheek and then I hear a zipper, and the rustle of his leather pants being lowered down those masculine looking legs. Damn it, if only I wasn't blindfolded. My hands aren't bound, so I could move it and take a peek, but I know I would be breaking the contract by doing so. As I am lost in thought, I feel the head of Master D's dick nudge my entrance ever so slowly. Holy Shit, this is really happening. This big, beautiful man is really fucking me, Madeline Shaw. Woo hoo, happy dance.

As I am pondering what a lucky girl I am, Master D thrusts his entire member into my opening, and my body quickly tries to accommodate him. It has been a while, and I know I am a bit tight, but the feeling is pure heaven. He doesn't move, allowing me to get used to his girth, and what a wonderful girth it is.

"I want you to become accustomed to my size, Charlotte, so we'll give it a few minutes before I move in you."

Are you fucking kidding me? He can keep his big dick in me as long as he wants. Just then, he starts to move in and out at a slow pace. I cannot take it, as I like it hard and fast. I move against him every time he moves back into me. A small groan escapes his lips, and I cannot believe that I actually might be satisfying my Dom.

"Charlotte, are you ready for the fast and hard that you have requested on your application?"

All I can do is nod, but he doesn't move and then I remember that I'm in training as a Sub and I respond, "Yes Sir."

Not any sooner did the word "Yes" leave my mouth and he slams into me, grunting as he does so. Master D blurts out, "you are so fucking tight! you are killing me here." The force in which he slams into me almost knocks me off my hands and knees, but I am strong from all the kickboxing I have been taking, and I hold my ground. My orgasm hits me so hard. I think I am going to fall apart. Just as I think this man has the stamina of a twenty-year-old, he pulls out and comes all over my ass. His cum streams down my crack and I can no longer hold myself up. I fall onto my stomach on the table.

"We aren't done yet Charlotte, please turn over and open your legs for me."

I don't know if I have the strength, but I comply. I hear a buzzing noise and before I know it, a very fast vibrator is on my clit, and I am screaming at the top of my lungs from the sheer ecstasy of it all. I come so hard and fast, I become disoriented. I then feel Master D's enormous cock enter me once more. Wow, talk about bouncing back so quickly. As he slams into me, the vibrator is never removed, and a third orgasm hits me.

Exhausted to the core, I close my eyes for just a moment. I don't feel my body being lifted from the table. Nor did I realize at the time that he wrapped my body up in a warm blanket. But when he unwraps me and slides me between the sheets of the bed, I know is in Master D's room, only then do I realize it.

Butch

After getting my thoughts in check, I enter the room. My beautiful Sub looks like she has dozed off. Cannot have a sleeping Sub, so I remove the blanket and place a pillow under her head. After asking her if she is ready for our next session, I walk to the small cabinet across the room to gather the necessary equipment. Remembering how she responded to the nipple clamps, those are the first items that I decide to adorn her beautiful breasts with.

I explain to her what is going to happen and the response as I place those clamps on her nipples turns me rock hard. I know she is probably dripping wet, and I am not disappointed. After playing with that delicious clit, I push one finger into her hot, wet pussy. No sooner did I insert a finger,

Charlotte feels like she is going to orgasm. After inserting a second digit, I grant her permission to release it.

After confirming she remembers her safe word, and giving her a bit more foreplay, removing both fingers in order to delay her second orgasm, I lift her from the table and have her get on her hands and knees. While she is assuming the requested position, I remove my boots very quietly. I don't want to give up what will happen next.

After she is on her hands and knees, I walk back to the cabinet to grab the soft crop. Without an explanation, my first swing hits her soft, round ass. She seems a bit stunned but hasn't used her safe word. I then hit the other butt cheek and massage it to help stimulate her.

Two more slaps and I cannot take it anymore. I grab her hips and gently move her towards the edge of the table, giving me the precise position for the next step of the session. In her application, Charlotte indicated she wants it hard and rough, and that is exactly my forte.

I then unzip my leather pants and move them down to my ankles, kicking them off so I have room to move. I ever so slowly run the tip of my dick over her wet entrance and push the tip into her soaked pussy. I wait for her tight entrance to relax and accommodate my size. As if she is anticipating my next move, I thrust hard and deep. Fuck, she is so tight; I have experienced nothing like this since I was fourteen and lost my virginity. I don't move explaining to Charlotte that I want her to become accustomed to my size. I feel like I am going to come almost immediately.

After asking her if she is ready for me to come hard and fast, all she does is nod. When I am about to pull out for her insubordination, she responds correctly with "Yes Sir." All I need to hear was the word "Yes" and I was gone. I thrust in and out of her so hard, I hope she doesn't have an issue walking tomorrow. She is so tight, hot and wet, I could fuck her all night. My stamina is usually long, but this beautiful curvy pixie of a woman has made me lose it and I pull out so quickly, spurting cum down her ass crack. The beauty of seeing my cum all over her ample ass excites me.

Charlotte falls forward on the table. I lift her up and place her on her back, asking her to spread her legs for me. A new vibrator was delivered to this room today, and I will be the first to use it. It might be small, but it packs a large punch. I turn it on and place it in the spot that I know will be the most effective. Sure enough, Charlotte screams as her second orgasm hits. I cannot wait any longer. My cock is rock hard, and I need to fuck her one more time tonight. Still leaving the vibrator in place, I slam into her waiting wet and tight pussy. Before I know it, Charlotte once again experiences an earth-shattering orgasm. I spill my seed into her hot, warm womb and then slowly remove myself from the table.

After dressing, I see that Charlotte's breathing is steady and I cannot believe she has fallen asleep. I grab a warm blanket and wrap it around her, and carry her to my room. After removing the blanket, I go into the bathroom, returning with a bowl of warm water and a washcloth, and administer the aftercare she deserves. I have never lost control like that. Charlotte is definitely getting under my skin. I cannot see her with anyone else in the club.

Madeline

As I slowly open my eyes, I see that the room is lit by candles everywhere I look. A very soft smell of lavender surrounds me. I feel a hard body behind me, and I see muscular arms wrapped around me. Master D is holding me as if I were a precious gift.

Master D feels me stir and reaches over and hands me a bottle of water, instructing me to drink to stay hydrated. I would prefer a good glass of a dark porter right now, but hey, my body feels like it has been through the ringer, so anything wet will work for me.

"Charlotte, tell me how you are feeling. Are you sore? Did I hurt you at all tonight?"

I am still exhausted, and he wants to talk? All I want to do is sleep. But I muster enough energy to answer him. "I am a bit sore, Sir, but in a good way. I really just want to close my eyes and sleep for a bit, if that is alright Sir?" I question.

Master D chuckles that sweet chuckle I am becoming accustomed to, and he whispers to close my eyes and he will be here when I am ready to wake and dress. I am so comfortable in his arms that I drift off into a wonderful, peaceful sleep.

***

While experiencing one of the most erotic dreams I have ever had, I hear someone calling Charlotte over and over, and rocking my body back and forth. "Go away," I mumble, but this person is persistent. I slowly open my eyes to see those familiar blue eyes.

"Charlotte, it is seven a.m. We need to get you up and dressed. I have a job I need to get to, but I would never leave my Sub unattended. I know we didn't have a chance to discuss subspace, and how it affects a Sub, and for that I am truly sorry. At our next session, we will talk through it first, before we play, so you have a complete understanding of what you experienced last night."

Seven a.m., shit! I have an appointment at eight a.m. with a new local organic vegetable farm. I fly off the bed as if it was on fire, as Master D hands me my clothes that I arrived in. I turn my back to him as I dress, which seems ridiculous, knowing that he already saw me completely naked and fucked me from behind, for Pete's sake.

After dressing, Master D excuses himself for a moment and returns with a 4x4 White Lightening from Starbucks. So that is why that question was on the application, ha! But I grab the drink and take my first sip. Yummy, just what the doctor ordered, or should I say the Dom, I laugh to myself.

Master D walks me out to the foyer and says that he looks forward to our next session. When did he get dressed? Shit, seven a.m.! I cannot believe I was out for the night, and he never woke me up.

"Until Monday, Charlotte, have a great week," he says, kissing me gently before he disappears down the hall and I head out to the waiting Uber.

I sit back and close my eyes, replaying everything that happened last night. Before I know it, the Uber pulls up in front of my restaurant. I thank him and I run to the back of the building, to the stairs that lead up to my apartment. I shower with record speed and make myself look a bit more presentable before my eight-a.m. appointment shows up. This is exhausting.

Chapter 7

Butch

I shower quickly at the club, forcing my thoughts off Charlotte. Shit! I can't believe we slept here together all night. This goes against all my rules. I admit to myself, though; it was amazing waking with her in my arms, something I could get used to. Okay, so no, I can't force my thoughts off her. She's really gotten to me. I still haven't decided if it's good or bad that she has.

I slip out of the building as fast as I can and drive to the station, hitting a coffee shop on the way for a large, strong cup and a breakfast sandwich. I sneak in the firehouse's backdoor and go directly to my office. I'm able to complete my reports on the weekend shifts and on the four trainees just in time for the meeting with the captain and fire marshal, who is also our district arson investigator.

I shake both their hands as I enter the captain's office. Greg 'Bud' Kleckner, is a grouchy old man, but one hell of an arson investigator with over twenty years of experience. He knows his shit. "Hi Bud, I'm glad you're here," I say, taking my seat. I lay out the call pattern over the weekend of the dumpster fires.

"Your arsonist was just working himself around the district," Bud says. He goes to the district map on the wall and traces the course of the fire reports, a perfect horseshoe shaped path. "I'll see what I can do to get surveillance footage pulled from businesses and streetcams near each fire. Maybe we'll get lucky and get this guy at multiple locations."

"Have there been any similar dumpster fires in other districts?" I ask.

"No, looks like you won the arsonist lottery," Bud says with a straight face. "Hey, which reminds me. I received your advanced notice of the fight next month at that gym and the request for the event permit. They won the lottery too. I've okayed the request based on their capacity limits. As long as they remain under two hundred and fifty in total attendance, I'll issue the special use permit. I'm heading over there after this meeting to meet with the owner, see the venue, and advise him of my decision, provided I don't find anything that would make me decline the permit. You want to tag along?"

"Yes," I reply. "I know the owner. Work out there myself. He's a good guy and will be very receptive to anything you dictate to approve the permit request. He wants to run the safest place he can."

"I'm glad to hear that," Bud says. "I'm tired of busting businesses after the fact and hearing that they didn't know they needed a special permit."

"Yeah, Stevens even asked me about how to request to have EMT or paramedics on site during the event. As I said, he is always safety conscious and takes care to follow the rules."

"Okay, good. Back to your dumpster fires. I'll visit those locations after we hit the gym," he pauses, and his lips tip into an uncharacteristic grin. "Like I hit the gym." He waves his hand over his girthy middle. "Anyway, you'll need to drive separate."

That was good. I need to send Andy a text to give him a

heads up on the fire marshal's impending visit so he can give the place a once-over to be sure there are no violations at the moment. If Bud was to find anything against code, that would sink his permit request.

Once seated in my car, I type out a quick text to Andy. *Heads up, surprise fire marshal visit to approve your event permit request in five minutes.* I hit send without re-reading it. Then I shift to drive. I park in the front of the gym on the street, behind Bud. I can see both Andy and Logan at the front counter through the large glass windows. I hope he saw the text message.

Bud and I enter. "Bud, this is Andy Stevens, the gym's owner and Logan, his number two," I introduce.

Bud shakes their hands, jostling the clipboard and pen to his left hand. "I need to do a spot inspection to issue the event permit."

"Sure," Andy says with a smile. "The fight itself will be in the basement area." He nods towards the back of the gym to the stairs, and he steps away from the counter.

Bud follows him. I follow Bud. Logan remains at the counter. Bud's head is on a swivel, checking everything out. Andy goes over to the load-in door and opens it. On the far back end of the gym, the ground slopes down, and a large garage door rolls up, creating a large doorway.

"We plan to leave this open during the event," Andy says. "I researched the regs for an event this size and the two egresses this door and the stairs back up to the first floor meets the requirement."

"And I see the mandatory number of fire extinguishers both down here and I saw them upstairs as well," Bud says.

"There is a security system with a battery backup for fire and carbon monoxide," Andy points out. "And of course, we have a no smoking on the premises policy."

Bud makes notes on his pad and fills in sections on his form. I watch over his shoulder as he checks off approved. He hands the permit to Andy. Then we all return to the first floor. I stand at the counter with Andy and Logan, watching the fire marshal leave.

Once he pulls away from the curb and his car leaves our field of vision, Andy slaps me on the shoulder. "Thank you for the heads up!"

"He's a good guy, but a stickler for the rules. Had he found even one thing out of compliance, no matter how minor, he wouldn't have approved the application and I didn't want you to fail inspection because of something small you may not have been aware of. I know downstairs is pretty much Mason and Blake's area and they don't care as much as you do."

"Yeah, we're working on that," Andy says. "They're on their last chance with me after we found the steroids and other enhancers down there a few months ago."

"I remember that," I say. It damn near lost him Kenzie when she saw him and Logan holding drugs when she walked into the office. "I'm surprised you said yes to them hosting this fight."

"Logan and I will be here during it, watching them. And it will be great advertising for the gym. Not only are they paying me a cut of the profits from it, I'll get fifty percent of the first month training fee for anyone who joins their program from the event. Everyone who comes will get a flyer with an introductory special MMA training price plus a full listing of everything the gym offers, with a special new member's rate."

I chuckle. "Kenzie?"

"Marrying a marketing person was good for business," Andy says with a laugh. "Within the next few months, we plan to roll out a bunch of other changes that should make the gym more attractive to potential members. I'm negotiating right now to buy the building space next door to expand into."

"That will double the size of your gym," I say.

"We're planning full locker rooms with showers, steam rooms, sauna, maybe even a whirlpool hot tub."

"Fancy. Are you planning to up your fees?" I ask.

"If we do it right, we won't need to," Andy says.

"Good luck with it. And let me know if Mason and Blake will pay for EMTs and a unit to be onsite during the fight."

"I will," Andy says.

Then I leave to go back to the fire house. I almost forgot that I am on duty until tomorrow morning. It's another great day in paradise.

Madeline

I almost forgot that I told Kenzie I would work out with her at the gym after I met with the new vendor, which I'm still shocked I made it home to shower and meet with him. The farmer turned out to have great looking vegetables I haven't been able to source locally before now. He even grows a variety of microgreens and mushrooms. I purchased a nice assortment to try out before committing to regular purchases.

My mind was already planning tonight's special that I would use them with. I was thinking a mushroom bisque, a charred rainbow beet salad with microgreens, and a crusted beef burger with microgreens, mint aioli and feta cheese. My mouth was already watering just thinking of the menu.

I found a parking spot right in front of the gym as a fire department SUV pulled away from the curb. I wonder if there was a problem at the gym necessitating the fire department. I found that wasn't the case when I pushed through the doors and greeted Andy. Evidently, the gym was going to host an MMA style fight later in the month and they had just passed a surprise inspection to receive the permit for the event.

"Are you going to offer any food or drinks at the fight?" I ask Andy. "I could cater it."

Andy chuckles. "I think your food is too high-end for what would normally be served at an MMA-style fight. Beer and hotdogs maybe, if anything. I honestly haven't even thought about it." He laughs some more. "So, I will bet you have never been to a fight."

I let a distasteful expression crinkle my face. "You would win that bet. I have no desire to see two men beat the shit out of each other. You know, on second thought, you may want to see about a food truck out in the parking lot," I suggest. "And you can keep all refreshments out of the gym space, too."

"Now that's a great idea," Andy says. "Kenzie will be back in a minute. She just ran Trina over to a friend's house to play. Why don't you hop on a treadmill or a bike and warm up?"

Leave it to Andy to remind me why I was at the gym. I reluctantly climb onto an elliptical and begin my workout.

Butch

Tuesday nights are normally slow at the Velvet Playroom. Monday and Friday are Dom-Sub nights. On Thursday, the club caters to Furries. I find it weird, but who am I to judge? Saturday night is for Swingers. We had to expand from our Dom-Sub preference to make the club turn a profit. Four nights of paying guests keeps us afloat, and allows Cosimo and I to work our normal, full-time jobs. But there are still things to be taken care of on the nights the club isn't open to members. I go in when I can on Tuesdays and Sunday's just to check the place out after the place has been used Thursday through Saturday, and on Mondays.

After checking on the guest logs and security cameras, I stop in to see Cosimo. He keeps regular hours at the club, even when it is closed. I think he likes his office at the club better than at the Cheshire offices.

"Hey brother, anything new on the calendar? I only have three sessions left with Charlotte. I am enjoying being back in the game," I share.

Cosimo turns from the window he was just looking out of and folds his arms across his chest. "Drago, I do believe you broke one of your long-standing rules last night, or should I say this morning?" He pauses for a dramatic effect and gives me a hard look. "I cannot remember the last time you had a Sub in your private room for over two hours. Was Charlotte in subspace so long that you couldn't get a handle on it?" he asks.

His tone is condescending. "Shit Cosimo, I was tired from working three long, back-to-back shifts when I hit the club last night. I probably should have cancelled the session," I begin. "But Charlotte is making great progress and will be a great Sub for the lucky Dom that takes her on. I accidentally fell asleep and woke up around six-thirty this morning."

"Drago, I think your Sub is ready for a public display with two Doms. That was also on her application. Are you game for that?"

"No fucking way, not yet! I am not ready to go that far with her. I want to push her to her limits first to see where her breaking point is. Perhaps in Session six we can go there. Do you have anyone in mind?" I question, sensing he does.

"Master Kurt has expressed an interest in possibly becoming her permanent Dom at the club. He wanted to know how she was doing, and whether she was looking for something permanent outside the club as well. His last Sub just became engaged to someone else."

Master Kurt is a fair and good Dom. Perhaps using him as the second Dom during session six might not be a bad idea, I think to myself, as I know Charlotte expressed interest in sex with two men on her questionnaire. "I will give it some thought," I answer. "I am going to make my rounds now. See you in about an hour."

Madeline

I was exhausted when I woke Saturday morning to the alarm at seven-thirty a.m. People really get up at this time of the day? Of course, most people got to bed before three a.m. But then, most people didn't run restaurants. I almost rolled over and went back to sleep, but I remembered I had promised Kenzie I would get to their apartment over the gym by eight to help her finish packing what she needed to move right away. She messaged me Friday to confirm the closing went well and that great house, just two blocks from the gym, was now officially theirs. She was excited, as well she should be, and I was happy to help her pack and move.

They were very lucky that they didn't have any date that they really needed to be out of the apartment. Andy owned the building. He'd eventually rent it to someone, but it would be when they had finished the move. They could move most of their things today, certainly the necessities, but take their time to move the rest. I knew her goal was to have the bedrooms, and the kitchen set up today so they could sleep there tonight.

I arrived at eight-thirty-five with a tall, iced vanilla latte for each of us. I needed the caffeine, but with it already eighty out, hot coffee was out. As expected, I found Kenzie in the kitchen at the apartment, boxing up food from the pantry and cupboards. I handed her the latte. "I figured you could use this."

"Yes, thank you," she says, taking it from me.

"Where do you need me?"

"Can you go in and pack up Trina's closet and the toys not packed yet? Don't worry about her dresser drawers. They'll just remove them with the clothes in them when they move the furniture. Only going two blocks makes it so easy!"

"Sure," I say. "Where is she?"

"At Andy's mom's house. She came over about a half hour ago and took Trina with her. The guys are all at the house already with the first load of furniture from my house." She pauses and laughs. "I'm glad I have so much there that we can use to fill the rooms of that big house. Combined with Andy's stuff from here, we might not have to buy anything right away."

"I can't wait to see it!"

"Thank you, again, for helping us move. I know this is really early for you."

"You have no idea!" I laugh. "Are there packing boxes in Trina's room to use?" I drop my bag onto the counter out of her way and prepare to get to work.

"Yes, and a marker to label the boxes. Don't worry about taping them shut, but make sure you fill them all the way. When the boxes are moved over, I'll probably have you put the stuff away in her closet so we can bring the boxes back and pack more into them. I know we don't have enough boxes, but then again, we don't need to do it all in one trip."

"Sounds like a plan."

I walk down the hall and into Trina's room. I smile as it is so cute. I've seen it before, but I still smile. There are frilly white lace curtains on the windows, the light streaming in bounces off the bubblegum pink and violet purple walls. The room is decorated with ponies and rainbows. The furniture is white and normally, the dolls and books are scattered all around, but now they sit in boxes as most of her toys were packed in four large boxes that were lined up under the windows. I open her closet and begin placing the shoes in the bottom of the first box. The clothes are packed next. I leave them on their hangers and loosely fold them into the box. It didn't take long to fill the boxes, as Kenzie had most her stuff already packed.

When I return to the kitchen to tell her I'm done, I see she is just finishing filling three coolers with items from the refrigerator. "Let's run these coolers over to the house," she says. "We'll probably have to do another trip or two."

"Okay," I say. "I've got Trina's room done."

"Fantastic. Thank you. I'll text Andy and let him know." She taps out a quick text and then we haul one of the largest and heaviest of the coolers down the stair case into the gym. Her car is parked out front. It takes us both to carry it. We return to the apartment, and I grab one of the others. I'm out the door ahead of her.

Butch

Brian Porter, Andy's friend, who filled in for me as a groomsman at the wedding, and I are on our way back to Andy's apartment over the gym. He cleared all his tools from the back of his dark blue panel van to be able to haul furniture and boxes. Andy and Logan are still at the house arranging the furniture from Kenzie's house. We'd all met at her place at seven and loaded as much as we could in vans, pickups and a box truck Andy rented. Andy asked us to get Trina's bed and other furniture from her bedroom. He wants her to be able to sleep in her bed at the new house tonight. And what a nice house it is! I'm really happy for Andy and Kenzie. This house is perfect for them, and it is only two blocks from the gym.

We pull around back and park beside a little red, brand-spanking-new Cadillac CT5-V Blackwing. "Oh, sweet Jesus! Look at this." I am practically drooling. "I wonder who drives this beauty!"

"Seriously, Butch? We both know you could easily go buy one if you wanted one," Porter says.

He only recently learned of my connection to Cheshire Winery. It's not something I broadcast, and his comment irks me. "If I went out and bought everything that catches my eye, I quickly wouldn't have the means to buy anything. Having a few bucks in the bank isn't about flaunting it, as far as I'm concerned. It's a cushion, but I still work for a living."

I can tell by his facial expression he feels bad for saying it the way he did. He knows I'm a firefighter, knows I put my life on the line and don't sit back relying on old money. "Well, both of your rides are pretty sweet too," he says. He flashes me a smile. "I hope this car is gone by the time Andy brings the box truck. It's blocking where he'll need to park the truck."

We mount the back stairs. The screen door is open, and we catch sight of Kenzie at the door of the inner hallway. "Hey, Andy sent us to get Trina's bed and things!" I shout to her.

"Come on in and take as much as you can fit in the van. I'm just running some of the cold stuff from the fridge over."

Brian and I go in. "Do you need me to carry that cooler down to your car?" I ask. "It looks heavy." And she is pregnant, shouldn't be doing any heavy lifting.

"Nah, I got it, thanks!"

She leaves and Brian and I go to Trina's room. We disassemble her bed, which is already stripped of the sheets and blankets. I see them in the top of one of the many packed boxes in the room. "We might as well take as many boxes as we can, too. Her dresser and desk won't take up too much space."

"Yeah, we can stack the boxes on top of the furniture,"

Brian agrees.

Madeline

"Oh, Kenz, this house is great," I say to her after she gives me the grand tour. "The kitchen alone is to die for!"

Kenzie laughs. "I knew you'd love the kitchen."

"I love all of it. And it is nice to see your furniture again. I know it was only a couple of months that your house sat vacant, but didn't you miss your stuff?"

We're in the kitchen. Andy and Logan are upstairs, putting the beds together from Kenzie's house in the two spare rooms. They'll use Andy's bed in their room. Her living room and dining room furniture were nicer than his, so they were already arranged in the two front rooms. Her kitchen table set was set up in the kitchen. Andy's kitchen table would go out in the sunroom, and his living room set would be used in the family room off the kitchen.

"No, I can't say I did. Don't get me wrong, it's nice to see my living room and dining room furniture in the front rooms. They match the color scheme the previous owner had so we don't even have to paint these rooms, but Andy's furniture worked for us fine at his apartment, and now we can use it all."

"It was meant to be," I say, giving her a hug.

We put the cold food away in the fridge, a stainless steel, four-door French, top of the line, refrigerator. To. Die. For!

"What now?" I ask.

Kenzie taps several boxes that sit on the counter. "We are going to use the everyday dishes from my place." She calls out while pointing where she would like the plates, bowls, and cups to go. "Can you please unpack the dishes for me?"

"Sure." And I get to work.

A short time later, Andy and Logan come into the kitchen. Logan looks worse than I did. Not only is he tired from a late night, but he is also hung over. That's obvious.

"Do you want to finish my latte?" I ask him.

He takes it and downs the last third in the cup in one drink. "Bless you, kind woman," he says with a wink. "I knew I liked you for a reason beyond your hot body."

He flashes me his killer, flirty smile. I really do wish I'd gone there the evening of the wedding. If he was half as good in bed as the confidence he projected, I'm sure it would have been a hell of a night.

"Maddie, where did you park at the apartment?" Andy asks.

"Where I always do, around back, up against the gym."

"Can I have your keys? We're going to bring the box truck over for some furniture, and I need to be sure the back area is clear enough to maneuver the truck."

"Oh, sure," I say, pulling my keys from my bag. I hand them over to him.

"I'll probably move it to the side lot, if that's okay," Andy asks.

"Sure, wherever you need to put it, is fine."

"We'll be back," Logan says in his best Terminator voice, and I chuckle.

"The Texan Terminator," I say to Kenzie as the two men walk out of the room.

Butch

It doesn't take us long to pack up all the furniture and most of the boxes in Brian's van. We head back to Andy's new house. We meet Andy and Logan coming out the front door.

"Damn, we hoped to catch you at the apartment. We're going to bring the furniture and boxes from the master bedroom over now. I want us to all be able to sleep at the house tonight. My mom will bring Trina back with lunch for us too," Andy says. "She's making lasagna."

"Oh, I do love your mom's lasagna," I say with a smile. She's not even Italian, but can she cook!

"Leave Trina's furniture for now," Andy says, pointing at Porter's van. "Drive back over and give us a hand. That king-sized mattress and box spring was a bitch to get upstairs. It will not be easy to get down."

We drive back over to the lot behind the gym. The little red Caddy is still parked in the way. I'm surprised when Any throws Logan a set of keys. He gets out of the truck and moves the car.

"Whose is that?" I ask.

"Kenzie's friend, Madeline. She rode over with Kenz. She's unpacking the kitchen at the house."

"Nice," I can't help but remark.

"Looks like you two will finally get to meet today," Andy says.

I take a look again at her car after we park the box truck at the base of the stairs from the upper deck. Anyone who drives a car like that I want to meet. But then, my mind strays to Charlotte. I wonder what she drives. I bet it's something sporty too. She strikes me as a ballsy lady in all aspects of her life. Yes, she'd drive a sports car.

We go into Andy's place and, as I recall, the mattress, box spring, and other furniture are big, bulky, and heavy. The four of us have our work cut out to get it down in the truck. The weight isn't so much the problem as we all work out and can lift it without a problem. It's the size of it. I chuckle to myself.

Size does matter!

As expected, the furniture is bulky and awkward to maneuver. We hump it out of the apartment and down the stairs, which are steep. We muscle it up into the box truck. Between the four of us, we get all the bedroom furniture out, as well as all the boxes packed up in the master bedroom and bathroom. We have room left in the truck. I know Trina's room is empty. I open the door to the third bedroom, Andy's mom's room.

"We're going to leave this room as is for now," Andy says. "But what do you think? Can we fit the living room furniture?"

The guys all agree we should be able to. We load everything but the television onto the truck. That'll go over in someone's car at some point. We grab a few more miscellaneous boxes and get those loaded, too. We completely fill the box truck.

Madeline

"All done," I call to Kenzie. All the kitchen boxes are unloaded.

"Me too," she says. "Let's go back and get the rest of the food from the fridge. Andy's friend Butch is there. I want you two to meet." She flashes me a conspiratorial smile.

"Kenz," I moan with a smile to show I'm not completely disinterested. I'm still keeping my options open, but I really am hung up on Master D and giving the lifestyle a chance.

"Humor me," she says.

We take the coolers. We'll need all three and may even have to do a third trip to empty the refrigerator at the apartment. And we are off. She backs out of the driveway and before I know it, we are again parked in the front of the gym. We stop briefly at the counter when we enter the gym and chat for a second with Ashley, who is running the gym today. I've warmed up to her. I really didn't like her much when I first met her, of course, I had also heard how cold she'd been to Kenzie, so I didn't think too highly of her just because of that.

We bring the coolers back upstairs and into the empty apartment. The kitchen table is still there, but the living room furniture is now gone. Kenzie crosses the empty room and goes out onto the back deck. "Wow they're fast," she says. "They're on the way back to the house already." Then she goes and peaks into the master bedroom. "Yeah, they got almost everything from our room, too."

"I can't believe how fast they were! You're nearly done here."

"Yes, it's gone smoothly. After the closing yesterday afternoon, when we got to the house, we found that Sue, the previous owner had everything clean. She mopped, vacuumed, disinfected the bathrooms. She even had the refrigerator spotless. We intended to spend hours cleaning but didn't have to. That's why we were able to do so much more packing. But I have a lot of unpacking to do."

"I'll help, don't worry."

"Oh, and I forgot to tell you, Andy's mom is bringing a pan of lasagna back for us all for lunch. Her lasagna is so good!"

"I'm looking forward to it," I guarantee.

Then I get busy transferring items from the freezer into the coolers while she finishes packing up the kitchen. Soon, I have all three coolers full, and she has four more boxes packed. As I try to lift the smallest of the coolers onto the table, I know I have messed up, forgetting how heavy the frozen items are. Rooky mistake. Kenzie tries to help me, but I'm not comfortable with her lifting something so heavy.

"Wait, this is not good. It's too heavy, Kenz. Let's get Andy or one of the other guys to carry these down to the car."

Kenzie's face lights with a conspiratorial smile. "I'll have Andy send Butch back over to help us with these and the boxes."

"That's not too obvious now, is it?"

"What?" She tries to play innocent. "Just because we have two friends who are awesome and happen to be single, is it wrong I want you to meet?"

"If he's that awesome, why is he single?"

"Andy told me he had a really bad breakup with his last girlfriend. Andy said he never told him why they broke up, but he suspected she cheated on him from the few things he did say about it. Trust me when I tell you he is amazing, and I can't imagine why any woman would cheat on him!"

"Fine, do whatever you want, but do it soon, before the frozen stuff melts."

Kenzie smiles and picks up her phone. She calls Andy. The timing is perfect. His mom is due with lunch in about an hour. He and Butch would come back over and move all we had packed. We'd have time to unpack it all in the kitchen at the new house before his mom arrived.

As Kenzie hangs up, my phone rings. I pull it from the back pocket of my shorts. It's Tammy, my assistant manager. She is opening the restaurant for me today and accepting the food order. "Hi Tammy."

"Boss, I think you need to come to the restaurant right now. I just got here and there is no electricity. I don't know how long it's been out. I don't want to open any of the refrigerators or freezers and let the cool air out, but I don't know if anything is spoiling, either."

"Oh, shit! You're kidding!"

Kenzie's concerned eyes fix on me.

"I left at eight and we had power then, so I'm sure nothing is spoiling yet. Did you check the breakers?"

"Yeah, and you're going to want to see the breaker box, too. I think someone messed with it."

"What do you mean, messed with it?"

"You'll see when you get here," she says.

I end the call and turn back to Kenzie. "I'm sorry. I have to go." I relay to her what Tammy told me.

"If you think someone intentionally cut the electric to your restaurant, call the police, Maddie."

"I will." The thought that it could have been Dave comes to me.

"And this fridge is empty. I know it won't hold as much as what's in your freezers, but feel free to store anything here," she offers. "And let me know if you need these coolers. I'll have them emptied within the next half hour. I can fill them with ice and bring them over if you need me to."

I give Kenzie a hug. "Thank you. I'll let you know." I'd feel terrible if I had her help me when I was supposed to be helping her move.

"And if you have no power tonight, and need a place to sleep, we're leaving Andy's mom's room intact for now. You know the code to the locks, feel free to come stay here for as long as you need."

I hug her again. "Thank you so much. Let me get to my restaurant and I'll let you know what's going on."

I grab my purse and leave through the back. Trotting down the wood stairs off the deck, I look around and momentarily panic, not seeing my car where I parked it. Then I remember Andy moved it to the side lot. I walk around to the side lot and there she is, my little red pride and joy.

When I hit the unlock button on the door, it didn't unlock. Oh, crap. That's right, Andy moved my car. He has the keys. I pull my phone out of my back pocket again, preparing to call Kenzie. Through the side door of the gym, Logan comes out. I thought he was over at the new house.

"Hey," he calls, jogging towards me. "I have your keys."

"Oh, good, thanks!"

"You heading back to the house? Can I catch a ride with you?" he asks as he hands them to me.

"No, sorry, I'm not. I have a small emergency at the restaurant. But I can give you a ride if you want." I open the door and slide behind the wheel.

"Nah, that's fine. I can walk."

"Andy's heading back here to load and move more over. You might want to wait and help him." I start the car.

"I'll do that," Logan says. He closes my door for me.

I roll the window down. Even though the car has been parked in the shade, it is hot inside. "I'll see you later." I shift to reverse to back out of the parking spot and then I pull out of the lot. At the stop sign, I see the box truck pull into the back driveway of the gym. Andy and Butch are back. Damn, I missed meeting him again.

Butch

I'm in the box truck with Andy. We may actually get the last of the furniture and boxes moved with this trip. As we near the driveway that runs behind the gym where we will again park to load, I see that sweet little red car pull out of the gym's parking lot. I get the slightest of glimpses of the driver, female, dark hair in a messy bun, the loose tresses blowing around in the breeze. She has dark sunglasses on that dominate her face. Logan is jogging back towards the stairs to the deck. Good!

With his help, we'll get the truck loaded quicker. I can already taste Andy's mom's lasagna.

We park and go upstairs, and as expected, Kenzie's friend had just left. When Kenzie tells us she left because someone may have sabotaged the electric at her restaurant, I think about our arsonist. Could it have been him upping his game by moving onto structures? Creating an electrical fire from a short in the breaker box is a much different MO than the accelerant used in the dumpsters, so I immediately dismiss this idea.

Andy scrolls through the contacts on his phone. "I'm going to text Maddie the contact info for a friend, an electrician and tell her to use my name if she needs him. Teague may be able to get her fixed today if he knows she's a friend of mine."

"Was he at the wedding?" I ask.

"No, he couldn't make it," Andy says. "He was out of town."

"I hope someone can get her power back and fast. She has so much food inventory that will spoil if it isn't kept cold. I offered her use of the fridge here and the bed, if she needs it tonight. It's way too hot to sleep without air conditioning," Kenzie says.

Andy, Logan, and I, move the three heavy coolers out to the truck and the rest of the boxes from the kitchen. Kenzie kept packing as we moved them and she had two more boxes done, which completed packing up the kitchen. We moved the kitchen table and chair set out too. One more trip through the apartment confirmed all that was left to move over were the two television sets. We put them in the back of Kenzie's car. That was it. Kenzie leaves to drive the televisions over to the house while we do one more sweep of the place. Except for the things in the bedroom his mom slept in, we'd moved everything out of the apartment.

Then we leave and climb into the cab of the truck.

"If Maddie does end up staying there tonight, let her know she can knock on my door for coffee or anything else she may need," Logan offers with a sexually suggestive air to his words.

"I doubt she'll be knocking for a booty call," Andy says laughing.

"You never know," Logan says, making me laugh as well. "She was considering it the night of your wedding."

"So, is she one of the few women in the city you haven't slept with Logan?" I ask. His sexual promiscuity is legendary. I'm quite surprised I haven't encountered him at the club. At some point, I probably will. He has to run out of women, sooner or later. Of course, he has no idea about my involvement in the club and that is the way I preferred to keep it.

"Hah-hah," Logan says. "And no, haven't. Believe me, not for lack of trying."

"Wait, did I just hear that you struck out with her?" I ask.

"Fuck you, Butch," Logan says laughing.

Andy barks out a full belly-laugh as well.

Madeline

I check my phone at the stop light. It was going crazy with text messages. Several from Tammy, one from my food vendor, and one from Andy, sharing an electrician's contact info with me. I tap out a quick thank you to him. The light turns green. My mind has been trying to figure out what the hell I'm going to do if my electric can't be fixed in time to save my inventory. The fridge and freezer at Kenzie's apartment will only hold maybe a quarter of my inventory at the restaurant. Coolers and ice would save the refrigerated product, but not the stores in the freezer. I have a lot of money tied up in my inventory.

I walk into a three-ring circus. My new fresh produce vendor is there delivering my order as is the wine shop. Okay, neither of the orders need to be refrigerated, at least. My meat vendor is there too, that is the one that is the problem. And I'm glad that Tammy realized it as well. She didn't accept the order, knowing that we don't want to open any of the refrigerated or frozen lockers.

Then the fire department pulls up. What the fuck?

"I called them," Tammy said. "I smelled gas in the basement when I went back down to check the breaker box after we talked."

I rubbed my throbbing head. *Oh, my God! This can't be happening!*

A Lieutenant Cotter greets me. He sends several of his men into the restaurant. I send the meat vendor away without accepting the delivery. I promise him I'd call him back later and reschedule the delivery. So much for the special I was going to make tonight.

The gas company comes and fixes the cracked pipe in the basement. Lieutenant Cotter agrees that the damage looks suspicious, especially with the damage to the electrical panel. I call the police. The officers come while the fire department and the gas company are still there. I hate to do it, but I give the police information on Dave, citing that he is the only one I could think of who could have done it, the only person with motive. My hands shook with the realization that someone purposefully damaged both the gas pipe and the electric.

"What about Frank?" Tammy asks me.

"He's good at running his mouth. I don't see him

breaking in and damaging an electrical panel and gas line," I say. I hoped not, anyway.

Once the gas company assures me there was no threat of an explosion, I call Andy's electrician friend. Teague promises to come right away. He arrives as everyone else is getting ready to depart. He gets to work, pointing out and confirming what Lieutenant Cotter had said, that the damage in the electrical panel couldn't have happened by any way other than intentional sabotage.

I want to cry, but I know I have to figure out the menu for tonight with what is in stock. I could cry later.

Hours pass and my employees start to show up for work. My restaurant is due to open in less than two hours, and we have no electricity yet and no food prepped. We are booked with reservations. I didn't want to have to cancel them. The good news is that the first hour we'd be open there were only a handful of reservations. If the power is restored within the next half hour, we might pull it off with a limited menu.

Just then, Teague appears at the door from the basement. "I think we're good to go, but I'd prefer if you all wait outside while I throw the breaker."

I laugh nervously. *What does he think is going to happen when he throws it?* "Okay, but will you be alright down there?"

"Yeah, I don't think anything will blow up or anything, I'm just being careful."

I don't understand what he means, but I agree to clear out the place. The employees who were there had been sitting in the main dining room, either wrapping the silverware in the napkins in the daylight or cutting the lemons and limes that had just arrived in my food order.

We stand outside on the sidewalk and watch the lights come on inside and the lighted 'Toad and the Hoot Owl' sign in my parking lot to the side of the building comes to life. I breathed a sigh of relief. Shortly thereafter, Teague comes out the front door and waves us in.

"Okay, it's all fixed."

"Come into my office and I'll get you paid," I say. It didn't matter what the charge would be. He got me back in business. That was priceless.

"I'll bill you," he says. "But, also, I wanted to tell you I think you should change the locks and get a good security system. Someone did this intentionally."

I gaze at him with what I was sure was an outraged expression on my face. I knew that! The truth was, I wasn't sure who all had keys to the restaurant. I did plan to have the locks changed right away.

"You know Brian Porter, don't you? He's also friends with Andy. He puts in a good system with keypad locks. You can assign employees specific codes and then just disable their code when they no longer work for you without having to change the locks. And his security system can be monitored right from your phone."

"I-I know," I stammer. "After I have paid your bill, I'll see what I can afford."

"You can make payments to me if you need to and I'm sure Brian will set up a similar arrangement with you. Madeline, you can't afford not to secure this place after today."

"Thank you," I say. I know he's right and I appreciate that he'll take payments. I'm sure Brian will too.

I watch him leave in silence and roll it all around in my mind for just a few minutes before I pull my thoughts to getting dinner prepped. I step into a crowded kitchen. My staff is busy prepping what they can. Even servers and the bartender are in there helping! Salads are being made and other vegetables are being cut. Once again, I am so thankful I hired such good people. My thoughts go to Dave for a moment. Did he damage the electrical and gas line? I shake it off and get to work.

I look through the food lockers to see what I can pull together. More than half the menu will be off limits for at least half the night. I create appetizer and main course specials and price them extremely low to entice the customers to order them. I verbally go over the menu with Tammy as I'm prepping the specials and she takes notes. She'll print off special menus for tonight with what we can make. And we'll share that we had an electrical outage and hope our customers understand we did our best. That'll have to be good enough.

***

The night goes better than it started. None of the customers complain about the limited menu and my quickly thrown together specials are a big hit! Well, so is the pricing. I made little on them, but I kept the diners happy and well fed. I'm exhausted as I turn the lights off and lock up the restaurant. I'd been so busy I hadn't gotten around to messaging Brian Porter. I'll do it in the morning. An uneasiness hits me as I mount the stairs to my apartment. And I heard Teague's warning replay in my mind, that I couldn't afford not to enact better security after today.

By the time I unlock my apartment door, I'd decided that I would drive over to the gym and sleep in Kenzie and Andy's vacant apartment. I grab my phone charger and some clothes, and I leave. It was after midnight, technically Sunday, so I doubted Brian Porter would come today. I hoped he could come during the day Monday. I didn't think I'd feel safe sleeping there until I knew the restaurant was secured.

Chapter 8

Butch

I was scheduled at the fire station on Sunday, an additional shift I picked up to help out. It was a twenty-four-hour overnight shift. I hoped we wouldn't be too busy. I didn't want to be exhausted Monday evening when I would see Charlotte again. As I entered the house, I ran into one of my counterparts, Aaron Cotter. He was heading out.

I knew he'd have all the details of his shift recorded, but I stopped him anyway. After greeting him I ask, "how was the shift?"

"Busy," he says. "Our arsonist hit two more dumpsters."

That wasn't good news.

"And we rolled on a gas leak at that restaurant, The Toad and the Hoot Owl. It was deliberate. Someone damaged the gas line on purpose. Couldn't have been normal wear and tear or an accident."

"I thought there was an electrical problem there."

Aaron raises an eyebrow, questioning how I'd know that. I explain that the restaurant's owner was helping move friends I was also helping, and she got called away. That was how I knew.

"Yeah, the electric panel was hit too. Someone did a

number to try to shut that place down. An electrician was just arriving when we were leaving the scene, the gas line repaired by the gas company. I hope he got the electric fixed so she could open her restaurant, nice lady, and I know she was stressing about the amount of money she had in her food inventory."

Well, wasn't that something? Cotter got to meet her, and I still hadn't. I was offered that Saturday shift but declined it, as I had committed to helping Andy move. I shook my head. "Thanks for the update," I say, knowing he was eager to get home. I immediately go to my office, and I read through the reports. Not only did I want to see what was up with the arson reports, I also wanted to read the report for myself on the gas leak at the restaurant.

I didn't even know Madeline Shaw, but she was a friend of Kenzie and Andy's so, I checked into it. And what I found was alarming. Cotter wasn't kidding. Someone really did a number on that place. If the person had been just a little more skilled, they could have caused an electrical short that would have sparked a gas explosion. I was glad that the police had been notified. I wasn't sure if the fire marshal was notified or not. I saw no notes regarding it, so I picked the phone up and called Bud Kleckner. He didn't answer. I left him a detailed message and requested a callback.

Madeline

I was pleasantly surprised that Brian Porter came to my place on Sunday to give me a quote. I was even more ecstatic that he had the equipment with him and was available to install it right then and there! And as Teague had suggested, he even said he would accept installments for me to pay it off. I was getting the Friends and Family pricing and terms. Thank you, Kenzie and Andy! The system he installed was top-of-the-line, easy to operate, and as Teague had said, monitorable on my phone.

We were back to normal when we opened at four p.m. offering our full menu. I'd received the meat order from the previous day and had plenty of time to thaw what I needed and to prep it before my staff arrived at two. I'd slept good at the apartment over the gym the previous evening and was thankful Kenzie had offered it to me. What I also discovered in that apartment changed my morning shower. A rain shower head transformed a normal shower into an incredible experience. I planned to buy one for my place right away.

I'd invite Kenzie and Andy back for a dinner on the house very soon. Without them, I wouldn't have gotten the electric fixed so quickly, nor would I have the new door locks and security system from Brian. A free dinner was the least I could do.

I slept amazingly that night, back in my own bed, in my own apartment. Plus, I was exhausted after being up earlier than usual on both Saturday and Sunday. I was able to lounge in bed, as Kenzie and I had canceled our normal breakfast for the morning. I did have to put in a food order and pay some bills, but I had most of the day to myself. I was excited and let my mind wander to what the night may be at the club with Master D. After the stressful few days, a great release with him was exactly what I needed! I could use a couple of good orgasms. Hopefully, that would be in his plan for the night.

Butch

While I head to the ladies' locker room to meet Charlotte, fuck if I don't run into Catrina with her new Dom. I cannot believe that Master Michael is still with that bitch. She looks me straight in the eye and purrs, "Hello Drago. Long time no fuck."

I wish a hole would open-up and swallow her into the bowels of hell. Although I have a smile on my face, she knows better. How can I let her affect me like this after a whole year?

The only reason she is still allowed in this club is the fact that her daddy is the mayor and could close us down at any time. Master Michael extends his hand, and we shake, and they move on. I watch their backs retreat down the hallway and then I remember, I have a job to do. Charlotte is waiting in the ladies' locker room. When I arrive, Charlotte is standing outside in the hall. My blood is boiling. I am not in the mood for this shit. "Follow me and keep your head down, Charlotte."

The scenario I had planned for the evening didn't fit the mood I was in. I take her straight to a private room and I instruct her to bend over the Restraining Bench and tell her I will be tying her hands and feet to the legs of the bench. I see her hesitate, but she complies. I choose a wide flogger and explain to her I will administer a punishment for not following my explicit instructions.

"I don't understand Sir, what did I do to upset you?"

Madeline

"Think about it Charlotte, you are a smart woman. You should be able to figure it out." His words were clipped.

I don't like how he is talking to me. "Sir, are you seriously punishing me for waiting outside in the hallway? You were late, and I was concerned that I misunderstood your directions."

"As a Submissive, you are not to think, but to follow. Is that clear?"

Oh, fuck him! I am so pissed right now. If I wasn't tied down, he would get a swift kick to the balls. How dare he thinks I didn't understand what I was told to do? Just as I think that, the first smack of the flogger comes down on my ass. I cry out from the pain. Tears fall down my cheeks. The second smack is worse. I scream, "Paris!"

Butch

So enraged in my thoughts, I heard but didn't process my Sub's safe word. Cosimo barges into the room and grabs my arm as it comes down for a fourth hit. My Sub is crying hysterically, and I feel like shit. I know I lost all control. And I knew it had nothing to do with her. It had been running into Catrina.

"Get the hell out of here! You need to get your shit together! I will see you in my office when I am done cleaning up your mess!" Cosimo's voice is a growl.

I turn to leave the room without looking back. I can't see her red, tear-streaked face again, caused by my actions. What have I done? She put her trust in me and I fucked it up. How could I have let Catrina get to me this bad? My gut is in a knot. I know I deserve whatever Cosimo has to say to me.

Madeline

The man unties me. He looks familiar, but I don't think I know him. He stares down at my tear-stained face. He scoops me up and takes me to the same room that Master D has taken me after each session. It's the last place I want to be. I want to tell him to take me to the locker room so I can change my clothes and go home. But I also feel this horrible wave of exhaustion hit me.

"I am going to get a warm washcloth and wipe your face if that is okay, Charlotte."

All I can do is nod. Where did my voice go? I am completely shocked at what just happened. And I know if I say anything yet, it will be screaming and swearing that comes out of me, nothing civil. And he doesn't deserve that. He did nothing to me. He wipes my face and then he hands me a glass of water with two small pills.

"What the hell are these?"

"A light sedative to help bring you down from your

experience. You should be awake within four hours, and we can talk again about what happened if you would like to."

He covers me up. "Charlotte, there is a button next to the bed. If you need anything at all, please push it and I will arrive to help you."

"Can't you stay for just a few minutes? I just don't understand why Master D was so angry with me for waiting outside the locker room door. If that is what being a Sub is about, I want no part of it." He sits on the bed next to me. I feel completely spent and although I don't know this man, I sense I can trust him.

"He has some baggage that he apparently hasn't come to terms with. I know he has to feel like shit. And I know he will want to explain what caused tonight's episode. Please trust me when I tell you what happened is not what being a Sub is about and his behavior tonight is very much out of his character."

It dawns on me; I saw this guy at the gym. That's where I know him from. "What's your name? I saw you in the Stevens Street Gym the other day, didn't I?"

He smiles and nods. "My name is Cosimo. Master D is my brother. We are the owners of the club, although my dumbass brother has been out of the game for about a year, and after reading your profile, I thought the two of you would be a great fit."

"You two are the owners of the club?" Oh shit. That means they both know exactly who I really am.

"Yes, my brother works the security end of the club and doesn't have access to the applications and background checks that are run on each member. I am the only one who sees them. I promise your anonymity is secure as promised."

I have no other choice than to believe him. The pills must have kicked in, as I am suddenly fighting to keep my eyes open. All I want to do is curl up in a ball and sleep for a week.

"If you would like, I can stay here until you fall asleep."

"I would, Cosimo, thank you." My eyes start to close as I drift. I think I feel Cosimo's soft hands brush back the hair that had fallen into my face. Either that or I am already dreaming, but I don't think that is the case. I am strangely still aware of what is going on around me. Before I pass out, the thought comes to me that the brothers' hands and their touches are very different.

Butch

From Cosimo's office, I watch the scene in my private room unfold on the security cams. Although, due to the angle of the camera and the lighting, I can only see their silhouette. That doesn't stop the nasty head of jealousy that is rearing its ugly head in me. That fucker is moving in on my territory. Where is that bottle of bourbon? I plopped down on King Cosimo's throne and rifle through his desk drawers. I am shocked when I come across still pictures of me with both Catrina and Charlotte. What the fuck?

Drinking straight from the bottle, the bourbon burns all the way down. Getting shit faced is my number one goal tonight. Things went straight to hell faster than counting to ten. How could I have let that bitch affect me so badly that I actually lost control with Charlotte? I told her I would never hurt her and to trust me. Boy, did I screw this up. I was sure she would never forgive me, and I wouldn't blame her for that.

A few hours later, Cosimo enters his office. The look on his face finding me in his chair is priceless. His eyes immediately go to the empty bottle of bourbon sitting on the desk in front of me. I can see judgment in his eyes, and I don't need this shit right now.

"Okay brother, I can see you have something to say to

me. Let me have it. I know I fucked up, and that Charlotte is more than likely never coming back to me. I want to thank you for cleaning up my mess tonight, but did you have to enjoy it so much?"

"You think I enjoyed having to console a Sub who just had the most degrading experience of her life? Shit, Drago! She didn't deserve that punishment and you know it. What the hell is wrong with you? I gave Charlotte a sedative and told her I would check on her later."

He pauses and eyes me with anger. He waits. I say nothing.

"So, do you want to share with me what the fuck set you off like that? I haven't seen that side of you since the Catrina incident."

I scrubbed my hand over my face and breathed out the fire that was burning my chest. "Catrina, that's what happened. Did you know she would be in the club tonight, Cosimo? She's not supposed to be here on Monday nights. Damn it! I haven't run into her in almost a year, and she is with that asshole, Michael."

"That's it? Really?" Cosimo shakes his head. "Jesus Christ, Drago! It's been a year."

"Something reared its ugly head, and I lost my shit," I confessed. "Charlotte used her safe word, and I heard it, but it didn't even register. I was consumed with anger. If you hadn't barged in, who knows how bad it might have gotten?"

"Well, thank God I did. And I'll make sure that Catrina is never here again on a Monday night. Friday is her night, when you aren't here. I'll make sure that is enforced."

I can't believe the forgiving tone of Cosimo's voice. "I didn't put my Sub's safety first, and I will regret that for as long as I live. I wouldn't blame her for wanting a new Dom to take over her training. Hell, I wouldn't blame her for never returning to the club."

"Brother, you need to take some more time off, and I will talk with Charlotte before sending her home tonight to determine where she wants to go from here. I think you should be the one to explain to her why you lost your cool, but you should probably be sober for that conversation. If she is willing, I could arrange for her to come in on one of your days off from the firehouse later this week or next, so the two of you can talk about what happened and how to proceed."

Chapter 9

Madeline

Wednesday morning arrives, and my ass is still a bit red. I have no idea what made Master D administer the punishment he did. I have already canceled my session next Monday so I can get my head wrapped around everything that happened and what Cosimo explained to me. I need to decide if I'm going back to the club.

I decide hitting the gym is what I need after I receive my food order. I am starting to enjoy working on the equipment and the kick boxing class that I am now taking. Hitting things really relieves a lot of frustration. Kenzie isn't in. It's not like we had a date to work out together and I know she isn't always there, but I was hoping to see her. My fault, as I didn't contact her to ask. As I am about to finish up on the treadmill, I panic. I look over at the front door and see Cosimo headed my way. What the hell is he doing here?

"Hi," Cosimo says, coming up to my piece of equipment.

I'm flustered seeing him here, especially after what happened in the club the other night. "Hi," I reply, watching him cautiously.

"You canceled your next session," he says, dropping his voice very low.

Yes, I was able to do that online on the website. I nod I

did.

"I think you should come in and talk about what happened now that you have had some time to think about it before deciding."

I am winded from the speed I was going, pushing myself, so instead of answering, I shake my head no.

"Madeline," Cosimo says.

I like he uses my real name here, but used my club-name there, even when we were in the privacy of that sequestered room. I appreciate the thoughtfulness he has put into it.

"There is a reason you joined the club, fulfillment you weren't getting elsewhere. I want you to think about that and let that guide your decision more than the incident." He pauses as several other gym members walk by. "But I won't press you farther, here, now. Just think about it. Call me and let me know your thoughts."

He hands me a business card with only his first name and a phone number on it. Odd. I take it and tuck it into the pocket of my hoodie. He excuses himself and goes to engage in his own workout. I couldn't keep myself from thinking about what he said. Yes, there were reasons I joined the club. After experiencing what I had there already, was I ready to give that up? And what next if I did? I had known I wanted something like this, had craved something like this. By the end of my workout, I decided I had to call him and go back to at least talk with him. I'd call him tomorrow.

Butch

"I ran into Charlotte today. She cancelled her next few sessions online, so I suggested she call me to talk about it," Cosimo says as a greeting when I answer his call.

"Where did you run into her?" I ask. I'm just getting off shift at the firehouse. I toss my bag into the passenger seat of my car. I was on the last twenty-four hours.

"That doesn't matter," Cosimo says. "The point of this call is to advise you she cancelled, and I am trying to intercede."

Great, Cosimo is playing the hero. I'm sure he wants me to thank him, and I probably should. "Do you think she'll call?"

"I'm hopeful. There are reasons she joined the club to begin with. I reminded her of that. If she calls, I will try to get her to come in and talk with me. I prefer to see someone's face to gage how they really feel about things."

I drop myself behind the wheel and slam the door shut in anger. Damn him! I have a feeling he didn't just run into her. I'm sure he pulled her info and made sure to be where he'd run into her. She had to feel targeted by him and that may be enough for her to not come back. I'd be pissed if it were me and I felt my anonymity had been violated. "Will you at least try to get her to talk with me before she makes her decision?"

"I'll see how the conversation goes if she calls. But I agree. It would be best if she talks to you."

"It would," I agree as I turn the engine over. It roars to life. "Okay, I'm just leaving the firehouse. Let me know if you hear from her."

He agrees to.

I drive to the gym to have a good workout.

The shift wasn't too bad. My sleep was only interrupted twice, once for our dumpster arsonist, the second for an MVA with entrapment. The car was crushed in on the driver. We had to use the jaws of life to cut the poor guy out of the car. When we first rolled up on the scene, I was sure no one could be alive in that vehicle. That driver had been lucky.

I park in the side parking lot of the gym just as Kenzie pulls into the lot. Trina bounces out of the car and runs to me, all smiles. She greets me with a big hug. I love that kid!

"Hi Uncle Butch!"

"Hi kiddo," I answer. Then I give Kenzie a hug. It's odd that she had driven to the gym. She usually walks. "Hey Kenz, you feeling okay?" I worry about her and the pregnancy.

"Yes, just fine. Why?"

I point to the car. "You normally walk."

"Oh, I'm just getting back from picking Trina up from playing at a friend's house."

We walk into the gym together. Andy is at the counter. He smiles and gives Trina a hug before greeting me. "Your brother was in earlier," he says. "He left maybe an hour ago."

"Humm, is that a fact?" I say. I'm glad I didn't run into him here. I really don't want to see him face to face yet. I have to wonder when he ran into Charlotte. Could it have been here? Unlikely. "I'm glad he finally came in." I glance across the street at Cheshire. I wonder if he went back there after his workout or to the club. I'm going to guess the club so he could get a shower.

"You need someone to spot you?" Andy asks, pointing to the backroom with the weights.

"Yeah, if you're free."

"I wanted to do some lifting too," Andy says. "Let's hit it."

Madeline

"I'm very glad you called and have come in to talk," Cosimo says. He is sitting behind an impressive desk.

The guest chair in front of it where I sit is comfortable, but I can't relax. I don't know what to say, don't know what I want. I thought Master D, and I had something special between us, and I still can't believe he did that to me. I don't think I have come completely to terms with it. Whenever I think about it, I pendulum between being totally pissed off and wanting to cry. I push those thoughts from my head and stiffen my lip. I look Cosimo in the eye. "I haven't made a decision yet," I say.

"I understand." He looks thoughtful for a moment. "Tell me, Charlotte, what were your reasons for choosing to enter this lifestyle, for the role of Submissive?"

For a second, I panic. It was one thing typing it out on an on-line questionnaire, which was hard enough. It would be another saying it out loud to this man, who I do not know at all. Hell, I wouldn't even tell my best friend, Kenzie, about it. "I don't see why that is relevant." I almost referred to him as Sir.

His lips curve into a smile. "The role of a Submissive is, in my opinion, more of a calling. Having the courage to apply to the club and show up takes a special person, a committed person, a person with a sound reason to do so."

"You read my application. You know why," I say. I knew my voice is bordering on inflammatory, but I don't care.

He smiles again. I wish I could read what that smile means. "My brother had some demons come back to the surface that night, demons we both thought he had slayed. Everyone has demons they exercise in different ways." He pauses, pinning me with a stare. I don't know what he wants me to say, so I say nothing. Since I didn't speak, he continues. "What I'm getting at Charlotte is that everyone has reasons for everything they do. Would you agree with that?"

"Yes, I suppose so," I answer.

"Before the incident the other evening, would you have considered discontinuing your membership at the club?"

"No."

"Would you have requested a different Dom? Because you know, your contract gives you the option."

"I know it does," I answer, feeling defensive. I'm not

stupid. I know the terms of the contract I signed. His gaze is steady. He doesn't react to my near outburst. "And no, I wouldn't have."

"The Dom-Sub relationship is no different from any other. It's built on trust and devastated by the lack of it. People screw up and the other party must decide if they will forgive or not. But any real healing can only come from communication. Would you be willing to talk with Master D, hear what he has to say, and evaluate it for yourself if you can or want to forgive him?"

I think about it for a few seconds. "The only problem I have with any of that is that unlike any other relationship, the trust that exists in this relationship, especially for the Sub goes way beyond the trust you give to another in any other relationship."

Cosimo nods. "Very true. I am quite impressed with the grasp of this you have after four short weeks. That is even more a reason for you to talk with him before you decide. For your own closure, if nothing else."

That makes sense. Maybe in a few weeks I would be ready. I'm not today. I nod.

Butch

After receiving a text from Cosimo that he wants to meet in his office before the evening starts, all I could think about is Charlotte. I open the door to Cosimo's office, and as usual, he is on his phone, and he motions for me to sit down. Eyeing the open bottle of bourbon, I decide to make myself a drink before sitting down to hear what he has to say. He stops my hand before it reaches for the bottle, which pisses me off. He pulls the bottle away from me, which pisses me off more.

After hanging up the phone, Cosimo looks me straight in the eye. "You drank the last of my bourbon that you're going to drink Monday night. Until you get your shit together," he adds.

He eyes me with a stare I don't care for.

"I didn't know you still carried so many demons about Catrina and how it ended."

"I was going to marry her." My tone of voice is not nice. "So, fuck you very much that you don't think I should still be bothered by how it ended and by seeing her the other night."

"I spoke with Charlotte in person today and explained that, although what happened the other night was unacceptable, she must understand why she came to the club in the first place and whether she wants to continue with another Dom or have a serious discussion with your stupid-ass about what happened. That's how I left it with her. It's up to her to figure out how she wants to proceed from here."

"You fucking did what?" I shout. Does he think I cannot clean up my own mess? When he heard from her, he should have called me so I could have been the one she came in to talk with. I planned to explain I am a hot mess, and that I would never, ever, do that again to her. I can't voice any of that to Cosimo, though.

"Calm down Drago, hear me out. She needed to understand that was totally out of your character. I am trying to help you out here, because watching your sessions, I can tell that she is more than a Sub in training for you."

I grab his glass from the desk and swallow the bourbon in one gulp. I return his empty glass to his coaster on the desk, and then drop my head into my hands on my knees. When did this whole thing go in a direction I hadn't anticipated? I was broken, and someone like Charlotte deserved better.

"I gave her my personal cell and told her to call me when she was ready to restart her sessions, and if she wanted a new Dom to continue them. I also recommended that she just talk with you about what happened, even if it was to just get some kind of closure."

"There is not one Dom in this place I want to see Charlotte training with."

Cosimo refills his glass and takes a drink. "If a new Dom is her decision, then you will need to stay away. This is my fault. I was wrong to push you back into the game. You weren't ready."

"I know I have a wall around my heart. It was opening up to her. I care about her Cosimo, a lot. I want to keep training her." I knew I'd never let anyone else become her permanent Dom. I wanted her.

"That's solely her decision, not yours."

I nod my head, feeling a terrible headache about to come on. I really hope that I didn't permanently mess everything up with Charlotte. She is the most responsive Sub I have ever been with. I can see this relationship really going somewhere.

It's like Cosimo can read my mind. "This is more than just a training relationship to you, isn't it?

I don't have to answer. He knows. I can see it in his eyes.

"If I don't hear from her by Sunday, I'll call her to see if she is even considering returning to the club, so we will have a better idea of where to go from here? I also want to remind her we are closed this Monday, as it is the holiday and Tuesday is the makeup day. Her last email on the rescheduled club day, before this went down, indicated that she wasn't sure if Tuesday would work in her schedule or not."

"I'm on literally all weekend at the firehouse and on Monday the fourth. With all the illegal fireworks, plus legal ones that will be shot off, we are fully staffed. I'm off Tuesday through Thursday," I say.

"Okay, I'll let you know if I hear from Charlotte."

Chapter 10

Madeline

T he restaurant's reservations remain booked to capacity through the Fourth of July holiday weekend. Many of my staff requested at least one evening off, which I haven't been able to grant. That would be a third of our staff off each of the three nights. I get it, but that is the downside of working in the restaurant business. We are closed like normal on Monday the fourth, which is when the local fireworks will be shot off. Hopefully, they can plan things with friends or family on Monday.

I'm glad I've been busy since my last session with Master D. My thoughts are still reeling. I haven't called Cosimo back. I'm not ready to talk to him either. It's Friday, and I went to the gym this morning for one of Logan's kickboxing classes, which I am loving, and am thankful I didn't see him there again. But as I finish prepping my special and return to my office, my phone chimes a new email. It's the Velvet Playroom with a reminder that since Monday is the Fourth of July, the regular Monday events will now take place on Tuesday.

Not for me, they won't. I've cancelled my next few sessions. Kenzie and Andy are having a party at their place on Monday, the fourth. I plan to go and have a good time and forget about Master D for the evening. Maybe that friend of Andy's will be there, and I can meet him and see if there is any chemistry there. If nothing else, I plan to have several drinks, eat some good food and have a good time with friends.

I change into a clean chef's coat as some of my blueberry sauce splattered on the one I wore while prepping the specials. I created a special salute to the red, white, and blue, a raspberry, white chocolate, and blueberry sauce topped cheesecake. It looks delicious. Each slice will have all three toppings dripping from it in patriotic glory. And my bartender came up with a special white sangria with red and blue fruit for the weekend too. I just love when we can do themed desserts and drinks!

***

The entire weekend flies by in a busy, exhausted blur. I try to make the weekend fun for my employees who I know would rather be with friends at bar-b-ques and other parties. I break out desserts and drinks for everyone after our doors close to our patrons to enjoy during clean up. I thank them for their hard work and surprise them with gift cards to various local businesses to 'win' and 'steal' from each other during clean up games. Everyone walks out of work each night with a twenty-five-dollar gift card to some place different. I consider it a small investment to keep my employees happy. They may have preferred cash, but this was fun, and I had a good time thinking up the many different types of places to get the gift cards from. And staying that busy and planning it kept my mind off of what happened at the club Monday night.

Sunday night, we close at eleven, remaining open an extra hour because of the holiday weekend. It is one a.m. Monday morning when I close the back door, saying goodnight to Tammy, who stayed with me till we were done with everything. I watch her cross the parking lot to her car and then I mount the stairs to go up to my apartment. The hairs on the back of my neck stand up and a feeling I am in danger sweeps over me.

From the top of the wood stairs, on the small landing at my apartment door, I look over the area below. From here, I can see most of the side parking lot and part of the back of the alleyway. It's quiet. None of the surrounding businesses are open twenty-four hours. My restaurant is probably the business that is open the latest. The lack of people around when I close has never bothered me before now.

I'm sure it is just my imagination getting the best of me, but I feel as though I am being watched. My gaze sweeps across the side parking lot one more time. At the far end of the lot, my car is parked as always, but I think I see movement near it. I squint, looking hard at it and to the right of it where I thought I saw a figure dressed in black. But it's gone now, if it was ever there.

After staring at the spot for a few minutes, I decide I was seeing things. Nothing and no one is there. At least that is what I convince myself of. I unlock my apartment, using the new keypad of the security and lock system that Brian Porter installed last week, and close myself inside my apartment, leaving my worries on the other side of the door.

Before taking a well-needed cool shower, I pour myself a glass of a wonderful red blend and I lounge on my couch, sipping it. For some reason, that conversation with Cosimo last Wednesday in his office comes back to me. I know I eventually have to figure out what I'm going to do. I'm also going to have to figure out if I want to go in and have a conversation with Master D if for nothing else, just to get closure, as Cosimo suggested. He does owe me a huge apology, if nothing else. The question is, will I feel any better or any differently if he gives me that apology?

Butch

Monday morning at the firehouse arrives after an insanely busy weekend. Three dumpster fires, which is less than I expected. Our arsonist must have been distracted and is taking some time off because of the holiday. We had two structure fires, five fireworks-sparked dry grass fires, and thirty motor vehicle accident assists, with nineteen ambulance transports to the hospital. It could have been worse. And of course, the trucks from my house were in the Fourth of July Parade on Sunday. That's always a fun time.

I'm scheduled until seven a.m. Tuesday morning. Andy messaged me that they are having a bar-b-q and invited me to stop over at any point today if I can. I really wish I could. I never mind that I have to work most holidays and even when I am not scheduled, I usually volunteer to take a shift to help the guys with families.

Even though fires and car accidents are horrible for the people involved in them, I am glad we've been busy to help keep my mind off of Charlotte and how I fucked up. This waiting really sucks. But that is all I can do, is wait and hope.

Madeline

I'm shocked that I wake on the couch. The light is still on in my little kitchen. The glass of wine is nearly finished, standing guard on the coffee table in front of me. And I'm still in my white tank top I wear beneath my chef's coat, and my loose checkered chef's pants are still on me. I normally slide them off and put on a pair of shorts when I walk into my apartment, if I'm not going to sleep right away.

I rise and go to the window. I look out at my car, at the far end of the side parking lot. It's still there and looks fine. I think again about what I thought I saw. There is a row of leafy bushes behind my car. Maybe it was breezy, and I didn't realize it. It could have been just the wind moving the leaves.

***

Later that afternoon when I am ready to leave to go to Kenzie and Andy's house for the bar-b-q, I set the cheesecake in a sheet cake pan and the three sauces I made for the party onto the floor of the front passenger side of the car. I purposefully walk around the back of the car just to check everything out. I see no damage, no indication anyone was there, but then again, I don't know what I should be looking for or what I'd hope to find. I don't think I'll find a note saying, yes, I was standing here watching you last night. I chuckle to myself at that thought.

I shake it off and drive over to Kenzie's. I have to park up the block as there has to be thirty cars in their driveway and on the street, stretching out in both directions. I walk in the door beside the garage, into the kitchen. It's full of people, some I recognize, some I do not. I didn't realize this would be such a big party! I hope I brought enough cheesecake. Had I known there would be this many people here, I would have made two.

Andy's mom, Sheri, is in the kitchen, and she greets me with a hug. She is such a sweetheart. Kenzie hit the mother-in-law lottery! His youngest sister, Theresa, and her boyfriend Seth are there, which surprises me. I know the relationship between Andy and his sister is a bit strained. She showed up to the rehearsal dinner for their wedding at my restaurant noticeably pregnant and she hadn't told anyone in the family, including Andy and his mom. Andy and Kenzie handled it with class, as that is what they are, classy and respectful of everyone.

"Hi, glad you made it," Kenzie says, coming up behind me and wrapping me in a hug.

"Thanks for the invite," I say. "This is a much bigger party than you told me it would be." I hold up the sheet cake pan. "I would have made more cheesecake."

"I plan to cut it into small bites, and we have a half-dozen other desserts coming," Kenzie says. "Besides, I didn't want you in the kitchen all morning cooking. It's a holiday, your day off!"

I laugh. I wouldn't tell her it was made with the cheesecakes for the special dessert at the restaurant all weekend. "Thank you for thinking of me."

"I made sangria," Kenzie says with a smile.

I see that Sheri already has a red solo cup with her name on it, filled with Kenzie's sweet-smelling sangria. "Where's mine?" I laugh.

She helps me find room in her very full refrigerator for my dessert and then she points out the ample buffet of food. I grab a few bites of some yummy appetizers while she fills a solo cup for me with her potent sangria. We go out into their beautiful backyard, and I start to mingle. I'm not shy. I always talk to people at parties that I know, and I don't know alike. Brian Porter and his beautiful girlfriend, Tiffany, are the first people I go up to.

"Have there been any other incidents since last week?" Brian asks.

I'm hesitant to say anything about last night. Well, technically this morning. "Only in my mind." I laugh. "I'm being paranoid now." I then tell him about thinking someone was out by my car this morning.

"I didn't put any cameras to monitor the parking lot. I could if you want."

"No, really, not necessary. I'm sure it was my overactive imagination."

"You really should follow your instincts," Brian says. "If you feel weirded out, there is probably a reason for it. Don't discount if something feels off."

"Thank you, Brian," I say. "If I feel that way again, I may take you up on it."

I catch back up with Kenzie as Andy is taking the first

round of food off the grill to offer my help in the kitchen. After all, who, besides a chef, can handle total chaos in a kitchen? She introduces me to other gym employees and members who are also friends as I help her organize the food and refill it as the masses go through the buffet line, emptying plates and platters of appetizers, mains, sides, and chips. Andy's mom even made a pan of lasagna. I get the last piece.

I sit at a table set up in the yard with Andy, Kenzie, his family, and Logan. I've had four or five glasses of sangria. I feel loose and am having a great time. Logan and I trade harmless flirts. Damn, that man is hot! Not as hot as Master D, and there my mind goes back to him again. Shit! I'd been determined not to think of him today.

At some point later, I find myself alone at the table with Logan, exchanging flirty barbs. This is familiar territory. We interacted the same way at Kenzie and Andy's wedding reception. If I didn't know his reputation, I would think he's just a harmless flirt, but I know that isn't the case. He is not harmless, and he isn't just a flirt. He is most definitely a sleep with them once man-whore, and for someone like me, that is not harmless.

"I won't tell if you don't, darling," he says with the cutest Texas twang in his voice. "One incredible night." He flashes me an inviting smile. "Think of the possibilities."

"Why would I want only one night if it's as amazing as I think it may be? What good is it if you can't have it again?"

He laughs. "Oh, and it will be, but it's just a personal code I have. No relationships, no entanglements."

"Because most women can't handle just sex, no relationship. Is that what you're saying?"

"I'm not damning your gender, and you said that, not me." He chuckles.

Oh, he has no idea! "Let's just say for a second that a woman could handle a relationship that is purely sexual, no strings or expectations of anything else. And let's say it is amazing and earth-shattering, every time. That isn't something you would be interested in?"

"Let's turn that around. You and I have that no strings, amazing, purely sexual non-relationship." He points to Brian Porter's girlfriend, Tiffany. "And I get the opportunity to sample that. Do you have a problem with that?"

I know that would be a problem. I won't lie about that. "If it's amazing, why would you want to sample other opportunities?"

"Variety is the spice of life, darling," he says. "And it would be a problem for you, for any woman, and don't try to tell me it wouldn't be. Your last question answers that."

"Yeah," I admit.

He winks at me. "You let me know if you ever change your mind on that one incredible night." His gaze is cocky.

"And you let me know if you ever change your mind on the one-night thing," I fire back, just as cocky.

We both laugh as Margot, Kenzie's friend, Detective Margot Malone, heads in my direction. She must have just gotten off work and swung by. She's still dressed in her work clothes, a solid round-neck black t-shirt and beige dockers. Her gun and badge are at her hip. I've known her for many years. I get along with her well-enough, but we're not tight buddies. Kenzie is all we really have in common.

"Hi Margot," I greet.

"Madeline," she says with a smile and a nod. "What's this I hear about some problems you've been having? And why didn't you call me?"

"I don't know. I didn't want to bother you."

"The electric and the gas were messed with at your restaurant? A spark could have ignited the gas and killed someone. Kenzie said you have a problem with an ex-boyfriend. Do you think he could have done it?"

A knot forms in my stomach. "I gave all the info to the police officer that came to my place and took the report. I don't know if Dave would know how to sabotage it like that. Or if he even would. Brian Porter installed security cameras for me a week ago and so far, nothing concerning has been recorded."

"I'm glad you got new locks and cameras. You have my number. If you see this Dave character around, give me a call and I'll be happy to talk to him."

I laugh as I know how she'd be during that talk. She can be quite the hard ass when she needs to be. "I promise, if he shows back up or if anything else suspicious or concerning happens, I will call. I know how busy you are, though."

"I'm never too busy to help a friend," she says.

"Thanks. I appreciate it." And I do, but it's also kind of embarrassing. I'm not sure why, it's not like I've done anything wrong to invite this.

She points to my glass. "Call an Uber if you're near the legal limit or over. All the cops in the city are watching for drunk drivers this holiday weekend. There's even going to be a few checkpoints set up tonight."

I laugh. "Are you supposed to be warning people about that?"

She smiles. "I think it's better to give reminders than risk someone not thinking about it."

The rest of the evening is fun, and I meet and talk to a lot of people. Every time I glance at Logan, I can't help but think about what he said, and it gets my thoughts wondering about Master D. I hadn't even thought about it before now. Is he sleeping with anyone else? And does he wonder if I'm having sex with anyone? Does he care? There has never been anything spoken or written that speaks about other partners or that not being allowed.

Well, shit! This is just another thing I don't really want to think about. But I can't help it. Is Master D having sex with someone else right now either in a personal relationship or training another Sub? And do I even have the right to think about it? Or want to know? And do I really want to have sex with someone else? Can I really be the person who has sex casually, outside of a relationship, with no strings? I went into the arrangement at the club with that being part of the allure of it. But do I really think of what I'm doing with Master D as casual? I think I've already answered that in my feelings. Well shit!

Chapter 11

Madeline

After I get my food order in on Tuesday, I find myself at my desk fingering the card Cosimo gave me with his name and private cell phone number. I decide I do need to talk with Master D. I have to make a decision about the club, and I can't do that until I have talked to him. If nothing else, he owes me an apology and I do want it. I dial Cosimo, feeling determined.

"This is Cosimo," he answers.

"Hi, this is Charlotte," I say.

"Hello, Charlotte. It's nice to hear from you." His voice sounds formal or professional.

I pause, summoning my courage. "I do want to meet with Master D, but not during a session. You were right that I want to talk to him and let him explain, and I feel he owes me an apology." I know my voice sounds bitchier than I intended.

"He does," Cosimo agrees. "What does your schedule look like in the next few days?"

"I'm free today until four this afternoon. The rest of the week, I'm free from about ten in the morning until four. I could be free later, say after six, if that is all that will fit his schedule."

"Okay, let me get a hold of my brother and see what his

schedule looks like. I'll send you a text with a time to meet here. My office. Will that work for you?"

"Yes, it will," I say, my voice still bitchy.

"Okay. I will try to get this scheduled as soon as possible."

As I disconnect the call, I let out a heavy breath. I just know that I won't be able to sound any friendlier when I'm talking to Master D. I am still so pissed off. And if I'm being honest, very upset by what happened. I gave him my trust, and he betrayed it. I'm not sure if he can say anything to make that up to me or regain my trust.

I take care of a few other administrative tasks and then exit the restaurant through the back and mount the stairs to my apartment. As I glance around, I see a man with longish black hair and a shadow across his jaw and over his lip across the street, about a block away. I swear it's Dave! The man, whoever it is, ducks into the storefront in front of him, a new age bookstore.

"Oh, no you don't!" I say aloud.

I turn and go back down the stairs. I cross the street, dodging a few cars, and head right for the door to the bookstore. The overhead chimes tinkle as I open the door.

"Welcome," a sing-song voice calls from deep inside the store.

I've never been in this store before. A sign offers Crystals, Tarot Card, and Palm Readings, and all the other New Age trappings that aren't anything that I know about. I'm not even sure if I believe in any of it, for that matter. It's fascinating and a lot of people swear by it, but I'm just not into any of it.

I glance between the open racks of items as I make my way farther inside the shop. I don't see him, just two young women eyeing some beautiful crystal enhanced wind chimes with whimsical fairies hanging alongside the crystals. Wow, they are lovely. I may want to buy one myself.

I get to the back of the store without seeing the man who looks just like Dave. He was even dressed in jeans and a tight t-shirt, like Dave always wears. I didn't see his face clearly, though, to know for sure. And I have to know for sure. There would be no reason that Dave would be on the street my restaurant is on if he was not watching me, stalking me, or there to cause some more trouble for me. If it is him, I will call Margot.

"Can I help you with something?" the young woman with the vibrant purple hair and multiple piercings in each ear asks. It's the same voice that welcomed me as I entered. She has a pleasant smile on her face.

"I'm looking for the man who came into this store a few minutes before I did. Did you see where he went?"

"We're all looking for something," she says in that sing-song voice. "You've come to the right place to find it."

Oh, good, Lord! "No, I mean a real person who I saw come in here," I clarify.

She waves her arm in a motion like Vanna White over letters on the board. "Did you see him?"

"No, that's why I am asking you!" Yes, I'm getting irritated. I point at the arched doorway that leads into a hallway. "Did he go back there?"

Her face and voice take on a seriousness. "Only those seeking enlightenment, seeking to know their true selves, or seeking guidance pass through that arch. I sense that there are issues weighing on you. Your aura is disturbed." Her intense stare washes away and when she speaks again, her voice returns to that sing-song tone. "I've never seen you in here before. We offer a free introductory reading. It could benefit you greatly with a big decision that is dominating your thoughts."

"Sure," I say.

I walk into the hallway. Three doors are on the wall to my right and a door I suspect is the back exit is on the back wall. The first door is open. It's a bathroom. The next door is open as well. It is a small room with a few comfortable looking chairs clustered around a table. Decks of cards sit atop it. The last door opens as I reach it and an equally hippie-looking woman escorts out a young woman who looks to be about twenty. This room is identical to the one beside it except the lights on the two grapevine clusters that are in pots are on, casting a calming blue glow throughout the entire room.

I go to the back door, open it, and look around. No one is in sight in the alley.

"Miss, your free reading?" the front desk purple-haired woman calls to me.

I re-enter the store. "Give me a moment," I tell her.

By the time I make it to the front of the store, the two women I saw looking at wind chimes are gone. I wanted to ask them if they saw the man and help identify him. Damn. I turn around and come face to face with the purple-haired woman again. I want to be annoyed with her, but I can't be. She is so pleasant and makes me feel at ease. She tells me about the different crystals they have along the wall and their role in promoting energy, healing, and positivity. They are used in conjunction with readings by the practitioner.

"I sense you are unsure about a reading," she says. "May I ask why? You came in here looking for something. A reading may help you find it."

"Not unsure about it. I honestly have no experience with any of this," I say as I wave my hand at the crystals. "As I said, I followed a man in I thought was someone I knew."

Before I know it, I'm following her back through the archway and into the room with the blue lights. "This is Alanna, one of our practitioners."

"Hello and welcome," she greets me. "Please sit." She motions to one of the two chairs facing her.

"Hi," I say. "I've never had a reading before." For the life of me, I don't know why I am sitting here.

She picks up a deck of cards from the table, one of the five there. She begins shuffling them. "Well then, let's see how the cards will guide you. Many who come in have specific questions they want answered, maybe about their love lives or their careers. Others just want a general reading."

I watch her shuffle, evaluating her warm smile and large brown eyes that stare at me intently. "Let's just do a general reading and see what the cards say," I decide.

She continues to shuffle, and two cards fall from the deck. "When they flip out like that, we take them," she says. "First, we have Rest and Reconsider. And then Dedicated Effort." She lays the two cards next to each other, facing me. "I feel these two cards are trying to remind you of balance. You have a large endeavor you are focused on, just as the figure on this card. He is before a large mural he is painting. But just like he has to remember to rest, so do you. I feel that you push yourself and work comes first, but the cards are trying to remind you that if you do not give yourself rest, all your effort will go to waste as you will get burnt out."

I nod. Wow, that is pretty spot on. I do work very hard and take little time to rest. The club is the first thing in a long time I have done for myself. Dedicating one evening a week has been wonderful until last week.

"Seek," she announces as she flips over the next card.

The image is of a person sitting in the woods, with doves flying overhead. "You are seeking something that is eluding you. It's a good thing, but you are feeling unfulfilled in a way. I think the cards are telling you to keep seeking. Don't forget why you started your quest."

Okay, this is getting spooky. Yes, the club was the answer to a quest for my sexual satisfaction. Could the cards be telling me to stick with it?

Another card falls out as she shuffles. "Win or Lose, whether you're the winner at the top or on the bottom, you will still do what you Seek, what you have a passion for," she says tapping both cards. "This card joining the balance of the first two cards and the Seek card is a sign that you are heading in the direction that will bring you fulfillment if you keep everything in balance. Win or Lose, is a second balance card. It mentions both. It reminds you that you are doing what you're doing regardless of the outcome. For say, an author or a painter, they will continue with their passion regardless of if they make money doing it or it is just a hobby. They will continue regardless of if they win or lose at it. That isn't the point. The point is the fulfillment obtained from the action."

Hum, this one makes me think. Is this one speaking about the club or my restaurant? Could it mean times are going to get hard related to my business? This is an upsetting thought, given my success. If not work related, how could this card be applied to the club? Heading in the right direction to bring me fulfillment applies, but doing it regardless of the outcome does not.

She shuffles more. No cards come out on their own. She turns one over and lays it beside the others. "Moving On," she says. "This is usually about walking away from something in your life, moving on, closing a past chapter of your life and looking forward to the next. It could be you already have or you're about to." She stares at me, waiting for me to offer up insights from my life.

I nod. "Both have happened recently."

She shuffles again. "Let's see if the next card offers any clarity to it." A card falls from the deck. She turns it over. "Open Up, I feel this card is a reminder from the spirits to always be open. I don't feel you're a closed off person as you are always seeking. Maybe this is more on a personal level, a reminder to be vulnerable, to allow the other parts of you that you seldom open up to other people. I feel this is for the new chapter in your life that has come now that you're Moving On." She taps that card.

So, Moving On and Open Up. Maybe these cards are telling me to keep going with the club, but to request a new Dom. But would I really be able to open up to a new Dom after what happened with Master D? I'm not even sure I can be open with him again. I'm still so pissed.

She grabs another deck of cards. "Let's see what these cards tell us." She holds them up. Scoops of ice cream are on the front of the deck. "Ice cream cards are fun and perfect for summertime." She shuffles them. One is sticking out from the others. She pulls it and lays it face up, overlapping the other cards. "Cherry Vanilla, love, passion, and relationships. This is a feel-good energy card. It revealing itself after the Open Up card, gives strong connotations to your sex life and opening your mind and allowing yourself to be vulnerable in that arena of your life."

Oh, she has no idea, I think. I was the definition of open sexually. And in choosing to try the club, I was moving on from Dave.

She shuffles again and turns over a card. "Apple Pie, this card represents trust, integrity, and comfort. It's a warning to always stay true to yourself and never allow anyone to make you into someone you're not. It's also a reminder to take comfort in trusting. Someone who has your trust is there to help you stretch your wings and fly in a new direction. But as you soar, stick to your integrity and follow your heart."

I stare at her, not even knowing what to ask. Apple Pie is a lot to take in. Finally, the words form. "What if I trusted someone, and they betrayed that trust but want another chance? What if they are that person who was helping me stretch my wings, but something happened? How will I know if I should trust them or move on?"

She reaches over the table and takes hold of my hand. I feel a smooth rock in her palm. "You need to reflect on the totality of the cards, the meaning as they combine. You need to tap into your personal energy, your positive energy." She flips her palm open, and I see a deep orangey polished rock with hints of brown throughout. "This crystal is Carnelian from Botswana. It helps to amplify courage, confidence, and sexuality. I feel these things need to be amplified so you can trust in the cards the spirit guides have given you."

Butch

I'm at the gym. I've pushed myself hard for a solid hour, lifting more weight than I ever do. It feels good to physically challenge myself. Andy is on the bench beside me, and Logan is alternating, spotting us both. I'm trying to focus and keep Charlotte out of my thoughts. The longer it goes that we do not hear from her, the more I'm convinced I irreparably fucked it up with her. I want to apologize. I want to explain. I want to ask her to give me another chance, but I'm not sure how I will say it if I ever get the opportunity. And I know I have to wait until she decides she wants to talk. Hell, I could easily extract her contact info from the data base and go see her, but that would be a huge breach of trust and I know she'd never ever forgive me if I did that. But damn, would I like to!

"You must have had a hell of a weekend at the firehouse,"

Logan says. "You're pushing yourself hard, almost like a man possessed. You only do that when works been brutal."

"Do I?" I ask.

Andy laughs and brings himself to a sitting position. "You do," he agrees with Logan. "Is that arsonist still around?"

"Yeah," I say. "And yes, it was a busy three-day weekend with the holiday. It always is over the fourth. Dumb people, poor choices, too much alcohol, and fireworks don't mix. But that's the job. I'm not complaining. I'm sorry I missed your party, though."

"It was a good time," Logan chimes in. "And Sheri brought another pan of her lasagna."

"Damn, I'm really sorry I missed that," I say.

Andy stares at me as if he has something to say. I know that look. He knows something is bothering me and he's about to push me on it.

"Anything with Cosimo?" he asks.

I force a laugh. The guys think I am involved in the wine business and that is what Cosimo stays on my back about helping with. I hate lying to my friends, but the club and that aspect of my life are my business. I don't think they'd understand. "Always some shit with him," I say. "I've been on at the firehouse for four days straight, and after I take a nap, I have to go in and help him with a few things." I never give any specifics.

"I know it's the family business, your legacy, but I don't understand how he doesn't realize how much you work at the firehouse," Logan says. "It makes me glad I'm an only child."

That makes me laugh. Logan's parent's sure did a number on him. It's a good thing he had no siblings for them to equally mess up.

My phone chimes a text message. I pull it from my pocket. Cosimo. "Speak of the devil," I say, holding the phone up. But a smile comes to my face when I read the message. Charlotte wants to come talk to me, and Cosimo is asking what my schedule looks like for the next few days. Relief! Maybe I have a chance with her. But then the thought that she just wants to tell me off and slam the door on me or on Sub training in general floods over me, wiping the smile from my face.

"Something wrong?" Andy asks.

"Yeah, Cosimo," I lie. "I guess I'm going to see him before that nap." I pull myself from the bench.

"Hey, you agreed to try my new kickboxing class," Logan says. "One starts in fifteen minutes."

"I need to head out and swing by my place to get a shower before I go see what King Cosimo needs," I joke.

"Soon there will be a full locker room here. Showers, you name it. I've got plans to expand the place," Andy says.

"That'll be great," I say as I grab my bag. "I'll catch you later."

"You can use the shower in the apartment upstairs. Seems a waste of time to go home only to come back here to help your brother."

Andy points across the street to the Cheshire headquarters building. He assumes that's where I'll be going. He is right about one thing; it would be ridiculous to go all the way home only to come back this direction. I can shower in the bathroom in my private room at the club.

"Thanks, but I think I will show up as is," I laugh. "Will remind Cosimo that I have a life he is infringing on."

Both Andy and Logan laugh.

Kenzie is at the counter. I say goodbye to her on my way

out.

Madeline

I take an Uber to the gym, where Kenzie currently is. I'm going back over that way to pick up my car. I did leave it last night and take an Uber home as I was way too drunk to drive. I have to believe that I wasn't the only one. Everyone at their party seemed to be having a great time. I'm dressed in my workout wear as one of Logan's kickboxing classes starts in ten minutes, and I might as well take it while I'm here. I can walk from the gym to my car after and that will give me enough time to get home, shower, and then get my specials at the restaurant prepped before I open.

It really is amazing to me how much I enjoy working out, something I didn't think I'd ever feel. Kenzie was right. A good workout boosts my energy levels. It doesn't wear me out, which I thought would be the case. And I can already see definition in my muscles and a better tone to my body everywhere.

I push through the front door and greet Kenzie, who is at the counter. Andy approaches from the back, from the weight room. We make small talk for a few minutes, and I again thank them for the invite to their party the night before. I tell them I plan to take Logan's class and then go get my car.

They laugh. "A lot of cars were left last night," Kenzie says. "I'm glad everyone had such a good time. It was a great way to celebrate the new house, too."

"Trina looked like she had a great time," I say. "She was so excited to bring people up to the baby's room." I'm honestly so jealous of the energy Kenzie has. They've been in that house for just over a week, and she has everything unpacked and she already painted and set up the nursery. As it turned out, the bedroom they moved Trina into was painted in rainbow colors and Trina loved it just the way it was, so Kenzie didn't have to paint or decorate her room.

Kenzie and Andy both smile fondly. "She is so excited about the new house and the baby. I don't think she understands how long it will be before the baby arrives," Andy says.

"Hey, are you coming to take my class?" Logan emphasizes the word 'coming' with an added twang to his voice and a flirty smile in my direction as he approaches the counter as well.

"Interesting choice of words." I smile as I say it. "Yes, I am." I think about how awkward it would be to see him and talk with him if I had slept with him. It is much better to keep things as they are, flirty with lots of innuendo.

Kenzie and Andy both laugh.

"You know the way to go down," he says, flashing me that grin. Then he steps away from us, heading towards the bathroom.

The class is in the basement. "I do," I agree. "And I really need this today. I'm not sure, but I think I saw Dave down the block from my restaurant earlier. That makes me want to punch and kick something."

Kenzie's face contorts into a grimace. "You need to call Margot."

"I said think. I don't know for sure it was him."

"Doesn't matter," Andy says. "Call Margot."

"I will after class," I agree.

***

As usual, I am dripping wet with sweat when class is over. There were over a dozen people in class, but somehow, Logan always makes me feel like he's working with me alone. I'm sure everyone else feels the same way. The man is good at what he does. I chuckle to myself with the realization that he is probably good at everything physical. If only those Tarot Cards had advised me to go towards him. I didn't get that feeling at all, though.

With a quick goodbye to Kenzie as I fly past her at the counter, I rush out and walk the two blocks to her house so I can retrieve my car.

"Don't forget to call Margot," she yells as I pass.

"I promise!"

After I am seated behind my wheel, I hit dial on my phone and place the call to her, expecting to get her voicemail. I'm surprised when she answers as I shift to drive. After I tell her that I think I saw him earlier today, a feeling of foolishness washes through me. And I don't even tell her that I had a Tarot Card reading while I was there. I know that was crazy and very much out of character for me, but it was nuts how it did help me think more clearly about everything.

"Not that it's illegal for him to be on my street, but really, if he wasn't coming to see me or there to cause some trouble, he has no reason to be there. And he's not into anything New Age, so I can't buy he was there to go into that store."

"Plus, he was gone in the few seconds it took you to cross the street and enter it," Margot says, her voice sounding tight. "But if they don't know him in there, why would the woman behind the counter lie for him?"

I know exactly why any woman would. His panty melting smile. It's too bad he didn't have what it takes to back that smile up. "He's attractive, and he knows how to use that to his advantage."

"Give me a description of the woman you spoke with. I'll pop in and see if she will admit to me he passed through. And I'll try to get a positive ID on him from her too. Text me a picture of him, will you?"

"I will, thanks. Let me know what you find out. And Margot, as a thank you for your help, come in for dinner whenever you can. I'll treat you to dinner on the house. You plus one, of course. It's no fun to eat out alone."

"Thanks, but you don't have to do that. I'll call or text you later." Then she ends the call.

Butch

Being in my private room at the club brings a flood of memories, welcome images of Charlotte, and unwanted recollections of Catrina. Funny, I had not thought of Catrina once when I was in this room with Charlotte. How did running into her and exchanging a few words with her have the power to throw me down such a horrible spiral? I really thought I'd dealt with all those negative thoughts and feelings, more or less. Well, enough to function, I guess. It appears I truly haven't dealt with all those feelings because if I had, I wouldn't have reacted as I did.

I know Cosimo is going to ask me if I've gotten my shit together. He's also probably going to ask me what I plan to say to Charlotte now that she's agreed to come talk to me. I wish I had an answer for him. I don't yet. All I know is that I still feel like a piece of shit because of how I acted and what I did to Charlotte. I'm glad we were so busy at the firehouse all weekend. It kept my mind off her and this situation I caused, for the most part. But now I am off for four days. That's four days too long to have an idle mind.

Part of me wants Cosimo to set the meeting up right away, to get it over with. The other part of me wants it to be scheduled several days out to give me some more time to think about what to say. I'm sorry isn't enough, but I'm not ready to tell her how much of a fucked-up mess I still am because of another woman. That just seems insensitive and weak. Some

Dom, huh?

Cosimo is not in his office when I get there. I text him to discover he is still at the winery. It will be over an hour until he comes into the club. Well, shit. I could have gone home for that nap. I decide to go to the security room and check some video surveillance footage from the past few days. After all, Thursday, Friday and Saturday evenings were all club nights. Had yesterday not been the Fourth of July, it would have been a Dom-Sub night. That's tonight, though. Had I not fucked up with Charlotte, I may be enjoying her this evening. Maybe. She originally had not said she could come tonight. I know the club will be less busy tonight as it is not our normal night, and people have busy lives outside of the club, jobs, children, and children's activities.

I flip through the security reports and club attendance records for the past few days. Catrina and Michael were here on Friday night. Great. Then I notice Catrina was also here Saturday night, for Swinger's night, with a different man. What the fuck? I know I'm an idiot for doing it, but I can't resist. I bring up camera footage to see her with the guy, a body builder-looking type. He doesn't look familiar at all to me, thank God! I scan the footage to see them in the orgy room. Jesus, Catrina has no limits. I'm disgusted watching the number of men and women she engages with. I'm not judging her, but I'm disgusted because I was ready to make a commitment to her and thought that she could make one to me.

I wonder if Michael knows of her other activities. Or is their Dom-Sub relationship a club only thing with each of them free to have other trysts? Of course, he may be like I was, not even thinking to ask or set expectations. When I exit out of the camera feed, the thought that weighs on me is, how did I not see who she really was? Even when I caught them together, she didn't act guilty of anything. She laughed in my face. That had to be what stung the worse.

My phone chiming a text message brings my thoughts out of my head. I'm shocked to see I've been sitting here for over an hour. The text is from Cosimo. He's in his office. My mood goes from bad to worse. Fuck!

His office door is open. I go in and plop down in one of his guest chairs. His eyes wander over my face, or should I say, my scowl. I can tell he's reading my mood, and he knows it's not a good one.

"How were things at the firehouse over the weekend?"

"Busy."

"I thought you'd be relieved, maybe even happy that Charlotte reached out and wants to come talk."

I let out the frustrated sigh that needs to escape. "I don't know how I feel," I admit. "She could be just coming in to tell me to go fuck myself."

Cosimo laughs. "I would be quite surprised if that is the case."

He waits. I say nothing.

"Have you unpacked any of this baggage regarding Catrina that you are obviously still carrying?"

I run my fingers through my hair. "You know, I thought I had before I agreed to take on Charlotte. How I reacted surprised the hell out of me."

"It's been over a week. Have you come to any peace?"

Now the back of my neck gets a rub. "I know. I don't want Charlotte to walk."

"I was referring to you and peace over what happened with Catrina that made you react as you did."

I knew what he meant. I was just avoiding answering.

"Yeah. She's a piece of work that didn't deserve the feelings I had for her. She isn't capable of, and she doesn't have the emotional depth to be in the type of relationship I want. How I reacted last week was because I was still carrying hurt from it. I no longer am carrying that. What happened wasn't on me. It's on her."

"I'm not sure hating her is any healthier for you," Cosimo says.

"I've hated her for over a year. That's nothing new. What is new is I no longer feel hurt. And I know it wasn't my fault. It was all hers."

Cosimo stares at me like he wants to ask me something or argue with me about it. Lucky for him, he remains quiet. I'm sure I would have bitten his head off. Finally, he nods. "When do you want to meet her?"

"See when she can come in on Thursday, the day after tomorrow. I'm free all day and evening. I want a day to catch up on my sleep. I didn't get much over the three-day weekend."

Cosimo's eyebrows lift. "And a day to think?"

"I care about Charlotte. I want to make sure I am rested and yes, that I have thought out what I'm going to say to her."

"You owe her an apology, for starters," Cosimo says.

"You don't think I know that?" Now he's really pissing me off. "I've got this. I fucked it up and I will make it right." My voice is commanding. "And don't think for even a second that you're going to be in the room when she and I talk!"

Cosimo raises his hands in surrender. "I'll contact her and let you know the time."

Madeline

I'm up to my elbows in duck parts, literally, when I realize the fresh ginger that I know was there when I received my order is nowhere to be found. What the hell? "Tammy!"

She pokes her head into the kitchen. "What's up?"

"I received fresh ginger this morning." I hold up my hands. "Can you check the chillers? I don't recall putting it away, but I can't find it." I glance again at the prep counter. I would have left it here, knowing I'd be using it this afternoon.

Tammy laughs. "That was some great party you went to last night, huh?"

"It was but has nothing to do with the missing ginger."

"Okay," she agrees with a patronizing smile.

She checks everywhere but cannot find it. I send her to the store to buy some to replace it, but I know it was there this morning. This isn't the first time something I knew was in my order later went missing. Only Tammy and our bartender are in, have been in today. Neither of them would take it. I know even considering they would, is silly. But where the hell is the ginger?

After I finish getting the special prepped, I pull up the camera of the backdoor area on my phone in the security app. It captures the back of the delivery truck and me viewing and checking off the order. I watch it replay. As I run one of the bins of produce into the kitchen, Ernesto, the delivery driver, dumps a bin of greens atop the bin of herbs and fresh spices and sets the empty bin back into the truck. I then take the overflowing bin inside.

How odd. Why would he mix those items? I go to the chiller I know I sat that bin in and bring it out to the prep counter. Sure enough, the ginger and my other spices are beneath the greens. Odd he'd do that and not mention it, but at least the mystery is solved.

My phone rings, it's Margot. "Hello," I ask, anxious to hear what she found out.

"Madeline, it's Margot," she says sounding all business-like.

Yes, I know it's her. I saw her name come up on the incoming call on my phone. "Hi Margot. Did you find anything out?"

"The woman in the store admitted that a man passed through before you entered. She thinks it was Dave Walsh, but she couldn't be sure."

"Why wouldn't she admit that to me this morning?"

"He told her he was planning a surprise for his girlfriend and he thought you saw him and it would ruin the surprise if you knew he was in the area. He convinced her in two seconds not to confirm he was there. Then he slipped out the back," Margot says.

"Are you shitting me?" I explode. "I am so angry at that woman!"

"Easy Madeline," Margot says. "You cannot blame her for wanting to believe him. You said yourself he can be charming."

I groan out loud. "I know."

"Text me his contact info and address. I'm going to pay him a visit the next chance I get," Margot volunteers.

"I will. And thank you, Margot," I say. I hesitated getting Margot involved sooner, but I now think it's a good idea. She will scare him to leave me alone, I'm sure. I'm immediately distracted by my phone ringing again. The number that comes up is familiar, but it is not programmed into my phone, so I do not get the caller's name. "Hello," I answer.

"This is Cosimo."

My chest tightens. I glance around the kitchen confirming I am still alone in the room. "Hi. Did you get your brother's availability to meet?" I don't say his name out loud.

"Yes, he is available anytime on Thursday," Cosimo replies.

"Okay. I can be there at two that afternoon." I know my voice is matter of fact, no warmth at all.

"I'll let him know," Cosimo says. "Text me when you arrive, and I'll let you in."

After we end the call, the Tarot Card reading invades my thoughts. I reach into my pocket and pull out the crystal, cupping it in my hand. Courage, confidence, and sexuality, yeah, I'm going to need to have this on me when I meet with Master D. I just hope he says something that will make me want to continue with him because right now I'm not sure I'd throw him a life ring if he was drowning. If he doesn't have magic words that wow me, I then have to decide if I'm going to end it altogether or request a new Dom. Though I guess I don't have to decide any of it on the spot. I could tell him I'll think about it and get back to him. Yes, that's a good idea. I should go in there planning to do that.

Chapter 12

Butch

Two o'clock Thursday afternoon comes way too quickly. When I'd left the club on Tuesday, I went for a long ride to clear my thoughts. I opened the bike up out on one of my favorite country roads. I ended up way out in horse country. It was remote. The houses and horse farms were few and far between, with trees, green pastures, and fences stretching as far as the eye could see in all directions. It was quiet and peaceful. I didn't see another soul for over an hour as I sat on my bike in front of a small creek that babbled over some pebbles with the most pleasing, relaxing sound I've heard in some time. I watched the water flow, and I thought.

That at-peace feeling remained with me on Wednesday and this morning. I took care of some personal errands and I worked out at the gym both days as well. But now, as I sit in Cosimo's office at the club waiting for Charlotte, that peaceful feeling has evaporated.

Cosimo's phone, sitting on the desk, chimes and lights up. He lifts it and views the display. "Charlotte is here." His voice is flat. He'd asked me when I entered what I'd planned to say. He was miffed when I told him he wasn't getting a preview, that I had it and it was on me.

"Let her in and make yourself scarce."

"I'll tell her I'll be waiting in the lobby. No matter what happens, see her back to the lobby. I don't want her wandering around alone," he says, eying me cautiously.

"Like I need you telling me about security," I reply.

He gives me a thin smile before he leaves the office, leaving the door open. I rub the back of my neck and take a deep breath. I can't be anything but honest with her and then let the chips land where they may. Funny, going into a burning building doesn't faze me. But the fact that Charlotte could tell me to go fuck myself scares the living shit out of me. I know in my heart that if she walks on me, I'm done here. And my heart will never open to anyone else, no matter how long I live.

Charlotte

As I stand at the entrance to the Velvet Playroom, I grasp the crystal in my palm, my hand deep in my sundress pocket. Courage, confidence, sexuality, I repeat in my head. I'd spent some time each morning the last two days holding the crystal and meditating on the cards and the meaning of each, as well as thinking about why I came to the club in the first place. Do I suddenly believe in all this Tarot Card and crystal stuff? I don't know. But it makes as much sense as anything else.

The thoughts that weighed on me as I considered what I was going to do became straightened out and clear during each meditation session. I came to the club to begin with to get sexual satisfaction, which I had. I had opened myself up and trusted, which was freeing. Not being the aggressor for a change was fulfilling in an odd way. I had never thought what happened, could. The shock stayed with me still. If I was to walk away now, I would be glad I had the experience. I felt no regret towards any of it except how it may end.

The one thing that still nagged at me was what I'd do if I did walk away. I doubt I would ever have another sexual experience or relationship that would be as fulfilling as the first three sessions here had been. And even though this was supposed to be sex with no strings, no expectation of a relationship, my conversation with Logan at the Fourth of July Party proved to me that I probably was not capable of that. Already, I was hoping for a permanent club relationship with Master D. Taking it a step further, I had to think about if that would be enough or if I'd want more, eventually.

I scan my keycard and pull the door open. I enter the club like I had those three times previously, however, this time it is not in operation. It is broad daylight and I find myself face to face with Cosimo. He gives me a warm, welcoming smile. I fight to return it. I feel a little guilty I have been so gruff to him. None of this is his fault, and he has been nothing but kind to me. With that thought, I force the most pleasant expression on my face that I can.

"Thank you for setting this up," I say.

"Of course," he says as he closes the door. He ushers me through the entry and then heads for the hallway I know leads to his office. "My brother is waiting for you in my office. He asked I escort you, but do not come in with you. But of course, what you want is what is most important."

"That's fine," I say as his open office comes into view. I stop and turn to face him. "Thank you for everything you have done. I will get back in touch with you within the next few days and let you know my decision." Damn, there's that unfriendly voice again.

He nods. "I understand." He points to the office. "All I will ask of you is that you listen to my brother with your heart to decide your path. I can tell you that whatever he says will be genuine. He's a good person, and he knows he crossed the line and abused your trust."

I simply nod. It takes me a few seconds to make my

feet move to bring me into the office. When I step inside and see him standing there, my head feels light, and I have to remind myself to breathe. I'm sure I am beaming a look of pure bitchiness at him. I can feel that my chin is jutted out and my nose is raised into the air, accompanying the tight scowl that my lips are set in.

He beams a small grin my way. His eyes are locked on mine. "Hello, Charlotte. Thank you for coming in to talk with me."

"I'm here to listen," I say. Yeah, a bitchy tone in my voice.

He nods. He motions to one of the two guest chairs in front of the desk that are facing each other. He is standing on this side of the desk too. I take a deep breath and I sit down, not surprised when he sits in the other chair, facing me.

Butch

I knew Charlotte wouldn't make this easy on me, and man, was I right. That look on her face is cold. She sits, but she is not relaxed. She is poised on the edge of the seat, at attention, ready to bolt from the room. I can't say I deserve any other response from her at this point. I only hope my words and honesty will smooth things over. If nothing else, I want her to accept my apology and forgive me, even if she never wants to see or talk to me again.

I lean towards her, my elbows on my knees. What I'd really like to do is take her into my arms while I say what I have to say. And I can't help but notice how stunning she looks. Her makeup is applied lightly compared to how it looks when she comes in for a session. Her hair is loose, cascading in soft waves all around her beautiful face.

"I am so sorry for what happened," I begin, my eyes locked on hers. "You didn't deserve that, and I was wrong for how I behaved." I pause, watching her reaction. It seems like my words caught her a bit off guard. Did she not expect for me to immediately offer up an apology? "To make it even worse, you used your safe word, and I didn't stop. That is unforgivable. But I hope you will forgive me, after I have told you all I plan to." I search her eyes. I see no hint of her thoughts. And she doesn't speak. She is waiting for me to continue, so I do. "I have not been active here at the club for the last year. I've handled the security for my brother as I promised I would, so I didn't shirk my responsibilities. But engaging as I did with you hasn't been anything I have wanted to do."

I reach out and cover her hand, which is poised on her knee, with mine. I don't know if telling her about Catrina is smart or not, but it's what I've decided to do. I need to have physical contact with her when I tell her, though, and I'm glad she doesn't pull her hand away.

"There was a woman I was with here, who I loved and wanted a committed relationship with. I was ready to propose marriage to her when I found her cheating on me. I had not seen or talked to her since then, but I ran into her that night, here with that man, right before I met you for our session. I mentally was not right from that encounter with her. I'm not offering this as an excuse for my behavior with you, as there is no excuse. But I'm telling you to explain why I was not myself. I thought I'd dealt with all my anger over her betrayal, but I obviously had not. I'm dealing with it now and trying to move past it. I didn't realize I was still carrying the hurt from it, but I was."

Charlotte just stares at me. I wish I could read the thoughts in those beautiful brown eyes. Her gaze has softened, and she hasn't thrown my hand off hers. I take that as hopeful. I wish she would say something, though. I keep my eyes on hers and give her a few more seconds to process what I told her.

"Again, I am very sorry for what I did to you. What we've had is very special to me and I am angry with myself for fucking it up because of how I reacted to seeing and speaking with her." I do not vocalize it, but I know that if I was ever going to trust my heart to another woman, it would be Charlotte.

I wait because what she has to say to me now will impact the rest of my life.

Madeline

I'm numb, completely shocked by what Master D has just told me. I'm even more shocked than I was after what he did. I look down and see that he still holds my hand, but now he's gripping it in both of his. My right hand is still in my pocket, holding onto the Carnelian crystal. His eyes are boring through mine. I see honesty in them. And a pleading urgency. He needs me to respond to what he's just said. I have no words, though. I just have my thoughts, which are slowly coming to me now that the shock is wearing off.

I didn't expect such honesty from him. And I certainly didn't expect this to be about another woman. I'm also confused by his statement that she cheated on him. First, I can't imagine what any woman would want, that he couldn't give them. And secondly, I'm confused that in a club full of sex in front of others and with multiple partners, there is something called cheating. I want to ask about that, but not yet.

What I can see clearly is his remorse. He is truly sorry for his actions. I also see vulnerability in him. It's not easy for anyone to open their heart and apologize as he is. I know for a man to confess to being hurt by a woman's betrayal is rare. Most men do not lay their emotional scars out in the open for anyone to see. Women cry and eat tons of ice cream when they have been hurt romantically. They confide in their girlfriends. Men do not. Most men do not even tell the next woman in his life how badly the last one hurt him. That is taboo and considered weak.

He's still staring expectantly at me. I gaze at our joined hands to break eye contact. His touch had always felt so good, comforting, exciting, stoking something primal in me. Today, I feel his desperation in his touch, and I feel a connection to him, an emotional one. Today it is all about emotions and feelings, which puts our relationship on a different plane. Would it go back to purely physical after this point? Was it really ever purely physical? For either of us? He's just admitted to falling in love with his last partner, who I assume was his Sub. Maybe he can't keep it separate, either.

"I need some time to think about what you've said," I finally say. "I appreciate your honesty and I appreciate you admitting you were wrong. Thank you for that and for the apology. I hope you can put that relationship in your past, where it belongs. You were hurt, and that sucks. Shame on her for doing that to you."

"And shame on me for allowing it to hurt you," he adds.

I slowly nod. "I should go."

His expression is unreadable.

"I need some time to think and process your apology," I say.

He looks disappointed. "Of course," he says, coming to his feet.

His hand still holds mine, and he helps me stand. We stand very close together. He reaches out and lightly strokes one hand over my face. His eyes hold mine. And I'm sure he is thinking the same thing I am. This could be the last time we see each other or talk to each other. This could be the last touch, the last caress. That thought makes me sad.

"Thank you for coming in to talk, Charlotte," he repeats.

"Thank you for the apology and the explanation," I

repeat.

He leans in and presses a soft kiss to my forehead. His lips linger and he pulls me slightly into him. I take comfort in the physical proximity, wanting to lean all the way into him, wanting him to wrap his arms around me.

But he doesn't and neither do I.

After a few more moments, he pulls away and steps towards the door, breaking all physical contact with me.

"If you have no questions for me, I'll show you back to the lobby where Cosimo is waiting for you."

"I have one," I say. "Why did you agree to be or volunteer to be my Dom?"

Butch

Wow, that question is not one I expected. I envisioned a hundred other questions. I had thought out all possible questions and was ready with considered replies for each. Not this one, though. "My brother is the one who reads all applications. He and he alone, to maintain anonymity for our members who want it. We take that seriously. He approached me after reading yours, thought we would be a good match."

"Has he approached you with any others over the last year?" she asks.

"No," I reply. "Just you. And he was right. It was a good match. Just don't tell him as much."

This gets her to give me a small, natural smile. "I won't."

I'm disappointed when she passes me and exits the room. I would have preferred she had a barrage of questions. I follow her down the hall as she makes her way back to the lobby. As promised, Cosimo waits there. He rises from his seat as she approaches. Then his eyes flicker to me. I know he's trying to gage my mood to know how it went. My face is purposefully blank.

"Are you ready to be let out?" he asks Charlotte.

"Yes, thank you," she says. Then she turns back to me, and I feel like I've won the lottery when her gaze settles on me and it's not full of anger or loathing. "Master D, can you give me and your brother a moment, please?"

"Certainly," I answer, a bit surprised.

I turn and walk back down the hall. I'll wait in Cosimo's office. Once there, I help myself to a glass of his bourbon. I retake my seat and my eyes fix on the one she sat in. I replay the whole damn meeting in my head looking for a clue to what she may decide. I'll admit, her request to talk to Cosimo threw me. Did it mean she has decided? And if so, what does that mean?

I check my watch when Cosimo enters. This can't be good. It has been exactly four minutes since I poured my glass, three fingers, neat. I watch Cosimo pour himself a glass and take his seat behind his desk. Just once, I'd love for him to sit on this side with me.

"Well?" I ask.

"She's not angry any longer." He takes a drink. "She asked me one question. What is considered cheating in this lifestyle? So, I assume you told her about Catrina."

"Not her by name. Just the act that broke us up, that I had not resolved yet when I ran into the bitch last week."

Cosimo looks worried. "I surely hope you didn't phrase it that way?"

"Of course, I didn't." I gulp down a drink. It wonderfully burns all the way down.

"I explained the different levels of intimacy, commitment, and expectations that couples here at the club adhere to. I think she understood."

"Must have been a quick explanation," I say. I have to wonder how thorough it was. I hope it didn't leave her with more confusion.

"It's pretty simple. Going behind someone's back and not being up front about having sex with someone else is cheating. I don't care what lifestyle you practice."

"And she didn't give you her decision?"

"No," Cosimo replies.

"I honestly don't know what her decision will be. It occurred to me when we finished talking that today very well could be the last time I see her or talk to her," I admit.

"And how does that make you feel?" Cosimo asks.

"Have you been watching Doctor Phil or some shit like that?" I ask. Cosimo asking me about my feelings. What the fuck?

He chuckles. "No, but I do care about you, brother. And I feel I pushed you when you were not ready, so I am partially to blame. It was good to see you back in the game, though. I will admit that."

"Charlotte is special," I say after finishing my drink. "If she comes back, so will I. If not, I'm done."

I'm emotionally drained. I set the glass down on the desk and without another word, I leave his office. I exit the building and I get on my bike.

Madeline

As I drive back to the restaurant, the overwhelming feeling that invades me is sadness. Master D's ex-girlfriend had to be out to hurt him. In no other relationship could a woman tell her man she wanted to have sex with another man and have him line it up for her, which is what she could have done.

If she'd wanted to, she could have been fucked by multiple other men and Master D would have organized it for her and stood and watched. The only reason to do it as she did was for the thrill of getting away with it or to hurt him. What a bitch!

I park my car and cross the parking lot, heading for the stairs to my apartment. I see two other employees' cars are parked with Tammy's. I know she'll take care of everything to open the restaurant on time today. I already prepped the specials and left instructions for the staff anticipating that I may need some time to think about my meeting with Master D before I am ready to be 'on' with smiles and energy at the restaurant.

I enter my apartment and pour myself a glass of wine, a full-bodied cabernet. I remove the Carnelian crystal from my dress pocket and set it on the table beside my wine glass. I can see Master D's eyes locked onto mine. I can still feel his desperate grasp on my hands. And I can feel his tender kiss on my forehead. You'd think I'd be getting off on the power I hold, but I'm not. I know it is up to me if I see him again. I have the distinct feeling, though, that if I say I am done, it will crush him far worse than his cheating girlfriend did.

But the logical side of me says let's be very clear. I had three wonderful evenings with him and one horrible breach of trust. If he was any other guy and if this was any other situation, would I even consider seeing him again? No, no way in hell. So, I consider why this is different.

I take a sip of wine and can almost hear Cosimo's request to listen with my heart to his brother. Cosimo, the matchmaker. He has a vested interest in me returning, doesn't he? He won't want to admit he was wrong. And it is a business to him. He makes a profit off of membership fees. Come to think of it, I have never seen him in Dom's clothes on the floor during any of my visits. When he rescued me from the unwarranted punishment that Master D was giving me, he wore his suit and tie, like always, like today. So, does he own the club but not partake of the lifestyle? Then I remember the questions on the application. The club does cater to other sexual proclivities. Maybe the Dom-Sub thing isn't his game.

I force my thoughts away from Cosimo. He's not even part of this, doesn't factor into the decision I need to make at all. What I do think about is that I wanted Master D to hold me today. The almost chaste kiss he pressed to my forehead left me wanting more. Even with what he did to me, I wanted a physical connection to him. His hands holding mine did not repulse me. I wanted to feel his hands glide over my body. I'm actually getting worked up thinking about sex with him.

I guess I've made my decision. And strangely, I accept his apology and I do forgive him. I can understand why he snapped, why he was so angry. He wasn't angry with me. I was just there. I do need to have some rules in place though in going back, my rules that are not negotiable. I will have to talk with Cosimo about that. And then I'll have to talk to Master D.

My eyes go again to the Carnelian crystal. Courage, confidence, and sexuality. Wow, those all do apply to how I have approached this. Maybe there is something to this Tarot and crystal stuff.

Chapter 13

Butch

I t's Friday morning. I wake to a text from Cosimo asking when I can come into the club. Fuck. Does he never let up? I message back that I was not planning to come in at all and I sure as hell am not coming in during operational hours. I know that Catrina and Michael will be there tonight, and I will now do all I can to keep distance. I haven't talked with Cosimo since I left his office yesterday afternoon after talking with Charlotte. I thought he'd stay off my back for a few days at least.

I'm surprised by the return text message. He heard from Charlotte with her decision, and he wants to see me to deliver it. I pick up my phone and hit dial. Fuck no, not on his terms!

"I'm at the club, working from here this morning. When can you come in?" Cosimo asks.

"I'm not coming in. Tell me over the phone. What is Charlotte's decision?"

"Charlotte has decided to return to the club on Monday for her next session and hasn't requested a new Dom. So, I suggest that you keep your head together, brother, and don't fuck this up."

This is the best news! "I need you to set some rules with Catrina."

"I just got off the phone with Michael and he agrees that they will not be visiting the club on Mondays until your training with Charlotte is done. Apparently, Catrina was a total bitch during their session after you ran into each other, and we both agreed you two will avoid each other," Cosimo says.

Thank God! "Make Friday their permanent night. And you may want to feel Michael out to see if he is aware that Catrina is visiting the club on Saturday nights for Swingers Night as well, without him. I saw her name when I was reviewing the security logs."

Cosimo moans.

"Or don't. I don't care. I just don't want a security incident at the club if he finds out while there and it comes as a surprise to him," I say.

"Are you sure that is the only reason? Don't you secretly want Catrina to get rejected by him?"

I bark out a laugh. "As they say, Karma is only a bitch if you are. Catrina will get hers at some point, without my help. And I know I should be pissed at Michael for his part in her betrayal, but I always thought he was a decent guy before, so I'd like to think he was as duped as I was by her."

Cosimo laughs as well. "That's quite forgiving of you towards Michael."

"Well, it helps to know that Catrina is still up to her same games behind his back. I really wish her father wasn't who he is, and we could kick her ass out of the club. But I get it. We operate with his approval. If he wanted to shut us down, he could."

"It's tricky," Cosimo agrees.

I'm glad he's the one that gets to navigate the political shit related to the club. He's good at it. I'm not.

Madeline

I feel a sense of relief, knowing I made the decision about Master D. I had a good conversation with Cosimo about returning to the club. One, I have removed my permission for restraints. I will not be tied to anything in case Master D loses his shit again. I want to be able to walk away on my own if I need to. Two, I have also removed my consent for physical punishment, floggers, whips, and the like. I am proud of myself. I stated it calmly to him without embarrassment or fear. I was confident and courageous! Yes, I gripped the Carnelian crystal in my palm as I spoke with him.

I was thrown for a loop when Cosimo asked what I wanted Monday's session to be like, given the situation that occurred. He said I could dictate this one, to ease back in. I told him no. I wanted Master D to plan it as he has been, taking into consideration the two new limits I have dictated. I think that's fair. I would hope that whatever he plans is spectacular, given that I am trusting him again. But that trust is tenuous. If he abuses it again, I am done. I told Cosimo that.

"I'll pass everything we've talked about onto my brother," Cosimo promised.

Now that I'm thinking about it, how crazy is this? I talked with Cosimo about sex with his brother. Isn't that just insane? And I was okay with it, confident even. I'm not sure I even recognize myself any longer, but not in a bad way. I am a different person now than when I walked into that club the first time.

I have let go of a lot of the sexual taboos that I and many people have accepted. If it feels good and everyone is consenting, there is nothing wrong or immoral about any sexual behavior. I am even more sure now that I can never go back to regular sex again. I just need to get a handle on if I can really be involved in this relationship without wanting more.

And I know I need to talk to Master D about expectations and if this is an open or an exclusive sexual relationship. I think just for preventing STDs, I need to know.

***

It's Friday afternoon and I sit at my desk in my office of the restaurant, replaying that conversation I had with Cosimo this morning in my mind. My specials are prepped. I have an hour before the restaurant opens. My staff is getting the restaurant set up and ready for what looks like it will be another busy Friday night.

My cell phone ringing brings my thoughts out of that call from this morning. It's Margot. "Hi Margot," I answer.

"Hi Madeline. I wanted to let you know I finally caught up with Dave Walsh. I don't want to worry you, but I got some bad vibes off that guy."

"What kind of bad vibes?"

"Let me just tell you I've been a cop long enough to know that when something isn't quite right that you become very careful. Dave Walsh is as hinky as they come. He, of course, denies being anywhere near your restaurant on Tuesday, denies he harbors any anger towards you. But I know he damned well does. Be careful, Madeline. I don't have anything on him to arrest him for, just this gut feeling that he's up to no good."

"What can I do?" I ask.

"Make sure everyone in your life knows that he shouldn't be around, especially your staff there at the restaurant. I'm not convinced he didn't have something to do with your electric and gas problem. He won't account for his movements, so I can't even try to corroborate an alibi for when the damage was done to the gas and electric or even the other night when you felt someone was watching you as you went up your stairs to your apartment after you closed the restaurant."

"What do you mean, he won't account for his movements? Doesn't he have to?"

"It doesn't work that way. I don't have a warrant. I don't even have probable cause. He doesn't have to talk to me at all. And even if I did have enough to bring him in for questioning, he could lawyer up and refuse to tell me where he was during those times."

"That just isn't right! Don't victims have any rights? I know he can be on my street, but he has no reason to be except to cause me trouble. Why do I have to just take this and worry?"

"I'm sorry, Madeline. Yes, that's the way it works. Until he tries something or is overtly threatening, he can stand on the sidewalk watching your business all day and there is nothing I can do about it. I talked to him though, and he knows he's on my radar. That's usually enough to dissuade most scumbags."

"And the others?" I ask.

"It fuels some, pisses them off to act. That's why I said be careful. You have your new security system with the cameras. Keep the system armed and check your camera feeds. If he pokes around or breaks and enters, that will give me what I need to officially pick him up. And you may want to try to not be alone too often, just for a week or so."

"Margot," I complain. "I can't expect anyone to babysit me. And to have restaurant staff come in early to be with me when I receive my orders or while I prep food is going to cost me money."

"If you're alone, he will be more brazen. I don't think he will approach you if you're not alone. Just consider it."

"I will, thanks," I say.

"And call me if anything isn't right or if you get hard proof on him," Margot says.

I promise I will, and then take a second to get my thoughts straight.

Butch

I pop into the club late Saturday morning to check on things from Thursday and Friday evenings. I picked up a twenty-four-hour shift at the firehouse that starts this afternoon at two p.m. I'm barely through reviewing the security logs when my phone chimes an alert from the firehouse. They are calling me in early. This can't be good.

I swing by Cosimo's office to let him know that my first job is calling me in early and that I will be back on Sunday evening to review the logs and footage from Saturday evening's Swinger's Playfest. My bike is waiting for me in the parking lot. I hop on and speed to the firehouse. Nothing feels better between my legs to clear my thoughts than a motorcycle humming, other than a very petite curvy brunette Sub. I'm still soaring with excitement and relief that she will return to the club on Monday.

As I pull in, all the men are standing in full uniform in front of the firehouse. My first thought is, who the fuck died, and why wasn't I told? As I get off my bike, I see the Chief standing with my men. This cannot be good, but I keep a cool head and head over to the Chief, wishing like hell I was in my uniform.

"Sir, I received a text to report to the firehouse. Have I missed something, or has something happened that I should be aware of?" I ask.

The Chief chuckles and extends his hand out to me. We shake and then he begins. "Congratulations Butch, or should I say District Commander Dominante?" He smiles wide.

"Attention!" Lieutenant Cotter barks, and I only now see he's there.

The assembled men come to attention.

"Promotions have gone through. You scored high on the written exam and received extra points for your bravery during the warehouse fire last month, plus points for your years of service," the Chief says.

I am stunned. I forgot I'd taken the test several months ago. "Thank you, Chief. Do you know yet which district I'll be assigned to?" I am thrilled but a bit sad though, as I know it will not be district one. They never assign a newly promoted officer to his home district. I know the men at this house and in this district well. It's a good team and we do great work together.

"District Three," the Chief says. "The District Commander's office is at Station Thirteen."

I nod. Districts Two and Three are the two districts newly promoted officers are always assigned to. They are the smallest of the districts in the city. District Three consists of four firehouses that house four engine companies, one ladder truck, one ambulance, and one tanker truck. From what I know of the staff assigned to District Three, they are a good, competent team. Station Thirteen is a small house, built in the nineteen-fifties, but it's well maintained. It's in a good location, with lots of strip malls and businesses around it. It'll be a lot quieter than what I'm used to at Station One, as all the command staff and dispatch are quartered at this campus.

"Thank you, sir," I say.

"You have earned this Drago."

The team claps and hoots and hollers their congratulations. I am still in shock. I never expected to be promoted after only taking the test one time. The Chief and I walk into the firehouse, the rest of the team following, where there is a small reception set up with appetizers.

Bud Kleckner wanders in, as does other command staff to congratulate me and grab an appetizer or two. Everyone shows up whenever there is free food. "When you get a chance, I want to touch bases with you about the nuisance fires in the dumpsters," he says.

"Sure, after this."

"So, you won't officially take over District Three until August first," the Chief says, "but I'm going to start including you in meetings. Marty Sanderson from Station Six is being transferred and will replace you here. He'll report to you next week for you to begin turnover to him. That'll free you up for some of the meetings I'll schedule you for and for you to start to make appearances over in District Three."

"Yes, sir," I say. "Marty's a good guy, a competent fireman, and will make a good Lieutenant for the team. He'll fit in well with the team here."

"I thought so," the Chief says. "I'm on my way over there now, to have a similar announcement with his team and to personally deliver the news to him as well."

"I almost forgot to ask, what is up with Commander Brown, who I'm replacing? He's not retiring early, is he?" I had heard he was having some health issues.

"Yes, it's not public knowledge, but he has been diagnosed with lung cancer. He'll go out on a permanent medical disability."

"Damn, I'm sorry to hear that," I say. "And I'm sorry, that's the reason I'm being promoted."

The Chief clasps my shoulder. "You deserve the promotion, Butch. Take the job and do the city proud."

I strange bittersweet appreciation settles over me. I'm

not as elated as I should be. Between the fact that I am being promoted as Brown is ill and I will transfer to a different team, this promotion doesn't feel as good as I thought it would.

I return to my office to meet with Bud. "Mahoney, over at Thirteen is pretty self-sufficient. That team runs well. Twenty-four is going to be more of a challenge to you," he says. "You're going to want to spend some time over there to see for yourself how it runs."

"I know Twenty-four is a bigger house with a lot of new fireman assigned there," I say. I'll take his word for it. Bud should know the dynamics of each house. He interfaces with all of them.

"A third of their staff are recently out of training," Bud says. "Fritz is next in line for Shift Commander. I expect that promotion to go through in the next few months for him, so you're going to have a leadership hole over there."

John Fritz, the Senior Commander over at Twenty-four, is a good man. If he does get the Shift Commander position, it will be well deserved. I'm sure there will be a lot of shifting of officers throughout the districts in the next month or so. "I thought you wanted to talk about the arsonist," I say.

Bud chuckles. "He hasn't hit anything in District Three yet. He is widening his circle, though. He hit a dumpster over in District One last night. I've put out a communication to all districts to warn business owners to move their dumpsters away from their buildings. So far, no structures have caught on fire from the dumpster fires, but you know as well as I do, it's only a matter of time."

"Yeah, I'm surprised it hasn't happened yet, either."

The Velvet Playroom is in District One. I make a mental note to tell Cosimo about the fires and to have someone be sure the dumpster is far enough away from the building. I'd already made sure the dumpsters are away from the Cheshire Winery headquarters and administrative offices, here in District Five as well as over at Stevens Street Gym. I'd also alerted the Downtown Merchants Association to advise their other members.

After most of the command staff have gone home for the evening, and those on the overnight shift are all who are left, I call Cosimo. First, I warn him about moving the dumpsters. Then I tell him the news of my promotion. He is very supportive and congratulates me, telling me that I deserved the promotion. He wants to celebrate and is going to make reservations for dinner some place to celebrate on Wednesday night when there is nothing going on at the club and both he and I are available. He'll text me the plans on when and where, after he gets the reservations made.

Later that night, as I settle into my rack at the firehouse, and I close my eyes, Charlotte's face and her incredible curvy body are the only thing I see. If things were different, I would be sharing this wonderful news with her. I can see her in my bed every night making love to her all night long. I drift off to sleep with that thought in my mind. I have lost my heart and soul to a petite little brunette, whose real name I don't even know. The scene on Monday will be the most important scene we have shared, and it must be perfect. I have a plan.

***

"Are you sure this is how you want to play this session, brother?" Cosimo asks in that snide way he has.

"I gave it a lot of thought all weekend," I say. My gaze flickers to the clock on his desk. Charlotte will arrive within the next half hour. There is no time to come up with another scenario for this evening, even if I wanted to. "I thought of nothing else, actually. I fucked up, and this is how I can right it."

"You don't think giving her the exciting club experience

she came here looking for would be more appropriate?"

"I think after what I did, I need to pull out all the stops to show her it will never happen again and that I treasure her. I need to regain her trust before I can make her fantasies come true."

"I suppose so," Cosimo concedes. "I have reserved the patio room for you, per your request. Good luck."

I can tell from the way he says it that he still questions if this is the best way to handle tonight. But I am confident it is. I have an agenda. And I do believe this will solidify Charlotte in my life. She questioned what cheating was in this lifestyle and I'm not sure if Cosimo's answer confused her. I need to talk about this with her. I think she needs a session that has less of a club feel to it and more of a seduction when she least expects it. When we talked, there were a lot of emotions that were underlying. Those emotions can never be discounted or forgotten. They will be a part of our relationship from now on. The Genie is out of the bottle. This will not be just a sexual relationship any longer. It can't be.

So, I walk back through the entry and confer with the receptionist to be sure she will give Charlotte the instructions I need her to when Charlotte checks in. Then I go to the elevator and go up to the Patio Room. I hadn't used this room in a very long time. I had actually considered using this room to propose to Catrina in. I'm so glad I didn't.

I flip on the overhead lights, setting the lighting to starlight. The fountain in the corner cascades the water over the rocks into a splash pool with a soothing sound. The many trees and other foliage look so real in this lighting. Under my feet, the soft grass-like carpet finishes the illusion that we are outside. To my right, the bistro table has the fake flickering candle and the open bottle of wine with the two glasses I placed there before I went to meet with Cosimo. And two chairs pulled up to the table sets the mood that we are going to have a glass of wine and talk like two civilized adults. Little does she know I plan to seduce her until she drops to her knees in front of me, begging me to be the best Dom I can be.

My lips curl into a smile at the thought of it.

To my left is the couch-like sectional set where I will make love to her. Yes, I will make love to her. I have fucked her. I have eaten her pussy. But I have not shown her I treasure her by making love to her like no other man ever has or ever will.

Tonight, I will, and she will understand that there is a place for that within this lifestyle, too. The Dom-Sub relationship can have many facets to it. On her questionnaire, she had expressed interest in having sex with two men at the same time. That is a fantasy I will gladly arrange for her next session. I want her to know that any sexual fantasies she has I will arrange and fulfill. But I want an otherwise exclusive relationship with her, inside and outside of the club.

Master Kurt has expressed interest in being her permanent Dom. Hell no! But I am not opposed to allowing him to service her to help realize her fantasies with me. I will have to have a discussion with him at some point. But not tonight. Tonight, is for Charlotte.

Madeline

I pull myself from the Uber and approach the door into the reception area of the Velvet Playroom. I have so many emotions rippling through me. Even more so than the first evening I came here. Depending on how this evening goes, this could be my last visit here. I'm giving Master D another chance. His apology was sincere, but I am a firm believer in the old adage, hurt me once, shame on you, hurt me twice, shame on me.

When I reach the reception desk, I'm surprised when the woman there tells me that tonight, instead of reporting to the locker room, I'm to use the elevator and go upstairs to the second floor, room P-one. She points to the elevator across the lobby, which I never really noticed before. "You are expected, so just enter when you arrive."

I thank her and cross the lobby. As the elevator rises, my nervousness does as well. I look down at what I'm wearing, a simple black sundress with sunflowers on it, and flat sandals. Nothing fancy, nothing nice. I don't even have on great underclothing as my outfit has always been provided.

Room P-one is directly across from the elevator. I pause outside of the door for a few minutes, wondering if Master D has changed his mind about continuing and he plans to talk with me here to end it. Maybe this is his office, knowing that he is part owner of the club. After struggling to make the decision to return, that would be just my luck.

Finally, I suck in a deep breath and open the door. Stepping inside, I am shocked to see the amazing room. There are trees and flowering bushes. My gaze is immediately drawn to the corner where there is a waterfall flowing over rocks, a real waterfall! The water is actually running. And overhead, the dark night sky is lit with stars, lighting the entire space into this magical, starlit effect that is mesmerizing.

"Good evening, Charlotte," I hear Master D's voice from my left.

My gaze shifts, landing on him as he approaches from a sectional sofa-looking patio furniture set. His hair hangs loose, hanging over the collar of his black dress shirt, that is tucked into black jeans at his waist. The sleeves are rolled up to his elbows, creating a casual look that accents his nice body well. He holds a single red rose in his hand.

"Good evening, Sir," I reply.

He takes my hand in his when he reaches my side, and he presses a warm kiss to my palm. Then his stare locks with mine. The corners of his eyes crinkle with his smile. "You look lovely this evening." He hands me the rose.

I glance down again at myself. "I'm confused, Sir."

He chuckles. "Would you like a glass of wine?" He motions to the little bistro table and the bottle that is open sitting with two wine glasses and a flickering candle.

We've never shared an alcoholic beverage before a session. I'm still very confused. "Yes, thank you, Sir."

He pours us each a glass and takes my hand again once he has handed my glass to me. He leads me to the sectional. "Please, sit," he motions to it.

I take a seat in the middle of the cushion behind the small table. He sits beside me. He raises his glass. "Will you join me in a toast?"

I nod I will, still very confused.

"To second chances and a deeper relationship than we've enjoyed before this point."

Deeper? What does he mean? He's watching me expectantly. I tap my glass to his and bring it to my lips. Mm, a rich red blend with amazing undertones of dark fruit and chocolate. The color is brick red with hints of garnet. The nose is a luscious mix of blackberries and cherries with the sweet chocolate holding its own. I didn't get a look at the bottle, but I plan to before the evening is over. I don't know what to say, so I remain silent and return the look of expectancy to Master D.

"Thank you for coming in this evening," he says with a smile. "I am humbled and honored that you have returned to me."

"Sir, did Cosimo convey to you my new terms?"

He bows his head. "He did. They will be honored. I understand. I need to earn your trust back. I wanted us to talk this evening. That is why we are here and not down in the Playroom. I need to be sure you are okay with everything, and I wanted the opportunity to explain a few things to you in a leisurely, quiet setting with no pressure."

He sits his glass onto the table in front of us, and then takes mine from me and sits it beside his. He shifts in his seat, so he is facing me. I do the same, curling a leg beneath me, so we sit facing each other. I set the rose beside my wine glass. He takes my hands in his. Excitement skitters through me when he raises my hands to his mouth and presses hot, wet kisses to each set of my knuckles. His eyes remain locked on mine as he does.

"Cosimo told me you asked him what is considered cheating in this lifestyle," he says.

I nod again. "His reply was a bit confusing," I admit.

Master D smiles and nods. "Charlotte, as your Dom, I will make all your sexual fantasies come true, even if that involves others in our play. I will push you from your comfort zone to bring you erotic sensations you want and maybe ones you never dreamed possible. We have not talked about expectations, exclusivity, or a relationship outside of the club before, but I think it's time we do, given the emotions that passed between us when you and I spoke in Cosimo's office. Trust isn't just necessary for the physical and sexual, it's vital for exhibiting emotions as well. Don't you think?"

"Yes, Sir," I say. "I think it's even more important when discussing emotions."

He nods. He is still holding both my hands in his. "As I'm sure Cosimo told you, there are many different relationships possible. Some in this lifestyle simply have encounters at the club to satisfy their sexual needs. They may have full lives outside of the club that include a significant other that they have a sexual relationship with. The two worlds never intersect. Others have their sexual needs fulfilled here, but no sexual life outside of the club and the two parties promise to be exclusive sexually in all aspects of their lives, but they never interact outside of the club. A third option would be a relationship of exclusivity inside and outside of the club, a relationship spanning both worlds. Cheating would be when either party, in any of those scenarios, step outside what is agreed upon by the two people. Does that make sense?"

I think about it for a second. It sounds so simple, except I'm unsure if I can accept that having sex with several people is not considered cheating.

"So, let's say a Dom-Sub pair agree to be exclusive and have an at the club relationship only. If either have sex with anyone else, inside or outside of the club without the other knowing and approving, that is cheating, but if the Dom wants to introduce multiple partners at the same time he is there and the Sub is willing, inviting another person at the club to join their play is not considered cheating. It is done within the confines of their club relationship, with both parties approving of it."

I nod. That makes sense. "It has to do with communication and approval by both people."

"Correct," Master D says. "Before now, we haven't spoken about exclusivity as an expectation, but I would like to."

I watch his eyes come to an intensity I've never seen in them. He brings one of my hands to his lips and presses a long kiss to my palm. Then his lips reach to mine. The kiss he gifts me with is incredible. It is soft, slow, and passionate. His tongue explores my mouth leisurely as he pulls me onto his lap and cradles me with his strong arms. I can feel his hard member press up against my pussy, which sits atop his arousal. The kiss lasts a long time. One of his hands holds me behind my neck, keeping my face where it is for his mouth to make love to mine. His other hand holds my back, so my body is held in place.

When our lips separate, I am breathless. I'm dripping wet and my pussy is aching with need. I want him inside me. I want him to do what he wants with me. I'm tempted to slide from his lap and assume the Sub position at his feet.

"I would like us to be exclusive inside and outside of the club," he says. "And with this discussion, I need to declare to you my intention of remaining as your permanent Dom, if that is what you would like."

Wow! I am shocked. My thoughts are reeling. I'm not even through the training yet to decide if this lifestyle is for me. I've committed to nothing but the six sessions, of which this is technically number five.

Before I can say anything, he continues. "But I do not want an answer to the permanence of this relationship today. I want you to think about it and consider it over the next two sessions. I would like an answer on the exclusivity question, though."

I don't even have to think about it. "I can agree to the exclusivity."

A smile spreads over his face, reaching his eyes. "Very good. And I can agree to exclusivity as well. I want to be completely honest with you, Charlotte. I am also wanting a relationship with you outside of the club, to be defined at a later date, when you are comfortable with the two worlds intersecting."

I suck in a breath. "You do?" I have not even considered this possibility.

He smiles again and his face draws close. He drops his forehead against mine.

Butch

"Charlotte, sexually, you fulfill me completely. I can keep sex and emotions separate, but I don't want to with you. Over this last year, I have come to know exactly what I want and what I don't want. I think I've come to a greater understanding of myself than I've ever had. I know I won't be fulfilled in all aspects of my being if we keep our relationship limited to the club." She remains silent. I know that I want to share my life with someone who wants to be there, who is all in, but I won't tell her that now. I think it would overwhelm her and push her away. "But as I said, I don't want you to answer any of that right now. I want you to enjoy your next two sessions and think about it. And nothing in this relationship will progress faster than you want it to."

She stares at me with a gaze I cannot decipher. Finally, she nods. "Thank you, Sir, I will think about it."

"And now, Charlotte, to prove to you that I do have feelings for you, and that I do treasure you, I'm going to make love to you. I'm not going to fuck you. I'm not going to play out some scene that I think will check off a fantasy you have. I, as a man, am going to make love to you, as a woman, from my heart. Do not mistake a single kiss or caress as anything but intended for you and you alone on an emotional and physical level."

I angle my head to kiss her, half expecting her to pull away. I'm thrilled that she does not. She returns my kisses. We kiss and our hands explore for a leisurely length of time. It's not that I dislike normal sex, it's just that it normally doesn't do it for me like my preferred Dom-Sub play does, but tonight I find the kisses and caresses fulfilling. I'm intoxicated by Charlotte's touch, by the taste of her mouth, which fuels me to want to place intimate kisses to her other lips until she explodes in orgasmic bliss, which will make her beg me to repeat the attention with my eager cock.

I truly would love to tie her to the couch as I pleasure her and push her past her normal boundaries. But I know I must wait until I regain her trust. Another time, I promise myself. So, I pull up the skirt of her dress and pull away the black panties she has on. I press her legs apart as I drop to my knees in front of her. I kiss a trail up her inner thigh. She lies back on the couch, where I pressed her while still kissing her face and neck. Now it's time for me to savor her incredible pussy.

Her body rocks at the first lap of my tongue. Her scent and taste are heaven. I spread her legs wider and plunge fingers into her. A moan escapes her gaped open lips. I increase the intensity of my attention and am surprised when rather quickly her pussy clenches around my fingers, nearly crushing them, and I am rewarded with a deluge of her amazing juices while she gasps out a perfect sound of pure erotic ecstasy.

I tongue little circles around her hard nub, knowing I am hitting the ultra-sensitive spot in just the right way by her trembling and the gasps of pleasure that fill the room. I continue until I know she is on the cusp of a second release. I quickly free myself of my confining jeans and way too hot shirt. I then remove the dress and her black bra so I can gaze at her. We are now both completely naked. I give her breasts attention as I slide her off the sectional and onto my awaiting, stiff cock, nearly coming as her steamy, drenched core surrounds me.

"Ride me," I murmur against her breast where my mouth is nipping and sucking.

Her hands go to my shoulders, and she complies, riding my cock, which bounces her gorgeous breasts in front of my face. I aid her with one hand under and cupping her perfect ass. The other hand cannot help but tangle in her hair, holding her in place. Her mouth gapes open and all I can think about is that mouth around my cock. Using the hand in her hair, I guide her mouth back to mine and I kiss her, plundering the inside of her mouth with my tongue, imagining every sensation to be on my cock instead of my tongue.

She sucks my tongue, her fingernails digging into my shoulders, her pussy clenching my cock as she rides faster. Her body shudders, moans escape her, but she doesn't stop until I feel a shattering release roll through her accompanying a guttural scream and gasp, her entire body going rigid.

I re-arrange our position so that her ass is on the edge of the couch. With both hands beneath her ass, I lift it to me, to the perfect fucking position for me to unload my pleasure. She wraps her legs around me. I piston into her with abandon, which makes her legs flop open, unable to hold on. She is splayed wide in front of me, and I have the best view of my cock plunging in and out of her swollen, glistening pussy. Just the sight of it makes me explode. I nearly collapse.

Chapter 14

Madeline

I t's another hectic day. I receive my food order, thankfully with no issues, and get busy right away prepping my specials for the night. After, I prep for a meal that has been requested for a special private dinner party to celebrate a fireman's promotion, one Drago Dominante. Wow! That is some name. I'm looking forward to meeting this man and his family tonight. Tammy talked with the requestor who booked the event. I didn't. They want a large, family style traditional Italian dinner, which I am thrilled to whip up. They've even arranged for a wine delivery from a local winery, Cheshire, which I normally don't stock.

I have my wait staff come in early to set up for the private dinner event, which will take place in the secluded back room. I love having this space for these private dinners. It gives the guests a great venue for their events. The front of the house is fully booked with reservations for the night as well.

I buzz along, taking care of everything that needs doing and even have time to go up to my apartment and take a shower before the restaurant opens. I trot up the stairs and find a floral delivery box on the landing at the top of the stairs outside my door. I scoop the box up and carry it inside. I recognize the flower shop it is from. It is just around the corner. I wonder who it could be from as I open the box. I know

Cosimo has all my info. Did his brother, Master D, have him send it?

Monday night was incredible. I'm still on cloud nine by how it went, and I am so thankful I went back to the club and kept him as my Dom. I am still bowled over that he made love to me as he did. I would never have thought that plain old vanilla sex could be so erotic, so orgasmic! And the fact that he proclaimed that he wanted to keep me as his permanent Sub, have an exclusive relationship, and have a relationship outside of the club eventually was so unexpected.

Unboxing it, I find a beautiful bouquet of wildflowers in a beautiful pot, the ends of the flowers stuck into the wet floral foam. But instead of a lovely aroma wafting from them, I smell something terrible, a horrible mildewy smell that instantly triggers a headache. I search for a card to tell me who they're from, but I find none. The smell is overwhelming, so I bring the bouquet outside. Below the stairs is the dumpster. I toss them into it and then return to my apartment. Maybe a nice hot shower will rinse the smell from my sinuses.

Twenty minutes later, as I turn the shower off, the headache is worse. The steam and hot water didn't help at all. I haven't had a doozy of a headache like this in a long time. I forgot how debilitating they can be. I hate to do it, but I call Tammy to tell her I'm sick and she'll have to handle everything this evening. I know if I go downstairs, the smell of the food will make me throw up.

I'll have to stop at that florist tomorrow and see who ordered the flowers. I have a bad feeling it was Dave, and he did something to the water in the foam to make it smell so bad. Retribution for Margot's visit? I wouldn't put it past him. With that thought, I take a handful of Tylenol and I lay on the edge of my bed, closest to the bathroom, in case I do have to throw up. My head hurts so badly.

Butch

I have to say I am genuinely excited about the dinner party that Cosimo planned for this evening to celebrate my promotion. I've always thought he didn't approve of my career choice of being a fireman because our family is well-off, and he wanted me to go into the family wine business. But he has been supportive of it recently, proven by his insistence on planning this dinner. It's at a restaurant in my precinct that I have never eaten at, The Toad and the Hoot Owl. I'm sure Cosimo goes to many restaurants on a regular basis, but I didn't know he frequented this one.

I left the bike at home and have the BMW convertible, so I park towards the far end of the lot, and I'll be damned if I don't see the little red sports car that belongs to Kenzie and Andy's friend Maddie. It's only then that I recall that their friend is a chef and owns this restaurant. Holy shit, I'm finally going to meet her. Not that I am interested in any other woman at this point.

Charlotte has my body and soul. I smile for the hundredth time since Monday night, recalling the sex we enjoyed. I now understand addiction. I would do anything for another hit of her, another taste of her pussy, another thrust into her core, another kiss, another caress. I made love to her, and I will again. I also want to tie her in place, gag her, spread her legs and make them remain open to me for as long as I want to lick her, finger her, and fuck her. I want to combine all aspects of erotic play and lovemaking to create the most stimulating, orgasmic encounters we can, many of them that will last far into the future. I want her in my bed and in my life. I wish she was here with me on my arm this evening. Well, she didn't say no to any of it, so there is hope.

When I walk into the restaurant, Cosimo is at the main bar, drink in hand. He greets me and ushers me to the back to a private room. Not only are several of my friends and crew from my firehouse there, but my entire family is also there. Mom and my sister, Gabriela, and a few of my cousins who live in the area are standing around the room chatting. Something pulls at my heart strings, making me feel emotional. It has been a long time since the family has come together for anything other than a wedding or a funeral. It really means the world to me that they are all here to celebrate this with me.

As I look around the room, I see Andy and Kenzie Stevens at the end of the table, smiling warmly at me. I hadn't told Andy or anyone else outside of the firehouse about the promotion. The fact that Cosimo reached out to them to invite them, knowing that Andy is probably my best friend outside of the firehouse, makes me really appreciate my brother. I know we have a complicated relationship, Cosimo and me, but when he does things like this, I can't be mad at him about the other stuff.

I make my rounds, greeting everyone and thanking them for coming. When I get over to Andy and Kenzie, she gives me a hug. Andy shakes my hand and then pulls me in for an embrace. "Precinct Commander, huh?" Andy asks with a smile. "Why didn't you tell us about this big promotion when you were in the gym last?"

I shrug. "I don't know. It just didn't come up in our conversation."

"This is a really big deal," Kenzie says. "We're very proud of you, Butch,"

"Aw, Kenz, thanks," I say and give her another hug.

Just then, a line of servers come into the room with dishes in their hands that smell amazing. Everyone takes their seats. Dinner is served family style. Calamari and mussels start the parade of plates. Of course, Cosimo has chosen the perfect wine from his private reserve to go with the appetizers. Cosimo explains that this wine has a deep yellow color, with mineral fragrances. He goes into so much regarding the grape, the growing, and even the bottling of this particular wine, including that it is decanted and not filtered before bottling. I know this is his thing, and he loves to talk about the wine. I just know that it tastes amazing.

The next course comes out, large bowls of mixed green salads arrive. I am so touched and how happy and relaxed everyone appears, except for Cosimo. I know he is trying to look like he is relaxed, but he's not. I've never seen him so uptight. He also keeps watching the door and the waitstaff like he's nervous about them. I'm not sure what's up. I'll have to talk to him later.

Before the main entrees are brought out, the wait staff removes the glasses used for the wine we drank while eating our appetizers. Clean red wine glasses are brought out, and several bottles of the everyday wine from our public stock arrive at the table. The red blend is one of my favorites. Then the main courses arrive. Plates of Lasagna, Chicken Carbonara and Shrimp Fra Diavolo arrive, piping hot. Being from an Italian family, I can verify that this place is as close to home cooking that you can get!

That's when I realize we haven't met the chef yet. Normally, in a place like this, the chef would have come out and introduced herself by now and asked how the food was. After the dessert is devoured, I go over to where Andy and Kenzie are.

"Hey, isn't this your friend Maddie's restaurant?"

"Yes," Kenzie answers.

"Where is she? I'm kind of surprised she hasn't come into the room," I say.

"She's sick tonight, a migraine," Kenzie says. "She prepped all the food earlier and then got a headache so bad she is in bed."

"Oh, that's too bad. I was looking forward to finally meeting her," I say. I chuckle a bit. "It's as though there is a conspiracy to keep her and I from meeting."

"Nothing that sinister," Kenzie says with a laugh.

And she'd know. Sinister circumstances were what led to the two of them getting together. Thank goodness Andy was the guy in the bar that she met after she had been drugged by a co-worker. Things would have turned out much differently for her had she not met Andy that night. I still wonder how she is mentally right after all that went down. No, I don't wonder. I know it was Andy that made sure she got the mental health help she needed to move past all that. And what they have is amazing. To find a love like those two have is something I admire. And it inspires me that just maybe, it could happen to me too.

As the evening winds down, several of the guys are going to hit the local bar by the firehouse, but I decline, determine to get a good night's sleep. I say my goodbyes to my family and friends and head home. I am truly touched by everyone's support this evening. The world feels right in all regards, professionally and personally.

Madeline

I spend most of Thursday in bed with the headache, though it is dulled quite a bit. The only time it really throbs is when the sound of the garbage truck pierces the otherwise relative quiet. I decide I must have a virus, that maybe I was going to get sick anyway, but the horrible smell of the flowers just hastened it, or worse yet, it wasn't the flowers at all, just a virus. I may have thrown out a perfectly innocent bouquet of flowers. I still need to get over to the florist and see who sent them.

I feel badly that I dumped all aspects of the restaurant on Tammy and the rest of the staff. But they are competent,

I remind myself, and Tammy is paid very well to manage the place, which she hardly ever does alone. I rarely take a day or two off, even for an illness, so it's not like me doing this is commonplace or unfair. If nothing else, I guess it's a good test of my staff.

Friday morning, I feel much better. I eat something more than toast, which was all I ate Thursday, and I even manage a cup of coffee. By the time my food order arrives, I know I have kicked whatever it was that had me down. I feel back to my old self. We have another private party booked for the evening. It's a party of twenty-five, and the food choice was left up to me. I plan a nice variety from my regular menu to make it easier for myself.

I keep meaning to get over to the florist to inquire who sent me the bouquet. I really want to know, but one thing after another on Friday diverts my attention and before I know it, my staff is arriving for their shifts. We are booked solid with reservations, plus that private party.

The private party turns out to be a reunion of a group of Marines who served together in the same unit twenty years ago. They re-found each other on social media and planned this get together. The organizer lives in Lexington, and he found out about my restaurant and our private back room for events like this from Kenzie. He's a member of the gym, he tells me. Wow! She is such a good friend helping to promote my restaurant.

They have a great time. I hear a lot of laughter coming from the room. They tip my servers well. Unfortunately, though, they won't leave. Dinner is served and cleaned up. Desserts are devoured. More drinks are ordered, and still, they stay ordering round after round of drinks and even a few more appetizers. My restaurant made a lot off them. Finally, at one in the morning, I go back to the room and tell them we are closing, and they have to leave. I direct them to another bar I knew stayed open until three. Then we get busy with clean up.

Chapter 15

Madeline

The clean up after the private party is a bitch. The last staff member leaves the restaurant at 3:00 a.m. I drag myself upstairs to my apartment for a nice cool shower and some needed sleep. I am hot, sweaty, and exhausted. I set the AC down to sixty-two as I enter the apartment. I stand under my new rain shower head and let the cool water run down my body. After experiencing the shower at Kenzie and Andy's apartment with this fixture, I went out and bought one immediately. It is a game changer!

I put on my boy shorts and tank top and sit on the edge of the bed. The room has cooled nicely. It's almost frosty, just how I like it when I sleep. As I lay down, I think how happy I am that Kenzie introduced me to these soft 1800 count sheets. Who knew how great these little splurges on luxury would make me feel? The shower head and the sheets remind me that I am so thankful she is in my life. I really need to send her a thank you for referring her gym member to me for the private party booking tonight. I really made a lot from that booking. With happy thoughts, I turn the light off. My down comforter envelopes me in a cocoon and I fall asleep immediately.

My dreams start out so beautiful only to become very scary. I wake and am coughing uncontrollably. I open my eyes to total darkness. The electric is out, but I hear the smoke alarm wailing. What the hell is going on? I jump up out of bed and hit the floor. The apartment is full of smoke, and I am having a hard time breathing. I crawl towards the door out of the apartment. At the bottom of the door, I see a glow which I'm sure is fire on the other side of it. I make my way to the bathroom and crawl into the shower. I turn the cold water on to wet myself and a towel. A loud explosion rocks the room, knocking me off my knees. Everything goes black.

Butch

I have finally fallen asleep. It is nearly dawn. We had four dumpster fire calls through the night. Our arsonist was active. We need to get this son of a bitch. The stationhouse alarm goes off again. I jump out of my bed, pissed at the thought that it could be another dumpster fire. Doesn't this fucker have a job he has to sleep at night for? Even worse, the alarm bell has interrupted one of the most vivid fantasies I have ever had. My watch says it's nearly five a.m. Shit! I'd only gotten an hour of sleep since the last call.

We suit and gear up. I hop into the front of the engine truck beside the driver. As we fly down the street, lights and sirens blaring, the radio is relaying info on the structure fire from the police on the scene. It's not a dumpster this time. The address that we are headed to sounds familiar, but I don't know what building is at that location. I can picture the intersection, old downtown buildings with street parking, a few with side parking lots.

When we pull up to the address, my heart drops. The Toad and the Hoot Owl is engulfed in flames, and it doesn't look good. I suddenly remember that Kenzie's friend Maddie lives over the restaurant. And I know she is no longer staying at Andy's old apartment over the gym. Andy said she was there the one night only.

I direct the driver to pull through the parking lot and

bring the truck as close to the back of the building as we can get. Black smoke billows out of the structure. More police cars arrive and set up a perimeter. I jump out of the truck and start barking orders to pull hoses so we can get inside that building. Neither the Chief nor the Shift Commander are on site yet, so I am in charge until one of them arrives.

I run over to the two police officers that are standing there with lights shining up at the second story of the building. The engine from fire house number four was also called and they have just arrived. I direct them to come around back and pull their hoses alongside my crew. The apartment is over the back of the building. My crew will make entry into it. I want crew four to enter the first floor on the back and to also work on that dumpster.

"I know the building owner lives in an apartment up on the second floor. Did she make it out, officers?" I ask.

The first officer to my left points his flashlight beam to the external wood staircase. Most of it is shrouded in smoke. I can't tell if it is on fire or if that is just the smoke from the structure fire below. "We didn't see her get out, got no report she did. But we didn't try to get through the smoke to check on her. It's too thick."

I shake my head. "I'm glad you didn't."

I evaluate the space. The ladder truck will never fit back there. It's narrow. In evaluating a secondary point up top to make entry, if needed, I realize the dumpster is up against the building and it too is on fire. Shit. Is that where the fire originated? I know from the notes I read when Cotter responded last week. He had his crew move it away from the building. How'd it get moved back? And when?

By this time, both crews from the engines have the hoses pulled, and the water is switched on, combatting the fire on the first floor from the back. Through my radio, I hear that the District Commander has also called in help from a third firehouse to ensure the fire does not spread to the building beside it and his car is just pulling up in the front. I turn the handling of the scene over to him and don my mask and tank.

I take up a position with one of the hose crews and share my plan to see if the staircase is on fire or just obscured from the heavy smoke. We have to get into that apartment and look for the resident, who I happen to know is Kenzie's best friend, but I don't share that info with the team.

As we mount the stairs, I hear through my radio that the third engine from station number two has pulled up and has pulled hoses. They will assault the fire from the front. The ladder truck is just pulling up in the front as well. They'll hit the second story and the roof from there. Then I tell my crew on the engine in the back to get a jet spraying as high on the second floor as they can, so we can make entry. The only lucky thing about fires in the downtown is that most buildings are brick. Had this been a wood structure, it would be too late to get upstairs to search for occupants.

I see the hose on the dumpster has pretty much put it out, but inside the place is an inferno. The glass on the back of the building is all busted. I know the fire marshal will be called to investigate, but I sure have to wonder if an accelerant was tossed through the windows. I have a hard time believing the dumpster spread inside with such a raging fire, especially as the fire was all the way to the front of the building when we arrived.

We lead with the spray from the hose and inch our way up the stairs. So far, the wood is intact. No flames. The wood landing at the top of the staircase in front of the door looks dicey. It could have sustained some fire damage as the flames are rolling out of a vent beneath it. Even the bottom of the door looks charred from it.

"Keep the hose on that vent," I order. "And hold on to me and Dip as we make entry." It is standard procedure that two enter and two remain behind to rescue the first two if needed. They will also keep the water directed where it will be most useful to help prevent the spread of the fire.

I carefully step onto the wood landing, placing most of my weight on the side farthest from the side of the building where the vent is spewing flames. I use the ax and crack the door. I don't see any flames in the apartment, not even coming up through the floor. I hope like hell we can get in there, search, get her, and get the fuck out before this floor collapses into the firestorm on the first floor.

I feel a tap on my shoulder and turn my head to see Dip Randall, standing beside me inside the smoke-filled room. Now that he is inside as well, I can move forward to search. It's as black as smoke gets in there. You can't see a damn thing. We make our way in, spreading out to thoroughly check the room.

I hear more glass breaking and then a loud explosion rocks the building.

"Shit!" I better get my ass moving.

I come to a door jamb. The door is open. My flashlight, penetrating the smoke only inches, reveals a bathroom. I see no flames, just the thick black smoke. I press forward, my eyes searching as I go. The building shudders once more and the large rain shower head comes off, dropping into the shower. My eyes follow it and I see bright pink cloth. A figure, wrapped in a wet towel, is slumped over in the shower stall. I lift a small, curvy brunette up, waist high, by grasping her under her arms. She is out cold.

"Coming out with one unconscious female," I broadcast.

I replace the wet towel over her face. Good thinking on her part to protect her lungs a bit from the heat and the smoke.

I'll give her some air from my mask when I get her out of here if the ambulance isn't on site yet. From the shudders I felt, this whole place could go at any minute. I retrace my steps back towards the door.

I meet back up with Dip, just feet from the door. Out on the landing, we see a ladder extending into the apartment, lying on the wood slats that are completely black. As I reach the threshold, I see the ladder is bent, forming the walkway down the staircase for as far as my eyes can see.

"Staircase is compromised," comes through my radio.

The stairs are still there, but the crew must have determined them unsafe. Dip traverses the space and mounts the ladder first. I hand the woman I assume to be Maddie over to him. Another of our colleagues is on the ladder below him. He spots Dip as he descends with the woman over his shoulder. After they are down, I transfer myself to the ladder and hustle to descend. I'm nearly to the ground when there is a very loud explosion, knocking me off the ladder, and the entire building collapses in on itself with flames cresting high above the twisted remains of the Toad and the Hoot Owl. Damn, that was too close!

I hustle over to the stretcher from the ambulance where Dip has laid the woman. I remove my helmet and air mask. Two of the house's best paramedics are treating her. They have an oxygen mask on her. As they push her hair back from her face, I get my first good look at her, and I feel like I was hit in the chest. Could this really be Charlotte? I move in, not caring if the paramedics think I'm overstepping. I turn her head to the side and check her for the heart shaped birthmark. And sure as shit, it is her. My heart fills with rage. She could have been killed. Was this the work of our arsonist?

Before I can say or do anything else, Andy and Kenzie run up and start rapid firing questions about their friend.

"Guys, you have to move back so the paramedics can treat her," I say. I lead them a few steps away. "What are you doing here?" I'm still shocked it's Charlotte.

"We saw the smoke and I'm signed up for the local text alerts. The text gave the location of the fire, and I just knew it was the Toad and the Hoot Owl," Kenzie says. "Look, I'm the closest thing to Maddie's next of kin here in Lexington."

"I get it," I say. "She's going to need you. Stay here and let me check on her condition." I step back over to the front of the ambulance. They already have her loaded in. Charlotte is coughing and her eyes are open. She momentarily locks eyes with me, and I see recognition in her return gaze. But then Kenzie rushes in and climbs into the ambulance with her. She hugs her tightly.

"Maddie, thank God!" Kenzie says.

Charlotte, I mean Maddie, is still coughing.

"Ma'am, you can't be in the truck," Jeff White, one of the paramedics, tells her.

"Consider me her sister," Kenzie says.

Jeff looks my way. I nod. I turn to Andy. "Kenzie can't ride in the truck. You and Kenzie should meet her at the hospital. She's awake, she'll be fine, may not even be admitted. I assume you'll take her to your place?"

"Yeah," Andy replies.

"Let me know when you get her home. I want to talk with her," I say. Boy do I ever!

"Will do," Andy says. He slaps me on the shoulder. "Thanks."

In his eyes, I see appreciation and true thanks. He knows she'd be dead had we not arrived when we did. That's why I do this job, to make a difference and save people. He calls to

Kenzie, and she gets out of the ambulance. Just before the door is closed, I see Charlotte staring at either me or the flames in the remnants of her restaurant. Then the door is swung shut, removing her from my view. Jeff White scurries to the driver's cab and the ambulance drives off.

I turn back and survey the scene. We still have some work to do before we can say the fire is struck. But I do know that the loss is complete. The building is a burned-out shell. At the far end of the parking lot, tucked in a corner out of harm's way, I see her little red car. I'm relieved it was parked far away from the building and it hadn't been damaged in the fire. Charlotte's business, her home, and everything else she owns has been destroyed. At least that little beauty was not.

Charlotte

As I open my eyes, I realize where I am. In an ambulance. My chest is burning, and I can't stop coughing, even though I have what I know is an oxygen mask on. I do a quick mental evaluation of my body. I don't feel in pain anywhere except my chest. I try to take the oxygen mask off so I can ask the paramedic who is hovering over me if I'm okay, but he stops me and tells me to leave it on. I know it isn't causing me to cough, but it has me feeling claustrophobic.

Just then, the paramedic moves and my eyes lock with Master D. He's standing in the doorway dressed as a fireman. Am I unconscious? Is this some weird sexual fantasy scene playing out in my head? Next thing I know, Kenzie is in the ambulance hugging me. It's barely light out. What is she doing here? I concentrate on calming the coughing. The oxygen is helping.

"Andy and I will meet you at the hospital. Don't worry. We'll help you with whatever you need," she assures me.

Then she jumps down, and I see Master D still standing there, staring at me. Behind him, I see a burning, partially collapsed building. As the back doors are shut, I realize that building is all that is left of the Toad and the Hoot Owl. I re-close my eyes, hoping when I again open them, I will find that I am tucked in my bed, and this has just been a nightmare.

***

That, unfortunately, is not the case. I am vividly aware of everything that happens at the hospital. I have an IV in my arm that the paramedic put in right before Kenzie climbed in. I'm wearing wet, smoke-soaked pajamas. Kenzie is allowed in the treatment room with me. She confirms the building is completely gone. My purse is gone. My IDs and credit cards. All my clothes, all my things, gone. Even though she promises that she and Andy will help me with everything and will take me home to their place, I am devastated. I worked so hard to build my restaurant. I saved. I put every penny of my inheritance into it. I worked seventy hours a week to make The Toad and the Hoot Owl a reality and it is gone.

A nurse comes in and changes me into a hospital gown. I am breathing easier now, but they still have a nasal catheter delivering oxygen. They'll leave me on the oxygen until the fluids they're giving me through the IV are done running into me, probably another hour. They're not going to admit me. Andy has gone home to get me some of Kenzie's clothes to wear out of there.

"How did you know my place was on fire?" I ask Kenzie.

"I'm signed up for the emergency text alerts for the area. It sends text messages when intersections are shut down after a crash or during a fire."

"What were you doing up so early? And where's Trina?"

Kenzie smiles. "She spent the night with Ashley last night. Andy and I get up early. We were headed to the gym for a workout when I got the alert."

"You really get up that early?" I repeat. "What's wrong with you?"

Kenzie giggles. She squeezes my hand. "I love you, Maddie. I'm so glad you made it out. They hadn't even brought you over to the ambulance when the second-floor caved in. We could have lost both you and Butch. Damn, that was too close."

"Butch?" I ask.

"Our friend, the fireman I wanted to fix you up with."

Chapter 16

Madeline

I awake to unfamiliar surroundings, and then I remember everything I worked so hard for is gone. What could have happened? My staff and I are very careful to make sure everything is turned off, candles are blown out, etc. The impact of what has happened hits me like a ton of bricks, and the tears start to flow down my cheeks.

I know I need to see the devastation for myself, so I put on my big girl panties, and get dressed in Kenzie's clothes that I wore out of the hospital. They are on the foot of the bed where I left them when we got home to Kenzie and Andy's house around noon and I was exhausted, so I borrowed something to sleep in and I went to bed.

I splash some cold water over my tear-soaked face and open the door to soft voices filtering up the stairs. I slowly walk down a few steps, not wanting to eavesdrop, but I hear my name, and it isn't Andy's voice.

That voice? Where have I heard that voice? Curious, I continue down the stairs to find the source of the voices. Andy and his guest are standing in the kitchen by the island. Andy's eyes meet mine. His guest is facing Andy, so all I see is his broad shoulders, tight ass and long black hair in a leather strap. No. Fucking. Way! And then he speaks, and I know that this is

Master D. I really did see him standing in the open ambulance doorway.

I remember Kenzie mentioning Butch. Is it possible? Should I continue to the kitchen, or shrink back upstairs? Neither Kenzie nor Andy are going to appreciate how we know each other. Just as I decide to turn and go back upstairs, Master D turns around. The air in the room disappears. I feel like I am going to faint, and yup, down I go.

Butch

Andy and I talk about the fire. The Arson Investigator is currently on site and will supply me with a full report by day's end. Just then, Andy looks up, smiles at someone behind me. I turn to see what he is smiling about, thinking Trina is there, and that is when I see her. Those beautiful brown eyes that have dominated my dreams. Just then, her eyes close and she starts to crumble. I catch her right before she hits the floor. Andy tells me to take her back up to the guest room and he will text Kenzie to let her know what happened.

Andy meets up with us in the guest room with a bottle of water. I have already moistened a washcloth and have it on her forehead. "You got any smelling salts?"

"Not here," Andy said. "Should I get your first aid kit from your car?"

"Nah, she's already coming around," I say.

"I'm sure the reality of the fire just hit her and overwhelmed her." Andy states. "That restaurant was her dream. She poured every penny she had into it."

My phone chirps and I see a text from Bud Kleckner. "The fire marshal confirms it was arson," I say.

"Maddie just had Porter put in a security system. He should be able to pull security footage from the cloud storage."

He pulls his phone from his pocket and taps out a message. "I'm contacting him now."

"That should help, thanks. After you get it for me, I'll forward it to the arson investigator."

Just then, Charlotte's, oops, I mean Madeline's eyes open. I'm really going to have to be careful what I call her. She opens her eyes with a panicked look. "Arson?" she asks. Her gaze is locked with mine. She knows who I am.

"Maddie, this is our friend Butch," Andy introduces.

I smile. "Hi Maddie. It's nice to meet you," I say.

Madeline

Are you fucking kidding me? Master D is Butch, Kenzie and Andy's friend that she wanted to fix me up with. I used an assumed name. Why couldn't he? I guess I just assumed his name really started with a D. "It's nice to finally meet you too," I say, taking his lead.

"The Arson Investigator is currently at the restaurant and will supply me with a full report. I'll keep you informed," he says in an official voice.

"I want to go to the restaurant now," I state.

Butch and Andy look at each other and they both shake their heads no. "You really don't need to see it yet. Give yourself a day. It's a total loss," Master D, I mean Butch, says.

"I am going, and no one will stop me. That was my dream, and I want to see what might be salvageable."

"There's nothing salvageable," Master D, Butch says. "And it's not safe to even try to go in there. Besides, the arson investigator hasn't released the scene yet. It's all cordoned off with yellow tape."

It feels like he's thrown a bucket of ice water over me.

"Nothing is salvageable?"

He sits on the edge of the bed and takes my hand in his. It's familiar and comfortable for him to hold my hand. "I'm really sorry. No, nothing is salvageable," he repeats, gently and with a sympathetic expression on his handsome face.

Tears leak out of my eyes again. I can't stop them. I haven't felt this lost, hopeless, or sad since my grandmother died.

I feel him squeeze my hand again. "It's going to be okay," he says. "I know Andy and Kenzie are here for you, but I will help you with whatever I can." There is a pause. "I know you don't know me, but I want to help you. The fire marshal and I will both interface with your insurance company to help file and speed along your claim."

"And you know your credit cards were melted, not stolen. You can call and order rush replacements to come here," Andy said. "You should have them in a day or two."

His statement almost makes me laugh. Almost. Shit. That's right. I have no money, no credit cards, no clothes, nothing. Thank God for good friends.

"Where do you bank?" Andy asks. "You can probably get a replacement debit card handed to you to access your checking or savings accounts."

"Yes, that will be at the top of my list."

"I'll get access to the fire scene, even if it is unstable. I can search it and see if I can find anything, say your car keys. If not, I have a friend at the Cadillac dealer. We can get you a new set of keys without much fuss."

"And of course, you can stay here for as long as you need to," Andy offers.

"Thank you," I say, my eyes going between them. Yes, thank God for good friends, though I'm not sure what to classify Master D or Butch as.

"A replacement driver's license will be trickier. The DMV will require proof of identity and residency in Kentucky. The good news is, you own a business, so you most likely have an accountant that can supply you copies of your tax documents with your full Social Security number on it. But you will still need either a birth certificate or passport," Master D, Butch says.

"I have my birth certificate and passport in a safe deposit box at my bank," I say, only now realizing how much of a pain in the ass it's going to be to get everything replaced, least of all my clothes. I'll have to get replacement credit cards first, business and personal, so I can buy some clothes, shoes, necessities. I wonder how long it takes to get an insurance payout.

Master D, Butch must have read my mind. "Most insurance companies are going to pay out within a month of the fire, so you won't have to carry balances on your credit cards for too long. And this was clearly arson, which you are not a suspect, so there shouldn't be any delay in getting the payment to you."

I wonder if I'm not a suspect because I nearly died in the fire or because Butch, Master D, knows me. I know in most restaurant fires, they look to see if it was turning a profit and if not, they suspect the owner.

"Okay, so, your plan should be to go to your bank to access your safe deposit box to get your passport and to get a new bank card. Order replacement credit cards, and then go to the DMV to get a replacement driver's license. And don't worry about the insurance claim. The fire marshal and I will get that started for you. I'll just need you on a call to the one-eight-hundred claims line with me," Master D, er Butch says.

I'm exhausted, and the thought of having to do all that today or tomorrow completely psyches me out. I just want to curl into a ball and go back to sleep for a week or two.

"Not today though, tomorrow," Master D, Butch says, with a comforting pat on my shoulder.

"Kenzie will be happy to run you around to accomplish anything you need to," Andy says.

"Where is she, anyway?" I ask.

"She ran to a store to get you some things. You can borrow any of her clothes, of course, but she thought you'd at least want new underclothing and a few other things."

"That's so sweet of her. I'll pay you guys back for anything she buys."

"I'm not worried," Andy says with a smile. "I'm pretty sure she put a new toothbrush and toothpaste in the bathroom, and there is shampoo, conditioner in there for you if you want to get a shower. She should be home soon."

I run my fingers through my hair. It feels disgusting, and it reeks of smoke. Ugh! I realize I slept in the bed with my hair and body filthy and smelly. I should have taken a shower before I laid down, but I felt so exhausted when I was discharged from the hospital. I barely remember the drive here or walking up the stairs. "Thanks, I will."

Master D., Butch nods at Andy. "Give me a moment with her, will you?"

"Sure," Andy says, not even appearing fazed by his request. He leaves the room and closes the door behind himself. Huh? Does Andy know how Master D. and I know each other? Does he know about the club?

"How are you really?" he whispers softly, the back of his

hand caressing my cheek.

I stare into his eyes and a feeling of safety floods over me. I shake my head. "I don't know. Exhausted, sad, in shock." Tears prick my eyes again. I let out a hard breath. "In shock about the fire and shocked you are here and that you're the Butch that Kenzie has wanted to introduce me to."

He chuckles that familiar laugh which warms my heart and sets me at ease. "I was quite surprised when I recognized you, too."

"So, now what?" I ask.

He looks thoughtful. "Do you prefer I call you Madeline or Maddie? I can't very well call you Charlotte in front of anyone outside of the club."

My cheeks heat. "Yeah, I really don't want my friends to know about my other life."

"It's safe with me. Andy doesn't know anything about my ownership and involvement in the club, and I prefer to keep it that way for both our sakes."

I'm glad we're on the same page. "So, Butch." I smile.

"I do want to help you with whatever I can. I'm a lieutenant with the fire department, well, now a District Commander. I just got promoted last week." She stares at me, waiting for me to finish my thought. I'm sure an odd expression has settled on my face. I tell her what I'm thinking. "Ironically, the fire at your place this morning is probably one of the last ones I'll be going into as a firefighter. District Commanders rarely go into the site and search for victims as I did this morning."

"Wait, was that party at the Toad and the Hoot Owl this past Wednesday for you?"

He smiles again. "Yes, I thought I would finally meet you

at your restaurant? Kenzie and Andy were there for my party, and Kenzie told me you had a migraine."

"I rarely ever get sick or have headaches, but that night, I had a horrible headache develop at the beginning of the evening. I'd just gotten my specials prepped and my staff informed of the evening's plans, and I had time to go up to my apartment to change clothes. There was a box of flowers left for me that smelled terrible and triggered a headache so bad I had to lie down. Did either you or Cosimo send them?"

"I'm sorry, no, they weren't from us. Was there no note with them?" he asks.

"No, I've been meaning to go to the florist to see who sent them, but I was still sick all-day Thursday and didn't have time Friday."

He looks thoughtful for a moment, like he's really concentrating on something. "I don't want to scare you, but we need to make it a priority to find out who sent them. And has anything else odd or concerning happened besides the gas and electrical issue the day Andy and Kenzie moved?"

Oh shit! That's right, he probably doesn't know about Dave and everything I've been dealing with. Oh my God! Could Dave have started the fire? "I need to call Margot. Do you know her? Detective Margot Malone?"

He shakes his head that he does not know her.

"She's a good friend of Kenzie's. I talked to her last week. I've been having problems with an ex-boyfriend. She talked to him, told me to be careful of him, got a hinky feeling off him."

Butch

Now I get a really bad feeling. "We've had an arsonist setting dumpsters on fire for the last few weeks. No structure fires have resulted from them. Your dumpster was blazing when we arrived on site, in addition to the interior of the building. When did it get moved back against your building? I know Cotter had it moved when he was out for the gas leak."

She looks at me with confusion. "I don't know."

I can tell she is thinking hard to remember.

"I know it was below my stairs Wednesday night. I stood on the landing outside my apartment and threw the flowers into the dumpster from there."

"An accelerant was used inside your restaurant to spread the fire. Andy has reached out to Brian Porter to get all the video recorded on your system since he installed it. We hope it will show the arsonist," I say. "I can't say if it is related to the dumpster fires and the guy just escalated by hitting the interior too, or if this is something different."

I can tell she is overwhelmed at this point. I don't blame her. This has been a lot. I make a vow to myself that I will be there to help her rebuild her life and I will work with our arson investigator closely to make sure we get the son of a bitch that did this to her. I cup her cheeks between my hands, and I reach my lips to hers.

After I give her a gentle kiss, I pull back and flash her a supportive smile. "Please let me be here with you and help you rebuild your life. If we establish a relationship after this point, Andy, Kenzie, and everyone else will only know that we finally met today, and we hit it off."

A beautiful smile curves across her face. I'm glad I could bring her a glimmer of joy today. "Thank you, Butch," she says, emphasizing my name and smiling wider as she says it. "I will appreciate any help you can give me."

I lean in, wrapping my arms around her and I hold her, which is what I know she needs.

After several long, enjoyable minutes, she pulls away. "I

need to get that shower."

"And after, please try to eat," I say. I hand her water bottle to her. "And hydrate very well in the next few days."

She takes a drink and then stands up. "You know, it would have been really uncomfortable to come face to face with you at the restaurant during your promotion party. Isn't it just crazy you booked it there, not knowing who I really was?"

"Yes, just crazy," I agree. After she closes the bathroom door behind herself, I let the smile on my face fall. Not crazy or random. But I can't wrap my mind around why Cosimo would do that, book my party at her place, knowing damn well who she was.

Chapter 17

Butch

I send a text to Cosimo asking when he will be at the club. I'm there. He is not. It is mid-afternoon on Sunday. I purposefully stayed away Saturday evening, as I didn't want to run into Catrina if she was back for another Swinger's Saturday Playfest. But I did need to come in and check the security logs from the three nights. I also have lingering concerns regarding the attempted entry into our data through the firewall. Danny, our IT guy, keeps assuring me the security is robust enough to stop any hacks. But the fact that someone is trying is disturbing.

I receive a text back that he is not sure when or if he is coming in. I want to talk to him face to face about why he booked my party at The Toad and the Hoot Owl. Damn him, he had to have ulterior motives, but for the life of me, I can't figure out what they could be. Upholding our member's anonymity is a fundamental principle at the club. And after I had just gotten Charlotte back to the club, why would he risk that, risk me losing her? Certainly, he knew that if she'd come face to face with both of us at her restaurant, her place of business, that she'd be mortified and completely weirded out. Especially because she'd know that he knew exactly who she was. It boggles my mind.

I send him a reply text that I am on at the fire station

Monday through Friday this next week from eight a.m. to five p.m. I add that I will not be in Monday evening and that Madeline, yes, I use her real name, is cancelling her session because her business, The Toad and the Hoot Owl, burned to the ground early Saturday morning.

My phone immediately rings. Cosimo. "Hello."

"Burned to the ground? Jesus Christ! Is she okay?" Cosimo asks.

"If you want to talk to me about her, I suggest you get your ass in here," I growl.

"I'll be there in fifteen," he says.

"I'll be waiting in your office."

Given that he will be here in fifteen minutes, tells me he's at the main offices at Cheshire, across from the gym. On a Sunday afternoon. He works far too much. No wonder he is wound way too tightly. That won't stop me from laying into him though.

The look Cosimo gives me when he comes into his office is another great one. He's dressed as casually as he ever gets outside of his house, crisp blue jeans and a polo shirt. I'm sitting there in cargo shorts, sandals, and a t-shirt. I'm also sipping his bourbon.

"I see you've made yourself comfortable," he says, setting his phone onto his desk. He goes behind it to the credenza and pours himself a glass as well. "So, tell me about this fire."

"The alarm went off at just before five a.m. Saturday morning. My truck was first on scene. The entire first floor was engulfed in flames. I knew from Andy at the gym that their friend Madeline lived over the restaurant. Long story there. I pulled her unconscious body from her shower. We got her out just seconds before the building collapsed in on itself. A few other engine crews were working on the first floor. They pulled out, knowing it was about to go. No one was injured."

Cosimo blows out a loud breath. I can tell he is very much bothered by my narrative. "Thank God for that." He downs a gulp of his drink. "Is she okay?"

"Madeline was treated at the scene by our paramedics and transported to the hospital. She wasn't admitted. She's at Andy and Kenzie's house. I talked with her there on Saturday afternoon. Imagine my surprise when we laid her onto the stretcher in the ambulance and I saw my Charlotte." I know my voice isn't friendly.

He has to know what's coming as he stiffens. "I'm glad she's okay. I'm assuming the restaurant was a total loss."

I nod, staring at him with anger.

"That's a shame. It was a nice place. I hope she can rebuild."

"Really? That's it?" I pin him with a stare that if looks could kill, would.

He stares back at me but doesn't speak.

"You planned my promotion dinner. Why the hell would you have it there?"

A smirk curves his lips. "Why do you think? Jesus Drago. Why do I have to push you into everything? It was way past the time for you two to drop the alias bullshit and expand your relationship. I knew neither of you would freak out in front of her employees, yours, our family, and your friends."

"Are you fucking kidding me?" I demand.

"How long would it have taken you to move the relationship out of the club? A few more months? Six months? A year? That's what you wanted to happen, isn't it?"

I am shocked. He crossed the line this time. It wasn't just my life he was fucking with; it was hers.

"So, are you going to have communication with her outside of the club now?"

"Yes," I admit begrudgingly, still figuring out what to say to him regarding his interference.

"You're welcome."

"Oh, no you don't! She wanted anonymity, and you didn't have the right to out her to even me."

Cosimo chuckles. "Jesus Drago, always taking the moral high ground. I only did it because you're my brother and I want you to be happy. I could see what you could not about her. I knew you would want to keep her as your permanent Sub that first night. By the second, I knew you would only be satisfied if you expanded your relationship outside of the club. You've been a mopey mess for the last year. That's why I pushed you."

I am shocked. I can't believe Cosimo would do this, that he would think he has the right to decide this for me and for her.

Madeline

I sip a wonderful glass of wine and look out of the sunroom windows at Andy and Kenzie's backyard. It is Monday evening. I cooked dinner for the Stevens family, including Andy's mom, whipped up a simple berry summer salad with feta and grilled chicken breast. Cooking for them is the very least I can do. I'm happy to give back as they have already helped me so much.

It was a busy day. Kenzie and I started at the bank. I received counter checks and a new debit card. I took out five hundred in cash to last me a bit. I accessed my safe deposit box to get my passport and birth certificate, and then we went to the DMV to get my replacement license. We had all that done by noon. Kenzie then treated me to lunch. Then we went shopping, and I bought cosmetics and some clothes. We swung by my cell phone carrier's store, and I got a replacement phone. Next was the post office, and I filed a change of address for my business and personal mail to go to Kenzie's house. Our last stop was the Cadillac dealer. I got a replacement set of car keys, well a key fob, but calling it a set of keys is the saying ingrained in my brain.

We swung by my restaurant to get my car, and I couldn't stop the tears at seeing my dream destroyed. It hit me in a way I didn't think it would. It was as if seeing it made it more of a reality than it had been, even though I knew it had been destroyed. Kenzie wouldn't drive away, expecting me to follow until she was sure my tears had stopped, and I could drive.

I even stepped as close as I could to gaze inside the brick walls and saw that everything was a charred mess. Butch and Andy had been right. There was nothing salvageable. I couldn't wrap my mind around that. In such a short amount of time, everything that I had worked so hard to create was gone.

"Not gone," Kenzie had said, trying to soothe me. "Waiting to be rebuilt. That's what the insurance is for. You can build it back better than it was."

That offered me little comfort.

My replacement credit cards that I ordered on Sunday with one day delivery arrived just before dinner. I now have ID, cash, and credit and debit cards. I have a purse, clothing, and cosmetics. Kenzie even insisted on buying me a necklace with a charm that dangles that says, Strength in a beautiful script lettering. She said it will remind me that I have it. I have it on right now.

"So, what are your plans tomorrow?" Kenzie asks.

She is sitting across from me at the table and chair set that was in Andy's kitchen at the apartment. I'm sure she knows I am lost. I want to talk to Butch, Master D, but I won't tell her that. I just want to hear his voice. We talked on Sunday afternoon. He'd called Andy and Andy handed me his phone to talk on. We did that phone call to the claims department of my insurance company to report the fire. I wrote down Butch's cell phone number so I could program it into my phone when I got the replacement. I am so happy I was able to take care of that today too. I figure when I go up to bed, I will send him a text and see if he can talk. I know he worked today, but I don't remember what hours he worked.

"I guess I need to start the process of rebuilding. Now that I have a phone, I need to contact my vendors, my accountant, probably even my attorney. Butch said he'd help me contact a company to remove the rubble from the site once it is cleared by the fire marshal to do so, so I can think about rebuilding. I'll need an architect and builder." I blow out a breath. "I haven't even started yet, but I am already exhausted by everything that I will need to do to rebuild."

Kenzie reaches across the table and grabs my hand. "Rome wasn't built in a day. This is a marathon, not a sprint." She pauses and chuckles. "Can I possibly come up with another cliché?"

I chuckle too. "I know it's all true. It's going to take time and patience."

"You'll get there. And Andy and I are here to help you anyway we can."

She is just the sweetest, best friend. Tears pour out of my eyes again. I have never cried so much as an adult. I'm an emotional mess and I hate it.

Kenzie strokes my arm. "Cry as much as you need to."

She knows me so well.

"And then get really pissed off. Someone did this on purpose. We're going to find who did it and get his ass arrested. Margot even said attempted murder charges will be added to the arson charges."

"When did you talk to Margot?" She has my attention.

"I called her Saturday afternoon after we got home from the hospital, while you slept. She wants to be kept apprised of all developments. I know she's already looking at Dave for it."

I let out a sigh and shake my head. "I'm not sure I believe he would be capable of it. I don't know." I take another drink of my wine and then gaze out over the back lawn again at nothing in particular.

Just then, Andy leads Butch and Brian Porter into the sunroom. My eyes lock with Butch. Yes, I have to think of him as only Butch when we are with friends.

"Hi Maddie. I am so sorry about what happened to your restaurant," Brian says.

I shift my eyes to him. New tears fill them. "Thanks, Brian. I'm honestly still in shock."

He nods and a sympathetic grin curves his face. "I bet." He sets a laptop on the table and takes a seat beside me. "The good news is we had the cameras watching everything." He taps his laptop. "We have good footage of a lot of things. Butch told me about the flowers that made you sick a few days before the fire, and I even have footage of them being left by your door. Plus, I found a few other things over the three weeks since the system was installed that look pretty suspicious to run by you before we turn this footage over to the arson investigator and the police."

For the first time since Saturday, I'm hopeful. "I want to

see the footage from the fire first," I say. Butch stands behind me and places a hand on my shoulder. Kenzie moves to a chair beside Brian, and Andy stands between the two of them so that everyone can see the laptop.

Brian's lips form a sympathetic smile again. "I thought you would. So, what I've done," he says, opening the laptop, "is go through all the footage since the system was installed. As you know, the camera recording only activates when there is movement. We put in four cameras, one focusing on the front door and window from inside, two on the back door, which also captures the bottom of the stairs leading up to your apartment and part of the alleyway, and the fourth inside the restaurant capturing most of the main dining room and the doors into the bathrooms and the kitchen." He pauses and smiles. "We got good coverage with the placement of the cameras."

"The night of the fire," I remind him.

"Hear me out. Since I've got three weeks of camera footage on four cameras and we know arsonists often visit the site they will set on fire, I wanted to make sure I screened your footage and pulled out anything suspicious to have a smaller file. All of it will be turned over. I made a separate file of the four cameras from the first instance of the arson until the cameras cut out. But I also pulled out all the things I found suspicious for you to review so we can narrow it down to the truly suspicious for the police to review first. Does that make sense?"

"Yes," I admit.

"Now, the night of the fire, I found nothing suspicious on those cameras all evening and as you and your staff cleaned up, except that dinner group. Jeez, they just wouldn't leave, would they?"

I chuckle a little. "Yeah, I made a lot off that private

party. And they tipped the staff very well. I felt terrible basically throwing them out at one a.m., which is a full hour later than I normally close. One a.m. is what's dictated by the city though, so I had to kick them out then. Did you see something suspicious regarding them?"

"No, not at all," Brian said. "No one even gave as much as a glance back at the door when they finally exited." He clicks a few keys and brings up the back door recordings on a split screen. "Here is you, locking up the back and going up your stairs for the night."

I watched myself on the recording.

"The cameras did not record again until four thirty a.m." He clicked the keys again. "Here is the back door camera footage from both cameras." The footage again plays from the two cameras on a split screen. First, an alert hits the system of a power interruption and then a figure in a black mask, wearing a black hoodie and black pants, approaches the back of the building. "The power supply was cut to the building and then two minutes later this guy approaches your building." He'd paused the footage. He restarts it. "There, he just broke the back window into the kitchen. That's some sort of protective mat he's lying on the broken window frame."

Next, I watch the guy do it and climb inside my building. He has a black bag in his hand.

"If you remember, my system has battery backup on the cameras, so they'll keep recording during a power outage, but not the door or window sensors," Brian says. "He knew there was security and an alarm system on the building. He cut the power in the alley before entering the building so no alarm would trip."

My anger is off the charts as I watch this guy. He had a mat to lie over the broken glass. He has a bag with what I'll assume is what he used to start the fire. This was planned, premeditated, and fully thought out.

"Next, here is what went on inside," Brian says.

From the main dining room camera, I see him creep into the dining room, through the door from the kitchen. He removes one bottle that looks like a water bottle from his bag, and he sprays a trail all through the front of the restaurant, over the bar, near the front door. He uses three bottles, emptying liquid. He places the empty bottles back in the bag before pulling the next full one out. Then he leaves a trail of the liquid on the floor back to the kitchen.

Brian then switches to the backdoor camera feeds again and I see him exit the building. He pulls two more water bottles from his bag, unscrews the lids and shoves what looks like paper into the top of them. The black bag goes into the dumpster. He drizzles some liquid into the dumpster and then a bright flash shows fire. He lights the paper at the top of one of the bottles and tosses it into the dumpster, the other he throws through the back window. There is a bright flash of light, which I know is the fire erupting in both the dumpster and from inside my restaurant.

Oh, my fucking God! I feel like I'm going to pass out.

"And here's the inside of the dining room. Your arson investigator will confirm this is the fire following the path of the accelerant."

The footage activates with a glow coming to the room from the kitchen, where the door was left propped open. The glow increases as flames race across the floor from the kitchen into the main dining room. And in a matter of seconds, fire is everywhere! It runs up the bar and spreads over all of it. It climbs up the walls and dances over the tables.

And I know while this is happening, I am right upstairs sleeping, unaware that fire is ravaging my restaurant. And the arsonist knew I was upstairs sleeping too. This thought makes me dizzy.

"The only thing that saved you, Madeline, is that he didn't set fire to the back room specifically, and that is the area that was right below your apartment," Butch says.

"So, are you saying he wasn't trying to kill me?"

"He obviously didn't care if he did or not, but if that was the point of setting the fire, unless he was inept, he would have saturated the area below your apartment with the accelerant as well as the stairs to your apartment," Butch answers.

I drop my head into both hands. I feel Butch's comforting hand caressing my shoulder. I wish I could just curl up in his arms and drop my head against his chest. Not that he could make any of this go away, but the physical connection would help.

"I know the guy wore a mask and hoodie, but does his size and shape seem familiar?" Butch asks, giving my shoulder a gentle squeeze.

After a few quiet moments, I pull it together and raise my head. "I don't know. Won't they be able to build a profile or something and predict his height and build from the cameras?"

"Yes, our arson investigator and the police will do that," Butch says.

"Okay, the flower delivery. I want to see it."

Brian clicks a few more keys. "I'm going to show you what each of the back cameras caught separately, so the view is bigger."

The feed from the first camera plays. The first clip is a man with what is clearly that delivery box in his hands. He approaches from the alleyway. The box with the flowers in it hides his face. He crosses right in front of the back door to my place and disappears, heading towards the stairs up to my apartment. The second camera's feed is played next. It captures his back after he's passed the back door to my place, and it shows him as he rounds the dumpster and mounts the stairs. I don't get a good look at him in either clip. One thing is for sure, it is clearly not the same figure that set my place on fire. This guy is shorter and fatter.

"Now the feed from after the box was delivered. The time stamp is one minute later."

The camera feed records him stepping off the stairs. The flower box is no longer in his hands. He walks back towards the camera, his face angled down. At the last second, before he is out of frame, he raises his face and looks into the window at the back of my restaurant. Brian pauses the recording there and zooms in on him. Anger spreads through me like the fire did through my restaurant.

"That fucking weasel!" I explode. "That God-damned fucking fraud fuck, mother-fucker!" I glance around at the others. I'm sure I look and sound like a crazy lady. "That's Frank Blanchet!"

"Frank Blanchet?" Kenzie repeats.

"Madeline, who is Frank Blanchet?" Butch asks.

"A rival chef," I say, nearly growling. "He deliberately made me sick."

"I have this same guy on film doing a few other suspicious things over the course of the three weeks," Brian Porter speaks up.

"He was near my restaurant other days, too?" I can't believe it.

"Yes, I have him in footage on four other occasions,"

Brian says.

He shows us the footage. Frank was right outside my restaurant on multiple occasions. One of my sous chefs, Enrique, hands him fresh vegetables on one occasion, lemons on another, and even a bottle of liquor. At the time, I noticed some of the items I had run low on and wondered how I had failed to order the correct amount.

The last clip Brian plays really pissed me off. Frank was inside the front of my restaurant near the bar, talking with two of my servers, no doubt trying to lure them away to work for him. They sure looked chummy. So, one of my sous chefs and two of my servers kept a friendly relationship with Frank after I had to basically kick him out of my restaurant. Unbelievable!

I now had to wonder if everything ever missing, or I was running low on, had gone into his greedy paws. That was theft as far as I am concerned. Theft by Enrique, theft by Frank! "I want to press charges against both Frank and Enrique for theft. I want Margot to be the one who talks to Frank about those flowers. I don't trust anyone else to come down on him. He poisoned me. He made me sick on purpose with those flowers. He took things from my restaurant, things I paid for that he had no business taking."

"Easy, Madeline," Brian says. "All things will follow a process. I've worked with the police before. I'll make sure these recordings are placed in Margot's hands. She'll want to watch them before she interviews you. She's going to need everyone's names and contact information." He hands me a small pad of paper he pulls from his shirt pocket. "Write down what you have on Frank and Enrique."

I shake my head. "I have their phone numbers, but their addresses and other info is with my accountant in my files. I'll have to get it tomorrow."

"Then get it tomorrow," Butch says, squeezing my

shoulder. "Porter is right. This is going to take time. You're going to have to be patient."

"I'll text Margot and have her come over as soon as she can," Kenzie says.

"I have all this taped footage in a cloud repository that I will give the fire marshal and any law enforcement agency access to," Brian says. "I can also supply flash drives if they want, and I can walk them through it just like I just did for you."

"Thank you," I say. I'm still trying to process that it was Frank that poisoned me and made me sick, and that several members of my staff welcomed him inside the restaurant when I wasn't there. Enrique even gave him items I had purchased, shorting me of them when I needed them. I knew that Frank and several of my vendors were tight. I had to wonder if that was why some of the things happened, too. Damn! I knew I would now be suspicious of everything.

"Okay, I'm going to take off now," Brian Porter says, closing his laptop and standing up. "Let me know if you need anything else, Madeline."

I stand as well and wrap my arms around him to give him a hug. "Thank you for spending so much time going through the footage and copying out the important stuff. I still owe you for the system you installed. I promise you I will pay you once I receive my payment from the insurance claim."

"I wasn't concerned," he says.

Kenzie and Andy walk him out, leaving Butch and me alone in the sunroom. He moves in close and wraps an arm around me, drawing me in for a hug, which I really need. "Are you okay?" he asks.

I nod against him. "Yes, no, I don't know."

"You have to feel very shocked and sad after seeing all of that," he says.

"It's surreal. I'm so glad I had that camera and security system installed, otherwise we wouldn't know any of it. I'm so overwhelmed by everything I'm going to need to do," I admit.

His arms tighten around me. "You'll get through it, but you will need to take it one day at a time, one task checked off at a time."

Butch

I can feel her relax in my arms. I wish I could lie beside her tonight and hold her as she falls asleep. Well, maybe I can. I press a kiss to the top of her head, watching the doorway to the kitchen. It's a bit too soon for Andy or Kenzie to see affection in the form of me kissing her anywhere. Holding her is a sympathetic gesture any person with a heart would extend to another in emotional need, so I don't care if they walk in to me embracing her.

I have to grin a bit when I think about her F-bomb laced rant. I have never heard her swear like that, but I don't blame her. I would want to kill someone who did what that Frank chef-guy did. Whatever he poisoned those flowers with was toxic. It could have done damage to her that she doesn't know about yet. I'm thinking a visit to her doctor isn't a bad idea. I'll bring that up after that cop friend of theirs gets Chef Frank to admit what he poisoned her with. By the sounds of it, they are all confident that she will get him to confess. I hope so. I don't want to have to tell Madeline that justice isn't always obtained. What you know to be true and what you can prove with evidence in court are two different things.

Kenzie and Andy re-enter the sunroom. Neither reacts to seeing her in my arms.

"Margot texted back. She'll be by in the morning to talk

to you about the video surveillance after she meets with Brian. She's taking him up on his offer to walk her through it," Kenzie says.

Madeline straightens and pulls out of my hold. She nods. I watch her rub her forehead. She looks exhausted.

"Where's Trina tonight?" I ask, realizing I haven't seen her since we arrived.

"She's going to spend a few days with my mom," Andy says. "Mom came for dinner and then took Trina home with her."

"I haven't had the chance to get dinner yet," I say, hoping to use it as a segue.

"I'd offer you some of the wonderful chicken breast berry salad that Maddie made us for dinner, but we ate it all," Kenzie says.

"Thanks, I wasn't angling to raid your refrigerator," I say with a laugh. I turn to Madeline. "I see you're having a glass of wine. Would you like to come with me to have another or maybe some dessert while I get a bite to eat? I said before I'd like to help you rebuild. I have some contacts in the trades and some experience in construction permits. I'd like to help you get your plans together, so as soon as the insurance claim funds are paid, you can get right on it. If you have your plan written out, it will be much easier."

Her lips curve into a beautiful smile. "Thank you, Butch, yes. I'd like that." She turns to Kenzie and Andy. "You don't mind if I," she begins.

"Oh, heavens no," Kenzie cuts her off. "Go, get to know Butch, have a good time. You deserve it. You have the code to the house to get in if we're in bed."

I smile. Kenzie wanted to introduce us for so long. She

has to be loving this.

"Oh, I doubt I will be that late," she says.

"And feel free to come back in and hang out as long as you want after," Andy says, his eyes fixed on me.

I nod. I plan to.

Madeline and I leave. I have my BMW. The top is down. It is parked beside her little red car. I open her door and close her in. Wow, the two cars do look good parked next to each other. "I'm so glad that little beauty was parked far from your restaurant." I nod to the car.

She chuckles a little. "I've always parked it in the far corner of the lot to try to keep the doors from getting dinged up by my customers. I'm glad it was spared by being parked where it was."

I start the car and it roars to life. I back out of the driveway and drive towards a casual restaurant near the firehouse I like. I'd like to take her some place really nice, but given how we are both dressed, the place I'm heading will do. They have full bar service, wine, great desserts, and I can get a steak and baked potato, which is what I have a taste for. I glance over at her. The sun shines on her face, the breeze is whipping around the loose locks of her hair in her messy bun, and she looks relaxed, unlike she did earlier. This has to be as close to perfect as life can get.

After I put the car in park in the lot, I reach my hand over to hers before turning the car off. I raise it to my lips and brush a kiss over her knuckles. A beautiful smile curves across her lips. "Thank you for coming with me."

"Thank you for the invitation," she says.

"We can spend a lot more time together now, if you like. If not, please do not feel any pressure to do so," I say.

"I don't feel any pressure from you, and I truly appreciate all the help you are offering me. I don't want you to feel obligated to help me, though."

I nearly laugh out loud. Obligated? "No, it's my pleasure to help you. I told you last week at our session that I wanted to expand our relationship." I pause and chuckle. "So much for giving you a few weeks to think about it."

"I think fate, the spirits, or whatever you believe made the decision for me," she said with a smile, appearing to be happy with it. "I trust you, Butch."

"That means a lot to me," I say. I cup her cheeks and draw her in for a kiss. Then I nod to the restaurant. "Let's go in."

Madeline

Butch is really something! He had my heart as Master D. He saved my life as the firefighter who carried me from my burning building. I am just amazed how comfortable I am with him and how seamlessly our in-club relationship has spilled over into our new out of club relationship.

We get seated in a booth, and I am surprised that he asks me to slide over and he sits beside me. He hands me a pad of paper and a pen. "For you to make notes." He smiles. "This is a working dinner to get your plans made. You will feel better if you have some plans, a direction. I cannot even imagine how devastating the fire and the loss of your business have been."

"I got a lot accomplished today. That felt good." I tell him about all the running around that Kenzie and I did.

He chuckles. "I'm exhausted just listening to your day."

Then it dawns on me that today is Monday, and we were supposed to have a session at the club. "Today is Monday."

He smiles. "You say that like you just realized it."

"I did," I confess.

"No worries. I talked with my brother yesterday and told him about the fire and that we would not be there tonight."

"Oh, thank you for taking care of that," I say.

The server comes by. I didn't even look at the menu. Neither did Butch, but he orders a strip steak and baked potato. "You had red wine back at Andy's house. I'll get a bottle. You pick it."

I lift the wine menu from the table and quickly glance through the red wines. I was drinking a red blend. I find one I know will go good with his steak and with chocolate as I intend to get a chocolate anything for dessert. I order it and then quickly look at the dessert section of the food menu. They have a flourless chocolate cake that looks delicious. I order that as well and tell the server to bring it with his steak, I'm only having dessert. She laughs.

***

We enjoy a lovely evening. We linger and drink the entire bottle of wine. He also helps me make a lot of plans and a to do list for when the rubble of my restaurant is released by the arson investigator. He has a friend who is an architect. He text messages him while we are there. His friend, Tuck Lowden, agrees to start working on plans for my restaurant rebuild right away, before the insurance payout. He promises that his friend will not only suggest layout elements that will keep the cost low but also be able to help me with finding the right builder. He makes me an appointment with the architect tomorrow.

As we finish our wine and prepare to go, I realize how nice the evening has been. I felt relaxed and the extreme sadness I felt since the fire has been replaced by something else, determination to rebuild now that I have a plan. I finger the charm on the necklace, Strength, yes, I have strength. This is going to make me stronger, not break me, with the help of my friends. I am so grateful to Kenzie and Andy, Brian Porter, and Butch.

As we walk out to his car, I have to wonder what would have happened between us if Kenzie had fixed us up rather than meeting as we did at the club. Or even if we would have met at their wedding. Would we have hit it off? And what about the sexual aspect? Then I dismiss that thought. Everything happened the way it was supposed to.

"Madeline?" he asks.

I snap out of my thoughts and find that we're standing beside his car. He has my door open and is waiting for me to get in. "Oh, I'm sorry. I was in my own head for a second."

He steps into me and presses a kiss to my forehead. I immediately drop my head against his chest and lean into him, craving the physical connection. I'm flooded with the thought that I am exactly where I need to be. I feel optimistic that the new chapter of my life, the post fire chapter, will be the best yet. And I think back to the Tarot Cards. Moving On and Open Up. Wow, had they predicted this? Or did they come up to give me guidance at this point, to serve as a reminder that life is full of new chapters, and I must open myself to trust others?

"I'm sure you are still exhausted," Butch says.

"I am," I admit. "But I'm also focused now on what I have to do to rebuild. Thank you for your help with that." I pull away just enough to look up at him. "I am excited to meet with your architect friend tomorrow. I am glad I can get started on it right away, without having to wait for the insurance money."

"I work normal day shifts the rest of this week, but anything I can do, let me know. And I hope we can spend some more time together this week."

I feel the smile pull at my lips. "I'd like that."

The sun has dipped below the horizon. The faintest glow is in the distance to the west where the last rays of today's sun are reaching up. Darkness and a sprinkling of stars are to the east. The air has cooled, and the humidity has eased. It is a pleasant drive back to Kenzie and Andy's house.

I yawn as he puts the car in park in the driveway.

"I'd like to come in for a bit," he says.

"I think I just want to go to bed. I'm beat," I say. I can see disappointment wash over his features.

"I'd like to hold you as you go to sleep."

I'm sure I blush. "I'd like that, but Kenzie and Andy."

"Are asleep. I'll quietly let myself out after you're asleep. Their bedroom is in the back of the house. They won't hear my car. Besides, Andy did invite me to come back in."

I find myself nodding yes without really thinking it through. We go straight up to my room. I change into my pajamas in the bathroom, a little tank top boy shorts set I bought that afternoon. I feel an odd sense of modesty. He has seen me in sexy getups of his choosing and naked and here I am hiding in the bathroom to change my clothes. This guest room though is perfect with its own bathroom. I open the door to see him seated on the bed. He's kicked his shoes off. This feels one hundred percent different from our interactions at the club. It's odd.

He rises and pulls the covers back. The room is cool as Andy and Kenzie run their air conditioning set low to sleep, just as I do. I cross the room and come over to the bed, dropping myself between the sheets. I scoot over to the middle of the bed, and he follows me in. The sheets are cold and not only do goose bumps form, but I can also feel my nipples have hardened. Butch sees it. His eyes are fixed on my chest and an erotic smile is pulling at his lips.

Butch

Holy fuck, this is one of the best sights I think I've ever seen. Charlotte, Madeline in an innocent looking baby-doll pajama set, the tank top portion clinging to her full chest with erect nipples, sliding into bed, where I am going to hold her. But fuck, if my mind doesn't immediately think of all the erotic things I'd like to do to her body.

I slide in beside her, pulling the covers over us both. I roll into her, pulling her body close to mine. I'm sure she can feel my erection, which is pressing into her. My hands cannot get enough of her even though I know she is beat. Unable to stop myself, I grasp her face and pull her lips to mine. The kiss is lengthy, and my hands roam to more intimate places on her.

When she pulls away and yawns deeply, I remember how horrible her last few days have been and how exhausted she is. I return my hands to her back and cease kissing her. I will my erection down and I just hold her. I'm sure she would have welcomed sex, but within a matter of minutes, her breathing evens out and I know she has already drifted off to sleep.

I linger for about a half hour, holding her sleeping, relaxed form tightly. It feels good and I wish I could just close my eyes and sleep with her all night. But that isn't something I want to explain to Andy just yet, not that he would have a problem with it. We are going to have to work something out though. I imagine she'll stay here for at least a few weeks to a month until she can gain her bearings and she gets the insurance payout that will allow her to figure out a permanent place to live while she rebuilds. She and I are not at a point yet that inviting her to stay at my house makes sense, but that is something I can see in the not-too-distant future.

Before I fall asleep, I do pull myself from the bed. I carry my shoes with me down the stairs. I cut through the kitchen intending on slipping out through the side door and come face to face with Andy, who is standing before the open refrigerator. Shit.

He is surprised to see me. "Butch?"

"Sorry, didn't mean to sneak up on you," I say.

"Is Maddie okay?"

I chuckle at that question. I point upstairs. "She's sleeping."

Andy definitely looks confused and intrigued. I can see the unasked questions across his face. "I was just letting myself out. I'll see you later."

"Yeah," Andy says as I head for the door.

I chuckle into the night air. I'm not going to confirm or deny anything. Not that he'd be one to ask or judge. I'm sure that had I stayed all night and met him in the kitchen tomorrow morning, he wouldn't say or think a thing. But I wouldn't do anything to make Madeline uncomfortable and if I read her correctly, she would be uncomfortable with it right now.

I drive home, enjoying the cool night air whipping over me. I love this convertible. A realization comes to me that even though I didn't have sex with her tonight as I would have liked, I am at peace in a way that I haven't been in over a year. I think I have finally let go of the betrayal and all the ugly feelings regarding Catrina.

Chapter 18

Madeline

Kenzie's sunroom is quickly becoming one of my favorite rooms in her house. There is a light breeze blowing through the open windows this morning and it's not too hot yet. I slept in until ten a.m. and was greeted by a note in the kitchen telling me to make myself at home. They were both at the gym.

I made a cup of coffee and am sitting in the sunroom sipping it and reviewing my to do list to rebuild that Master D, Butch and I made last night. As I sit there, I convert the to do list into a master project plan and timeline, complete with tasks ordered in a chronological sequence. If my insurance payout comes within a month, I could have my place rebuilt, up and running in as little as six months. My appointment with his architect friend, Tuck, is at two this afternoon.

A smile is on my face, recalling the evening and how much I needed to just be held by him when I went to sleep. I wish I could have woken beside him, but I know he has been at work for several hours already. I know he works varied shifts, so I don't know how a real relationship between us is going to work. But I'm not going to allow myself to stress about it.

I realize how surreal this is. Just over a week ago, I had not even decided if I was going to stay at the club. A week ago, yesterday, I was sure I was, and I was considering an outside relationship of some sort with him. And here I am today, knowing he and I will have a relationship and considering how we can sleep all night beside each other. I'm not ready to have that aspect of our relationship be public knowledge or have him come down Kenzie's stairs with me in the morning. Besides, I know that probably isn't something they want to have to explain to Trina. I know I am going to have to find some place to live. I cannot stay here indefinitely.

I lift my phone from the table and tap out a text message to him. *Good morning. I slept great last night. Thanks for staying with me while I fell asleep. I hope you have a good day. Talk to you later.* I re-read it before I hit send. It sounds the way I want it to, not too clingy or girlfriend-ish.

Then I start to attack some of the items on my to-do list for today. First, I call the phone company to see what my options are to get my restaurant phone line transferred to either my cell phone or another cell phone entirely. I get a helpful advisor who gets me set up with a cheap cell phone that I can pick up at the local store this afternoon. She even calls that store and gets the manager on the line to get it set up for me. Then she helps me access my restaurant's voicemail. I change the message to inform my patrons that the restaurant is closed due to the fire, and I will change the message with updates when they are available. I don't indicate that the place is a total loss, and it will be months and months before I reopen. I have a few catering gigs on my schedule, and I have to figure out what I'm going to do about them. I know I don't want to cancel any of them.

I'm amazed I keep it together and don't cry during the call.

Next, I contact all my vendors to inform them, though several already knew as they'd tried to deliver product either yesterday or this morning. I had to tell them that I wouldn't be able to pay my past invoices until I got my insurance payout in about thirty days. I was happily surprised that none of them had an issue with that. They all wished me well and gave me their sympathy over the fire.

I called my accountant. He, too, knew about the fire. As his office was local, he said he'd been shocked when he'd seen it driving by on Sunday. We set up an appointment for later in the afternoon, so we could go over my finances. I needed to know where I was financially and what funds I could access, so I could plan accordingly.

I had to leave a voicemail for my attorney. She was a sole proprietor, her office in the living room of her home. She didn't have an office staff, not even a receptionist. I wasn't sure what I had to discuss with her, but it just seemed logical I should meet with her.

When I disconnected the call, after leaving her a voicemail, my text message tone chimed. It was Margot. She'd just finished reviewing the security camera footage with Brian Porter. She asked if she could stop by within the hour. I was just getting ready to tap out a reply when Kenzie came into the kitchen. She saw me in the sunroom and smiled, heading my direction.

"Hi," she says. "Isn't this room perfect to have your coffee in?" She takes a seat across from me.

"Yes," I agree. "I've been taking care of some calls." I lift my phone up. "Margot watched the footage with Brian. She can come by in about an hour."

"That's great," Kenzie says.

I tap out a reply to Margot. "I'm anxious just to get that over with," I say to Kenzie.

She nods at my pad of paper. "What's that?"

"My plan. Butch and I brainstormed over dinner, well,

his dinner, my dessert." I smile. "He is experienced with what needs to be done after a fire. He helped a lot."

"I'm so glad you too have hit it off," she says.

"Okay, yes, I will admit he is pretty great," I say with a smile.

Kenzie is beaming. She's probably already planning the wedding. I smile wider at this thought.

"Well, you know he is welcome here anytime. Any of your friends are. And you know you can stay as long as you need to. Andy and I are both glad to help."

"Thanks, Kenz. That is so nice of you both."

"I'm glad you're making progress." She nods to my list, where I already have several items on my master plan checked off.

"Yes, so, after I meet with Margot, I have an appointment with one of Butch's friends, who is an architect, to start the conversation of rebuilding my restaurant. Then I meet with my accountant after that, but I'll be back in time to make dinner. I looked in the refrigerator when I got up and I plan to do something with that sausage, maybe a sausage, kale, and potato casserole with cheese."

"That sounds wonderful," she says. "We are going to get so spoiled by your cooking."

"It's the least I can do."

"Well, we appreciate it. I'm just back for an hour or so, going to have some lunch and then need to get back to cover the counter at the gym this afternoon. I was going to invite you to come work out, but it sounds like you have another busy day."

"Yes, busy," I say, tapping my list. "But productive. And I feel better having a list of what I need to do in what order, with an expected timeline. I had something similar when I first set out to open The Toad and the Hoot Owl, a project plan, if you will. I have that now and it is helping to get on with my life. I don't feel as lost today as I did since the fire."

Kenzie grabs my hand across the table. "Oh, sweetie, I am so sorry you are going through this."

I finger the necklace she gave me. "I'll come out even stronger on the other end of this."

She smiles and nods. "Yes, you will."

***

Kenzie has gone back to the gym before Margot arrives. With her is a man she introduces as the arson investigator, Bud Kleckner. That's when I realize I haven't heard back from Butch yet. I'm surprised I have not. I invite them in, and we sit at the kitchen table as the temperature outside is near ninety and the sunroom is no longer comfortable, not even with the ceiling fan on.

"We watched the camera footage with Brian Porter," Margot says. "I understand you saw it yesterday."

I nod. I hadn't realized they would watch it together. "I want to press charges against Frank Blanchet for delivering those poisoned flowers. I was sick for two days."

"I will talk to him," Margot guarantees. "I have to warn you. It's going to be your word against his. You don't have the flowers any longer. There is no physical proof that there was anything wrong with the flowers to make you ill, or even any proof you were sick."

"Are you kidding me?" I demand in outrage.

"Calm down, Madeline," she says. "I am going to do everything I can to get him to confess, but you need to know that I can't arrest him."

I suck in a deep breath. "What about theft? He took food items that were not his. I did not authorize him to have them."

"I'm sorry, Madeline. Your staff handed the items to him. I can get them for petty theft, but I can't charge him. The bottle of booze was the most expensive item. I'd put your loss at under two hundred dollars."

"I want you to talk to my sous chef and threaten him with theft charges. See what he says about why he did it."

Margot nods. "I will, but in the end, you know you'll just have to fire the guy. Have you had any contact with him or your other staff since the fire?"

"No. I only talked with Tammy, my manager. I had her contact the staff and tell them about the fire. She was to tell them that there would be communication later this week from me. But that was late Saturday afternoon before I saw the footage and knew about the theft of my inventory."

"Maybe you can withhold about two hundred dollars of his last paycheck to reimburse you for the loss."

I laugh, a sick sound. "Like two hundred dollars is going to help me at all."

"It's something," Bud speaks up. "And not knowing what your insurance deductible is, it will help." He shrugs. "I'm glad you had the cameras. The footage gave insight to the arsonist's activities. I wish every arson fire I investigate had camera footage of the perp."

"Butch told me there had been a rash of dumpster fires over the past few weeks. Do you think it was the same guy?" I ask.

"I can't say one way or the other. The lab is still analyzing the accelerant used. Usually, arsonists keep to the same MO and the same accelerant. This is the first time a structure has been lit. It looked in this case that the fire in the dumpster was to destroy the bag of evidence."

"Besides Dave Walsh, is there anyone else you can think of that you've had problems with who may have wanted to burn down your business?" Margot asks.

"Only Frank Blanchet, though I don't know why he'd want to kill the golden goose that is supplying him with my inventory." I know my voice sounds gruff. "For the life of me, I don't know why he'd poison me with those flowers. Of course, I don't know why he went out of his way to attack me in that food critic article either. I hadn't had any contact with him in months. My only guess was when I got that great write up, he was jealous of my success."

"We have to assume the damage to your gas line and the electric panel was done by the same person who set the fire," the arson investigator says.

I didn't know he knew about that. "Do you think that was an attempt to set a fire that didn't work?"

"Crude, but it could have caused a gas explosion if done correctly."

"So, what happens next?"

"We investigate and try to find proof of the arsonist's identity. We're pulling security footage at neighboring business and street cam footage in the area to try to see someone who matches our guy's description or someone with the bag. He had to put the mask on someplace. Often that's how we get them."

"And I'll be pulling everything I can on both Walsh and Blanchet to place one of them in the area at the time of the fire, cell phone records, camera footage around where they live and the routes they would take to go from that point to The Toad and the Hoot Owl," Margot adds.

I nod, not very hopeful. "And you'll press Frank about the flowers," I bring up again. "That has me really pissed. I wish I had proof I was poisoned."

"I'll let you know how it goes," she assures me. "And I will be paying Dave Walsh another visit. I plan to tell him he is my main suspect in the arson case. The guy caught on your security footage could be him, body size matches."

"Thanks, Margot," I say.

Kleckner comes to his feet. "I'd like to tag along on that visit. I can often get a read on arsonists when they're interviewed."

"I'd welcome you on that interview," Margot says. "You should tag along when I talk to Blanchet as well. He physically doesn't fit the physical profile of the arsonist, but that doesn't mean he didn't hire someone to do the deed."

After they leave, I am left staring out the front window, feeling deflated. I get what Margot was saying. You cannot arrest someone without proof, but that doesn't mean I'm not angry. She's promised she will get back in touch with me after she has spoken to both Frank and Dave. I only hope one of them says something that incriminates themselves.

Butch

My morning has been one meeting after another. Most of them for the new job, and I technically don't even take the position and rank until August first, which is just under two weeks away. I appreciate I am being included in those meetings so I can hit the ground running when I assume command of the precinct. My stomach rumbles and I realize it is nearly lunchtime. Shit! I then realize I had gotten that text message from Madeline that I hadn't responded to yet.

I take a minute and tap out a reply, telling her I'm free, and if she wants to call, I have a minute to talk. I am in my office with a huge stack of paperwork in front of me and a sandwich and bag of chips I'd gotten from the food truck that visits the station and all our neighboring businesses daily. I hate to admit it, but I buy from them several days a week if I don't have time to go out to one of the local diners or sandwich shops.

My phone rings. Madeline. And a smile pulls at my lips, just seeing it's her. "Hello, how's your morning going?"

"Good, productive," she says. "I've gotten a lot done."

"Good," I say, opening the bag of chips. "I've been in one meeting after another for the last four hours. I'm sorry I didn't reply to your text message before now."

"No worries. I'm glad you did now and had a minute to talk. Margot and an arson investigator just left. I have to admit, I'm not feeling hopeful."

"Why, what happened?" I ask.

She gives me a recap of the meeting and all that was said. I listen carefully while I take a few bites of my lunch. I can hear the disappointment in her voice.

"Knowing someone did something and proving it are two different things. Don't be discouraged. They haven't even started to investigate yet." I take another bite of my sandwich.

"I know," she agrees. "It's just not fair. I was poisoned and my business and home were burned down. I have to have faith that someone will be punished."

"Yes, you do need to have faith. I know Bud, he's a good investigator. And from what I've heard about Margot, she's tenacious as well. Madeline, it hasn't even been a week. This is a marathon, not a sprint."

"That's what Kenzie said too," she says.

"You need to give the investigators time to investigate.

In the meantime, keep plugging away at your to do list. I think you will really like Tuck. Your meeting with him is at two, right?" I know damn well what time the meeting is. I'm just trying to distract her.

"Yes, and I have a meeting with my accountant after. Hey, I'm making dinner for Kenzie and Andy tonight. Would you like to come? I know they won't mind." She pauses and laughs a beautiful sound. "Kenzie is just elated that we are spending time together, knew we'd hit it off."

I also laugh. "We'll let her continue to take the credit. And yes, I'd like that. What time?"

"Dinner won't be until around seven," she says. "Andy has a client at the gym scheduled until six-thirty. But feel free to come any time before. I should be back to start dinner by five."

"Sounds good. I should get there around six. I want to get in a quick workout at the gym when I'm done here."

"Great, I'll see you later then," she says.

After we disconnect the call, I am hit with the realization that we have a relationship. Just like that. We are now spending time together, sending text messages and having phone calls. It feels comfortable. It feels right. I know I want to get her back to the club as soon as possible, too. Then we will have the relationship I want, that I envision for myself, a type of relationship that fulfills me in all aspects of what a relationship needs to be for me. I can only hope that is what she also needs and wants.

Madeline

Butch was right. I really like his friend, Tuck, short for Tucker. He is in an office in a warehouse loft in an industrial area of the city. This building has been converted to offices rather than manufacturing. The building, though, hasn't lost its charm. His one room office is huge, with plans and models on display all over the room, many of them hanging from exposed pipes. We sit at a conference table made from old reclaimed barnwood. He has the plat of survey for my building on the table. I'm surprised he's already obtained it.

"So, your new building will have to stay within the footprint of the old building, city regulations," he says. "And we are limited to two stories, as the original building was. But we can do anything we'd like on the inside. You had dead space in the front of the building and an apartment on the back. If we are creative, we can increase the floor space of your kitchen and dining area by tapping into that space."

"I like living over my restaurant, so I don't have to go too far at the end of the night," I say.

"Okay, how much square footage do you need? I'm thinking to increase seating capacity, we could create a loft space on the second floor in the front of the building with guest tables and keep your apartment in the back."

"I like that," I say. "And I had this great backroom area for private parties. I could also seat guests there as regular dining room floor space, but I could close it off for the private party. I'd love to have two of those rooms that could also be opened up to create one large private room."

"We can do that," Tuck says. "There are a few great, low cost, moveable wall systems that will make the space transform rather easily for you."

"That sounds good," I agree.

We work together for an hour, laying out my wish list for the new Toad and the Hoot Owl restaurant. Besides the increased private party dining space, I want a larger bar area, maybe even one within the larger of the two private party spaces. My kitchen doesn't need to be increased in size, just laid out better for prep, especially if I'm going to continue or increase my catering side of the business. I decide while I'm meeting with him that I need to grow the catering side while I have no restaurant to have a steady income.

My meeting with my accountant shows me more potential revenue than I anticipated to help me rebuild. I forgot about the inherited IRA that I have to spend within ten years of my grandmother's death. There is fifty thousand dollars there that will help with the rebuilding process. Yes, I will have to take a hit on the taxes for it, but when better to have to pay taxes than when my income is low, thus putting me into a lower tax bracket.

We also go over the final payroll for my employees. I tell him to process but hold my sous chef, Enrique's last check. I have to talk with my attorney first to see if I can withhold it due to his theft of the merchandise that he handed over to Frank Blanchet. He'll have the checks ready within a few days. He also suggests I hold a mandatory staff meeting where I'll distribute the checks. I like it! This way I can talk to my employees to let them know I am going to rebuild and to see who I can retain for help with the catering I plan to do. I will still need some staff for it.

I plan to talk to my friend Makarios over at Agathias Restaurant and ask if I can use his place to have a meeting with my employees one day before they open. I can't think of anywhere else I can do it. And Makarios has already reached out to me with his condolences on the fire and the loss of my business. He said to let him know if he can do anything to help. Well, the use of his dining room for a staff meeting would help a lot.

I am feeling much more hopeful and upbeat when I return to Kenzie and Andy's house. I pour myself a glass of wine and get dinner started. That optimism doesn't last very long. Margot calls and asks what's for dinner. She's spoken to everyone on her list and wants to fill me in. I know that Kenzie and Andy won't mind if she comes for dinner too, and I am making plenty. She'll arrive by six-thirty.

I take my project plan for rebuilding and my glass of wine back out into the sunroom. It's in the shade now and much more comfortable. I fill in the call to Makarios and the employee meeting as items on my master plan. Even though the restaurant is closed, I still have that off-sight catering gig coming up this weekend that I don't want to cancel. I need to figure out a rentable fully stocked commercial kitchen location to prepare the food for the event, which thank God they only ordered appetizers and small plates. I add this item to the list. I already have a van reserved to transport everything I need to the event, which is at someone's home.

Tammy and I will need to work together some place to plan it, though. I wonder if Kenzie and Andy will mind me using the table in their sunroom or their dining room table as an office? They've already done so much to help me; I hate to ask. With no other options, I decide that I will ask them after dinner.

Kenzie arrives home first. I fill her in on our dinner guests. As expected, she is fine with it. She gets the plates down and sets the table while I make a garden salad to go with the casserole. Margot arrives just minutes before Andy and Butch come through the door.

I'm hit with a surprisingly happy feeling when my eyes lock with Butch's. I hope we will get a few minutes alone to talk. I place the serving dishes on the table while everyone, but Kenzie, takes a seat at the table. She's retrieving her salad dressings from the refrigerator. I pour myself another glass of wine. I'm the only one drinking. Kenzie is, of course, pregnant, and Margot is still on duty. Both Butch and Andy have bottles of water, so healthy. I don't care. I sip my wine and enjoy it.

"So, are you going to tell us what you discovered today?"

I ask Margot after everyone has filled their plates.

She glances around. "I shouldn't talk about this to everyone, but I am counting on none of you repeating this."

"Jesus, Margot, you know us all. No one here is going to divulge confidential information," Kenzie says.

"Besides, Bud Kleckner filled me in this afternoon," Butch says. "But I am anxious to hear your thoughts."

I'm surprised to hear this. If he'd arrived earlier, I wonder if he would have told me what Bud said. "Margot, please."

"For the most part, Kleckner and I are on the same page. He didn't like Dave Walsh anymore than I did at our first meeting, but Walsh did seem more likeable today. He actually asked if you were okay, seemed concerned. It could be he was just inquiring, as it would be what a decent person would do, and maybe he didn't want to seem indifferent or even worse, anxious to hear about injury coming to you."

"Kleckner said he played dumb when you told him he was a prime suspect," Butch says.

"Yeah, his outrage wasn't believable. And he had no viable alibi, was alone in bed at his apartment with no witnesses," Margot says. She holds up a forkful of the sausage casserole. "This is really good, by the way."

"Thanks," I say. "How long will it take to get his cell phone records to see if he was in the area of my restaurant or at home during the fire?"

Margot chuckles. "You've been watching too much television. To get that info, we first have to have a judge sign off on it. I typed up the request and submitted it today. It's being reviewed. Given the dumpster fires, we want to look at Walsh's records for them to. Neither Kleckner nor I want to have to go back and ask a second time if the accelerant turns out to be the same. We should have the lab results by the end of the week. Unfortunately, Madeline, these things take time."

"After talking to Dave again, do you think he did it?" I ask.

"That's not a fair question to ask me, Madeline," Margot says. "I haven't had time to look into him enough to know."

I can tell she has more on her mind. "What? There's more. I can tell. I know you well enough."

"I shouldn't say this, but yes, I think he did it. First, he wasn't surprised to see us there. And he wasn't surprised he was being interviewed by an arson investigator, so he knew arson was suspected. As I said, his outrage wasn't believable. It was bad acting, at best. There was something that just didn't ring true about him."

"Kleckner thinks he's good for it as well. Got a real hinky feeling off him," Butch adds. "But he didn't like Chef Frank, either."

"Yeah, that guy is a piece of work," Margot agrees. "I sure hope I can lock him up for something, but unfortunately, being an ass hole isn't a crime."

"Did he admit to leaving the flowers?" I ask.

"Not at first, denied it and threatened to call his lawyer. I showed him the pictures of him there with the box and then without after he came back down the stairs and he said, yeah, what of it? It's not a crime to leave a bouquet of flowers. When I told him they'd been laced with something toxic, he demanded I supply the lab report to that effect. Cocky motherfucker."

"If he doesn't admit to poisoning them, you can't charge him, can you?" I ask, getting angry. He's going to get away with it.

"We're a long way from accepting it at this point. I have other things up my sleeve to do to try to get him to admit it.

He did, though, seem to be shocked to be a suspect in the arson. The one thing that was suspicious is he asked if we'd captured the arsonist on camera too and did that person look like him," Margot said.

"That's thinking pretty fast on his feet if he didn't previously know the cameras were there," Andy remarks.

"Yeah," Margot agrees. "He should have been so stunned we were accusing him of arson that he wouldn't have been able to think about it. It almost made me think his shock of being an arson suspect was contrived."

"Or shocked because he knew he was not the one onsite lighting the fire," Butch says. "Kleckner thinks he may have paid for it to be done. But we are a long way from proving that."

"I'm not so sure," Margot says. "I will want a few more formal interviews with him. I have a feeling his story will change a few times."

"What about my products walking out the back door and going into his hands?" I ask.

"He claims he paid for the items," Margot says.

"Does he have receipts?" I demand.

"I then went and talked to Enrique, nice kid, but misplaced loyalty," Margot says, ignoring me. "You need to fire him."

"It's not like I have a business to employ anyone right now. Did Enrique admit to doing it?"

"Yes, finally, when I showed him pictures," Margot says.

"What do you mean, misplaced loyalty?" Kenzie asks.

"He bought Frank's sob story about not having everything in place to open his own restaurant. And you, being the bad guy in this story, kicked poor Frank out before he was ready. He says that Frank has supply and cash flow issues and, in Enrique's mind, helping Frank with a few items that you could easily replace is not theft."

I am shocked. That's what Enrique really thinks of me? I rub my forehead and sigh. The problem is, Enrique is a good sous chef, available to work anytime I need him. Had I not seen the video of him giving Frank my inventory, I would have tried to keep him on somehow to help with the catering gigs. But now, there is no way.

"Did Enrique corroborate Frank's statement that he paid for the stuff?" Kenzie asks.

"No, he did not. And we don't have any money changing hands in the footage," Margot says. "I'll mention it to Frank next time I talk with him, but that's no smoking gun. It's merely something to use to try to trip Frank up. I'm sorry I don't have better news for you, Madeline. But remember, we are at the beginning of our investigation."

I set my fork down. I've lost my appetite. With my eyes closed, I rub my forehead again. I feel a hand on my upper back.

"Marathon," Butch whispers.

I nod my head. Then I take a deep breath and reopen my eyes. "Thank you, Margot."

"These things take time," Butch reminds me. "You have your plan to rebuild. That's what you need to focus on now."

I know he's right. "Yes, thank you for the reminder."

Margot gets a call, and she leaves quickly, but not without taking the remainder of her meal in a paper bowl with her. The four of us are left at the table.

"Excuse me for a few minutes," Butch says, holding his phone up. "It's my brother and I have to call him." He steps outside.

So, I ask Andy and Kenzie about using either their dining

room table or a portion of the sunroom for an office. I need to be able to leave some things out and there is no desk in the guest room I am staying in.

"I can do you one better," Andy says. "I was going to rent my old apartment above the gym to my little sister Theresa and her boyfriend, Seth at a ridiculously low cost to help them out, but she's being a princess and said the stairs won't work for her, being pregnant or with a newborn." He pauses and chuckles. "Never mind that I lived there with Trina as a newborn and those stairs never bothered me or my mom. So, anyway, you can have the apartment if you want it. It's three bedrooms and you can make one into an office, even hang a sign outside the backdoor that it's your catering company or however you'd like to designate it. You are welcome to live here as long as you need to, but I figured you may want your own space."

Tears come to my eyes again. Damn! I hate that I am still feeling so emotional. Kenzie just nods and smiles at me. It's obvious they had talked about it.

"Thank you, guys, for everything. I will not ever be able to pay you back for everything you are doing to help me."

"Your one of my best friends, Maddie. No thanks are needed. You'd do the same for me," Kenzie says. "And you do not owe us anything. We don't expect you to pay us back."

I know I would do the same for her. I smile and nod through my tears. "Thank you for the apartment. I'll take it," I say. "How much will the rent be?" I ask as an afterthought.

Andy grins. "Low and you don't pay until you have extra money and can afford to, or if you want, you can work the main counter in the gym for me, say, twenty hours a week in trade for it. I can always use extra help at the gym."

"That will help so much," I say. "And I'm sure I will have an extra twenty hours available in my schedule."

"And I was thinking," Kenzie says, "to make a little extra cash, you could set up a smoothy bar in the gym, maybe even offer healthy grab and go sandwiches or salads. We're expanding and getting more members to the gym every day. We have a huge expansion planned in the next few months if everything goes as we hope."

"Okay, yes, let's see how my plans progress, but that could be a good way for me to earn a little extra money every week. I've already decided that while my restaurant is being rebuilt, I need to expand my new catering business, which thanks to you two and catering your wedding, I just started. I got four gigs scheduled over the next few months without even trying."

"And I'm sure once you put it out there that you're open to catering events, that you will get many more," Kenzie says.

"And if our expansion goes as planned, we will have double our gym space," Andy says. "If you want a little café inside the gym, we could plan that into our design. It would be up and running long before your restaurant is rebuilt. You could order a few industrial pieces of equipment and do your catering work from there. I'm sure we'll easily come to an agreement for the rent. You're a friend, Maddie. We'll make it work as the whole point of this is to help you."

"Oh, wow, that would help so much. I'm going to spend nearly all I make on this catering job this weekend. Between the cost of the food, the rent of the commercial kitchen to prep it, the van rental, and my staff costs, I'm only going to come out with about a hundred dollars. And that's only because it was in the contract that the client is supplying all table linens, and place settings. If I had to supply those, I'd be in the red for this job."

"If you want some marketing help, I'm happy to help," Kenzie says.

"I will take you up on whatever you can do," I tell her. "But only if you let me pay you."

"You can pay me after you make some money off my plan," Kenzie says. "We can start with free advertising in our gym newsletter, the community social media pages, and the downtown merchants' association newsletter. I previously looked at several other low-cost options for the gym, so, I'll revisit those as well."

"I trust you," I say. "Figure out an advertising strategy and just tell me how much it'll cost."

Kenzie chuckles. "We'll implement one advertising avenue at a time so I can track the results. Besides, I don't want to overwhelm you with clients. Oh, and that reminds me, you need to change the message on your website and phone line from the restaurant is closed due to the fire, to advertising your catering menu, pitch it for your customers to enjoy their Toad and the Hoot Owl favorites."

"That's a great idea," I agree.

Chapter 19

Butch

I am gripping my cell phone so tightly that my fingers hurt. My anger right now is off the charts.

"Drago, did you hear me?" Cosimo says.

"Yes, I'm just trying to process what you said." I pause and breathe out. "Are you sure?"

"I'm sure no one got inside. All the cameras were functioning. But the damage to the door lock and keypad on that back door is unmistakable. Someone tried to break in."

"Okay, I'll order a few cameras for outside surveillance on our doors. Just having cameras inside monitoring who comes in the doors is no longer sufficient." I think about the cameras outside of Madeline's restaurant that identified Frank and the arsonist's activities, and I know cameras outside are vital.

"And we'll need a new door sensor and keypad unit. I have the door secured for now. But in doing so, I've eliminated an emergency exit."

I think for a second. It's Tuesday. "I can have a new one installed by Thursday when the Furries arrive. The club won't be in use over the next few days, so it's not an issue. Just make sure that any staff that may be in, know."

"Okay," Cosimo says. "How is Charlotte today?"

For the first time during our conversation, I smile. "She's better, has a rebuilding plan now, something to focus on."

"That's good. If there's anything I can do, let me know."

"I will. Thanks. I'll be in either Wednesday or Thursday after work when the parts arrive. Thank you for understanding that she has needed me to be with her." And I've needed to be there too, but I won't tell him that.

I step back inside and hear the tail end of their conversation. Madeline is going to move into Andy's old apartment over the gym. While this is great news, I have to wonder if it is due to the fact that Andy basically saw me sneaking out last night. Not that he'd judge or think anything, but I'm sure he wouldn't want to have to explain it to Trina.

Madeline and Kenzie fill me in on the entire plan, including Madeline working part-time at the gym in exchange for rent. Kenzie also has offered space for her to set up a smoothy bar and a spot to sell grab and go sandwiches and salads. This gets me thinking. The gym is across the street from Cheshire. And Cosimo has complained about the lack of lunch delivery in the downtown area.

"Let me run this by you," I say. "I won't mention it to Cosimo until you let me know if you want to do this, but you know the corporate offices of Cheshire, my family's winery, are across the street from the gym. Maybe you could offer lunch delivery a few days a week to the employees. They could put their orders in on your website and you could deliver lunch. I think you could make a decent profit to make it worth your time."

She smiles wide. "Wow, yes, that would be great. I could make gourmet sandwiches and salads up in the apartment, don't need any special equipment for it."

"Okay, I'll talk to Cosimo then," I say.

"I'll help you make up some flyers with the menu, delivery days, and how to order," Kenzie offers Madeline. "Would Cosimo let them be handed out to the staff at Cheshire?"

"I'm sure he would," I say. "And it would be great advertising for the gym as well."

"If I do set up a small café in your gym expansion, I could brand everything as The Toad and the Hoot Owl to go at the Stevens Street Gym, giving both of our businesses exposure."

Andy nods. "We can even revisit the plans to get you an outside door. If things go as planned with our acquisition of the building next to the gym and the build-out of our space, I don't see why you couldn't be open for business in as little as three months."

Madeline looks genuinely excited. "That would be fantastic. I guess I need to update my master plan again." She laughs.

Madeline

I sleep so much better that night, having a plan and a place of my own to live. The next morning, Kenzie and I leave to go shopping to get what I need for the apartment, towels, kitchen necessities, including a few basic pans and bowls I will need for my catering and my favorite coffee machine. Since they were using her dishes and silverware at the new house, what Andy used was still at the apartment. I don't need to buy those. I will need to make a detailed inventory of what kitchen essentials are in the apartment. I'm sure I will need to buy a few more things to be able to run a sandwich and salad operation.

On our way to the store, we pass an estate sale. Score! Within a half-hour, I have a kitchen table set, a desk and chair for my new office, and a small living room set. Kenzie calls Andy, and he promises that he and Logan will pick the furniture up within the hour and move it into the apartment over the gym. I'll be able to sleep there tonight! And I know I want to invite Butch to spend the night with me.

We hit the grocery store. I know there is nothing in the fridge at the apartment, so I buy a lot. Kenzie does her weekly shopping, too. The back of her car is full by the time we return to her house to unload her groceries first, taking the time to only put away her cold items. Then we go to my apartment. I smile. My apartment. I have my own place again. I feel a strange mix of euphoria and hope that I haven't had since the fire.

She parks in the back, and we carry what we can up the stairs. It'll be several trips to get everything inside, I'm sure. When we enter, I can't believe it. Andy and Logan have the furniture inside set up so nicely. The living room set I bought looks great in the space, like it was made for the room. The kitchen table set is perfect beneath the light in the kitchen. I go looking for the desk, and I find they've even moved the bedroom furniture from the spare room into the master bedroom. The desk is in that spare bedroom. Trina's pink and purple bedroom sits empty. Kenzie assures me I can paint it and make the room into whatever I want it to be.

"Wow, just wow," I say. I am so humbled that they took care of all this for me.

Kenzie embraces me. "Welcome home. It's yours until your place is rebuilt."

"I slept so well last night, having a plan and knowing where I was going to live. You and Andy have been lifesavers!"

"Come on, let's get the rest of your groceries up here," Kenzie says. "You don't want that ice cream to thaw."

"No, I do not want that," I say with an exaggerated dire-sounding voice. We both laugh as we trot down the stairs.

Madeline

I am so grateful to my friend and fellow restaurant owner, Makarios. It is Thursday at one in the afternoon. He gladly offered the dining room of Agathias Restaurant for me to have a staff meeting. All of my employees are seated before me, all of them, including my sous chef Enrique. They all greeted me so warmly, several with tears in their eyes regarding the fire that destroyed my restaurant, their place of employment. Several have already found new jobs. I'm happy about that. I will need to decide who to keep on to help with the catering jobs, or I guess more appropriately, I'll have to see who can stay on. Tammy has already agreed to, knowing that she will keep her manager position when the restaurant reopens. She'll be a big help during the rebuilding process, too.

I inform my staff that I have already contracted an architect and a builder to rebuild the restaurant. I am hoping to reopen in as little as six months. I guarantee they can all have their jobs back when that time comes, but I understand some will have new jobs that are working well for them, and they may not want to return. I tell them I will gladly give them good references for any job they apply for. I promise to stay in touch. I thank them for all the hard work they did, helping to make The Toad and the Hoot Owl as successful as it was.

Then I tell them about my plans to run catering jobs until the restaurant is rebuilt. I have already secured an industrial kitchen space to rent to prepare the larger jobs at. I'll use it for the job this weekend. Besides Tammy, I need one more person to help prepare and work the event. I'm thrilled that over half of my staff raise their hands. I have a sheet of paper ready to receive the names of those who would like to be contacted to work future catering jobs. I pass it around.

It is an emotional meeting for me. And at the end, as I call each employee and hand them their last paycheck, I hug them, thank them, and say goodbye to each of them. I know I probably won't see many of them ever again. I save Enrique's check for last. I also notice that he has signed the sheet of paper indicating he would like to work future catering jobs for me. I know Margot talked with him about the theft of the food items he handed over to Frank. Does he think I don't know?

After calling his name last, as I did all the others, I hold his final check in my hands. "Before I think about giving this to you, Enrique, I need to know how long you have been handing over my inventory to Frank Blanchet?"

"It was just a few odds and ends to get him through occasionally. It's not like it was a regular thing," Enrique says, with little guilt or remorse.

"And did he pay for these odds and ends?" I ask.

Now Enrique looks guilty. "Well, not in cash that went into your receipts for the night, if that's what you're asking."

I shook my head. "So, let me get this straight. I ordered the product. I paid for the product. After you gave it to him and I needed it, I had to take time out of my day and go buy it in a store, paying retail for it, and you don't see this as theft?"

"Theft?" he repeated. "No, I loaned the items to him. It's no different from when you call Makarios to acquire product, like that night last month you needed to replace the lamb."

"The difference was, I called Makarios, who paid for the lamb, not one of his sous chefs who did not and did not have the authority to supply it on his behalf. Makarios knew the product left his restaurant. And I paid Makarios for the product. When you handed these odds and ends over to Frank, I didn't know about it, and I did not get paid."

"It wasn't that often," Enrique insisted.

"I saw four instances in three weeks. I know Detective Malone showed you those photos. One was an expensive bottle of liquor. I spent more on that bottle than this paycheck is for." I tear up his paycheck. "You're fired and don't use me for a reference."

He looks dumbfounded by this. "Fired?" he finally asks.

"You stole my product and gave it to Frank Blanchet," I say.

"I don't see it that way," Enrique says.

"I don't care how you see it. I'm withholding your last paycheck to reimburse me for that bottle of liquor. I'm within my rights to do so. You're lucky I am not pressing charges against you for theft."

Butch

I'm happy the replacement door scanner and security cameras for the door came in quickly. It's Thursday evening and I am at the club installing them. I came here straight from work to get it done. I'm still pissed someone tried to break in and I have to wonder if it was a random attempt, or did whoever tried to get in know exactly what type of business this is? From the front, it appears to be a cigar bar and humidor. Only club members would know what it really is.

Not that I am proud of it, but we do exert a certain threat against any former members, be the departure be their idea or ours, not to disclose the club. This would be the only hint that our family was once involved in the Mafioso back in the old country. It's what my great grandfather had to do for his wine business to survive. They got out of all of that and have never dabbled in it since, and certainly not in our U.S. businesses. Besides, the promise to never disclose the existence of the club is part of every member agreement, so as far as I'm concerned, threatening to disclose pictures of them at the club, should they go public with what the club is and who else frequents it, is fair. But that has never been necessary.

This entrance is not our primary entrance. It could appear to be just an apartment, or a store room housed in the mostly commercial building on this block of commercial buildings. The back alleyway is for delivery and trash trucks. Behind the alley is a privacy fence with gates and a large public parking lot on the other side. That is where most of our members who drive to the club park. The door on the side of the building with the driveway beside it is where the Ubers come and go from. And no one enters or leaves the club through the cigar bar, though there is a secret door into the club and out of it in the hallway of the cigar bar, just in case. I was told by the realtor when we bought the building that it was a holdover from when the space in the basement was a speakeasy during prohibition. None of our cigar bar employees even know the rest is there.

I have the card scanner replaced quickly. The cameras take a bit longer as I have to drill into the building to affix them, even though they transmit wirelessly over the club's secure internet. I notice that while I work, the whole area is quiet. No one in the neighboring businesses uses this alley much in the afternoons. I'm sure that had to be when our intruder tried to get in, when it was quiet. When I am finished installing them, I go inside and do the hookup from the cameras to our network. And then I take a look to be sure the angle of the cameras is giving me what I want them to. All looks good.

When I am finished, I stroll into Cosimo's office to let him know it is done. The Furries should start to arrive within the next half hour. I open his office door without knocking. He is on his cell phone, and he motions for me to come in and sit.

As usual, he's discussing something about the vineyard in Italy. I don't think my brother ever sleeps. I feel extremely bad for the person on the other end. My brother is so passionate about his vines, and from this side of the conversation, something has gone wrong.

When he ends the call, he looks up at me and gives me that smirk that I have seen a million times as we were growing up, that same smirk my father used to have. Something is up, but I cannot figure out what. I'm surprised when he throws his cell phone across the room and then lets out a huge sigh.

I walk over to the wet bar and pour a generous amount of bourbon, which he accepts. "What's happening at the vineyard, brother?" I ask, hoping it is not as bad as the conversation made it sound.

"One of the buildings that houses the bourbon barrel-aged red blend caught on fire and burned to the ground. For some reason, the sprinkler system didn't go off as it should," he states. "I have my safety manager on it, but that is a lot of money I lost today."

"Brother, I am so sorry. If there is anything I can do to help, please let me know. I know how much that first bottling meant to you."

"It was worth a lot and yes, I nurtured those grapes personally." He pauses and shakes his head. "Anyway, how is Charlotte?"

I smile. "Good. She's started her plans to rebuild her restaurant. We're going to take this next Monday off, but I think we will be back at the club after."

"You're spending time with her still?"

My smile broadens. "Yes. It's been nice. It's been a smooth transfer of our in-club relationship."

"You're welcome," he says smugly. "I only did what I did, booking your promotion dinner at her restaurant to push your relationship to where I knew you wanted it, needed it," he tells me again.

I merely nod. It's water under the bridge at this point.

I watch my brother drink the entire glass of bourbon down. He looks like he lost his best friend. Cosimo leans back in his chair and closes his eyes. Within a few minutes of quiet, he is asleep. I silently get up and leave his office, closing the door soundlessly behind me. Finally, the man is resting. I admit, I am starting to worry about him. When did he get wound so tightly?

I go to the security office. Since Cosimo is sleeping, I decide I have to stay at the club to supervise tonight. I send Madeline a text to let her know I won't be stopping over after all. I find myself smiling when she calls.

"Hi," I answer. "I'm sorry I can't stop by. I have to help Cosimo here."

"No problem," she says. "I'm always up late. If you change your mind or get out earlier than you think you will, just text me."

I slept at her new place, Andy's old apartment, the night before. We christened the bedroom, the shower, the hallway, and the kitchen counters. A lust filled smile spreads over my face as the memories come to me and heat me up. "I will. How'd your staff meeting go?"

I listen to her narrative of the meeting as I flip through security cameras, watching some of the Furries enter the club. Most of them haul their costumes in large formal dress bags, oversized backpacks, and satchels. One guy cracks me up as his is transported in a guitar case.

I can tell that the meeting was very emotional for her, saying goodbye to employees she may never see or talk to again. I promise I will stop over, no matter how late it is when I'm done. I did enjoy falling asleep with her in my arms after fucking her on so many surfaces in the apartment. I enjoyed even more waking to the smell of our sex still clinging to us both, engaging in another round, and then getting even hotter in the shower before I went off to work and she went back to bed.

Madeline

It's hard to believe that the fire was only a week ago. Laying in my bed, in my new apartment over the gym, I hear the toilet flush and then Butch saunters buck-naked back into the room. He pulls the sheet from me, exposing my naked body to his greedy eyes. I love how he looks at me. He crawls up the bed, his lips pressing wet kisses to my slightly spread legs as he advances. He gives my pussy some special attention, getting me fired up quick. I'm disappointed when he continues to crawl up me, continuing with kissing my pelvis, then abs, and up to my breasts. He pauses there and eyes them, then flashes me that hungry look I love to see on his face.

"This is the perfect way to wake up on a Saturday morning," he growls.

"Yes, Sir, it is," I purr. It's getting easier for me to shift between normal relationship sex and when he wants to engage in Dom-Sub play. I can see it in his eyes, sense it in his demeanor.

"My precious Sub, with the perfect, perky breasts. You make this Dom very happy."

I smile shyly. "Yes, Master D. It is my goal to please you in every way."

"And you do," he says. "Do you know what would please me right now, though?"

I'd drop to my knees in front of him for instruction if he wasn't straddling me, his face near my breasts. "Please instruct me, Sir."

"I want to watch you get yourself off for me. Your nipples are not erect for me, my little lamb. With your hands, show me how I love your breasts. And then feed them to me when they are crying out for my mouth to pleasure them."

The games this man wants to play are fun! And endless! Are these types of things to spice it up that perverted or unusual that my previous boyfriends could not fathom them? I don't think so. And as I comply and massage, finger, pinch, and enjoy my own hands, imagining they are his as I stare into his eyes, I do get very turned on.

"Sir, I would be honored if you would take over. I just may orgasm soon," I say, as I press one of my nipples towards his mouth.

He clamps down hard with his teeth. It feels damn near as good as a nipple clamp. Then his steel-hard member penetrates me in one stroke, the fingers of his other hand taking the other nipple in an equally tight grip. He pulls on the nipples as he fucks me hard and deep. At the absolute perfect moment, he releases the pressure on my nipples and the wave that rolls through me is electric.

"Sub, I did not give you permission to come," he growls.

"Master, I am sorry," I apologize. "You are just so skilled with my breasts. What is my punishment, Sir?'

The look on his face is positively smoldering. He pulls out and moves himself, so he is sitting on the edge of the bed with his knees spread. "Get on your knees between my legs," he instructs.

I slide from the bed and take up the Sub position on my knees, facing him, just an inch from his amazing cock which stands at attention.

"This morning, for coming without permission, you will service me. I want to feel those lips around my cock. I want you to drink down every last drop of my seed."

He is so hard and long, and I will have to put that whole thing in my mouth. Holy shit! I don't know if I can do that without gagging. I look up at him. He has so much lust in his eyes. I know I am going to disappoint him. I am not good at this at all. Considering no man has ever made me feel confident about my skills with this sort of thing.

Remembering myself, I drop my gaze.

Master D places two fingers under my chin and angles my head so I can see him. "Charlotte, my sweet thing, you will be fine. We will take this slow until you are able to take my entire length in your mouth. I am then going to fuck you and make you swallow every last drop."

I have never swallowed before, as I was never able to bring a man to an orgasm this way. I am starting to panic, which will just create more of a problem for me.

"Breathe, Charlotte, stay out of your head. Trust me, little one."

Master D directs me to open my mouth, and he slowly places the tip of his penis on my lips. I tentatively lick the end like a lollipop. I taste myself mixing with some pre-cum on it. He moans, which I am going to take as a good sign. Slowly, he pushes in about an inch and I suck him in even farther.

"Slowly, Charlotte, you need to adjust to the length of my dick."

Ever so gently, I take him inch by inch. I am telling myself to breathe through my nose as he gets closer to the back of my throat. I can feel my gag reflex kicking in. I keep the chant in my head. You can do this; you can do this.

"Charlotte, look at me. I want to see what is going on in that pretty little head of yours. I am going to now set the pace and we will not stop until you have pleased me, and you have drunk every last drop of what I give you."

The pace he has set seems to be doable, and then as he

closes his eyes and starts to moan, the pace becomes a bit animalistic in nature. I don't know if I can hold out much longer. He has his hands in my hair and is pulling me in and out at a very rapid pace. All I want to do is please him, but I am now feeling like I am going to fail. Just as I think I am going to need to back away, Master D yells my name, Charlotte, and comes hard and long. I make sure to drink every drop, as I don't want to disappoint him in any way.

Master D then does something unexpected. He grabs me under my arms and puts me back up on the very edge of the bed. He instructs me to spread my legs as wide as they will go. He slowly trails his fingers up my left thigh until he meets the juncture between my legs. Slowly he wipes two fingers thru my pussy and then licks them.

"There is the taste I have grown to love, all honey and lavender." His fingers are now replaced with his tongue and what a wicked tongue he has. He sucks softly on my clit and then dives right into my wet, hot channel. I orgasm within minutes, but he doesn't stop. Back to my clit and he inserts two fingers and finger fucks me, all the while sucking on my clit. Another orgasm hits me without warning. That tongue should be labeled a weapon of mass destruction. Holy crap!

As I am trying to get a grip after that last orgasm, Master D gets up and lifts me. Then sits down with me on his lap. I snuggle into his embrace. Minutes later, he is hard and stiff again. "Charlotte, turn and face me now."

I do as he requests and as I am about to get comfortable, he slides right into my channel and tells me to ride him, ride him hard. He lies back on the bed, relaxed, as I ride him with more focus than I have ever given anything in my life.

Butch

I have been looking forward to this since I met Charlotte. That mouth of hers feels so good wrapped around my dick. I could see in her eyes that she was unsure of what to do at first. I wasn't sure if she was role playing, knowing I would want to instruct her, or if she truly is not experienced in how to masterfully administer a blow job.

As I talked her thru it, she relaxed. The feel of her mouth on my dick is pure heaven, and it is all for me. I have dreamed of that mouth sucking me off. I grab her head and set the pace. I know it is a bit rough, but the way her mouth feels, I don't know how long I will last. And her application had indicated she wanted it rough. To know that she is doing this for me, that she trusts me to take care of her, has me wondering why I hadn't claimed her before now. Her mouth is amazing.

As the pace quickens, I know that I will not be able to hold on much longer. Within minutes, I scream her name and shoot my load. She drinks it down like a pro and looks up at me and smiles. To her and my surprise, I grab her and place her on the mattress, her pussy at the edge. I instruct her to spread her legs wide. As I run my tongue along her slit and into her hot, wet channel, I taste my favorite flavors, honey and lavender. I quickly replace my tongue with two fingers, and suck on her clit until she orgasms, and I keep going until she erupts in a second orgasm. Yes, I am needy that way. By this time, I am so hard, I have to feel her riding me.

I flip us around, so she is sitting on my cock, and I lie back, getting comfortable. "Ride me," I order. She fucks me unlike I have ever been fucked. She is like a Sub possessed, possessed to please her Master. I erupt in a release so earth-shattering; I see stars and can't breathe. Only then do I realize that she is collapsed on top of me, completely spent.

Yes, this is a damn good way to wake up on a Saturday morning!

Madeline
I am exhausted by the time we load the food for the

catering job into the panel van I rented. Butch, Master D, woke me way too early! Not that I am complaining. OMG, the sex we shared was incredible. Sex out of the club is just as amazing as sex in the club with him. I now know what a full, satisfying relationship feels like. How had this eluded me all of my adult life?

"Maddie?" Tammy asks, her voice raised.

"I'm sorry," I say, only now realizing that I was in my own head. I know she probably asked something I didn't hear. "What?" My voice is soft and remorseful, communicating that I had not heard her. Dante, my bartender who helped prep the food, will help serve it, and bartend at the event, is standing behind her.

"Should we all drive separately? Will there be enough parking onsite for us to do so?"

I think about the house where the party is. It is out in horse country at one of the large homes with stables. The driveway is long, and I know they plan to valet park the cars of their guests all along it. I glance over at both Tammy and Dante's cars. Mine is in the lot where I rented the van. Andy's friend that he referred me to, to get my car painted, came through and had it done in one day. I'll bring the van back after the event and get my car. The little that may be left in the van will easily fit in my trunk. We are using stackable serving containers that look nice, but I picked up on the cheap. All the plates and linens are being supplied by the host, special family China.

I kept the food easy, cold canapes, finger sandwiches, a delicious caprese crostini, and some rich dessert bites, lots of flavor packed into tiny pieces. I have more than enough food for the expected two hundred guests at this engagement party.

"Yes, there should be more than enough room for you both to park onsite. And I won't need any help after it's over, we have cleaned up, and loaded the van with what little will be left to bring back."

They both smile. I know this was the desired answer so that when we are done, they can blow out of there and enjoy what was before now a rare Saturday evening off. Dante is a good bartender and I have already been contacted by a potential employer for a reference, which I, of course, gave a glowing reference of him and his bartending skills. I'm sure he will get hired quickly and I may not have him for future events. We'll see.

I crank the music up as I drive to get my blood pumping and get myself in the right mental zone. We arrive at the house forty-five minutes before the guests are due. That will give us plenty of time to set up. Our cars are directed to the drive that runs between the house and the stables, which, by the looks of it, those horses live better than a lot of people do. I pull up where the valet tells me to, along a service entrance into the kitchen.

Tammy, Dante, and I wheel and carry everything inside. Knowing I'd be doing more catering jobs, I sprung for a three tiered cart that would make things much easier. I'm glad I did. The gourmet kitchen we walk into is what every chef fantasizes about working in.

The party's host, Ella Isleson, the bride's mother, greets us. Her face has had recent Botox, based on the lack of wrinkles and firmness that hadn't been there when she'd contracted me for this event. She's dressed in a cool-looking summer tank dress that is tailored to her cute little gym-conditioned body. Okay, yes, I'm only a little jealous.

"Ella," I greet warmly, joining her in air kisses. "You are going to love the magnificent morsels we created for this event. The desserts are to die for!"

"Oh, I'm sure we will just love whatever it is you created,

Chef Madeline. I am just so happy you didn't cancel today's event with the horrible fire and all," Ella Isleson says with a very deep southern accent.

"The Toad and the Hoot Owl is more than a building that a fire can burn down," I say. "It's the food and the love my staff and I put into it." I motion to Tammy and Dante. "I believe you know Tammy, my assistant manager and Dante, my bartender? They'll be helping me serve your event today."

"Yes, of course," she says. She points towards the door on the other wall. "You will see where we have a table set up in there for the food and the bar, of course, for you, Dante.

We all head towards the door. But Ella delays me.

"Let your staff get started. I wanted to ask," she pauses for a dramatic effect. "I heard it was being investigated for arson, you poor thing. Did someone really do this to your incredible restaurant on purpose?"

"It appears that way," I admit. I put a smile on my face. "But I have already met with an architect, and I will rebuild as fast as I can, make it better than it was. In the meantime, I'm expanding my catering business, so please keep me in mind for future events and tell your friends and associates about my catering services."

She pats my hand. "That I will, dear."

The afternoon goes perfectly. My food is a hit. Tammy, Dante, and I work together well. I feel energized and in the zone. My mojo is back! I feel invincible. And I know that if I can get the catering gigs, I can pull them off and hopefully, make a decent living doing them until the restaurant is rebuilt.

The cost to rent the commercial kitchen is my biggest expense right now plus the cost to invest in the professional serving dishes like chafing dishes and such. For this job, China and linens were supplied, but future clients may want me to supply these. I'm going to have to figure out a low-cost way to acquire them. I'll also need some place to store them. I could use Trina's pink and purple bedroom as my store room but humping them up and down the stairs at the apartment is not an attractive thought.

As I drive the van back towards the city after the event, I decide I do need to take Andy up on his offer to build a little café with a few pieces of commercial equipment in his new gym build-out space. Doing my catering from there and storing my supplies and equipment there with street access will make my life easier. And I can have Tammy help me run the café as well as the catering arm, so the load will not be completely on me. I only wish I could do something to keep Dante. A good bartender for the catering jobs will be hard to find.

Chapter 20

Butch

Madeline and I have settled into a nice out of the club relationship. It is amazing how comfortable and comforting it feels. I slept all but one night at her apartment over the gym since she moved in and that was because I was on overnight at the firehouse that night. I picked up the shift to help out. I still haven't brought her to my house. I'm planning something big for when I do that.

It is the last week of July. In four days, I officially move into my new position at work, though I have spent more time in meetings and training for it than I have spent doing my current job. Commander Brown, who I'm replacing, is already out on medical leave. I've begun moving my things into his vacant office.

It's an odd transition time for me, both professionally and personally.

The one thing I am glad about is that Cosimo has left me alone. He's made no demands on me. Since replacing the keycard scanner and installing the cameras at the club last week, I haven't heard from him, and I haven't been back. Though today, I stop in as I need to plan my next session with Charlotte, Madeline at the club, our return.

It will be session six, her final session as a Sub in

training. This is a session that is so important to solidify her as my permanent club Sub. The week after will be the collaring ceremony, which is unnecessary for us as a couple, as we have committed to each other, but it is important in our club life. Having her recognized as mine in both my worlds is paramount to me.

It is Friday evening, Catrina and Master Michael's evening at the club, but I have to go in to talk to Master Kurt. I will avoid all public areas where I may run into them. I arrive early with hopes of being gone before they arrive. I have already reached out to Master Kurt to ensure he will be in early to discuss with me what I need from him.

First, I go to the security office and go through the logs. I check my club email to find a message from Danny, our IT guy. There were several more firewall breach attempts over the last week. But the hacker didn't get in. He is confident whoever it is will not penetrate the firewall. He just wanted to notify me of the attempts.

I review logs and footage from both Monday and Thursday evening, and nothing looks suspicious or odd. As I am finishing up some reports after reviewing the footage, there is a knock at the door. Master Kurt pops his head in and asks if this is a good time. I invite him in.

"As you know, Charlotte is at the end of her training. Cosimo and I both agree she is ready for something a bit more involved, including a second Dom."

A big smile blooms over Master Kurt's face. Yup, he is the perfect choice. "I have already made my interest known that I would like to be considered as her permanent Dom. So, yes, any scene you have in mind I am interested in."

I take a breath. I hate to burst his hopes. I don't think he'll be smiling after I tell him.

And he's not. "You're keeping her as your permanent

Sub?" he repeats. He's frowning and his jaw is twitching.

"The chemistry's there."

"Yeah, can't argue with chemistry," he agrees. "Well, congratulations."

"Thanks. But I want you to be involved in this scene. This particular fantasy was on her questionnaire," I say.

"Sure," Master Kurt agrees. "I'd love to be involved in it."

We spend a half hour together while I lay out my plans, including my limitations of his participation. He gives his input on his portion and we come to an agreement. Monday evening will be a night Charlotte, Madeline, will never forget. I am happy when Master Kurt and I part. He goes to his private room to get ready for the evening. I go to Cosimo's office for a pre-opening security meeting.

When the club is in use is the only time that we have security onsite. There are always four men there to ensure our members are safe from intruders as well as being there to keep the peace in case someone gets out of hand, and this count includes Cosimo and myself. I wasn't due in tonight and I am not staying, so the three other regular Friday night security team members are already there. Technically, I don't have to be there, and my work is concluded. I could blow out of there, but I have been absent for the last few weeks, so I feel obligated to be there. Plus, I want to give a few updates about the firewall breach attempts.

It's a quick meeting and standard in its content. I have turned on the system text updates that notify me as each member swipes their card and enters the club, watching for Catrina. I want to know the second that bitch enters, and I want to get out as soon as I can after. I scan my phone as each name pings it.

One name catches my eye. Master Lew has just swiped

in. This is odd. I happen to know that Lew Heller is not coming this evening. I ran into him at the diner I went to for lunch. He and his wife, club member Christina, were excited to be invited to go to Churchill Downs with an owner and watch the races in his private box this evening. It could be that their plans changed, but something nags at me about it. Maybe because Christina's card swipe didn't precede or follow his.

I jump up from the chair as if it was on fire. Cosimo looks up and has a look of concern on his face. He knows me too well, I guess. I don't want to sound the alarm that something is wrong, unless I'm sure, so I make an excuse about being late for something and get the hell out of there. By the time I make it down to the security room, I've talked myself into believing I'm just being paranoid.

I pull up the swipe and see it was done at the door I replaced the keycard reader at. This is not a door any of our members used to enter. Lew never has. Now my mind is reeling. I quickly log in and pull up the camera footage of that door. I don't know who the hell it is that has just swiped Lew's card. It sure as shit isn't Lew. As I flip through camera footage inside the club, looking for our intruder, I call Cosimo.

"We have an intruder," I say when he answers.

"Details?" Cosimo asks.

"Someone swiped in with Lew Heller's card at the door I replaced the reader at. It's not him. I'm looking at internal cameras trying to find this sonofabitch. Male, dark hair, slight build, maybe five-ten. Caucasian. Wearing jeans and a light colored short-sleeved t-shirt."

"Got it, keep looking. I'm texting our three security members. Let me know when you find him."

I display all the camera feeds on two monitors, my eyes sweeping over the images. The club is getting busy. There are a lot of bodies moving around the tiny blocks of camera footage.

What the hell? I catch sight of him going into the server room next door. A second later, I am at the door to our server room. Even though I want to break in and confront this guy, I think it through and call Brad, the strongest of the three security men on. He is tall and broad, more intimidating looking than the others. Then I quickly call Cosimo and give him an update.

As soon as Brad arrives, I swipe my card. I slowly open the door. I peer past the rack to where the computer is, and I see someone sitting at the station. I motion to Brad and then I creep into the room, Brad right behind me. I quickly subdue the guy. Being a skinning guy, he cannot put up much of a fight. And he is young, maybe eighteen. In the meantime, Joel, one of the other security men, arrives. I ask the guys to take him to Cosimo's office.

As I review what is on the screen, I let out a loud "son of a bitch" by what I see. And that's before I see the thumb drive that's plugged into the computer. I cannot wait to find out who sent this little shit and what the end game is.

A damn data breach! Our complete membership list was being downloaded. Names, phone numbers, email addresses, and status. This list would be a great way to blackmail the more prominent members of society. I couldn't wait to get a hold of this guy and get the information I wanted.

I log the computer off and bring the thumb drive with me to Cosimo's office. I enter without knocking to find the asshole standing in the middle of the room, facing Cosimo. His eyes look like they are going to pop out of his head. Brad and Joel are in the process of emptying his pockets. They lay the contents out on Cosimo's desk, cell phone, wallet, and a Velvet Playroom keycard. He hands it to me.

"Where did you get the club keycard?" I demand, leaning into the kid's personal space.

"I don't have to tell you shit, man. Go fuck yourself."

Wrong answer. I push him into a chair. Still leaning over him, I open his wallet and read his name. "Mark Heller. You're Lew Heller's kid, aren't you?"

His eyes go as wide as saucers, knowing he's busted. What a dumbass, bringing his license with him. I guess he didn't think he would get caught.

"Would you like to share with the group what the hell you were planning on doing with our membership list, of which your mother and father is on?" I ask.

"None of your business. You have no right to keep me here. My father is a very influential man."

"Are you sure about that, Mark? I bet if we scan that card, we'll find it's your dad's card. What would he think about you stealing his card from him? Compound that with breaking and entering, and trying to download a confidential list from a business, is daddy going to bail you out of this?" Cosimo asks calmly.

Mark Heller says nothing. He stares defiantly at Cosimo.

I had to give this kid credit. He had balls. He wasn't going to budge, but I knew a way to get him to talk. At least he was over twenty-one, so it wasn't like we were dealing with a minor. "Take him to Room 501," I tell Brad. "And make sure he gets the full treatment."

Brad stares at me for a moment and then smiles.

Room 501 has all the tools needed to give this kid the scare of his life. He will wish he stayed home tonight. "I will be there shortly. Strip him down to his boxers, briefs, or tighty-whities."

Cosimo eyes Mark Heller's pants. "My guess is boxers with video game characters on them."

After Brad and Joel muscle him from the room, Cosimo

closes the door. "You're going to have Mistress Yvonne scare him?"

"He's twenty-one," I say.

"Don't you think we should talk to Lew first?" Cosimo asks.

"Lew didn't secure his member card. I hate to ruin his night at Churchill Downs, but his son committed a crime."

Cosimo nods.

"I'm just going to have Mistress Yvonne scare him enough to find out why he's here and what he planned on doing with our member list. I'm not going to have her sexually fuck him up for the rest of his life."

Cosimo's lips curl into a smile. "I'm glad to hear that. We wouldn't want to misuse sex to harm him. And I'm sure Lew would agree with that. I'll get a hold of Lew. You go take care of his dumb shit kid."

"I'll let you know when we've gotten the info from him."

I leave Cosimo's office and then call Mistress Yvonne to meet me in room 501, telling her I need a favor. She purrs she would be more than willing to assist in any way she can. What a horny Mistress she is, and she loves them young. I'll have to be sure she understands the goal of the interaction.

I meet her in the hall outside of the door, explain what happened, and tell her what I need her to do. The smile on her face is so big, like a kid who just got a pony. She is one sadistic woman, but she'll do nicely to scare this kid and get the info I need. And who knows, Mark Heller might enjoy it. If he's anything like his dad, he will.

We enter the room and see Mark sitting on the bench. His hands are cuffed high to the wall the bench is against. He sits in just his boxers. Yes, Sonic boxers. Brad and Joel stand on either side of him. His pants are on the floor in front of him. I'm sure they were removed by Brad and Joel. The kid isn't looking so smug now.

"One last chance," I say to him. "What were you going to do with our member list?"

His jaw is set, clenched tightly. He shakes his head.

I nod to Mistress Yvonne, and she strolls over to Mark. As she bends down, her hands come to rest on his knees. I can see that he is feeling very uncomfortable. "I don't think you understand your position," Mistress Yvonne purrs in his ear. "We are not playing around. Well, I will be, but the security guys, no."

He says nothing. She runs her long, blood-red nails up his thigh. I see the marks she leaves on his white skin. He lets out a squeal and pulls down on the cuffs with his hands when she tucks her hand under the hem of his boxer and firmly grasps his balls. The cuffs don't give.

"These are mine now," she says.

"Get off me, you crazy bitch! I don't consent to this. That makes it rape!" Heller yells.

We all laugh. "Now you're getting the idea," I say. I dismiss Joel. Brad and I can handle this.

He pulls at the cuffs again, his eyes darting around in a panic as Joel leaves the room.

"Help! Someone help me!" he screams.

"Scream all you want," I say. "The room is soundproof."

After a few seconds of none of us showing concern at his screams, he stops.

"How many lovers have you had?" Mistress Yvonne asks him, her hand still in his shorts. She waits. He doesn't answer. "Tell me, is it women or men that get you hard, or perhaps little boys?"

"Jesus Christ, you're disgusting!" Heller yells. "Women, you sick bitch!"

"Okay, good," she purrs. "Have you ever pushed a girl or a woman a little farther than she agreed to? Made her say no more than once?"

I see in his eyes he has. I lean against the wall. This is where it will get fun.

"Ah, yes," Mistress Yvonne answers for him. "So, this is no different." She abruptly stands and goes to the wall with her whips, floggers, and the other tools of her trade. She grabs a particularly scary-looking flogger and a pair of nipple rings. "Except I use toys to push you a little farther than you'll agree to."

His eyes get even bigger.

"What are you doing here? What were you going to do with our member list? And how did you know the layout of our building to go straight to our server room?" I ask very calmly. "And was it you that tried to hack in past our firewall over the last month?" He is scared, but he still doesn't answer. "You tell me what I want to know and we're done here. I'll call her off."

"Oh, you are no fun!" Mistress Yvonne complains.

"You're not going to touch me with those," Heller says. The confidence is gone from his voice.

With no notice, Mistress Yvonne strikes his nipple with the flogger on his right side, then the left. He lets out a startled whine. She repeats it a few more times until they are erect. Then she secures the nipple clamps, a pair of particular rings that look rather barbaric.

"Ouch!" he whines. "That fucking hurts."

"Pain is an incredible prelude to ecstasy. When the two coalesce, the result is orgasmic bliss, which you will discover soon enough."

His shorts suddenly tent. Mistress Yvonne runs the bushy end of the flogger down his chest, down his unimpressive abs, and onto his lap, circling it over his enlarging cock beneath the Sonic boxers. The kid is scared and getting turned on at the same time. He's Lew's kid, alright.

Mistress Yvonne turns to me. "If you'd please?"

Brad and I grab his legs and pull his ass from the bench, stretching him out. We grab his shorts and pull them down his legs. We then pull the bench out from the wall so that he is in a somewhat reclined position, and we cuff his ankles to the floor, legs spread. He cannot move. Mistress Yvonne dances the flogger over the delicate skin of his erect cock.

"Pleasure," she moans. "But, if I were to strike, pain. Many of my playthings like the pain followed by the pleasure." She removes the flogger and runs her fingers softly over his head. Then she grabs him at his base and pumps him. "Or perhaps you'd prefer I get down to business on it?"

His mouth drops open and he gasps. He's enjoying it.

She abruptly stops and drops to her knees between his spread legs. "Or perhaps you'd enjoy my mouth, but I do warn you, I like to bite."

"Stop!" Mark Heller yells. "Don't bite me, please, Jesus Christ, don't bite my dick."

Mistress Yvonne grins that sadistic smile. Her tongue runs circles atop his weeping head. She makes a good show of it and his eyes are riveted on her tongue. His panting increases. He watches her, enthralled, enjoying the intense view and physical sensation and scared she will bite at any moment. I'm starting to wonder if he'll come before he cracks. But then I remember how skilled she is. She won't let that happen. She knows what we're trying to accomplish.

"Do you want to come, Mark? Do you want to spurt your seed all over my face?" She tears open her dress. "Or perhaps over my tits?"

Mark is getting even more turned on. "Yes," he moans.

"What were you going to do with our member list?" she asks, returning the flogger to his cock and gently swirling it over it. "I'll bring you to the most incredible orgasm you've ever had. I just need the questions answered."

When he remains silent, she brings the flogger down on his upper thigh. Ouch, that'll leave a mark. He jerks and lets out a scream.

"Pain and pleasure, my pet," she says. "The next time it falls, it will be on your glorious cock, but don't worry, my mouth will soothe the pain until my teeth cause more. For each answer, a pleasure-filled sensation. If you remain silent, pain, my pet."

"Yes, I tried to hack in," he blurts.

"Very good," she purrs. And she runs her tongue over his balls.

Mark moans in ecstasy, throwing his head back.

"What were you going to do with our member list?" I ask.

His eyes come to me momentarily. The look on his face tells me he forgot I was there. Then they dart back at her. "I was going to blackmail all of them, including my father, sick son of a bitch coming to this place for God knows what kind of sex."

"Oh, yes," Mistress Yvonne moans with delight, and then she engulfs his cock in her mouth, to which his eyes roll back in his head, and he hisses out a strangled sound. After a few seconds, she pulls her lips away. "No, no, no, you don't get to come yet."

Heller is close. He is trembling.

"Do you want me to make you come, my pet?" she purrs. Then she licks his shaft again.

"God, yes, please," he moans.

"Are you a sick son of a bitch coming to this place and enjoying this kind of sex?" she teases him in between tantalizing bites across his cock.

"Oh, fuck!" he groans. "Yes! That feels unbelievable."

She holds his head poised in her teeth and stares at him. "Answer me, my pet, or I shall punish you. Are you a sick son of a bitch enjoying this kind of sex? Do you want me to continue? Do you consent? Do you want me to make you come harder than you ever have in your short life?"

I'm not sure how she can talk so clearly with a cock in her mouth. Practice, I guess.

"Yes, yes, yes to all of it," he rattles off panting and moaning.

"Say it. Address me as Mistress Yvonne, beg me to make you come anyway of my choosing, grovel to me," she instructs.

I know we're done here. Mistress Yvonne has just converted him from an intruder to a member. If I read the young Mark Heller correctly, he will be a regular under her whip and chained to her wall. I nod Brad to the door. "Carry on, Mistress," I say. "Let me know if you need any help." I pat Mark Heller's cheek. "Enjoy. We'll leave you to your fun now. The Mistress will bring you by my brother's office after your session to sign your membership paperwork. I can assume we are done with your nonsense of wanting to extort our members?"

He gazes at me with an unreadable look.

"Answer the man respectfully, my pet," she whispers to

him. "And call him Master D."

"Yes, Master D." The words fly from his mouth.

I smile and nod. "I'll see you around."

I chuckle to myself as I move towards the door. As I exit, I hear him doing just as Mistress Yvonne instructed him to. Good boy. I go straight to Cosimo's office. I enter to find him watching the scene in Mistress Yvonne's room on his computer.

"We have a new club member," I say.

Cosimo laughs. "He's Lew's son, chip off the old block."

"Did you get a hold of Lew?" I ask.

"Yes. He said to entertain Mark, however we saw fit, and that he and Christina would head this way after the races. He isn't cutting their evening short, so it's a good thing Mark is enjoying himself."

I chuckle at that.

Cosimo takes a more serious tone. "They need to talk to him. Apparently, he found out about their lifestyle, and didn't know how to handle it."

"Mistress Yvonne didn't hold anything back, and I could see that Mark was scared shitless at first. But as you saw, he sure as fuck got into it. Technically, he committed breaking and entering, but we converted him to a member. That is a better outcome than pressing charges," I say.

"Agreed. I will talk with Lew and Christine when they come later. Mark will be released into their custody, but I will make sure that they tell Mark that if he does anything illegal like this again, his money will be cut off. That's usually enough to straighten out a trust fund baby."

"Have the new member paperwork ready for him to sign and collect the membership fee for him from Lew while they're in. Make sure young Mister Heller knows we have the footage. Hell, make it available to him. He may want to watch it repeatedly to get off."

Cosimo smiles. "So, give him the complete new member experience. And I'll make sure he books his next session with Mistress Yvonne before he goes."

"My thoughts exactly," I say. I nod to the door. "I'm going to head out. I'll talk to you later."

I swing by the security office after I leave him to make sure it and the server room are buttoned up. Everything is well. I head down the hall towards the exit closest to my car and I run right into Catrina, literally, a collision of bodies. We are both startled. That's obvious.

"Are you okay?" I ask her, righting her on her feet.

"Yes, thank you. Is everything okay? I heard there was an intruder in the building?" she asks.

"It was a false alarm," I lie. "But a good test of our security procedures. Don't worry. You and all members will always be safe here."

I'm surprised how calm I feel seeing her and talking to her.

"Thank you, Drago."

"You're welcome. Have a good night." I nod, and then I step around her and proceed to the exit.

When I push through the outer door and inhale the evening heat, I realize whatever had a grip on me regarding her, be it anger or hurt, it's gone. The only thing on my mind is driving over to Madeline's apartment so I can take her into my arms and fuck the daylights out of her. Watching Mistress Yvonne work over Mark Heller has left me horny and wanting to engage in some play with my curvy little Sub. Happy Friday night!

Chapter 21

Madeline

I take an Uber to the club, like usual, which feels odd as Butch, Master D, and I have spent so much time together since the fire. This will be our first night back, since discovering who we really were and establishing our out of club relationship. Butch said he could have picked me up and we could have driven in together, but he wanted this last official night of my training, session six, to be as the other five have been. I think he has something special planned for me. I have a smile on my face and a tickle between my legs, considering what it could be.

In the locker room, at locker number thirteen, which I have discovered is his number at the firehouse, I find a white leather corset and g-string set. It zips in the front. The bottoms are secured, tied with strings on both sides. Humm. Interesting. White for innocence or purity? I laugh. That sure as hell isn't the case for me, not with the five previous sessions plus all the sex we've had out of the club. And there are no shoes at all. So, he wants me barefoot?

I take a shot of the Pinnacle Chocolate Whip Vodka, enjoying the flavor in my mouth, holding it for a moment before I swallow it. And then I exit the locker room to find my Master D looking sexier than ever, standing in the hallway. He is bare chested, wearing those awesome leather pants that lace up over his impressive package, that I now know intimately. He too is barefooted.

He extends his hand to me. I place my hand in his and drop my gaze submissively. In anticipation of this evening, I am already wet. When he presses a wet, hot kiss to my palm, and then snakes his tongue out to lick it, I feel enough wetness hit the tiny g-string in my crack to soak it.

He walks me to the room with the stage. The room is packed. I'm shocked when he leads me up onto the stage. In the middle of it are two blocks, sitting about two feet apart. They come up to my knees. Above it is a bar with two handcuffs. I instantly go rigid. I had removed my consent for restraints. Had he forgotten? Or did he assume that since we now have a relationship, I'm okay with them? I know I look nervous as my eyes sweep over the audience. What am I going to do about this?

"Your choice, my little lamb," he whispers. "You can merely grasp the bar, or you can give me permission to clasp your wrists in the cuffs."

I feel bad, but I cannot consent yet. I drop my gaze. "If it would please you, Master D, I would prefer to grasp the bar."

"Very well," he says.

I can see he is disappointed. "Perhaps next time, Sir," I add.

He helps me to stand on the blocks. I reach my hands up and grab hold of the bar. Then he hops up on one of the blocks with me and he secures a blindfold over my eyes. I know I need to keep hold of that bar. I have an image in my mind of me falling if I let go. That would not be very sexy.

From somewhere behind me, hands snake around my middle and my corset is unzipped. The cool air hits my breasts. They are betraying how excited I am. I feel lips and teeth on my right breast. I recognize them as Master D's. Heaven. Then I feel another set of lips on my left breast, a stubbled face accompanying those lips.

Two sets of large male hands run up my legs. Two hands

wrap around my hips and cup, kneed, and caress my ass. The two techniques are very different. The other hand of each man is holding me inside my thigh, less than an inch from my pussy. Then I feel the ties on each side of the g-string pull and I'm aware it has been removed. I am standing there naked, except for the two faces covering my breasts as their mouths continue to ravish my nipples.

I feel fingers drag through my folds. I know I am already dripping wet. I feel one of the hands on my ass inch towards my dark hole. A finger circles. It enters my ass at the same time two fingers penetrate my cunt. Combined with the two sets of mouths on my breasts, the sensation nearly makes me come. The only thing I hear is my moaning. I note that it is so quiet in the room that you can hear a pin drop.

"Do not come until I have given you permission," I hear Master D say.

Both mouths are removed from my breasts. A second later, nipple clips pinch both sides. I feel an equal pull on them. I groan out, enjoying the pain. Then, a mouth covers my clit and its assault on it, combined with the fingers plunging into my cunt and the one finger wiggling and going in and out of my ass takes me to the brink. I feel a tongue run down my back from the nape of my neck to the crack in my ass. I pant and moan my pleasure, aching to be given the permission to come. I can't hold out much longer. I can feel every muscle in my body tremble.

"You may come," Master D says as I feel another pull on the nipples.

And I explode. I scream like I have never screamed. My entire body quakes. My knees go weak, and I damn near let go of the bar. No sooner do I recover and the fingers in both of my holes are removed. I feel a loss. Suddenly, a very large dick enters my cunt, and I am in heaven. It jabs all the way in. His rhythm becomes fast and hard, just the way I like it. I am on the verge of orgasming again when I hear Master D whisper in my ear to hold off if I can.

All of a sudden, I feel a presence behind me, and a dick enters my asshole slowly so I can stretch and accommodate it. I feel powerful lips crush my lips and the kiss was a panty dropper. Behind me, another set of lips press wet kisses to my neck. My mind is catching up, and it occurs to me that there are two men taking me. My fantasy has come true, two hot men fucking me and kissing me. And two sets of strong male hands are holding me and caressing me everywhere.

Master D's voice is in my ear again. "Come now and come hard." His voice is strained and grunting.

And when there is another tug to the nipple clamps, it's not like I could have stopped it. The sensations to my body are overwhelming. I shatter in the most perfect orgasmic tsunami. My body convulses. Hot white lightning sears the insides of my eyes. I crumble, no longer able to hold myself up on my legs or with my hands.

When the Dom that is fucking my ass comes, he loses control and fucks my ass harder than it has ever been fucked. I hear him groan out a guttural, nonhuman sound and I feel his breath on the back of my neck. Then he collapses into me. A second later, I hear Master D moan my name, Charlotte, as he comes, repeating the forceful fucking assault from the front.

I fall into strong safe arms in front of me, Master D's. The blindfold is removed, and Master D gazes at me with admiration. He kisses me deeply. I'm jealous he has any energy left to. When he pulls his lips away, I notice that the room is empty of all the other Doms and Subs. I wonder when they left.

In the corner of my vision, I see Master Kurt is the Dom behind me. He presses a kiss to my cheek. And then he pulls out of my ass. I shudder. Master D pulls out from my cunt and then removes the nipple clamps. There is a metal chain between the two clamps. I love the look of it. Master D and Master Kurt each gently kiss a nipple. As erotic as it felt as they worked the nipples while blindfolded, seeing both their heads on me, and gazing down, seeing both their mouths take a breast, is pretty fucking erotic too.

Then they both caress me with both of their hands again. I don't know how it is possible, but I am getting worked up again.

"Do you have one last orgasm left in you, Charlotte?" Master D whispers.

"Yes, Sir, I do," I reply.

"I promised Master Kurt a taste of your pussy," he says, while directing me to the sex swing at the far back of the stage.

He sits me on the open seat portion and places my legs up in the webbing stirrups. I am splayed open wide.

"That is the most beautiful sight," Master Kurt says. "Her ass is open where I fucked her, her cunt is dripping, and her clit is swollen and glistening."

I feel his mouth take my clit. His technique is so different from Master D's. He's rough on the sensitive tissue, sucking hard and flicking his tongue over it quickly.

"Enjoy this," Master D. whispers and then his mouth crashes into mine and his mouth is equally as barbaric as Master Kurt's.

When Master Kurt pokes fingers into both my holes, assaulting me with deep, fast, finger fucks, I don't last long. My entire body quakes and my screams are swallowed in Master D's mouth as he continues to kiss me with a ferocity I've never experienced.

I have a vague sense that I am carried into Master D's aftercare room and, after being washed and given a bottle of water, Master D cradles me in his arms and I fall asleep. Sometime later, I awake to him spooning me in his bed. His eyes are wide open, staring at me. He sits up, letting the sheet fall so I have a beautiful view of that rock-hard chest in the flickering candlelight.

"I have watched you grow into one of the most beautiful Subs this club or myself has ever seen. I know that you had a fantasy of two men taking you at the same time. I'm glad I could fulfill that fantasy," he says with a soft voice.

Butch

"You have fulfilled every fantasy that I have ever had, and you make every day special, just by being in it," she says. My heart soars with her declaration.

"How do you feel this morning?" I ask her.

She stretches and yawns. "My body hurts, but in a good way. It's morning?"

I feel a smile tug at my lips. "Yes, nearly six thirty. I need to get to the firehouse soon. I'll drop you back off at the gym on my way."

"I didn't even ask you, how was your first official day in your new position yesterday?" she asks.

"It was good, though I will admit my thoughts were on you and last night most of the day. Today, my thoughts will probably be replaying last night."

She laughs. "I will think of nothing else."

"I hope you can lie around and relax today," I say. I know she doesn't deliver lunch today, and she hasn't started working for Andy yet, either.

"I've never been this lazy in my life," she says. "But yes, I probably won't do much today."

"You deserve it," I say. And I realize that I would do

anything to make her life easier for her.

My thoughts jump ahead to next week. Next Monday evening is the collaring ceremony, an important night. That will be when I bring her to my house after the ceremony and declare my love. I have a week to plan the perfect night for her.

"I don't know if I deserve to be lazy, but I think I can take today to relax," she says.

I prod her to get up and get dressed. Then I drive her back to the gym. I pull around back and drop her at the bottom of the wood staircase leading up to her apartment. I watch her go in her door before I pull away. I know I am smiling as I drive across town to my new firehouse.

I have a packed day, meetings, inspections, and more meetings. I send her a text message around noon and am happy to hear she has been relaxing most of the day. I make plans to go right to the gym after work. I'll enjoy a good work out and then go up to her apartment for a shower. She's making something no doubt delicious for dinner. Then I plan to enjoy her body before falling asleep holding her in my arms.

As far as I'm concerned, life doesn't get any better than this.

Chapter 22

Madeline

It's Wednesday morning. After Butch left for work, I went down to the gym and took one of Logan's bootcamp classes. Unbelievable. Seven a.m. and I was exercising. After a shower and breakfast, I contact the insurance company to find out where we are with the settlement from the fire at my building. It's been two and a half weeks since the fire. I know it can take up to a month to get the check. I just want to know if they have a dollar amount decided yet. If I know the amount, I can move forward with the architect and builder. They want to meet me at the site today. The insurance company gives me the number I need. There will be more than enough to rebuild. I did have full replacement value in my policy, thank God! It's just going to take a little more time for the claim to be processed.

With this knowledge, I call Tuck, my architect, and agree to meet him and the builder he wants me to meet at the site of the Toad and the Hoot Owl. I'm anxious to see it, now that much of the debris has been removed. Now that I have a plan and am moving forward, I'm pretty sure I can stand at the fencing and not cry upon seeing my dream gone.

As planned, I arrive at noon. The fencing extends into the parking lot and two vehicles are parked in the drive, also blocking me from entering, so I am forced to park on the street.

The closest spot is a block away. It's a good thing I have on comfortable walking shoes. I had considered dressing up a bit for this meeting out of the casual clothes I've worn since the fire, but in the end, shorts, a t-shirt, and sandals won out. I even have my hair up in a messy bun.

Tuck Lowden stands in front of the fencing with a man I know has to be the builder. He is fit and looks outdoorsy, just what I would expect a man who works in the trades to look like. His name is Scott Ellis. I can feel the calluses on his hands when we shake as Tuck introduces us to each other. After small talk and pleasantries, we get down to business. I don't divulge the amount the insurance will pay out yet. I want to hear from them how much it will cost before I let on what I have to spend. I'm disappointed that Scott cannot give me a figure yet.

"So, this is how it works," Scott says. He has a rough-sounding voice, like he's smoked one too many packs of cigarettes. "I will take the final plan from Tuck and will work up all costs in a spreadsheet, every item for the build down to the last nail. I'll include all permits, which I take care of getting, and even the cost for the utility hookups. Then, we'll go over the spreadsheet and see if the cost is doable for you, and if it isn't, we start downgrading the materials and removing some of your luxury add ons."

I don't think I have any luxury add-ons. "Did Tuck tell you that I am looking to rebuild as quickly as possible?"

Scott chuckles. "Everyone usually is. As soon as you and Tuck can nail down the design of it and we can discuss building materials, I can get the spreadsheet done."

"The city requires the exterior to be stone or brick, as the original building was to maintain the integrity of the downtown area," Tuck says. "There are also a few architectural stipulations. Given that we want to create a loft in the front with additional seating, I want to see if I can get larger front windows approved. If we can't, I don't think we should abandon the loft, but we may want to redesign the space slightly and have the open loft space over the bar instead of at the front of the building."

"And I would encourage you to add an elevator if you're going to have an upstairs to meet ADA requirements," Scott says.

"That sounds like an expensive luxury item," I say. "Can't handicapped guests be seated on the first floor?"

"So, one night you have both your party rooms booked and the front of the restaurant is filled. A lovely elderly couple come in. Neither can do the stairs. You place them on a wait list for seating. Behind them, a younger couple come in and they are immediately seated upstairs," Tuck says. "The elderly couple gets mad and leaves. One, you've just lost revenue and two, that elderly couple can claim you did not provide reasonable accommodations to the ADA mandate and since this will be a newly built building, it applies in a different way than your old building did."

"And you never had second floor seating in the old building either," Scott adds.

"I suppose I could even have that loft space designed as a third private party room, so I don't lose seating on the main floor." I nod my head. "Okay, add a small elevator to the drawings. How much does that cost?"

"About thirty thousand," Tuck answers.

"That's a lot of money," I complain.

"Do you think your restaurant has the expansion capabilities to use all the additional seating the space will provide?" Tuck asks.

"Yes," I answer. "And with the two private party rooms on the first floor that can be transformed into one large room, I plan to dive into the banquet and private party business more than ever before. As it is now, I'm expanding my catering business while I have no physical restaurant to survive."

"Then the elevator would pay for itself the first year," Tuck says.

I know he's right, but thirty grand is a lot of money. "I want to keep a lot of the design elements of the new restaurant the same as the old. I picked up a lot of the decorations and the tables second hand. Will I be able to do that and store the pieces on site after it is under roof with windows and the doors locked?"

Scott nods. "As long as it doesn't look like the place is being used or lived in, it won't be an issue."

"What kinds of items are you talking about?" Tuck asks.

"The bar top in there before the fire, for instance, was obtained as a clearance piece at a quartz manufacturer's shop for a quarter of its retail price. I got it first and then matched the length of the bar to it. All my tables and chairs were mismatched. I got them by frequenting estate and garage sales. It saved me a bundle and gave the place charm. I'd like to do that again but will need someplace to keep it as I acquire it. And I'm not going to pay for a storage unit."

Tuck smiles and nods. "That will save you a lot for the rebuild as well. I'd say we can lay out approximate sizes. I'll give you a minimum and maximum size for each and we'll adjust it from there. That'll save you a lot of money."

"Okay, sounds good," I say, happy we're on the same page.

We step over to one of the two pickup trucks parked in my entrance that blocked me from entering. Tuck opens the back and unrolls drawings in the bed of the truck. I'm surprised to see that he's already got the design drawn. Wow!

It is just like we talked about. The private party space

that can be either open as regular restaurant space or closed to create two smaller party rooms or one large one, takes up the entire back half of the drawing except for a hallway and service area the runs the length of the space from the back door to the kitchen. He has a large, double-sided bar in the middle of the open room that the party rooms butt up to. It makes my bar more than double the size it was and allows bar service inside both party rooms.

"This design frees up the front of your restaurant for seating," Tuck says. "I've been in your place before and the bar is always packed. This more than doubles your bar stools and will more than double your bar receipts."

I notice that unlike my previous space, this one is mostly one large open room with some load-bearing pillars. "I could use free standing room dividers in between some of the tables to create more private spaces," I say, pointing at the main, open room.

"And that will help to buffer the noise too," Tuck says.

Somehow, he's managed to increase the square footage of my kitchen. He still has a small office for me and two bathrooms with four stalls each. He has stairs to the second floor, and the basement stacked on top of each other and enclosed in a wall.

He points to a spot near the bathrooms in the front of the restaurant. "The elevator will fit here."

Then he shows me two different layouts for the second floor. The first has a large picture window on the front to match the window below. The area above the immediate front of the restaurant is open, creating the loft space that tables will occupy. There is a small bar on the side, in front of the elevator and a single bathroom. The second design has the same windows that were on the original build, three small windows across the front. The loft space is open over the bar in the middle of the room and is much smaller of an opening than in the other drawing. There is a larger bar on the far left of the room and there are two, two stall bathrooms by the elevator.

"This second drawing of the upstairs gives me much more floor space and that larger bar if I want to use it as a private party room. The use of the additional space is amazing," I say.

"Well, if you notice in the drawings," Tuck says, flipping the pages, "your apartment size is decreased in the second drawing to give the restaurant more space by one hundred square feet."

In the first drawing, he gave me a separate bedroom space. In the second, the drawing is more like a studio apartment. One room plus a bathroom.

"Oh," I say with disappointment. "No, I hadn't noticed that."

"How much time do you really spend in your apartment? And do you entertain there?" Scott asked. "The footprint of the building is what it is. You will have to decide which is more important, restaurant space or personal space for your apartment."

He's right and I know it. And after my restaurant being shut down for as long as it will be, I will need as much space as I can get to earn the highest revenues from the space I can. I nod. "Go with the second drawing, even if you can get the larger picture window approved. One hundred square feet to seat guests is a hundred square feet to produce revenue."

"That's what I thought," Tuck says.

"I'll have the dollars plugged in and a cost estimate for you by the end of the week," Scott says.

We shake hands and I walk down the block towards my car. I pass by a little pub on the way and the smell of the pizza coming from the open door is amazing. I could go for pizza and a beer. I go in and am seated at a table in the open front window. They have a garage door type of window that they can raise and lower. It's pretty cool and makes it a great indoor to outdoor space.

Not wanting to eat alone, I place a call to Kenzie. The least I can do to thank her for all her help is to invite her to join me and buy her lunch. She's just heading out to go grocery shopping and lucky for me, she hasn't had lunch yet. She agrees to join me. I order my beer and place an order for a medium Margarita Pizza. It's her favorite.

When she arrives, I tell her about my meeting with the architect and the builder. I tell her I will have the full cost estimate from the builder by the end of the week and the check from my insurance company in about two weeks. I'm excited I can start the rebuilding process.

"Have you given any more thought to when you might start working at the gym?" she asks. "I know you've been very busy with everything."

"Yes, next week," I say. "I am so surprised by the number of salad and sandwich orders I've gotten the three days a week from Cheshire. Between those mornings being so busy and the catering jobs I've already picked up, both of which I have you and your marketing materials to thank, I haven't had time. I promise, though, next week I will commit to the twenty hours that Andy asked from me to cover the rent on the apartment. I also do want to have that grab and go sandwich and salad stand in the gym you mentioned. You'll have to let me know which days are busiest at the gym that will make it most profitable."

"I'll take a look at the attendance records when I go into the gym later this afternoon and let you know," promises Kenzie.

Our pizza arrives and I order another beer. It just tastes so good today. The weather is perfect for this table, and we linger and talk for a few hours while I have two more beers. I feel more normal than I have since the fire. Not that I usually day drink, but it feels good. I think I needed this.

Kenzie still needs to get to the grocery store though, so I pay the bill and we leave. Her car is parked in the opposite direction. I give her a hug and happily head to my car. When I am almost to my car, I see a few people standing next to the driver's side door. Did someone hit my car? Great, that is the last thing I need right now. But when I get to the door, I could only wish someone hit it, and left the scene.

In huge white letters, someone has spray painted the word WHORE on the entire side, spanning both the front and back doors. I am truly devastated. I don't give two shits about the car, but for someone to say that about me hurts me to my core. I take one look at it, and everything starts spinning. The last thing I hear is a man's voice saying she is going down and everything turns black.

As I open my eyes, I am very disoriented. What the hell is going on? I slowly sit up to ask why I'm on the ground. A man I don't know tells me I fainted by my car, but he was able to catch me before I hit the ground. Good, I didn't hit my head. He also called nine-one-one. Not good.

A police car pulls in behind my car. I stand up and step over to the cop. That's when Kenzie runs over. Apparently, she was driving by and saw me go down. She parked and rushed over.

"Holy shit, Maddie, are you okay?" she asks. Then her eyes go to my car. "Who the hell did that?"

"Someone spray painted my car," I tell her and the cop at the same time. "I'll give you one guess," I tell her.

"Have you been drinking today, ma'am?" the cop asks me.

Oh, fuck, that's the last thing I need. "Yes, but I wasn't going to drive," I lie. "My pregnant friend, Kenzie," I say, pointing at her, "is my DD today."

"I haven't been drinking," she swears.

"Why were you coming to your car?" the officer asks.

"To get my bag from the backseat," I say.

He peeks into the car and sees a bag on the floor. He then looks at Kenzie, to confirm that she was pulling up to give me a ride home, which, of course, she does. I'll have to thank her for lying for me later.

"But it wasn't the drinking that made me pass out. It was that," I say, again pointing at the spray painted word on my door.

"Can I see some ID?" the cop asks me.

Seriously? I pull my new driver's license from my purse and hand it to him. He looks it over. His eyes go in the direction to where The Toad and the Hoot Owl used to stand.

"Yes, that address is the building The Toad and Hoot Owl occupied. I am the owner and head chef; well, I was before it burned down but I'm going to rebuild. I was here earlier meeting with my architect and builder. Then I met my friend at that little pizza pub down the street to celebrate the plan to rebuild my restaurant."

"I'm very sorry for the loss of your building," the cop says. "I heard it was arson." He nods at my car. "Do you think that was done by the same person?"

"I'd bet you anything it was," I say.

"Besides the fire marshal, who's working the arson

case?" he asks.

"My friend, Detective Margot Malone," Kenzie offers.

"I'll take some pictures and file a report. I'll forward the report to her," the cop says. "The police report will be enough for you to file an insurance claim. You don't need to wait to do that."

"Oh great," I moan. "My insurance is bound to drop me. Two claims in two weeks."

"Neither are your fault," Kenzie says. "Can she go?" she asks the officer.

"Yes, after I write up the report and she signs it," he says.

Ten minutes later, I am sitting in the front seat of Kenzie's car, and she is driving me back to the gym. I cannot fucking believe it. I have a five-hundred-dollar deductible, like I can afford more money going out the window. And a shop will probably need my car for a few days to repaint it, so I'll have to get a rental car. I have a catering job on Saturday. Even if it isn't in getting painted yet, I certainly can't drive it with WHORE painted on the door. On top of that, I'll have to make a trip back to get my car when I'm sober. Fuck!

Chapter 23

Butch

I check my watch. I can't believe it is after six. I'm late. And I hate being late. I pause by my bike and send Andy a quick text message to let him know I'll be at the gym by six forty-five at the latest, depending on how bad traffic is. Yeah, six on Friday night. It's not going to be good. I've just left my office at Fire Station Thirteen, where I got stuck in a meeting that ran over with the Chief. I'd planned to be out of there by five thirty.

I survived my first five days in my new position. I can't believe it's only been five days. It feels like I've always been the District Commander. Thanks to all the prep leading up to my first official week, I was ready to hit the ground running.

Before I even straddle my bike, Andy's return message pops in. The ambulance and two paramedics have just arrived. I am thankful that Mason and Blake ponied up the money to pay for them and the unit to be on site during the MMA Event the gym is hosting this evening. I'm not planning to be on site officially, as a District Commander, as the gym isn't even in my district, but I will be watching out for proper safety and fire protocols. And I will be there to help Andy with anything he needs.

I know Madeline isn't planning to attend the fights, nor is Kenzie. Kenzie will be manning the gym's front desk. I even invited Madeline to come down and spend the evening with me. She invited me to come up to her place when it's over, instead. I, of course, will. I'm not scheduled to work tomorrow, so I plan to stay all night at her apartment. There is nothing better than waking to find her in my arms. Besides, I know she is still shaken up by what happened to her car. I have a horrible feeling it was done by the same asshole that torched her restaurant. I'm sure it is Dave Walsh. But knowing and proving are two different things. Thinking about him puts me in a foul mood.

I straddle my bike and turn it over. It comes to life with a throaty roar. The ride to the gym lifts my mood. Riding, the wind in my hair and the sun on my face, never fails to put me at ease. Traffic isn't as bad as I expected. I make it in twenty-five minutes. When I get to the gym, though, I am shocked. The first fight doesn't start for about a half-hour, but not only is all parking along the street taken, but the side parking lot is full too. I pull into the drive that runs along the back of the building, where a sign is made, pointing into the drive that says, 'Event Parking'. And the back area is packed with vehicles.

I pass the open load-in doors to the basement area. At least seventy people are hanging in front of the ramp to the basement. Peaking beyond them, what I can see of the interior looks crowded as well. Shit, they have a much bigger turnout than I anticipated. I hate to be a killjoy and count people to be sure they are complying with their capacity limit, but I can't let them go too far over capacity. I know Andy will understand and hopefully, he's already counting the number of tickets sold. Though, seeing the people gathered and the open door, I'm not sure how they will control entry of who has a ticket and who does not.

I pull up and park my bike to the side of the dumpster, which is pushed up to the building, just below the wood deck off the upstairs apartments. What. The. Fuck. How'd it get moved back against the building? Cars are parked in front of it, trapping it against the building so it's not like I can move it. Shit!

As I mount the stairs to bring my backpack up to Madeline's apartment, a food truck pulls in, followed by a beer on tap truck. Oh shit. This just turned into a three-ring circus. I have no idea where the fuck they are going to park. I watch as they decide to just park in the middle of the drive, in front of the crowd of people at the load-in doors. I take my phone out and text Andy, telling him I just arrived, and that he has a zoo behind the gym that he needs to look in on. At least the unit is parked in the side lot, and it isn't blocked in at all, in case it needs to transport a patient.

I continue up the stairs and knock on Madeline's door. She opens it and greets me with a smile. Then she frowns as she gazes out at the mob of people.

"That," she says, pointing out at the crowd, "makes me very nervous."

I pull her into my arms as I step inside. I kiss her lips as if my life depended on it. When our kiss ends, I know I have to try to put her at ease. "I will be down there during the fights, making sure all is okay. Then, when it's over, I'll come back up and I plan to stay the night."

She smiles wide and almost laughs. "You do, huh?"

I nod, a cocky smile on my face. "I don't work tomorrow. I thought we could sleep in."

"Sleep?" she asks with a raised eyebrow and a flirty smile.

"Or something a bit more fun than sleep," I clarify.

She presses her lips to mine, indicating she likes that idea.

"I'll be here all night," she says after our kiss. "Kenzie

took Trina over to Andy's mom's house and she's working the desk downstairs. Otherwise, I would have liked to have gone over to her place and watch movies. It's just as well. I have the file from the architect to review and mark up and the loan paperwork to complete. I like it I'm able to start the process to rebuild already."

I set my backpack on the floor along the wall. "I'll be back later tonight. Keep the doors locked." As I turn towards the door, I remember the dumpster. "One more thing. When did the dumpster get moved back against the building?"

"Is it?" she asks.

"Yes, it's right under the deck." I point at the door.

"Under it?" she repeats, shaking her head. "No, it wasn't there earlier, I'm sure."

"Maybe they had to move it to free up parking space," I say. But I don't like it. I'll talk to Andy about it.

I press another quick kiss to her lips and then I let myself out. By the time I reach the bottom of the stairs, Andy is out there, moving the food and beer trucks out of the way. He's directed them to park on the grass at the mouth of the driveway, near the street. The people move away from the building and follow the trucks as one large mass. That's one way to move them away from the building.

I trot over to him.

"Hey, thanks for coming to help," Andy greets me.

I nod at the group of people mobbing the trucks. "Do they all have tickets?"

"Only those with tickets are getting in. I have a feeling they go over capacity at the events at other locations, but I'm keeping a close watch on the count." He smiles. "Especially with the new District Commander here."

I laugh. "It's not my district, but I would have to say something if you are clearly over capacity. I'm glad to see the unit and our two men are on site."

"I told Mason and Blake if they didn't fund it, I'd lock them out of the gym. No ambulance and paramedics, no event."

I have to laugh at that. Yes, I can definitely see Andy telling them that and following through if they didn't. "Thanks. I'm glad we're on the same page. Hey, when did the dumpster get moved back against the building? I don't like it under the deck. It'll go up like kindling if our arsonist hits."

Andy's eyes go to the back of the building, to the deck and the dumpster beneath it. "What the hell? I have no idea. I'll talk to Mason and Blake. I don't think we'll be able to get the cars in front of it moved."

And where the dumpster was moved from, across the parking area and away from the building, was now packed with cars too, so there is no place to put it now. "We can move it after the event is over and everyone is gone," I say. "I don't want it there all night."

"Me either," Andy says. He points at the ramp leading into the basement of the gym. "Come back down with me."

I follow him. There are signs clearly posted that no food or drink is permitted inside. At the bottom of the ramp, I see barriers erected that theoretically funnel spectators to only enter at the right side, the left side set up as an exit. The twins, Mario and Marco, are stationed there. Mario and Marco are identical twins. They are both personal trainers and work the front counter for Andy some evenings when they don't have clients. They're in their late twenties. They have black hair, brown eyes, and olive complexions. The only way I can tell them apart is that Mario has long hair in dreads and Marco's is short. And Marco has more muscle mass, and he has more tattoos than Mario.

To the right side, the entry, two other gym employees stand. Tripp, another personal trainer who works out of the gym and runs a few of the bootcamp classes, is wearing his normal scarf tied around his head, his long sandy-blonde hair flowing over his muscled shoulders. Pete, a hard guy to get to know, stands beside him. Pete has short-cropped dark brown hair peppered with gray. His face is hard. He's one of those guys who has seen a lot, lived a hard life. He wears glasses over his steely gray eyes that focus on each person who passes through the entry as though he was memorizing their faces.

All four men have on their Stevens Street Gym tank tops, as does Andy. I'm sure Logan is around here some place, also wearing his Stevens Street Gym tank. I'm impressed that it's all hands-on deck tonight. Andy is taking security seriously.

"Butch is here in an official capacity tonight," Andy tells Trip and Pete as we entered. Then he looks at me. "Tripp and Pete both know to only admit those with tickets."

"And we're keeping a close eye on how many enter," Pete says. "I don't mean to talk badly about anyone, but I don't trust Mason or Blake to only sell tickets to capacity."

I couldn't help but smile. Pete always told it how it was. I glance around the interior, noting that it already looks packed. "Do you have a count of how many are inside?"

"We let in just over a hundred, but now that the trucks arrived, a lot of people have left to go get a beer," Tripp said. "The twins are stamping hands for re-entry."

As Andy and I walk deeper into the room, I glance around. The ring is lit with spotlights tonight that normally aren't there. There is tiered, bleacher seating on three sides of the ring. That is new as well. I wonder if it and the lighting are rentals or if Mason and Blake bought it. I have to wonder how many more events like this they are planning to host here. In the open area in front of the ring with no seating, a crowd is already gathered, standing in a large group. I don't like that at all.

I know Andy agreed to this event hoping to get more exposure for his gym, more members for both the regular gym as well as members who will train with Mason and Blake, which he'll take a cut of. By looking at this crowd, I don't think he will realize either. Most of these people are not fitness minded. They are here to watch two men beat the crap out of each other before they belly up to some bar and drink themselves into oblivion. I could be wrong, but I doubt it.

We come across Logan. He's stationed at the stairs that lead up to the gym. It is clearly marked 'Emergency Exit' with a lit sign. We clasp hands in greeting.

"You should be wearing a gym shirt tonight too," Logan says to me. Not only does his have the gym name on it, but it also advertises his bootcamp training.

I point to his shirt. "Is that working for you? Getting you new members?"

"Yeah, I already signed up ten women who want to come get sweaty with me," he says with a lusty grin.

Andy chuckles. "They're being given certificates to take the first class for free. But hey, if we get them in the door, we just may keep some of them. Kenzie says twenty-five percent will become paying members. We'll see."

We finish making a lap around the gym. There is another staircase in the front left-hand corner I had forgotten about. It too is lit with an 'Emergency Exit' sign. A handwritten sign is taped to the door. It says, 'Authorized Personnel Only'. I know it leads up to the small front room that Logan uses for many of his classes. It's a long, narrow room with Astro-turf flooring accessible only from the heavy weight room even though there is a glass door that spills out onto the sidewalk in front of the gym.

"We have the fighter's dressing rooms set up, up there," Andy says.

"Is that front door locked?" I ask.

"Yes, to prevent anyone from entering from the street. Anyone inside can get out."

I'm not worried about that. There are weights in that room. In an emergency, one could be thrown through the door or the windows, creating an exit. Just then, the door opens, and Mason comes into the room. Mason is a squat guy, kind of shaped like a fireplug. He stands a good foot shorter than me, but his muscles are well-defined everywhere. His nose looks like it has been broken several times and he has a few scars on his face that could use a plastic surgeon's touch. His brown hair is shaved close to his head, giving him a rough appearance. A mob enforcer is more approachable than he is.

"So, the fighters will come down this staircase to get to the ring?" I ask.

"Yes," Andy says. "Mason, Blake, the fighter's managers and trainers, and I will make sure the path stays clear when they are entering and leaving the ring."

"How many fights are scheduled tonight?" I ask.

"Five, each starting at the top of the hour. We're going to run five, five-minute rounds for each. We'll be done here by midnight," Mason answers. "Look, we've got everything handled." He puffs his chest out with some sort of self-granted authority, which pisses me off.

"We'll be watching capacity limits," I tell him.

Anger flashes over his face. He points to the garage door. "That'll remain open. My understanding is that as long as it is, no one will be counting how many are inside."

Now, I am angry. Didn't he read his permit? "Your understanding is not correct. An unlimited number of people can stand outside that door, but only two hundred fifty can be inside this building and that includes the fighters, their managers and trainers, Kenzie up at the counter and anyone else who is working out up in the gym. And you're damn lucky you were granted a number that high."

"Okay, enough gentlemen," Andy says. "Mason, two hundred fifty inside this space, period. Butch represents the fire marshal and has the authority to shut you down. And Butch, I know you will give him a little wiggle room on the number, applying that number to the spectators only."

I give Andy a look. Yeah, that technically isn't how the special event permit is written but given that the open garage door area creates a large exit, I can ignore a few extra people. A few. "Deal," I say.

Mason nods.

***

The night goes well. By glancing over the crowd during the rounds, I estimate that there has to be close to two hundred seventy-five spectators inside by the time the last two fighters begin their first round. But many are standing close to the garage door because there just isn't anyplace else to stand. In between fights, at least half of the crowd leaves to visit the food and beer trucks. I don't bust them for being over capacity.

I wandered outside myself, several times during the night, and was disgusted by the number of men I saw peeing on tires of the parked cars. I wasn't sure where the women were peeing. I probably didn't want to know. If they ever do this kind of event again, I'm going to tell Andy they need to rent some porta-potties.

There are also a lot of people lingering outside puffing on

their smokes. And I don't think they are all disposing of their butts in the many designated containers out there. I'm going to suggest to Andy that we hose the entire area down after all the cars pull out. I don't want an ember sparking a fire in the dry grass. And this will help to dilute the urine.

The one thing that appalls me through the night is Ashley strutting around the ring holding signs indicating the round in the skimpiest of outfits while the crowd of men shower her with whistles and catcalls. I knew she still did her ring girl thing on the first Friday of every month. I can tell Andy doesn't like it either. I see nothing empowering to a woman in this obvious show of tits and ass as the drunk pigs ogle and call to her. I thought it would be similar to the women at the club in their sexy apparel. It's nothing like it. For starters, we respect and appreciate a woman dressed to arouse. I see no respect from this group. Secondly, we dress as we do at the club, knowing we will participate in consensual play. She's dressed like that just to give a show and get these guys all hot and bothered. I have to wonder how many of these guys will jack off tonight or go home and throw a hump into their wife or girlfriend while thinking about Ashley.

Finally, the last fight is done. It's eleven thirty. I seriously can't wait to go upstairs and take Madeline into my arms. The crowd disburses immediately. The bright lights in the basement area are shut off. I expect a thank you from Mason for not saying anything about the headcount, but the best he can do is give me a nod when I tell him and Andy that the entire back area needs to be hosed down in case there is still a lit cigarette butt out there.

"I'll take care of that," Andy says. I sense he wants to be sure it's done and done thoroughly, and he doesn't trust Mason to do that.

"I did a sweep of this lower level and both staircases," Logan says, stepping up to us. "No one is inside."

"Come out with Andy and me," I say to Logan. "Let's get that dumpster moved away from the building."

"Yeah," Andy agrees. "And then I'll hose everything down. Mason, I want you to clean up all the cigarette butts tomorrow. I bet there are plastic beer cups everywhere, too. Cleaning that up will be on you."

Mason merely grunts.

We step outside into the warm night air. At some point through the evening, it clouded up. There is no moonlight or starlight. It's dark. I notice the light on the outside of the garage, across the parking lot from the building, is out. And neither of the lights upstairs outside of Madeline or Ashley's doors are on. No wonder it is so dark back here. I wonder why Madeline didn't turn the light on.

Then I hear movement coming from under the deck. A figure in black darts out from beside the dumpster just as an orange flame mushrooms out of it.

"Fuck!" I yell. "Andy, get the hose!" Out of the corner of my eye, I see Logan run after the figure who is running across the parking lot and ducking around the far end of the garage. Yeah, that fucker is not getting away this time.

"Mason, call nine-one-one and then Kenzie. She's still in the gym!" I hear Andy yell.

I take off running after the arsonist, too. I run behind the garage on the side closest to us.

"He's cutting back behind the garage!" I hear Logan yell.

I don't see either one of them. Then I hear a dog bark in the yard of one of the houses that backs up to the garage. I hop the fence and run full out towards the sound of the barking. Around the side of that house, I come face to face with a fucker in a black hoodie and black jeans. He stinks of smoke and sweat, and I get a nose full when I tackle him to the ground.

Logan joins us seconds later and between the two of us, we easily secure him, using his own hoodie to bind his hands behind his back.

I stick my face in his and want to pummel him. I recognize him, alright. "You must be Dave the dickless," I growl. "Because only a dickless asshole would set fires and try to kill his ex-girlfriend."

"I didn't do either. You just try to prove it, motherfucker. You won't be able to."

He struggles against us. "We caught you red-handed, asshole. The charge will be arson and attempted murder," I yell.

We drag him back to the gym. I hear the sirens from my old house in the distance, approaching fast. Andy is still dousing the flames in the dumpster. I trot over.

"You're going to want to hit the underside of the deck to keep the fire from spreading. The water will rain down on the dumpster. The deck is more important," I say.

Mason is standing around with his thumb up his ass, not sure what to do. Around the side of the building, coming from the side parking lot, is Kenzie, Ashley, and Madeline.

"Someone needs to call the police. We caught the arsonist!" I yell at them.

Madeline runs over to us as Kenzie places the call. I can see Madeline's eyes go wide at the sight of the man Logan and I are still holding.

"You fucker!" she yells. "You God-damned motherfucker!"

Then she does something that surprises the hell out of me. She throws a punch that is damn-near better than any of the ones I saw thrown tonight. Her fist makes contact with Dave Walsh's face, and I hear a horrible sound that I know is cartilage breaking. His head snaps back and immediately a torrent of bright red blood flows out of his nose. Shit! She just broke his nose.

"Nice right hook," Mason says.

Then she hits him again. This time with her left fist, making contact with his jaw.

She's winding up for a third punch when Mason pulls her off him. He's laughing. The rest of us are shocked.

"Easy, Madeline," I say. "We caught him lighting the dumpster on fire and he will be arrested. I'm sure the accelerant will match what was used to torch your place, as arsonists seldom switch up their game."

"Did you also paint up my car?" Madeline demands.

Walsh laughs at her. "Try to prove that too, whore!"

Mason grabs Madeline again as she pounces on Walsh. I'm secretly happy she lands another blow before Mason pulls her off.

Madeline

I can't believe it's really over.

"Are you okay, Madeline?" Margot asks.

She is sitting across from me at my kitchen table. Butch sits beside me, holding my hand on the table. Andy and Kenzie are on either side of Margot. The table is crowded with all five of us seated at it. Kenzie rises and grabs the coffee pot, offering to refill our cups. I'm exhausted. I just want to go to sleep. It's three in the morning.

"That depends. Do you have enough to hold Dave on? I know a judge will decide if he gets bail and can get out, but I'm not going to be okay if he's released," I say. I feel Butch squeeze my hand.

"It's very unlikely he will get bail," Margot says. "We found more accelerant in his car, and he was caught in the act of lighting the fire here tonight. He's a serial arsonist with the charge of attempted murder on top of it. And the fact that he threatened you and basically confessed to trying to kill you in front of police officers tonight will go a long way to keep him incarcerated pending his trial. Oh, and there was also a half used can of white spray paint in his trunk with the accelerant, though spray painting your car is not nearly as severe as the other charges."

It is quiet at the table. Margot takes a drink of her coffee.

"I want to be in that courtroom for his arraignment," I say.

"It'll be sometime on Monday. I can let you know what time," Margot says. "We should have a warrant to search his apartment later today. I'm hoping we find more there to add additional charges."

I nod as I yawn.

Margot stands. "It's late. I have everyone's statements. I'm going to go and get a few hours of sleep. You all should, too."

Kenzie and Andy also stand. Everyone departs through the door to the stairs in the interior of the gym. Andy will have the deck inspected tomorrow, or later today, as it is Saturday now. He will be sure it wasn't damaged from the fire before anyone walks on it.

Butch wraps me in his arms and guides me to the bedroom without a word spoken after everyone leaves. He peels my clothes off and then pulls the bedding back. I slide in and move to the middle of the bed, leaving room for him. Then I watch him remove his clothes as well. Tonight, he is Master D, in charge, directing me, and taking care of me. And that is who

I need him to be tonight.

He slides in beside me and rolls into me, pressing his naked body to mine, instantly warming me. And the feeling of safety that floods me is nothing short of miraculous. I was a bundle of nerves since the moment Kenzie called me, waking me, to tell me to get out of my apartment through the interior hall, until this very second. Even when I saw Dave held by Butch and Logan, even as I gave Margot my statement, I was on edge, until now.

I relax into Butch, appreciative of his presence, and instantly fall asleep.

Chapter 24

Madeline

I'm alone in my bed as I wake. I sit up and look around the room. The sunlight peaks in through the gaps in the curtains. I lift my nearly dead phone from the nightstand and am shocked to see it is nearly ten. I get up, use the bathroom, and pull on a tank top and a pair of shorts.

I'm thankful I got dressed. Seated at my kitchen table with Butch are Andy and Logan. That would have been embarrassing. Their voices are low, probably to not wake me. "Good morning," I greet them.

Butch comes to his feet and steps over to me. He presses a kiss to the top of my head. "I'm sorry if we woke you."

"No, you didn't," I say, my gaze sweeps between each of them. "What's up this morning?"

"I already had my guy inspect the deck. We were lucky. Only one beam needs to be added to keep it structurally sound, and even that he wasn't so sure it was needed. But I'll feel better, knowing it's been reinforced," Andy says.

"That's good. Did the back of the building sustain any damage?" I ask.

"No, we were lucky that we were out there when he hit it and I got water on it right away," Andy says.

"Andy, I am so sorry," I begin.

"You have nothing to be sorry for, Maddie," he says. "This is all on that psycho."

I laugh at that characterization of Dave. "Well, true, but he was coming after me."

"Yes, you are the victim," Butch says. "We don't blame victims."

"That's right," Logan seconds. "But I enjoyed watching you punch the shit out of him. I think Mason wants to train you and put you in fights." He laughs.

I smile as well. "I'm retiring after last night."

Logan comes to his feet and slaps Butch on the back. "You better treat her right, or she'll beat the shit out of you next."

Butch laughs.

"I need to get back down to the gym, too," Andy says. "It's safe to go out the back door and down the stairs. I wouldn't sit at the picnic table for too long, though until the additional beam is put up. He'll probably get to that tomorrow."

"Okay, thanks. I assume someone has told Ashley too?"

"Yeah, I sent her a text. I try not to talk to her the day after a ring-girl night," Logan says.

"At least now we know why she's such a bitch the next day," Andy says. Then his gaze flashes to me. "Sorry. There's a story there that I won't bore you with, but at least now I understand her issues a bit better."

"You can't help someone who won't talk to you or cut out things from their lives that are toxic," Logan says.

Andy shakes his head. "Her story to tell, not ours," he says. He walks to the door. "I'm glad we got him last night."

"Me too," Butch says. "I'm sure all our nuisance dumpster fires will stop now. I know our fire marshal will be at the arraignment and will press for remand."

After both Andy and Logan leave, Butch wraps me in a tight embrace. I drop to my knees and assume the Submissive pose. "Master D., I give myself to you."

Butch

My beautiful, vulnerable Sub is at my feet. She needs me to take care of her. She needs to turn over control to me. I would have been thrilled to make love to her this morning, knowing that she needs a physical connection. I am ecstatic that she needs me to lead her, and she is choosing the lifestyle this morning. I will give her the attention she needs.

I extend my hand to her. "Rise, my beautiful Sub."

She places her hand in mine and stands, dropping her gaze.

"Do you have anywhere you need to be this morning?"

"No, Sir. I am yours for as long as you want me."

My cock instantly hardens. I guide her back to the bedroom. "Watch me as I remove my clothes for you." I take my clothes off, watching her eyes the entire time as her eyes roam over my body. I can see her reaction to my ready cock. I will make this good for her. She needs it. "Now your clothes. I want to watch you take them off for me." After she strips, I look over her beautiful, curvy naked body, my eyes drinking her in for several long, silent minutes. She gets turned on by how I look at her. I lay on the bed, on my back. "Straddle me and sit on my face. I want to taste your pussy."

She smiles. "Yes, Sir."

She doesn't know it, but I am going to tongue her, and then pull back, repeatedly teasing her until she is crying for me to let her come, completely breaking her resolve to be a good Sub who obeys her Master and demands nothing. And then I will turn her over my knee and give her the most erotic spanking for it, followed by a kiss to her red flesh, followed by the best fucking of her life. Even the threesome fantasy fulfilled last Monday will fade in her memory compared to the shattering orgasms I will bring her. Nothing would give me greater joy today. I will use my entire body to bring her ecstasy. She deserves it and more.

I hold her hips as she seats herself as instructed. Then my hands glide up her flesh and grip her heavy breasts. Her body perfectly fits with mine to hold her fullness in my hands while she is seated on my face. I breathe in her scent as I press an open-mouthed kiss to her. I lathe attention on her with both my mouth and my hands. "Remember, Charlotte," I say into her flesh, "I will instruct you when you may come. Not until."

"Yes, Master D," she moans.

I tease her for nearly an hour, keeping her on the edge during that time. She is being a good little Sub though, crying out and writhing on me but not allowing her orgasm to overtake her. I know she cannot stand much more. And this time, when I taste the strong flavor of her nearing release, I do not let up. I suck harder on her clit. I have removed one of my hands from her breast and I have two fingers inside her hot, wet, tight cunt. I circle another finger against her anus.

She lets out a guttural cry. "Please, Master D. Please!"

I say nothing, but I keep going. My hand on her breast pinches her nipple tighter than any nipple clip, then releases it and she explodes immediately after with a scream and moan that tells me the release is shattering. The torrent of her juices that shower me is amazing. I want to flip her over and dive my throbbing cock into her dripping core. But there is one more thing I must do first. I flip her over my knee as she is recovering and I bring my hand down on her cheeks, right over her tight little ass hole. She screams out a startled cry.

"You came without permission," I say. Then I lean down and kiss her red flesh, blowing a hot breath over her ass hole. She wriggles. I dip one of my fingers into her juices and then trace around her anus in tiny circles, pushing further in with each movement. I slip my other hand beneath her, and my fingers assault her entire crack, clit and cunt. She tightens across my lap and gasps a startled whimper. "For disobeying me, I will finger you everywhere until you come three more times." I wait but she says nothing. "Do you forget how to reply, my naughty Sub?"

"Yes, Master D," she forces out, already moaning and panting.

It doesn't take long for all three orgasms to tear through her, each one more intense than the last. Then I position her on her knees, ass up, head on a pillow on the bed, and I take her from behind, smacking that perfect ass as I pound into her. She comes one last time, at my command, when she is moaning and writhing so that I know she cannot hold on any longer, her pussy crushing my cock. I join her in a dizzying release, nearly blacking out.

Then I pass out, holding my spent, and completely sated Sub in my arms. It is hours later when I wake. She is still asleep, cuddled in my arms. I smell the potent scent of our releases in the air, and it arouses me. I roll her to her back, and I kiss her. She comes awake when my lips take her breast, pulling one of her nipples into my mouth.

"Master D," she pants. I like that she's remembered herself and is still in the Sub role.

"Did you enjoy our play before our nap, Charlotte?" I ask, showing her I am still in Master mode.

"Yes, Sir," she says softly.

"I woke very aroused. My cock is throbbing for you."

A smile spreads over her face. "I am yours for as long as you want me," she whispers.

I spread her legs and gaze at her still wet, still swollen, blushing pussy. "That is the most luscious sight," I whisper. "Charlotte, Monday is the collaring ceremony at the club for the Subs in training. I told you before, I want you as a permanent part of my life. Andy and Kenzie already know we are together. I want to fall asleep holding you and I want to wake with you. I have fallen in love with you. Will you do me the honor of accepting my collar and continuing this amazing relationship?" So much for my plan to wait until Monday to declare my love for her.

"Sir, if I were standing, I would drop to my knees and bow my head before you. I would be honored to accept your collar and continue this relationship both in and out of the club. I love you too."

I am elated by her declaration. I roll onto her and press my ready cock into her waiting pussy in one thrust. She is mine. I knew it the first time I laid eyes on her. I knew it each and every time I touched her at the club, even though I tried to tell myself otherwise. My heart is open and exposed to her. I have given it freely to her and I know she will never break it. She will nurture and support me and arouse me as the best Sub I could ever have dreamed of. I make love to her, reveling in the sensations of having her. She brings my mind, body, and soul perfect fulfillment.

Madeline

I open locker number thirteen and I cannot believe it. The corset is in my favorite color, and the details of the corset are amazing. The rhinestones shine in the light. When I put it on, it fits like a glove. However, my breasts are really overflowing. He has made me look spectacular. No one else knows we have already come to an agreement. I'm not even sure if he has told Cosimo.

When I walk out at the appointed time, sans mask, My Drago is standing there, and I cannot see what is under his hooded eyes. Then my eyes wander below the belt, and I can see he is as hot for me as I am for him. I love our relationship out of the club. And I love this relationship in it.

"Thank you for agreeing to forego the mask from here out," he says. He offers his hand, and we walk silently down the hall to the main stage. The other Subs in training are all kneeling in a line in the center of the stage. Behind them is a padded bench where Cosimo sits. He brings me to the far-left side of the line. He runs his finger along my jaw and softly kisses me. Master D tells me to kneel, and I see the proud smile on his face as he addresses the audience. "You are all here to bear witness to a collaring ceremony. My brother, Cosimo, felt it was time for me to get back in the game by training a new Sub. Although that was the last thing I wanted to get involved in, I want to thank you, brother, for pushing me to take on the training of Charlotte."

"You are welcome, Drago. We have missed you," Cosimo says. "Our graduating Subs all kneel before you," he says, addressing the line of Doms on the left of the stage.

"Excuse me, my brother," Master D says. "I need to say more. Through her training, Charlotte exhibited the grace and beauty expected of a Sub with many years of experience. I know that I pushed her hard, but that was only because I realized very early on that she was mine."

I hear gasps in the room. And even though I am not supposed to, I glance up and into Master D's face. He stares at me with the most intense look I have ever witnessed, and I drop my eyes quickly. I know I have a huge smile on my face.

I feel his hand on my arm and he pulls on me to stand. He

gently places a kiss on the side of my cheek. The warmth that radiates from it calms my nerves.

"Charlotte, please turn around and lift your hair."

As I lift my hair, I feel his warm hands brush my neck, and then something soft is placed around my neck and clasped. I bring my fingers to it. I can feel a very supple piece of leather, with something hanging from the front of it. I can't wait to see what his collar looks like. The crowd applauds and Master D turns me around. He takes me in his arms and gives me one of his panty dropping kisses. I melt into him.

"More soon," he murmurs.

I sit at his feet while the remainder of the Subs accept collars from their permanent Doms and then assume a position at each of their feet. I still have not seen what my collar looks like. I know there is a party of some sort that is to take place after the ceremony.

That party turns out to be in this same room on the stage. Each of the seven Subs who graduated and accepted a collar are brought to an orgasm on stage by their Dom, while everyone watches. It is one of the most erotic things I have ever seen, a live porno exhibition. Some are fucked in various positions by their Dom, some are tongued and fingered. The last Sub to be collared goes first. I am last.

Master D leads me onto the stage, strips me of every scrap of clothing I am barely wearing, leaving me wearing only the stilettos. I am not surprised when he lies on his back on the bench. "You will sit on my face and not come until I command it to be so," he says.

"Yes, Master D," I reply. And then I dutifully straddle him and sit my pussy on his face.

***

At the end of the evening, instead of taking me to his

private room, I am surprised when he slides a black raincoat over my still naked body and leads me outside. All I am wearing is his collar, and the heals. A beautiful black stretch limo with a very official looking driver is waiting to open the door for me. On the seat is a single pink rose. He hands me the rose and motions me into the car. He takes the bottle of champagne that is chilling and pours us both a glass. I sip it. It goes down so smoothly.

The partition is up between us and the driver. I try to stay quiet as he again goes down on me, bringing me to another orgasm. He is not quiet when he slides his hard cock into me and thrusts into me until he is groaning in erotic misery, holding his orgasm off longer than I thought humanly possible. Before I know it, we pull up to a beautiful mansion in one of the most exclusive neighborhoods in Lexington.

"This is my home," he says.

I am shocked.

He gets out of the car when the driver opens the door. I am blushing and keep my eyes averted from the driver. Certainly, he heard us and knew that his back seat will need to be thoroughly cleaned.

As I enter the foyer, I see that candles are lit everywhere I look. The twin staircases that surround the room are absolutely stunning. I hear piano music in the distance, playing a beautiful melody. Without a word, he leads me by the elbow into a room on the left. The formal room is spectacular. It too is bathed in candlelight, which reflects off the gold accents warming the rich tapestry colors throughout the room.

There is another bottle of chilled champagne and two glasses. He pours us each another glass. Before he hands me one, his eyes wander over me. "We are alone here. Please drop the raincoat."

"Yes, Master D," I say, hoping that is the case. I let the raincoat slide from me. It drops to the floor around my feet. I stand naked before him. I love the lust filled gaze he scans my body with.

He hands me one of the glasses and he holds his up in toast. "You have made me the happiest Dom that has ever lived by accepting my collar. I love you Madeline, though at the club I would still like for us to use our club names. You wanted anonymity and I do believe that is still somewhat possible." He taps his glass to mine.

I sip the expensive grape.

"Move into my home here with me. I promise you will be loved and have a good life with me."

I nearly choke on the champagne. My eyes lock on his and I see he is serious. "Sir?" I ask with a startled smile.

He smiles wide. "I'm selfish. I want you at my feet daily. I want to have you every day downstairs in my well-equipped playroom. The two days the club is open for Dom and Sub play isn't enough. And I want to hold your naked body to mine every night when we go to sleep, only to wake in the morning and have you again before my morning coffee. I love you Madeline, and I don't want a day to pass without you knowing it. I almost lost you when I was a dumb-shit and I almost lost you in that fire. You have no idea how happy you have made me by accepting my collar."

"May I see it?" I ask, my fingers feeling over it.

He leads me into the adjoining room, a huge dining room with a table formally set for fourteen with gold rimmed China and glasses. An ornate mirror is hung over a buffet. I view the collar in the mirror. Holy Shit! The leather that makes up the collar is a pale pink and the pear-shaped diamond that hangs in the center must be at least four carats. I tell myself to breathe. I know I cannot possibly tell him that it is too much. Subs don't do that sort of thing, but shit, the money alone in the diamond would pay for a new state-of-the-art oven for my kitchen.

"It's beautiful," I say to him.

"I haven't felt the way I do when I am with you in a very long time." He turns my head and kisses me deeply. As I moan, he slips two fingers in my wet channel, moving in and out. Just as I am getting ready to orgasm, he undoes his pants, and they drop to the floor. He turns me around and commands that I drop to my knees and take him into my mouth. After his incredible orgasm in the car, how can he possibly be hard again?

Like a good little Sub, I do because I want him to feel as incredible as he makes me feel. I give him the best blow job I have ever given anyone. And not wanting to mess his gorgeous dining room, I swallow every last drop.

After, he pulls me to my feet. He motions to the table. "You did not answer my question. If you will move in, I want to announce our relationship to my family. They are due tomorrow evening for dinner. The question is, will you be here on my arm, Madeline Shaw?"

I feel my lips tug into a smile. "Yes, Drago Dominante. I would be honored to."

The End

Look for the other books in the Stevens Street Gym Series:

Book 1: Saved at Stevens Street – Kenzie and Andy's story

Click here to get it on Amazon

Book 2: Scorched at Stevens Street – Madeline & Butch's story

Book 3: Seduced at Stevens Street – Gia & Logan's story

Book 4: Seized at Stevens Street – Ashley & Blake's story

Book 5: Surrendered at Stevens Street – Faith & Cosimo's story

All books are stand-alone stories and while the story does continue from one book to the next, they do not need to be read in order.

Seduced at Stevens Street

Coming soon

Logan, Andy's number two at Steven's Street Gym, has a personal code—no relationships. He seldom sleeps with the same woman twice, as he doesn't want to give any woman the wrong message. But when Gia, a woman he knows he should stay away from, comes into his life one night, he finds he cannot stay away. There is something about this woman that gets into his system and takes hold.

Gia was stuck in a relationship that wasn't heading anywhere for too many years. She knew she wanted to get married and have children. The problem was, he didn't. She vowed to herself that she would never be with a man again, wasting her time, who didn't want what she did. Then she meets Logan. He is alluring, dangerous, and just what she needs in a one-night stand. The problem is, after that one night, she can't stay away from him, even though he is not looking for the same future that she is.

Acknowledgements

I truly say thank you, to you, the reader, for choosing this book. If you enjoyed it, would you please leave a review, so others might find this book to enjoy, as well? I would greatly appreciate it.

Thank you to my sisters, RK Cary and Margaret Kay, who also write their own series of Amazon Best Selling romance novels. RK published her trilogy, Destined & Redeemed and has several other Science Fiction/Fantasy stories in the works. Margaret is working on a collection of Military Romance stories in the Shepherd Security Series, 12 published to date. Both have been wonderful friends with the honesty that only a sister can give.

Thank you to my mother who shared with me her love of books. As a child, the wonderful example my mother set for me as an avid reader led my sisters and me to write our stories. She encouraged me to publish, and I appreciated her for her support. Sadly, she passed away earlier this year. I miss her immensely.

My friend, photographer, and graphic artist, Harry R., shot all of the covers for this series. Thank you, Harry!

The model for this cover is a personal trainer and a competitor in strongman competitions. Quint, thank you for modeling for this cover!

About the Author

Hello, I am Charlie Roberts. I live on a 40-acre farm with my husband, horses, and three barn cats. In addition to writing romance novels, I enjoy reading many different genres, quilting, sewing, jewelry making, and just about every other craft imaginable. I am also fitness-minded and work out at least four days a week. I believe as we age, exercise is a component needed to maintain good health. A healthy diet alone can't do it! The release of endorphins breaks my writers block whenever the creativity has slowed to a trickle and of course gives me energy for whatever I'm doing. This series came to be while spending countless hours at the gym and enjoying the well-built men who were around me.

Visit our website: www.sistersromance.com

Email me at: CharlieRoberts@sistersromance.com

Sign up for my newsletter to hear of newly released books at:

Subscribe to my Newsletter

I'd love to hear from you.

www.ingramcontent.com/pod-product-compliance
Lightning Source LLC
Chambersburg PA
CBHW020906200626
46814CB00001BA/193